Lower Education

A. M. Leibowitz

Supposed Crimes LLC • Matthews, North Carolina

Published in the United States.

First Edition

ISBN: 978-1-938108-52-5

www.supposedcrimes.com

This book is typeset in Goudy Old Style, licensed by Ascender Corporation.

For my husband and my children. Without our breakfast table conversations, my characters would have gone unnamed and my plot would have lost its thread. Your love and support mean everything to me.

Chapter One

A Tale of Two Meetings

PHIN PATTERSON sped east on I-90, his window down and his radio up in a desperate attempt to stay alert. The trees set back from the highway were only just beginning to bud, and the grass beyond the guard rails was brown. He had never enjoyed the drive to Albany; it was long and dull, particularly once one had passed Syracuse. This time, however, he had considered it worth the uninteresting trouble. He was on his way to meet with Donald Murdock from the New York State Education Department.

Murdock had promised it would be in Phin's best interest to hear what he had to say. He had offered a job that would pay significantly more than the other consulting jobs Phin had done—nearly as much as the last four months combined. That alone made Phin willing to suck it up and drive across the state. Besides, he was familiar with Murdock; he'd done some consulting at his request before, though nothing of this magnitude.

Upon arriving at the NYSED building, Phin circled until he found an available parking space. He stepped out of his car and stood looking up at the impressive building before climbing the steps. He took a deep breath and entered.

Five minutes later, Phin sat at a conference table in the board room three doors down from Murdock's office, waiting. The industrial clock on the wall marked the minutes Murdock kept Phin in limbo. Phin occupied himself by doodling on the back of an old piece of paper he'd left in his briefcase. When the door opened, he slid the paper underneath everything else and looked up at the two men who had just walked in. The older man was broad-faced with a full head of iron-gray hair, perfectly coiffed, and a lot of very white teeth. The younger man had a round, babyish face; he was otherwise rather dull-looking.

"Good. You're already here," the older gentleman said. He gestured at the young man. "This is Greg Stevens."

Phin nodded at Stevens before rounding on Murdock. "*You're* the one who wanted to speak with *me.* The less time this takes, the better. I have other clients." Phin tried to make his voice sound bored, without much success.

There were only two reasons a tag-team of NYSED representatives would have summoned him, and neither of them were social. Either they were going after a failing school or they were going after a particular teacher. He sat up straighter in his seat, assessing the suit-clad young man standing in front of him. Stevens was different from the old men who usually enlisted Phin's services. He shifted back and forth on his feet, not making eye contact with either Phin or Murdock. He must have been a junior tagging along with Murdock to play errand boy.

Murdock sighed. "You could at least pretend to have a better attitude this morning. I'm here to offer you something, but if you don't want it, the state's full of other consultants who would be glad to take the job." He pulled out the chair opposite Phin and slid into it. The young man hesitated before he, too, carefully took a seat.

"Then why did you ask me? Surely you had your pick of locals."

"I've seen you work, and I know you're up for the job. But if you don't want it..."

Phin narrowed his eyes. "I'm listening." He examined the pen in his hand and tried to look as though he wasn't already invested.

"You have a knack for making things clean, and that's exactly what we need right now. People trust you, Mr. Patterson."

He snorted. "They don't know me then, do they?"

"Likely not. But *I* do, and that's what matters here."

"What's that supposed to mean?"

"It means that if you do your job, you get paid, the state looks good, and everyone's happy."

"That's debatable," Phin sneered.

Murdock sighed again. So far, Stevens had done nothing other than sit mutely next to Murdock, shuffling papers and avoiding looking directly at Phin. At a glare from Murdock, Stevens shrank back, his face coloring and his hand shaking as he handed over an envelope. Phin amended his previous assessment of Stevens' purpose. The kid was just there as decoration to make Murdock more intimidating—his personal minion. *Wonder who he had to fuck to get his job,* Phin thought.

"Look, I'm just going to lay it out for you. We're sending you to do two things. First, you're going to evaluate the district's programs and weed out anything that might be draining emphasis away from math and language arts. You've seen it before—this is just standard procedure for a failing district." He paused to take a pen from Stevens' hand and make several marks on the page in front of him.

"And the second thing?" Phin prompted.

"You make it look like you're recommending downsizing because of poor performance, but you operate based on the list I'm going to give you."

"List?"

"Mr. Patterson, poor test performance isn't the only problem with this school. There are a few teachers who are responsible for making things difficult for us here in Albany. That cannot be allowed to continue. It is your responsibility to find reasons why their instructional methods are sub-par. I don't care how you do that, but that's what we're paying you for. Or, more accurately, what the school is paying you for."

Phin's lips twitched in spite of himself. "What makes you think I can pull this off? I'm not convinced the school is going to want to cooperate, and I know most teachers don't like to sell out their coworkers."

Murdock eyed Phin up and down; it made Phin want to squirm. "I'm sure you'll think of something." He leaned forward. "I hear you're an expert at *handling* difficult clients."

Phin coughed and looked over at Stevens, who flushed. Phin smirked at him, and Stevens' cheeks darkened. He lowered his gaze once more, angling his body away from the others.

"You'll go out there for the remainder of the school year. Testing is done and the results are in, though they won't be distributed to the school until September. We can't wait until then for layoffs, because as much as I don't personally care, it does 'disrupt the learning environment.'" Murdock made air quotes.

A snide remark came to mind, but Phin pushed it down in favor of business. "Uh..." He cleared his throat. "Just where am I going?"

"It's in North Cowell."

Shit. Phin swallowed hard and forced his face to remain neutral. *Does Murdock know?* Phin studied him, searching for a clue, but he found nothing. "Just where is North Cowell?"

"Southwest of Rome. Nearest city is Peroo." Murdock grinned. "Not much there to speak of. Should provide a good environment for concentrating on your job."

Phin raised his eyebrows. "So what you're telling me is that you want to ship me off to the middle of nowhere and find an excuse to fire—pardon me, *lay off*—a list of specific teachers under the cover of 'school improvement.' Is that about right?"

"That's a rather crude way of putting it, but yes."

"And we're not actually going to do anything for this town, but we're going to make them think we are by replacing half their staff?"

"More or less."

"Right. This list isn't based on their qualifications or their performance, is it?"

Murdock arched an eyebrow at Phin. "That depends on how you look at it. Some of them may or may not be putting their skills to work in ways that are not beneficial to the district or the educational system as a whole."

Phin tapped his pen against his hand. "Not that I care, but isn't that a bit unethical?"

Murdock waved his hand dismissively. "It's not my concern. It's not illegal, anyway. By shutting down or radically changing a school, the state can claim to be working toward improving education in New York."

"So, I'm just going to waltz in there and tell them how amazing—" he coughed "—this plan is, and they'll sign the papers?"

Murdock exchanged a glance with Stevens. "Not—not exactly."

Phin glowered at Murdock. "Yeah. That's what I thought. What's the catch?"

"If they don't comply, they will have two choices. A charter company can come in and take over, or the schools can be shut down and the kids sent ten miles away to the next town. It's up to them." Murdock cleared his throat. "That's why I asked you to come in. You're smart, Mr. Patterson. You had it right when you said they wouldn't just comply."

"Why am I doing this if it's already a failure? That makes absolutely no sense."

"It will when I show you this." Murdock pushed a paper across the table to Phin.

When he had finished scanning the paper, Phin looked up at Murdock. "They're already in process of privatizing."

Murdock's smile was condescending. "Correct. The school board has concluded this is their best option, but the parents and staff don't know it yet. Did you get a good look at the name of the company?"

Phin read it more carefully this time. He gave a low whistle. "EduText."

"Exactly. Your father's company is perfectly poised to reopen the school. EduText has quite a lot of experience in this arena. Of course, you do have some additional tools you can use if you meet resistance from the school. If they're willing to comply, we can send them further assistance for school improvement. You just have to convince them that you are there to functionally help them relieve the town of the pressure to perform better in regard to state standards. They need to trust you, Phin. They won't do that if they know—or even suspect—you're not fully invested in helping them. It's not your job to explain the charter. You can leave that to the school board. Your task is to legitimize the decision by making a report regarding whatever changes are necessary to make it happen—without letting anyone know that's why you're there."

Phin considered this. "All right."

"'All right,' what?"

"All right, I'll do it."

"That's it? 'All right'?"

"Yes. Was there something else I needed to say to make that more clear?"

Murdock sighed. "We'll have the team draw up the papers to make it official, and I'll get that list to you once I have it from the school board."

"You do that."

Murdock rose from the table. "Don't do anything stupid in the meantime," Murdock warned. He gathered his things and motioned to Stevens.

Stevens shoved everything back into his briefcase and stood up so fast he nearly knocked his chair over. Phin watched as he rushed from the room, followed by Murdock. Once Phin was alone, he ran his hand over his face, pulling slightly at his chin. He wasn't sure what he was getting himself into. Perhaps he would have been better off turning down the job. At least his local consulting work was a known entity. Murdock's plan was not.

He wasn't going to change his mind, though—he needed the money. All he had to do was to complete this one last job for Murdock, and then he could do his own work without having to rely on commissions from the state. There was nothing for it at that point. Phin would have to put in his time. The only upside to it was that after more than twenty years, no one there was likely to remember who he was.

Three weeks later, after putting his things in order for an extended trip, Phin was on his way to North Cowell. It was unusually hot for the end of May. Phin turned up the fan on his car's air conditioner; he couldn't recall ever before experiencing so much heat and humidity in central New York at that time of year. He glanced out the driver's side window. There was virtually nothing in this part of the state except long, winding roads and lots of swampland, dotted with the occasional hill, farm, or town. He checked his GPS. He was currently halfway between Syracuse and Amsterdam, heading south toward Peroo. From there, it looked like a thirty-minute drive into the tiny town of North Cowell. Phin decided to stop where he was for lunch, since it was at least another hour's worth of driving and this town appeared significantly larger than the one to which he was headed. He pulled over at a fast-food place.

The car was oppressive when he got back in, even though he'd been inside the restaurant only long enough for a light meal. For the thousandth time, he berated himself for allowing Murdock to suck him into this situation. It wasn't only the heat getting to him—the closer he got to his destination, the more tense he became. He hadn't been back to the area since just after he finished seventh grade. Even though it wasn't his hometown, it was close enough to the place he'd lived for the first nearly thirteen years of his life. There was no question that someone was likely to remember his parents—and not fondly.

Phin shut out all thoughts except navigating and trying to stave off the heat. After an oven-roasted eternity, the air conditioning kicked in and he drove on in peace. As he got farther away from Peroo, the houses thinned out. He sped along the endless stretch of County Road 27, fear-ing he had missed a turn. At last he approached a sign reading, "North Cowell, Pop. 1,930." He took in his surroundings: a two-screen drive-in movie theater, a gas station with a convenience store, and a few houses. Beyond them lay the town center.

North Cowell was clean and quiet. There were no traffic lights. As Phin approached the town center, he drove past what looked like a series of apartments and town houses. After that, there was a row of shops that wasn't quite a strip mall which featured a Mister Dollar and a restaurant advertising "Authentic Buffalo-Style Wings!" Phin found the latter highly entertaining for its bold, if inaccurate, statement.

Eventually, Phin came to an old-fashioned multistory house with an ornate sign out front informing guests that it was the Railway Penny Inn. The Victorian-style house was a bed-and-breakfast, the only place for non-residents to stay if they didn't want to drive all the way from Peroo. People were passing, some of them entering the diner on the ground floor for a cup of coffee or a newspaper. Guests ranged from a businessman in a three-piece suit to two college-age young women in cut-off shorts and flip-flops, with everything in between.

Phin got out of the car and leaned against it. He took a deep breath. This was it—possibly his very last chance to back out. Once he stepped over the threshold, he was officially on the clock and making a first impression on the people there. He closed his eyes and exhaled slowly, letting his professional persona drop into place. Phin opened his eyes and pushed himself away from the car. Glancing down at himself, he straightened his shirt and brushed his hands over the imaginary wrinkles in his pants. He squared his shoulders and stepped through the door of the Railway Penny.

Inside, Phin glanced around. The Railway Penny was reasonably nice, with a comfortable lounge and elegant but homey decor. To his right the cafe was just visible through the open doors. To his left was a small bar; it was dark and empty. Apparently, even with so little to entertain themselves, the residents of North Cowell didn't consider that an option at two in the afternoon on a weekday. Straight ahead was the front desk. Phin waited his turn behind a tall man in a ragged t-shirt and cut-off khakis. He pulled out his phone to read his messages while the other man checked out.

The t-shirt-clad man left, a mini suitcase in his hand. Phin hoped that meant there was now a room available. The only other option was to make the long commute from Peroo or one of the other surrounding towns. He followed the man with his eyes and then, once the man was gone, turned his attention to the front desk. When he saw who was behind it, a slow buzz of panic crept up his spine, and he almost turned around and walked back out. Murdock and the baby-faced NYSED employee—what was his name again?—could find someone else to do their dirty work.

After his initial alarm subsided, Phin realized that would mean giving up and crawling back home. He would have to return his up-front commission and explain things to Murdock, who would demand something in exchange for letting him off the assignment. Phin braced himself.

"I need a room." He stood partially behind the computer and kept his gaze averted.

It didn't make a difference. "Phin? Phin Patterson? Oh, my god." Victor Ellison swept out from behind the desk and came around to where Phin was standing. He grabbed him in a fierce bear hug and clung to him for a long moment. Vic pulled away and slapped Phin on the back. "How the hell have you been? And what are you doing here, of all places?"

"Jesus, Vic. Shut the fuck up. I can't have you making a scene right now." Phin tried to control his breathing. He should've known Vic wouldn't keep quiet.

Vic frowned and took a step backward. "Phin? What's going on?"

"If I'm going to tell you anything—which is debatable—it's not going to be here. This isn't information for the general public just yet."

Vic glanced around. "Fine. It's pretty slow right now, except for the cafe." He went back around the desk and reached underneath, producing a small sign that read "Back in Fifteen." He placed it on the desk with an old-fashioned bell next to it. "That'll do. Come into my office."

Vic motioned for Phin to join him behind the desk and led him through a door there. When they were both inside, he shut the door and waved his hand at the three swivel chairs clustered around a small table.

"Spill," Vic said once they were seated.

"All right. The State Education Department sent me here to do recon under the pretense of school improvement. They want to make it look like they're cracking down on schools that failed to meet the math and ELA standards."

"I'm sorry, I thought you just said you were sent by the Department of Ed." Vic's face contorted into an incredulous expression, somewhere between frowning and laughing.

Phin glared at him and nodded. "I did. Most of my work has been through Donald Murdock at NYSED, though technically I'm on the school's payroll. I'm an independent educational consultant." He leaned back and set his elbows on the armrests, steepling his fingers.

Vic groaned and ran a hand over his face. "Well, at least you're not still all wrapped up in your daddy's shit. Seems like you found someone else to help you screw people over."

"Not exactly."

"Not exactly, meaning what?" Vic narrowed his eyes.

"Not exactly meaning I might still be—a little—dealing with my father." Phin dropped his hands to his lap.

"Oh, hell, Phin."

Phin shrugged. "It's a living."

"You going to get out of that game before it eats your soul? That's what I did."

Phin's chest burned, and he gripped the arms of the chair. "Fuck you. It's not a game, Vic. I'm trying to do something good for once. I worked long and hard to be able to get out from under my father's thumb. I made my own connections to NYSED, and all I need is this one last commission before I can start over without their help. I'm going to do things my own way, making sure these schools stop getting dumped on. Someday, I'm going to find a way to put an end to this shit."

Vic snorted. "That's awfully noble of you. What happened to the selfish asshole I used to know and love?"

"I've changed, same as you. Besides, they're at least partly correct. These new state regs mean they need people to go in and clean things up. That's all I'm here for. If I can do this right—"

"You keep telling yourself that. It's no better than what your old man had you doing when you worked for him directly." Vic shook his head. "The day you change is the day I sprout wings. Just the fact that you took this work says a lot."

"Look, I just need to do this job and then it's like I said. I can branch out on my own. Do some real work." Phin looked away, avoiding Vic's eyes.

Vic straightened up and leaned forward, catching Phin's attention. "You're nearly thirty-five years old, Phin. I quit fucking people out of their money ages ago. You don't stop now, someone else is gonna own you 'til you die."

"That why you left?"

"Mostly. And partly 'cause I thought playing people was a pretty crap way to live. That was your father's business, and I'm not sure it isn't what's going on here, too." There was a flicker of something in his eyes, but Phin couldn't quite read it.

Phin studied his old friend. "What aren't you telling me?"

Vic looked away for a moment then trained a steady gaze on Phin. "You know what I think? You're already in over your head. I saw it coming, and *that's* why I took off."

"You never said a word. You just left."

"I know these suits, Phin. Your father wouldn't have hunted me down—this isn't a mob movie. But he would have ruined me, and he would have taken pleasure in it. Only reason he didn't try to track me was that he knew if he put too much effort into it, I could come back at him with accusations of discrimination, and they'd have been true. That bastard and his minions know what they're doing. I thought you were still in it pretty deep or I'd have gotten in touch. What you're doing now isn't any better—you're still lying to people, and you're still giving him power, even if it isn't direct."

"I see you're still a self-righteous prick. It's not like you didn't do everything that was asked of you and more when we worked together."

"And I see you still think you can come in and play hero while flushing people's lives down the crapper. How many people do they want you to fire?"

Phin squirmed. "It's not like that. The state's under pressure to pass these tests, and in turn, they're putting pressure on schools. I'm not on the payroll of either EduText or NYSED. Technically, it's the school that hired me. If this improves education then it's not all bad. And I'm not lying, exactly. I'm just...not giving all the information."

Vic scoffed. "Six of one."

"I guess that's fair." Phin shrugged. He desperately wanted to change the subject. "What's done is done. I'm here to do my job, with or without your help."

"What do you want from me?"

"Just a room." Phin paused. "And some information, since you're the only person I know here."

"Oh, that's all, is it? You want me to lend a hand in screwing over the people in this town, too?" Vic's words were harsh, but his face softened and he relaxed his shoulders.

"You going to help me or not?" Phin crossed his arms and leaned back in his chair.

Vic huffed. "I shouldn't, but I will."

"That's my man." Phin grinned. "Just like old times."

"Yeah, we'll see about that. First thing, we need to get you set up with a room." He sighed and stood up.

"Right. How well do you know this town, anyway?"

Vic looked up at the ceiling. "Been here five—no, six years. I'd say I know it pretty well." He turned his gaze on Phin, his eyes hard. "Why?"

"I think I may need more than a room. I need to know who's in around here. If I'm really supposed to be evaluating the school's performance, then I need to know whose ass to kiss."

"That's gonna be Dani Sloane. Everyone thinks the principal runs that school, but he's a tool. Dani's the real gatekeeper—no one gets past her." Vic narrowed his eyes. "You watch it with her, though. She's tough, and she doesn't take shit from people like you." Once again, an unidentifiable flicker passed across Vic's face.

"Yeah, I got it."

"You might also consider getting to know Alex Wells."

Alex Wells? He's here too? No way. No fucking way. Phin's stomach dropped and he stood still for a moment. He shook himself a little. "That's all I need to know for now."

Vic relaxed visibly. "I'll get your key."

Phin rose from his seat and Vic followed him. "How did you end up here, anyway?" Phin asked.

Vic shrugged. "I followed a rabbit trail. But that's a story for another day. Didn't really work out the way I thought it would." He led Phin back out to the desk and fished a key out from underneath. He handed it to Phin and drew up the registration. "Down the first hallway, last door on the right. First floor, farthest from the bar."

"Thanks. I owe you."

"You bet your ass you do."

Phin turned around and started toward his room. He considered flipping Vic off, but he merely raised his arm in a quick wave. On his way down the hall, Phin reflected that he wasn't sure whether Vic's presence was an asset or a hindrance. Only time would tell.

Chapter Two

Journey to the Center of the School

PHIN PREPARED himself for his meeting with the principal by reviewing the documents Murdock had given him regarding the school in North Cowell. Consulting work was in no way personal. The success or failure of a given school wasn't about whether the teachers cared about their students or even whether they were effective within the classroom. It was all about what could be measured by the standardized assessments, and this school had performed poorly for some time.

When he'd started consulting, Phin had entertained idealistic notions about helping schools provide rich learning environments. He'd been sure that he could escape the shrewd methods his father employed to get and keep clients. After several years of making a living by slashing funding, programs, and jobs, Phin had long since given in. If powerful people considered education a business, then so be it. Phin could easily play that game; he'd done it at his father's company for long enough to know how to fit in.

Before leaving his room, he glanced at his reflection in the bathroom mirror. He smoothed his sandy blond hair, which he'd had cut and styled for the occasion, and gave himself a cheeky wink and a smirk. Surely he wouldn't have any trouble finding someone to kiss up to. *Or something more. That usually works better*, he thought. There was always someone willing to provide dirt on a coworker, even in a school, for the right price. He would also need to find something entertaining to make his stay worthwhile. With any luck, he could have that *and* a successful trip. He'd secured his up-front fee by showing up, but the rest would have to wait until he'd done what Murdock had sent him to do.

Phin had the address of the school building in the file Murdock had sent with him, and he had discovered that it was within walking distance of the Railway Penny. The nice thing about being in such a small town was that everything in the town center was close by. The drawback was that it seemed like it was always slightly uphill. Logically, Phin knew that couldn't be true; but when his shins were aching from the umpteenth hill while exploring the town with Vic, his brain threw logic out the window.

Fortunately, Phin wasn't planning to wander the rest of the town first, so he figured the mile and a half walk would be relatively easy. He regretted the decision to go on foot long before he reached his destination. The unseasonable heat had not abated since his arrival. Five minutes into his trek, his feet felt swollen and overused, and sweat trickled into his eyes. He found it unfathomable that it could be so hot before noon. Phin hoped the building was air conditioned, for all the good it would do him given his state of sweaty disarray. There was no chance he would be able to freshen up before seeing anyone; that was too much to hope for. Instead, he prayed he wasn't in too rough shape to make a decent first impression.

Phin pulled open the front door of the brick two-story building. The cool air hit his damp skin, fanned in the breeze left by the door swinging shut. Phin leaned against a wall to collect himself. To his left were three closed doors. To his right was an open office, blocked off by a desk that spanned the length of the wall. Behind the desk he could see two more closed doors. He assumed the way in was around the corner. No one was in the outer office at the moment, which gave Phin the chance to catch his breath and put himself together. He didn't want to meet with the principal looking like he'd come from the gym. He closed his eyes and let his head rest against the wall. After a moment or two, he reached up to brush his hair back into place, keeping his eyes shut.

The soft, low sound of throat-clearing brought Phin back to his senses. He tensed, then opened his eyes. About ten feet away was an attractive dark-haired man who looked to be around Phin's age. His lips were curved slightly in poorly suppressed humor at Phin's expense. Phin's ears heated up, and he was tempted to glower back at the man, but that wouldn't send the right message. Instead, he kept his face neutral and waited for the other man to speak.

"Can I help you?" The man's voice was laced with amusement, though he was clearly trying to school himself into something more hospitable.

"I was sent by the State Education Department, and I'm here to see Gary Dettweiler. I have an appointment." Phin pushed off the wall and stepped closer, trying to seem casual.

"Our secretary handles the calendar. She isn't in the office at the moment. I can let her know you're here, though, and she'll get you in." He gave Phin a suspicious look. "What's this about?"

"I'm not at liberty to say."

The other man raised his eyebrows. Phin offered a condescending smile and drew himself up to his full height, shoulders back. The dark-haired man stepped back a pace without taking his eyes off Phin.

"All right," he said after several seconds. "Ms. Sloane is in the staff room. I'll tell her you're here." He turned around and walked off, his body language indicating Phin should stay put.

In less than two minutes, the man returned, accompanied by a woman who was possibly a couple of years younger than Phin. Her brown hair was pulled into a low bun into which she had stuck a pen. She smiled, but it was tight and didn't reach her eyes. The woman stepped into the inner office and stood facing Phin over the long desk.

"I'm Dani Sloane, the administrative secretary. You're from NYSED?" She sat down and pulled her chair towards the desk.

"Not exactly. I'm an independent educational consultant, but I was sent by NYSED at the request of the school. My name's Phin Patterson."

The woman's face tensed further. "What can I do for you, Mr. Patterson?"

Out of the corner of his eye, Phin caught the dark-haired man still watching him. He was leaning against the wall, his arms crossed and his jaw set. Phin angled his body so he could no longer see him.

"I have an appointment with Gary Dettweiler to discuss a few things."

"Of course." Ms. Sloane typed something and made a few clicks, but she didn't make any move to let Dettweiler know Phin was there.

"My appointment is at ten." Phin tried to keep the impatience out of his voice. *Why the hell is everyone here so hostile?*

Ms. Sloane muttered, "Mm-hm," and continued to type.

Phin struggled not to say something rude. He tilted his head, wondering about the best approach to getting what he wanted. He offered her what he hoped was a friendly-but-not-creepy smile. He let his voice drip with as much sweetness as he could, hoping she would catch the sarcasm. "It looks like you have quite a lot of work. Is there any way I can be of help while I wait? I wouldn't want my visit to make things more difficult for you."

The typing stopped. She looked up at Phin over the top of her computer screen. "Be careful what you offer, Mr. Patterson. I may take you up on that." She looked back down, but Phin caught the hint of a genuinely amused smile at the corners of her mouth, and she picked up the phone. "Gary? Mr. Patterson is here to see you. He says you're expecting him." She listened for a moment and then hung up. "He'll be out in a minute."

"I'm going to finish stocking my room." The other man, whom Phin had momentarily forgotten, turned to leave.

A tall, thin man appeared in the doorway of an inner office. "Hold on, Alex. Why don't you just get what you need and wait for us? That way I can find you later."

Alex. Is that *Alex Wells?* Phin glanced at him, searching for any trace of familiarity. His heart rate sped up significantly. *Oh, god.* His only hope was to pray Alex didn't remember him any better than he'd remembered Alex.

Alex shrugged, but Phin didn't miss the slight frown. "No problem." He stepped into the supply closet just as Dettweiler motioned to Phin to follow him to his office.

Inside the office, there was a round table surrounded by the sort of colorful plastic chairs often found in cafeterias. In one corner was a large bookshelf, of which every available inch was in use. There were books on education, leadership, and educational leadership, but the vast majority of the books were literature—everything from Shakespeare to Austin to Dostoevsky. Phin's eyes widened when he saw the collection, but he said nothing.

"Have a seat, Mr. Patterson," Dettweiler said.

Phin sat across the desk in a faux-leather armchair. He was reminded uncomfortably of the handful of occasions in which he had found himself in a similar position as a child, though the chair was far more comfortable than any he could recall.

"So," Dettweiler said. "You're the consultant we asked NYSED to send."

"Yes. I'm here to conduct teacher evaluations and put together a proposal for school improvement. As I'm sure you're aware, Donald Murdock at NYSED has recommended releasing some staff members and replacing others, pending the results of the state tests from last month. Following my evaluation, Mr. Murdock will contact you to collaborate with the school board to create a restructuring plan which will most likely involve closing and reopening under a charter."

Dettweiler sighed. "I'm aware. And I'm prepared to comply with any necessary procedures."

Phin scrutinized Dettweiler. In every previous situation involving school restructuring, the building staff were considered non-compliant; behaviors ranged from passively ignoring his presence, as Ms. Sloane had, to outright hostility once they knew why he was there. Not one building-level administrator had submitted to his inquiries without question. *No wonder Vic thinks this guy is a tool,* Phin thought. *He's awfully eager to help out the people responsible for firing his staff.*

"Pardon my ignorance," Phin said, "but I'm surprised by your willingness to cooperate."

Dettweiler didn't answer immediately; he closed his eyes and pinched the bridge of his nose. When he looked back up at Phin, he seemed resigned. "That would be because it doesn't matter what I think. I've already lost my job no matter what the state recommends, and as far as I can tell, the ball is already rolling on this. Since there's nothing I can do, I might as well make this as simple as I can."

Phin had the impression there was something Dettweiler wasn't telling him. He switched gears. "All right, then. One of the things I'm here to do is observe some of the classrooms and make suggestions regarding any immediate staff changes. The Department is looking to change the focus of the school from arts and sciences to math and ELA due to dropping test performance. Although the hope is to retain some of the teachers, some will need to be laid off, while others will need to be reassigned to other areas, provided they have appropriate certification."

"Of course. I can certainly provide—"

"Oh, that won't be necessary, Mr. Dettweiler. I have a list based on content area so I can get the most comprehensive picture of the school with the fewest classroom visits." 21

If Dettweiler was surprised, he didn't show it. He nodded. "I would be glad to assist you however I can, then."

"Good. Let's discuss a plan for making the classroom observations." Phin paused, considering how to phrase his request. "I think it would be best to restrict information to the fewest people possible. It could affect classroom observations if teachers believe their jobs are in jeopardy. For now, let's put this in terms of curriculum management."

"Of course," Dettweiler agreed.

They spent the next fifteen minutes outlining the first week. When they finally stood up, Phin was armed with a full schedule for the following several days. He shook hands with Dettweiler and they exited the inner office. Alex was still in the outer office, talking with Ms. Sloane. He looked up when Phin and Dettweiler emerged, but Phin couldn't read the expression on his face.

Dettweiler motioned at him to join them. "Alex, this is Phin Patterson. Mr. Patterson, Alex Wells. He's the school psychologist."

Phin's immediate thought was, *Shit.*

He'd been right about Alex's identity, and his job title made the situation exponentially worse. He never liked dealing with the counseling staff when he was on a job as it was. They could be difficult; they were often the hardest to sell on a school improvement plan. Phin had never quite understood this—after all, their jobs were rarely in danger, and if anyone could identify student needs it should be the counselors and psychologists. Yet somehow, he frequently failed to persuade them that he wasn't the enemy. In this specific situation, it could be even more of a challenge, depending on the functionality of Alex's memory.

On the other hand, Dettweiler was more cooperative than Phin was accustomed to, so perhaps Alex would prove to be equally willing. Phin extended his hand. They shook, and Phin tried to get a read on Alex. He didn't see any open hostility, which he took as a good sign.

"Well, come on, then. We can start by putting these things in my office. After that, I'll show you around the school." He thrust a stack of papers into Phin's hands and stalked to the office door. He shoved it open and didn't bother holding it for Phin. It swung shut, and he grabbed it just as it was about to smack him in the face.

Phin followed Alex out into the hallway and around the corner. The psychologist's office was located across from the nurse. It was a small room with one long table in the center surrounded by several more of the same colorful chairs as in Dettweiler's office. Two cushioned seats resided side by side along one wall, and there was a desk with a swivel chair next to them. A gray metal shelf took up most of the short wall opposite the door.

"You can set those on the table, Mr. Patterson."

Phin did as he was instructed, saying, "I wasn't aware that the school had an in-house psychologist."

Alex raised an eyebrow. "This district only has the one school. How else do you propose we test students who might have need for services?"

Phin furrowed his brow. "Some smaller districts share with others, and some only employ a part-time psychologist. You even have your own office."

Alex turned his attention to the stacks of papers on the table. "Well, we're in a unique situation. The town itself is more than a hundred and fifty years old, but most of the current residents haven't been here very long. There have been a lot of changes." He glanced up at Phin and frowned. "I'm sure you don't want a history lesson right now."

Phin had actually been thinking that the town's history might be interesting, but he wasn't keen to let on. Instead he said, "Ah. So you have a number of newer residents, then."

"Right, and a lot of kids who need support of various types. We have a large immigrant population, which means that we also have two language specialists so that we don't misidentify students—both those that do need help and those that don't—due to language barriers on our part. So, that's why I'm here full-time." He began stocking the shelf behind the desk, neatly arranging the supplies. He thumbed through the stack of photocopies and separated them into a row of bins, each labeled with the type of hand-out.

Phin stood by the door, unsure what to do while he waited. He crossed his arms and leaned against the frame. "Aren't you supposed to be giving me a tour?"

Alex paused and looked over his shoulder at Phin. "Were you in a hurry to be somewhere else?"

"Not really. I don't start observations until tomorrow."

"Then I have plenty of time to finish this before we go." He resumed his filing.

"What are those, anyway?"

"Mostly brain games. Students with needs are not limited to the ones who can't read or who have a diagnosed disorder or who are coping with emotional issues. Some of our students need extra challenges, so I keep a new set of puzzles each week, and the kids can come get them if they want." He frowned again. "I have no idea why I'm even telling you this. We should get going so I can show you around the school." He sighed and finished loading the brain teasers onto the shelf. "Let's go."

He stepped out into the hallway. Phin followed him, pulling the door shut behind him. Without checking to see if Phin was still with him, Alex set off.

Phin caught up to him. "I was hoping to ask you a few questions, Mr. Wells," he began.

Alex stopped abruptly and turned around. "It's doctor, actually, and I'm not sure how much help I can be. You're here to see how the classrooms and programs function. I don't do that." He turned his back to Phin and took up a rapid pace down the hallway.

Phin hurried to keep up. "I'm sorry, Dr. Wells. I just thought that perhaps you could continue what you were saying earlier about the town."

Alex slowed down and looked over at Phin. "Let's just get through the tour of the building. Wouldn't want you getting lost, now would we?" He pointed to a set of doors. "That's the elementary gym."

Running a hand through his hair, Phin sighed. It was going to be a long day.

The building was large and open. The school was two floors, with all of the elementary children on the ground level and the older students on the second floor. Each floor had four main sections. On the ground floor, the younger students were housed in one hallway and the older ones in another. To the right of the main office were the gym, library, and cafeteria. A third hallway branched off around the corner from the gym in which all of the music and art classrooms could be found. The second floor followed a similar pattern, configured slightly differently for the upper grades.

The tour didn't take long. For the duration, Alex kept a running commentary, doing a decent impression of a narrator for a dull nature documentary. As they rounded the corner by the gym, he said, "This is the old building, originally built in the seventies to replace the original school."

"This is the old building? Does that mean there's a new one?" Phin asked.

"The town had a brief swell in population about twenty-five years ago, so they built another school." He kept his back to Phin, always ahead by a pace or two.

Phin walked faster to keep up. "But you don't use it? Why not?"

"We do use it," Alex said. "That's where all the community education programs are held. We have a dance studio, English learners classes, and a variety of recreational programs. There's a community center and gym there, too."

They moved into the last hallway. They passed the music classrooms, and Phin was surprised to see that there was a set of science labs just beyond them. Each door was labeled with a different theme—Living Environment, Physical and Mechanical Science, and Computer Technology. Phin hadn't known that such a small town could sustain those programs. He made a note in his phone to look into the school's funding, since allocation of resources could explain the school's poor test performance.

"So, you mentioned a population dip and then a recent upswing—" Phin tried.

Alex turned around and frowned at him. "I fail to see how that's at all relevant to your job. If you really want the town's history, go over to the public library. I think there's a book."

Phin half expected him to add, *If you can read it.* He pursed his lips and trotted after Alex. He wasn't going to attempt to question him again; it was clear the man wanted to keep some distance. Phin hoped that they weren't going to be forced to work together in close quarters very often. Alex was already a pain in his rear.

Eventually, Alex deposited Phin back at the main office and returned to his own room without so much as a backward glance. Phin entered the office once more. Ms. Sloane was still seated at her desk, whistling softly while she typed. When she heard the door, she glanced up.

"Back from your tour, Mr. Patterson? How did it go?"

"Not bad. It'll take me a while to get used to the building layout." Phin smiled at her. "My official tasks don't start until tomorrow. Anything I can do to give you a hand, Ms. Sloane?"

Ms. Sloane raised her eyebrows. "There's always work to be done."

"Then let me help. And you can call me Phin, by the way."

She snorted. "Fine, then. I'm Dani." She waved at a stack of papers. "I don't normally do the photocopying—that's the aides' job—but one of our aides went home sick and left a stack she didn't get to. Teachers have been running their own, but these are for someone who's not in the building today. You can make yourself useful by following the instructions on the top sheet."

Dani returned to her typing, but as Phin grabbed the pile, he caught the pause in the clack of the keys and saw her peering over the top of her computer screen. It was only a flash and then she was back to work, but it was enough to make Phin smile to himself. He carried the papers into the copy room.

When Phin saw the instruction list, he nearly groaned out loud. He had assumed it was just a matter of running multiple copies of each page. As it turned out, whichever teacher needed them wanted double-sided packets, collated, stapled, and hole-punched. It was a substantial job, and it would take him a while, especially on a copier with which he wasn't familiar. He only had himself to blame; he was the one who had offered. He imagined Dani was out there laughing at him.

There was already someone else in the copy room; a petite, athletically-built brunette with a pixie cut was punching buttons on the machine. When it started, she turned to Phin. "Are you from the copier company? This will only take about ten minutes, and then it's all yours."

"Uh..." Surprised, Phin faltered. He shook his head. "I'm not—"

"I'm just going to go grab something I left in my classroom. Since you know the machine, can you just watch it while I'm gone?" She ducked out of the copy room without waiting for an answer.

While Phin stood there waiting for the copier to finish, another woman appeared in the doorway. She was considerably older than the first, tall and slender with gray hair and a lot of silver jewelry. He could smell her perfume, something floral but rustic. She had only a few pages in her hand. She turned to Phin. "I heard that. Ten minutes my ass. This thing's been acting up since last Thursday. Watch, two minutes in, it's going to jam." She leaned against the wall and studied Phin. "You're not from the copier company. Who are you subbing for?" she asked.

"Oh, um, I'm not," Phin said, caught off-guard once more. "I'm—"

The copier jammed.

"What'd I tell you?" The woman set her papers down on the table in the corner and began fiddling with the copy machine. "Damn thing does this every time the copy lady's out. I'm pretty sure it's possessed, and the demon inside it only likes her." She huffed and opened the paper jam compartment. "Doesn't help that Gia took off in the middle of her job. Some people." The paper came free and the blinking text on the copier stopped. "There."

The woman managed to restart the copy job. When the pages had resumed cheerfully spitting out into the tray, the woman turned to Phin again. "I'm Eunice Clark," she said, extending her hand. "And you are..."

"Phin Patterson." He didn't offer more details.

The woman blinked. "Phin Patterson? That's an unusual name. By any chance did you grow up in Morton Ponds?"

"Ye-es, but—"

A big grin spread over her face. "Well, damn, honey. I'll bet you don't remember me."

"Uh...no. Sorry." Phin racked his brain, trying to recall if they'd ever met before.

Eunice laughed. "I used to babysit you when you were tiny." She threw an arm around Phin's shoulders, and he tried not to stiffen. "You inspired me to go into teaching."

Phin twisted slightly to get a good look at her and raised his eyebrows. "I did?"

"Well, no, but it sounded good, didn't it?" She laughed again. "Now, I already guessed you're not here to fix this piece of shit." She waved a hand at the copier and eyed Phin. "Or was I wrong about that? Because if so, I just did your job for you."

"Nope. I promise I'm not here about the copier. At the moment, I'm just helping Dani—uh, Ms. Sloane—in the office."

Eunice scanned Phin suspiciously. "Hm. There's something you're not telling me. Well, no matter. We can catch up later. I'd like to know what you've been up to since you outgrew diapers."

Phin shifted on his feet. "Yeah, sure."

Eunice returned her attention to the copier, which was still churning out copies. "When Gia gets back, I'm going to let her have it. I'm tired of her leaving her job running so she can go do whatever, while I sit here for fifteen minutes just to do a thirty-second job."

Just then, the other woman—Gia, presumably—returned to the copy room with a textbook. She frowned at the copier. "I thought it would be done by now."

Eunice laid a hand on Gia's shoulder. "Oh, sweetie, the copier got hung up again, right in the middle of your extremely important job." Her voice was thick with artificial sweetness.

Gia's face fell. "I'm sorry. You're not mad, are you?"

"No worries," Eunice told her. "We fixed it for you. I'm sure you didn't *really* mean to leave it for us to take care of. I just hope all your copies came out right." She peered past Gia and winked at Phin, who stored the moment in the back of his brain for later use.

After what seemed like an eternity, Gia's copies were finished and she disappeared without looking at them. Eunice took care of her task efficiently and waved goodbye to Phin, giving him a conspiratorial glance on her way out. He was left wondering exactly what Eunice had done to Gia's copies that she would discover back in her classroom. Apparently, there was some Secret Copy Room Code he would have to learn before he would be able to blend in. He plunked his stack down on the table next to the copier and peered at the buttons. Phin had just figured out what he needed to do and had set the copier to its task when he heard voices in the outer office.

"Hey, Dani. You coming out with us later?"

"Probably, if I can convince Michael to watch Carlie and Jake. Just for a little while, though. Michael said he has something he needs to do after school, so I'll probably be late."

"I'll bet I know what that is." Soft laughter. "You should have a word with him about that. Nikki-Ann's mom won't be too pleased."

"Like you're one to talk, Alex. Jim used to tell me what you two got up to, and it involved a lot of sneaking around. At least Michael's honest with me, and at least it's only a girl."

"I guess." Alex's voice sounded suddenly tense. Phin swallowed. He remembered vividly all the things he'd hidden from his own parents during his teenage years. From the sound of it, Alex must have had similar memories. Maybe they had more in common than Phin had thought.

"God, I'm sorry, Alex. I didn't mean—"

"It's fine. I know you didn't."

"I'm sure you didn't come in here just to ask me about Michael. What do you need?"

There was a substantial pause and then, "I wanted to know what you thought about this whole thing. You know—State Ed sending their vultures."

At that point, Phin, peeked around the corner. Alex was standing in front of Dani's desk. She had pushed her chair away from her computer and was looking up at him. Phin held his breath.

"Not much I can say at the moment," Dani murmured, tilting her head in the direction of the copy room, then glancing over at Dettweiler's closed door.

Alex nodded. "I got it. Well, whenever you have a minute."

"Sure," Dani told him. "See you tonight, then?"

"All right. If Michael's back in time from his not-really-a-date."

"Very funny, Alex."

Laughing quietly, Alex left the office. Phin returned to the copier. The first of the packets was done; three more to go. He sighed heavily. He didn't relish spending the next month playing Copy Guy for the school. It was his own fault, really—he was the one who had offered to help. Good thing he would be able to start his real work in the morning.

Chapter Three

At the Bar, Two Boys

By THE time Phin returned to the Railway Penny, he was a mess. The day had only gotten hotter, and Phin had had to walk home because of his earlier foolish mistake in not taking his car. He ducked inside and sprinted to his room in order to avoid having to talk to anyone before he was properly clean.

He felt much better after a shower. He sat on the bed and contemplated his options. Vic had given Phin a room at the back of the ground floor, which meant that he was on the opposite side from the bar and wouldn't have to deal with the late traffic and noise. It also meant he had easy access to the community kitchen. Unfortunately, Phin hadn't had time to go shopping and therefore had no food. Unless he wanted to go to the store, his choices were limited to eating in the Railway Penny's diner, finding another local place, or driving thirty minutes north to Peroo. He settled on the first and made his way back out toward the front of the inn.

When Vic spotted him, he waved Phin over. "Heading out?" he asked.

Phin shook his head. "Thought I'd just stay here. It's convenient for now. I'll have to go shopping at some point, though."

"Yeah, that's the one thing I miss about Buffalo. No decent grocery stores. Closest Wegmans is up in Peroo, and that's a haul from here." He shrugged. "At least there's the farmer's market."

"Good to know," Phin replied. "You didn't really call me over here to ask me about food, did you?"

"Of course not. Did you have the chance to meet Dani yet?"

Phin hesitated. "Yes. But I didn't have much chance to talk to her." He leaned on the desk and lowered his voice. "I was hoping maybe you could help me out with that. You obviously know her."

Vic's eyes hardened and his lips tightened. "Absolutely not."

"Come on. It's like old times. Why don't you want to do this for me?"

"I already told you why not," Vic hissed. "You're forgetting I know exactly what you plan on doing, and I'm not gonna let that happen. Find someone else to screw around with."

Phin scowled. "Who said anything about screwing around? I just want to talk to her."

"Sure. And later on, I'm going to tap dance naked on this desk." Vic stood up and leaned into Phin's personal space. "I meant what I said."

Without flinching or backing off, Phin replied, "You always did think you had the right to play moral compass for me."

Vic wasn't giving in either. "That's because I had to rescue your ass more times than I can count." He shook his head. "This is why we can't work together, Phin."

"Are you blaming me for the way you disappeared without a trace? Because that's not my fucking fault."

"You sure about that? Your way of doing business destroyed us once. You gonna let that happen again?"

"Fine." Phin sighed and retreated. "At least get her to talk to me so I can find someone else." He held up a hand when Vic opened his mouth to protest. "You can be there if you feel like you need to babysit me."

For a moment, Vic just stood there, his mouth set in a thin line. Eventually he, too, sighed. "All right. I'll make it happen. But once you have what you need, you leave her the hell alone. Clear?"

"Perfectly." Phin spun around and stalked to the diner without another glance at Vic.

He tucked himself away in the furthest corner of the restaurant, taking his time and leaving a generous tip. He slipped out, glancing at the front desk from behind a tall plant outside the diner. Vic was no longer on duty. He'd been replaced by a blonde girl bearing a generic expression of teenage boredom. Phin stepped around the plant and walked past the desk. When the blonde girl saw him, she sat up straighter and tried to pretend that her artificial smile wasn't merely so the guests wouldn't be offended. He half-smiled back and turned the corner into the bar.

North Cowell didn't have much in the way of entertainment. There was the bar at the inn, and on his tour of the town, Phin had seen a bowling alley and a couple of churches. Vic had pointed out one or two other things, but Phin didn't remember where—or even what—they were. Vic had said that on the weekends, some of the locals drove to Peroo or one of the other larger towns nearby, but the bar in the Railway Penny also did fairly good business.

It was a weeknight, so Phin assumed the bar wouldn't be too full. He stepped inside, only to find that a good-sized crowd was already there. He made his way to the bar and snagged a seat on one of the stools.

The bartender, a pretty, dark-haired young woman who looked barely legal herself, asked, "What can I get for you?"

Phin ordered a beer and sat sipping it slowly, facing out into the room. He was so wrapped up in people-watching that he almost missed someone sitting down next to him. When he swiveled around to see who it was, he choked back a groan. He must not have been subtle enough in his effort to suppress his reaction, because the other man turned to look at him.

"Mr. Patterson."

"*Dr.* Wells." Phin stuffed down the urge to sneer. "I'm a little surprised to see you here."

Alex shrugged. "I'm meeting a couple of friends. Better than drinking alone." He looked pointedly at Phin's glass.

"Yes, because I have so many friends here to join me. What, exactly, is your problem? You've been rude to me all day."

"You, mostly."

"So why are you sitting next to me, then?" Phin gestured at the half-dozen other empty stools.

"Because it bothers you." Alex grinned.

"Obviously you drop your mature attitude when you leave school grounds." Phin curled his lip at Alex before turning back to his drink. "You could at least keep a respectful, professional distance if you're going to be hostile."

"You really don't remember me, do you?" Alex asked. He shook his head.

Fucking hell. Do I deny it, or do I tell the truth? He didn't answer; he just sat there, keeping his eyes trained directly ahead and breathing slowly to calm his rapidly increasing heart rate.

"That's what I thought." Alex's voice cut through Phin's indecision. "I may remember every detail of what you did, but you don't."

"No," Phin said, swallowing hard. "I do. I just hoped we could put that aside. It's been over twenty years." He snorted. "Have you really been carrying that drama around in your head all this time? That's pretty sad."

Alex rolled his eyes. "I've moved on, but some things leave more of an impression than others. You spent a year tormenting me after we'd been friends." He shrugged. "Seeing you here brought a lot of it back."

Phin tried a different approach. "We were kids. People change."

Alex scoffed. "I'm sure they do. But you seem to be doing pretty much the same thing you were doing when we were twelve, only now you get paid by the state to bully people. Tell me, how many people are you here to fire?"

Panic rose in Phin's throat, and he willed himself to calm down. Alex couldn't possibly know the truth; he was only guessing based on what other districts had done. "First of all, it's your school that's paying me. Second, what makes you think I'm here to fire anyone?"

"That's what they do to schools on the watch list. I know how this works."

"I'm not here to fire anyone," Phin said. That, at least, was true; someone else would take care of that.

"Right. I don't know how you sleep at night." Alex's eyes bored into Phin, giving him the urge to get away.

Phin sat up straighter and squared his shoulders. He hardened his features and met Alex's glare. "I sleep fine, thanks, knowing that I'm contributing to the improvement of education."

"Keep telling yourself that." Alex turned away again.

They didn't speak for several minutes. Phin took a slow, deep breath and hoped Alex wouldn't notice that or the beads of sweat on his forehead. He shouldn't have been foolish enough to think Alex would have forgotten what Phin had done no matter how many years it had been since they'd last seen each other. He sipped his drink and avoided any further conversation.

The door opened and Phin looked up to see Dani Sloane standing there. This was as good a time as any to have a word with her outside the school, not to mention a good excuse to exit his conversation with Alex. He stood up and set his glass on the bar.

"Where are you going?" Alex asked.

"I don't see what business it is of yours, but I'm going to go talk to Dani." Phin gestured towards the door. "Guaranteed she'll be better company."

Phin felt the press of fingers into his forearm and looked down. Alex's hand was cool against his bare skin, and it sent a chill up Phin's spine. He raised his eyes to meet Alex' gaze.

"Why?" Alex asked.

"Get to know her better, of course."

"I doubt she's your type," Alex said through gritted teeth.

Shaking his arm free, Phin looked Alex up and down. "From what I recall, she's not exactly your type, either. What makes you such an expert all of a sudden? My interest in her is purely professional."

"Right. Which is why you couldn't wait until you return to the school tomorrow." Alex folded his arms and looked directly at Phin. His eyes, a rich, chocolate brown, softened. In a soft voice he said, "I know more than you think I do. You're capable of finding someone else to hook up with."

Phin's breath caught in his throat, and his pulse sped up again in a way that had nothing to do with fear. He had to tighten his muscles to avoid sucking in his breath, taking in Alex's wavy, dark hair, his olive skin, and the light stubble on his chin. There was no harm in responding. Leaning closer so that he was in Alex's personal space, he lowered his voice in both pitch and volume. "Is that so? Are you suggesting that *you're* more my type?" He reached out and let his fingers brush against Alex's arm.

A muscle in Alex's face twitched, and his Adam's apple bobbed. He pulled away. "As if."

Phin gritted his teeth. He knew he hadn't misread the signals; he'd worked that angle long enough at his father's company. Alex was intentionally messing with him. *Damn psychologists*, he thought.

To make up ground, Phin said, "Then it shouldn't bother you if I want to talk to Dani, or even take her home with me later." He stepped back

"Screw you," Alex said. "She's my dead cousin's wife, not that it matters to you. Leave her alone."

Keeping his face neutral so as not to reveal his surprise, Phin said, "She's an adult, and I'm not sure she would appreciate you trying to protect her virtue or whatever it is you're doing." He turned and began to walk away.

"I was right," he heard Alex call after him. "You're exactly the same jerk you were when we were kids."

Phin didn't respond. Shaking, he stalked towards the place where Dani had been standing. She was no longer there. He looked around for her and discovered that she was already talking to Alex, and they were seating themselves at the bar. He watched them for a few minutes then shook his head to clear it. Alex's words had hurt, perhaps because Phin knew there was at least some truth to them. As he stood there taking in the sight of Alex and Dani laughing and chatting, he knew what he needed to do. He had to make Alex believe that he had changed. Without bothering to examine it more closely, he returned to his room to contemplate his next move.

Dani worked her way through the tables to the bar. Alex was already there, talking to Phin Patterson, the man who had been at the school that morning. Alex had his arms crossed, and he was frowning. When his face relaxed, Phin rested a hand on his arm, but Alex jerked away from him. When Phin walked away, Alex sat down at the bar and put his head in his hand. Dani waited in the shadows by the wall until Phin neared the exit before she approached Alex.

When Dani arrived at the bar, Alex stood and greeted her with a half-hearted hug. She slid onto a stool and dropped her purse at her feet. Alex sat down next to her. She ordered a soda.

"Not drinking tonight?" Alex asked. He sounded tired.

Dani shook her head. "Not on a weeknight, and not before the kids are in bed. You know that."

"Yeah, well, after today, I figured we all needed something stronger."

They sat in silence for a few minutes. Alex fiddled with his glass, but he didn't take a sip. His shoulders were hunched and his gaze trained on the television above the bar. His eyes were glazed over, though, and he didn't react when something happened on the screen that caused a ruckus from a group of men in the corner booth.

"All right, what's eating you?" Dani finally asked.

"Jerk from State Ed," Alex replied.

Dani shrugged. Phin wasn't any different from the person the State Education Department had sent the previous year. Being behind on state tests wasn't new to the school, even if NYSED's way of addressing it was, relatively speaking. "I don't see how he's any worse than the others." She pursed her lips and looked up at the ceiling. "Well, other than the fact that he's apparently here to tell us what the suits want us to change. Last year it was just an informal visit with a list of things we were supposed to improve."

Alex shook his head and looked over at her. "It's different."

Dani closed her eyes and huffed. "It obviously seems that way to you, anyway. I actually thought he was a lot nicer than most of the people we've had to deal with."

"I'm sure that's what he wants us to think." Alex turned towards her. "Why are you defending him, anyway? I didn't think you were all that thrilled to have someone stalking us for a month."

"And you were the one who wanted to know this morning what I thought of him. So, I'm telling you."

"You know, I thought you might be more on our side. Earlier, you made it sound like you had something to say about it, and now you're all full of how great he is."

Dani frowned. "I never said he was great, only that he isn't any different from the last person they sent. He's not the problem—whatever it is Gary's not telling us is."

"Trust me, Phin Patterson is definitely a problem."

She set down her glass on the bar and wrapped her fingers around it, tapping them one at a time and considering how to answer Alex. She looked at him sideways, and it hit her. She sat up straighter and turned to face him.

"You think he's cute," she said. She bit the inside of her cheek to keep from smiling. "And it bothers you because you know he's here on state business."

Alex glared at her. "I do not! And as you said, he works for the state. That's—unethical, at best. Even if I did find him attractive, there's nothing I could do about it."

"So you *do* think he's cute."

Alex dropped his head into his hands and growled. "No!"

"Oh, come on. He's exactly your type. Tall, blond, blue-eyed, well-dressed—"

"It would never end well. He's there to evaluate our school. Anything unprofessional between us could cause more problems than it's worth. Besides, as I pointed out before, he's a jerk."

Dani rolled her eyes. "I never said anything about there being something between you. He's probably straight. Can't you just appreciate the eye candy and let this pass? Seriously, just admit he's hot."

"Whatever," Alex muttered, turning back to his drink. "He's not straight. Your observational skills are terrible, Dani. And I thought you said cute."

"That too." She smirked. "He has a nice ass."

"Please, just shut up now."

"Gladly. Eunice and Gia are here, and you know how they get if they sniff matchmaking." Dani paused. "Actually, it might not be a bad idea if you said something. Poor Gia still seems to think she's got a chance with you." Dani raised her hand and waved to the others. "They're coming."

"Well, thank God for small favors." Alex swiveled around in his seat and stood up to greet Eunice and Gia.

"Hey, you," Eunice said, parking herself on the stool Alex had vacated. "Should we find a table?"

"I can't stay much longer," Dani told them. "I promised Michael he wouldn't have to put the little ones in bed."

"You don't have to go too, do you?" Gia pointedly ignored Dani in favor of speaking to Alex.

Dani rolled her eyes behind Gia's back and caught Alex's attention. She winked at him, and he finally cracked a smile.

Eunice had already moved on. "So, new guy was in the building today. Subbing, maybe, but I've never seen him in there before. Dani, you know anything about it?"

"Only a little. He's not a sub. He's from State Ed."

"I know him, by the way," Eunice said. She motioned to the bartender.

"You do? How?" Dani frowned.

"Used to babysit him when he was in diapers." Eunice laughed. "I lived next door to his grandparents."

Dani snickered. "Then you don't really *know him*, know him."

"I know his family." Eunice reached over to take her drink. "His father's a real piece of work. His grandmother's pretty nice, though. I think she and my mother are still friends."

Alex leaned around Gia. "You used to babysit him?"

"Sure did, till I left for college when he was about three."

For the first time since they arrived, Alex laughed. "Oh, that's fantastic."

Dani poked him. "I'm sure he's a very different person now that he's an adult."

"Very different," Eunice agreed. "I would make a comment, but it would sound creepy coming from me. Gia, you saw him. What did you think?"

"Cute. *Very* cute. Nice ass."

Alex choked audibly on his drink, and Dani smacked him on the back slightly harder than necessary.

Gia continued, "Wait, wasn't he the copy guy?"

"Gia, didn't you hear Dani? He's from State Ed." Eunice huffed.

"Oh. Well, he's still cute." Gia grinned. "It was super nice of him to fix the copier, too." She frowned. "Too bad he couldn't have done it before it ruined half my packets this morning. For some reason, it flipped it so the back side of every page was upside down."

"I think being around kindergartners all day is causing you to lose brain cells," Eunice suggested. "He wasn't fixing the damn copier! And who cares what he looks like? I want to know what he's doing here." She twisted back and forth on her stool.

"Isn't it obvious?" Alex asked. "He's the one they sent to do their dirty work. I'll bet he's making a list of all the programs we have to cut."

"I think we just need to wait and see," Dani said. "He said that officially, he's an educational consultant. His job is to help us create a school improvement plan. That doesn't sound so bad. We've been in trouble for years." Gary—the principal—hadn't informed her of anything other than the barest facts. Instead of telling the others that, she went on, "Let's assume he's telling the truth until we have the chance to see what happens."

While the others continued to discuss what she'd said, Dani collected her purse from the floor by her stool. She straightened up and slung it over her shoulder. Alex glanced over at her.

"Want me to walk you out?" he asked.

"Sure." Dani knew it would give him an excuse to escape Gia.

Eunice stood up. "Heading out?"

"Yeah. Michael said he's got a lot of homework tonight."

Alex snorted. "Homework. Right." Dani smacked his arm.

Gia tilted her head to look up at Alex. "You're not leaving too, are you?" Dani had to turn away so she wouldn't be caught laughing. As it was, Alex noticed and pursed his lips together.

"As a matter of fact, I am. I'm pretty tired." He moved away from Gia.

"Have fun, you two!" Dani called over her shoulder as they walked toward the door.

Alex walked Dani past the Railway Penny to the row of houses next door. Neither of them said anything until they reached the porch. Dani fidgeted, searching for words.

"You all right?" Alex asked.

"Yeah. Just thinking that something feels...I don't know, off. Do you trust me?"

Alex lifted his eyebrows. "Of course."

"I don't want to say anything until I've had a chance to check things out because you know how involved Eunice has been in the shit with the school board all year. But Gary's not telling me something, and I want to find out what it is. Can you not ask me about it until I do some digging?"

"Is this about Phin—the NYSED guy?"

Dani furrowed her brow. "Sort of, but it's more about what Gary's been doing in those meetings with school board members. Just let me work on it, okay?"

"Fine. You'll fill me in later?"

"Of course." She smiled at him.

He peered at her, and he narrowed his eyes. "There's something else. You sure you and the kids are good?"

"Yes." She looked away. "I should go in."

Before Dani could reach for the doorknob, Alex pulled her in for a quick hug. "Get some rest, okay? I'll take the kids off your hands on Friday so you can have a break."

"You're a lifesaver," Dani told him.

"I know." He grinned, and she punched his arm.

They said goodnight, and he turned around and walked away, headed back towards the parking lot at the back of the Railway Penny. Dani watched him go, wondering again what Phin had said to him earlier to upset him. She hoped they could work it out at least long enough for her to find out what was really going on.

Chapter Four

How to Screw Friends and Influence Schools

Seated at the desk in his office with the door shut, Alex tapped his pen against the table, reading through the application in front of him. He scrawled a note on a separate sheet of paper before laying the pen aside and rubbing his eyes with his fingers. Sighing heavily, he pushed everything away from him and sat back.

The light tap on his door startled him. He gathered the papers and tucked them into a folder then called, "Come in."

He cringed when he saw the tall blond man in the doorway. Phin smiled, and there was something condescending in it. Alex shoved his folder under a binder and stood up.

"What were you working on?" Phin asked, leaning around Alex to peer at his desk.

"That would be confidential," Alex informed him.

"And it also might be relevant to my review."

Alex glared at Phin. "It's not. What do you want, anyway?"

"Just to ask you a few questions." Phin stepped further into the office.

"About what?" Alex folded his arms and eyed Phin as he looked around the office.

"Just some standard things about your procedures for tracking students with educational needs." Phin crossed the office to the shelf, tilting his head to read the titles on the binders there. "What are these? You have one for each grade level."

"They're what I use to help teachers create action plans. You know, you could ask any classroom teacher and they'll tell you everything you need to know."

Phin ran his finger down the spine of one of the binders then pulled it off the shelf. "Right, but you're the resident expert. Teachers can only tell me how they refer their students, not what happens afterward between you and the district." He opened the binder.

"Give me that." Alex snatched the binder back, snapped it shut, and replaced it on the shelf with a huff. "Look. If you want to see them, just ask. I don't keep student information in there—that's all in the locked files in the main office. You could probably have permission to read some of the IEPs, as long as you use copies where identifiers are eliminated."

"I see. I'll have to check on that, then." Phin inspected the rest of the shelf, examining the books and the color-coded bins. "You are impressively organized," he remarked, pulling one of the bins down to peer inside.

Alex gritted his teeth. "Stop messing with my filing system, please."

"Sorry. Just looking." Pushing the bin back and turning around, Phin smirked.

"Why are you really here?"

Phin held out his hands. "I told you. I want your expert opinion. You're responsible for making sure these kids are on the right track. Do you also do counseling?"

"No. That's Lilia Wardynsky down here and Raquel Yeminez upstairs." Alex frowned. "You should know that. Come to think of it, you should also already know how kids are placed for special education."

Phin sighed, and it still sounded like he was patronizing Alex. "I'm here because I'm trying to be nice. I have to work at this school for the next month, and we might as well get along." Another insincere smile. "I'll make you the same offer I made to Dani. I'm at your disposal. If you need help, I'm willing."

A shiver ran down Alex's spine. He flashed back to their meeting in the bar and wondered exactly what Phin meant by that. "In between all those classroom observations and meetings with Gary, right? No, thank you. I'm fine." He turned his back on Phin and pretended to reorganize the shelf.

"Dr. Wells—"

Alex spun around and threw his hands in the air. "Why are you still here? Go find someone else to bother."

"What if I think the information you have is more valuable?" Phin crossed his arms and tilted his head, jutting out his chin.

"And what if I think you're wasting your time? I have nothing here that would be of interest to you."

The corner of Phin's mouth curled upward. "I would say you're mistaken. There's plenty here for me to take interest in." His gaze traveled downward slowly, making Alex feel exposed.

Heat spread across his face, followed by a surge of anger. Placing his hands on the table and leaning toward Phin, Alex replied, "I don't know what kind of game you're playing, but it won't work on me. Is this how you've handled your other clients?"

"I have no idea what you're talking about."

"Yes, you do."

"All right, you got me." Phin chuckled softly. He moved in closer and lowered his voice. "I once signed an entire multi-year textbook contract on my appeal alone." His smile faltered, and he looked away briefly. He snapped his attention back to Alex and narrowed his eyes. "You're not the most difficult client I've ever worked with, though it's close."

"I'm not your client. There's no reason for your behavior."

Phin licked his lips. "I didn't make a mistake in the bar the other night."

Alex's pulse jumped, and he had to swallow several times before he could answer. "Enough. If you have something you need, you can get it from someone else. Whatever you're selling, I'm not buying it." He straightened up.

Following his lead, Phin backed off. "Look. I'm trying to be pleasant here. I realize we don't have a stellar history, but the least you could do is act like a professional."

"Because that's how you're behaving, right?"

Phin slammed his hands down on the table. Alex flinched, but he stood his ground. "I'm not asking for much, Dr. Wells. I just want the chance to sit down and talk with you about your official policies. Like it or not, you are the expert on your job."

Alex set his mouth in a thin line and glared at Phin. "Fine. But let's not pretend that we don't know each other. You can drop the formalities. I'll meet with you again on one condition."

"Oh? What's that?"

"We keep it strictly to questions and answers about the school's policies. Nothing else. Are we clear?"

"Perfectly. When would be a good time to start?"

Before Alex could answer, a slender, dark-haired boy poked his head inside the office. "Oh. Are you busy?" he asked in a softly accented voice.

Phin arched an eyebrow. He stage-whispered, "Your students don't need to make an appointment?"

Alex didn't answer. "What can I do for you, Josue?"

"Um...can I talk to you for a minute?" Josue looked down at the floor.

"And that's your cue," Alex informed Phin. "Out."

"I'll stop by later to set up that appointment," Phin replied. He turned around and walked out.

Alex watched him go, and his eyes traveled involuntarily downward, inspecting Phin's backside as he retreated. His ears heated up when he realized what he was doing. Shaking himself a little, Alex returned his attention to the boy in his doorway, hoping he hadn't noticed anything. "Come on in." He motioned to the seats at the long table.

Josue stepped in and Alex closed the door. "You have a minute?"

Glancing at the clock, Alex said, "Just a few. School's almost out." He tilted his head. "Do you want to see Miss Yeminez instead?"

Josue shook his head. "No. It's about...that thing I told you. She wouldn't get it. I mean, not like you."

"All right." Alex settled himself at the table next to Josue.

Josue sat silently for a minute, his folded hands resting on the tabletop. At last he said, "I didn't talk to my parents."

"That's all right. I told you to take your time. There's no one right way to do this."

"I know." He looked at Alex sideways. "I came out to my brother."

"Oscar?"

"Yeah."

Alex nodded. "How'd it go?"

"Good, I guess. He didn't freak or nothing." Josue stretched his arms out and cracked his knuckles then sat back in his seat.

"Is that what you came here to tell me?"

"*Sí*." He fidgeted. "I mean, no." He sighed. "The guy I told you about. I talked to him, too."

"All right," Alex said. "What happened?"

Josue shrugged. "He said he needed to think about it." He swore quietly in Spanish. "I think I maybe got him mad."

"Give him time. He asked you for that." A nervous twinge stirred in Alex's gut. "Did he—did he say anything else?" Alex held his breath.

Frowning, Josue replied, "No. Why?" He sat up in his chair. "Did he say something to you?"

Alex exhaled. "You know I can't tell you that. For now, don't assume anything unless he says it, okay?"

"Yeah, I guess." He paused and then gave a tiny smile. "Want to hear about Oscar?"

Josue stayed for a bit longer, filling Alex in with more details on what had happened with his brother. When they were through talking, Alex opened his door to find Michael standing there, about to knock. Alex stepped back to let him in, but he remained hovering in the doorway.

Without a word to Alex, he said, "Josue, you ready?"

"Yeah."

"Michael," Alex said.

"What?"

"I'm taking Carlie and Jake after school. Make sure your mom knows where you'll be if you're going out."

"Whatever." Michael turned his back on Alex and stalked off, Josue in tow. He leaned toward his friend and said, "What were you doing in there, anyway?"

"Nothing. 'S cool." Josue called over his shoulder, "*Gracias*."

"No problem, Josue."

Alex shook his head and went back into the office. He closed the door then sat down at his desk, pulling the folder out from underneath the binder. With a heavy sigh, he opened it and retrieved the papers, spreading them back out on the desk in front of him. He glanced at the clock, making a mental note of how long he had until Carlie and Jake were in his care. Working steadily, he could finish before they arrived in his office. He picked his pen up and resumed writing.

Dani leaned forward and pressed her lips against Vic's jaw, kissing and nipping gently. He was situated on the love seat with Dani riding his lap, their clothes strewn across the living room and their groans of pleasure rising around them. She was in Vic's half of the two-family house they shared, and they were benefiting from their friendship. It was a rare evening when none of Dani's kids were home. Alex had taken the younger two for ice cream and miniature golf over in Morton Ponds; Michael was out with his friends. Dani knew what that meant: they were probably four-wheeling up on Old Stan's property. Old Stan would make sure they didn't do anything too stupid.

They moved together toward resolution, Vic finishing first and taking Dani with him. Once her heart rate had slowed, Dani gingerly pulled off and flopped next to Vic on the sofa. He rose to divest himself of the condom and clean up. While he was occupied, she took the opportunity to freshen herself somewhat and get dressed. She was still shaking a little from their near-frantic session. Tugging her shirt back into place forcefully, she shut out the nagging thought that she and Vic would eventually need to decide what this was. She flopped back on the couch, listening to him rummage around in the other room.

Vic had been good to her over the years, and he had been there for her after Jim's death. He was grieving too, but not in the same way. Dani still wasn't exactly sure how their relationship had evolved. They had never had a conversation about it; it simply was what it was—taking care of each other and occasionally enjoying the perks of being friends with benefits. They'd kept it private; not even Alex knew everything.

Vic returned to the room with two glasses of water. Dani pulled the coffee table closer to the sofa and he plunked the glasses down on it.

"God," he said, still sounding slightly out of breath. "That was incredible." He reached out and rubbed the back of her neck.

Dani smirked. She loved to hear him talk about it that way. She picked up her glass and took a long draught of water. Holding the glass against the top of her knee, she leaned back. "Someone from State Ed was at the school the other day," she said. "He had an appointment, but he hung around afterward. I think he was trying to get information out of me."

Vic's eyebrows shot up, and he tilted his glass a little too far, spilling water down his chin. After he wiped his mouth, he muttered, "He moves fast."

"What?"

Vic looked over at Dani, his expression unreadable. He sighed. "You're talking about Phin Patterson, right?"

"Yes. How did you know?" Dani crossed her arms and pursed her lips, waiting for him to answer.

"I...uh..." Vic cleared his throat. "He's staying at the Penny. I might have told him to go speak to you about the school."

Dani snorted. "Well, you could have warned me. Supposedly, he's here to make recommendations for school improvement." She smiled, remembering Phin's attempt to charm her. "He was hitting on me, I think." Her thoughts wandered back to the bar, and she frowned. "He might have been hitting on Alex, too."

Vic's face had gone from somewhere between guilt and exasperation to scowling in under three seconds. "That figures."

Laughing, Dani replied, "Alex hates him."

"He does?" Vic's eyebrows rose once more.

"So it seems. Alex had to play tour guide at the school, and from what I could tell, it wasn't overly friendly." She giggled. "Plus, he bitched about it at the bar the other night before Eunice and Gia showed up."

"About him hitting on you?"

"No, about his being at the school and having to show him around." She decided not to mention the other part of their conversation. "Why are you so bent out of shape about a little flirting?"

"I sent him to talk to you, not make a move on you." Vic reached over and squeezed her hand. "Good thing Alex has a clear head. He should keep an eye on him just in case."

"That won't be a problem, I'm sure. But you and Alex both need to lay off. I'm a grown woman. As it happens, I'm not particularly interested in this guy. But if he's not being honest with us about why he's scoping out the school, a little charm might go a long way."

Vic's mouth was set in a thin line. He didn't say anything for a moment, and Dani wondered if he was going to bring up Jim. It was an argument they'd been having on and off for the better part of six months. "Aren't you the one who keeps saying I need to move on with my life?"

"This isn't what I had in mind. What reason could you possibly have for getting cozy with Phin? I'm not sure it's a good idea. You know, that way. Talk to him, but don't get too close."

Dani felt heat rising in her cheeks. She had just told Vic she wasn't interested in anything other than working him over for information, and he was treating her like a teenager going out on a first date. "I don't see why—"

Vic held up his hand. "Fine. Just be careful, okay? Guys like him take what they want and leave a mess for other people to clean up."

"What aren't you telling me, Vic?"

"Nothing. Forget I said a word about it." He leaned against the couch, tipped his head back, and closed his eyes.

Dani remained silent for a moment, resting her head on Vic's shoulder and looping her arm through his. Eventually, she said, "He seems like a nice enough guy. I don't know much about him, though. I just thought maybe I should let him in a little, see if I can find anything out. If he's interested, maybe I could..." She trailed off and looked at Vic out of the corner of her eye.

Vic turned his body towards her. "I can tell you anything you want to know about him."

And there it was. "Oh?" She feigned surprise.

He sighed. "I know him."

"I got that already. *How* do you know him?" She leaned forward, keeping her eyes locked on Vic's.

"We went to school together." He pulled his arm away and folded his hands together. He twitched his thumbs.

"And?" Dani laid her hand lightly on Vic's arm.

"And we used to be friends. Now we're not."

"And..." she nudged him.

"And he's..." Vic paused. "He's not the most honest person I've ever met."

"I see. Well, what do you recommend, then?"

Vic leaned back on the couch and closed his eyes. "Why don't we just invite him here?" He cracked one eye and peered at her. "That way, we can all keep an eye on him together."

"All right. Next week, then? I'll see if Eunice and Gia want in on it too. I'll bet Gia could sniff something out."

"Fine."

It was clear to Dani that she wasn't going to get anything else just yet. Instead of continuing that line of conversation, she asked, "You want to go again before the kids get home?"

Vic shook his head. "It's getting late. They're not going to be out much longer, and I have to get back to work. I'm on for the rest of the night."

She stood up. "All right. I think Alex is coming over for dinner tomorrow. Should I hold everyone off until your break so you can join us?"

"Sure." Vic rose to his feet to walk Dani out.

Dani snagged her keys from the table by the door. She turned to look at Vic. His features had softened, so she knew he had calmed down. He leaned over and gave her a light peck on the cheek.

"Good night," she said, and she stepped out into the warm evening.

Phin had successfully avoided Vic for two days after their confrontation. Now he needed to get out of North Cowell for a while. Everything about the town felt confining to him. It wouldn't have mattered to him if the bar at the inn had a live band and free drinks all night; he couldn't stay there for his entertainment. Leaving meant passing Vic on his way out the door. He'd already seen Vic come in around eight to relieve the blonde girl. He would have to take his chances.

The weather had cooled somewhat, but it was still warm enough that Phin didn't bother with a jacket. He grabbed his keys and headed out. Vic's attention was directed at something else, so Phin hoped to sneak past unnoticed. He moved as quickly and quietly as he could without appearing strange to the few people passing by.

It was not meant to be. The minute Phin passed the desk, Vic's head shot up and he called out, "Phin!"

Phin balled his hands and pinched his lips together to keep from making a frustrated noise. He composed himself by taking a few deep breaths and then turned around. "Yeah?"

Vic motioned him over. "I need to talk to you for a minute."

Leaning on the desk, Phin asked, "About what?"

"It's all set. I did what you wanted me to. I worked it so Dani's interested in talking to you. You'd better be careful, though. You know what I'll do to you if you try using your usual methods." He furrowed his brow. "Also, would you mind telling me just what the hell you said to Alex the other night? Dani's under the impression that Alex—how did she put it? He hates you." Vic crossed his arms.

Phin licked his lips and swallowed. "I didn't say anything to him."

"I find that hard to believe. Look, I told you to talk to them, not make them suspicious and angry. You want my help? Then stop antagonizing everyone I send your way." He put his hands on the desk and leaned forward. "Give it to me straight, Phin. What's going on?"

"First tell me why you're acting like it's your job to keep track of Dani. I had the same conversation with Alex. Him, I understand—he says she was married to his cousin or something. But you? I don't follow."

Vic just stood there for a moment, and Phin could see the internal debate. At last Vic said, "I don't need to tell you anything. Dani's a friend."

"Then I don't need to explain anything to you, either." Phin turned away.

"All right! I'll tell you," Vic said.

Phin turned back around. "I'm listening."

"Dani's a friend," Vic repeated.

"Yes, you've already said that. Get to the part where you tell me why that's important." Phin tapped his fingers impatiently on the desk.

Vic sighed. "When I came here, I had no one. She and Jim—he was her husband—took me in. They didn't ask any questions, just accepted me. Jim gave me a job here and made me co-owner just before he got sick. Then, after he died, Dani, Alex, and I only had each other." He paused and looked away for a moment then returned his gaze to Phin. "I love her, Phin. And I can't have her find out that I worked for the bastard who's about to ruin this town."

Phin scoffed. "Please. 'Ruin' is overstating it a bit, don't you think? You've always thought you were so much better than me. Guess you can't play that game anymore."

"You know what? Go to hell. You asked, I answered. Besides, it's your turn now. What did you say to Alex at the bar the other night?"

Instead of answering the question Vic was really asking, Phin replied, "I asked him if I was his type. He got pissy." Phin shrugged.

"You know that's not what I meant. I know Alex pretty well, and I doubt that would've been a problem if he hadn't already had some issue with you."

Phin didn't answer immediately. When he'd moved to Buffalo just before eighth grade, he had been determined that no one would ever know about Alex. What had happened between them was their secret. If Alex hadn't told Vic, then Phin wasn't going to either—at least, not the whole story. He decided he might be able to put Vic off by giving him enough of the truth to satisfy his curiosity and leave it at that.

"We went to school together. Before I knew you. We...weren't exactly friends." Phin held his breath, hoping Vic wouldn't press.

Vic looked thoughtful. "I wondered about that. I figured out you grew up in the same town, but it was bigger back then, and you left before high school. Huh. Makes sense, though. You *were* kind of an arrogant jerk in school." He snorted. "A lot like now."

"Hey! I've changed. Sort of." He looked Vic in the eye. "Are we okay, then?"

"We'll see."

"I promise not to try anything with Dani. Anyway, all I want out of her is her trust. I'm sure I can find someone else to give me information if I have to."

"You'd better. Meanwhile, I suggested Dani invite you to have dinner with us. She thinks it will give us time to catch up on old times." Vic grinned. "That wouldn't be so bad, as long as you can keep things civil. And also keep your trap shut about anything having to do with my work for your father."

Phin scowled. "Of course I can. I don't want to screw this up."

"Good." Vic pulled a book out from under the desk. "Now, get out of here. You might try that new bar up in Peroo," he suggested as he settled himself back in his chair. "Live jazz tonight."

Phin turned around and headed for the exit. He glanced back over his shoulder at Vic, who had the book open and his eyes trained on the page. Sighing heavily, Phin released the tension he'd been carrying through their conversation. As long as he played it more carefully with Dani, he would be able to count on Vic to help him out. Relieved, he set out for Peroo. With any luck, he might wind up having a very good time by the end of the night.

Chapter Five

A Secretary's Tale

Dani arrived early for work. She wanted some time to herself to set her things out and enjoy the quiet before the official chaos of the school day began. The previous week hadn't been bad; she'd expected much more upheaval with Phin stalking teachers all day, but he'd remained unobtrusive. Still, it would be nice to have a few minutes of peace before everyone showed up for the staff meeting.

She plunked her purse and a cup of coffee down on the desk and began sorting through the drawers, looking for a pen. She needed to make a list; lists were a guaranteed way to clear her head, and doing it by hand gave her more time to think than just typing it into a schedule. Gary had left her a dozen tasks he wanted accomplished before noon, including several phone calls. She located a small tablet of paper in the third drawer down and set it out on the desk.

A smile crept across her face when she thought about Phin and his mild flirting. While she had no interest in him herself, she had a good idea who might. Phin was due to observe two of her friends that week, and she decided to grab them on their way in. She scrawled herself a note with a few ideas to pursue later.

By the time she'd organized her to-do list and tidied her desk, most of the staff had arrived. She waved to the high school secretaries as they came in and scanned the entryway for Gia. When Dani spotted her, she motioned Gia over.

"What's up?" Gia asked. She shifted her bag higher on her shoulder.

Dani tried to sound casual. "I was wondering if you wanted to meet up after school."

"Sure." She furrowed her brow. "What about your kids, though?"

"You could just stop by my place," Dani suggested. "I'll send them to do their homework while you're over."

"Okay." Gia tilted her head to the side. "What's going on?"

"Nothing much. I just have a question for you, that's all. About that thing we were discussing at the Penny."

Gia grinned. "You mean the guy—"

"Shhh! Yes. Just don't say anything, okay?"

"No problem." Gia gave a one-shoulder shrug. "I'll talk to you later, then."

"Yeah."

Gia stepped away from the main desk and turned the corner. Dani kept her eye out for Eunice and finally caught sight of her, struggling with two large bags. Dani jumped up and exited the office to get the door.

"What is all that?" Dani asked, taking one of the bags and sagging under its weight. "Ugh. This weighs a ton."

Eunice grunted. "Potting soil. The kids are planting beans today. They get to take them home over the summer, but we have a few weeks for them to get the plants to sprout. We're going to see what happens under different conditions."

"Oh. You want help taking this to your room?"

"Sure." Together they hauled the bags to Eunice's classroom. Dani was grateful it was only a few doors down the fifth grade hallway.

When they had deposited the bags by the coat closet, Dani said, "Gia's coming over after work. Any chance you could join us?"

Eunice eyed Dani. "Probably. Why?"

"I think we need to talk about some things. You know, like at the bar the other night."

"Oh. Yes, I think you're right. I take it you have something in mind?"

"I might," Dani admitted. She leaned against the door. "I'll fill you in on the details later."

Eunice raised her eyebrows. "And I assume whatever you're thinking has something to do with our Miss Gia?"

"Of course." Dani smirked. "Not going to say any more right now, though." She glanced around.

Eunice nodded. "Good idea. Well, thanks for the help. I've got to get to that meeting."

They returned to the front of the building together then parted ways. Dani reentered the office and sat down at her desk to begin her tasks. She had all day to figure out how to explain things to Eunice and Gia; for now she needed to concentrate on work.

An hour into the school day, Phin arrived. He greeted Dani, and she handed him his visitor's badge. He clipped it to his belt loop and scrawled his name on the sign-in sheet while she pulled up the schedule so she could find the list of classrooms he would be visiting. For the next two weeks, he would be observing teachers at the elementary level before moving upstairs to check in on some of the high school classes.

Dani peered at Phin over the top of her screen. "I see you're in third grade this morning. That's the B wing, room three. Think you can find it all right?"

"I think so." He put his hand to his pocket then reached in and withdrew his phone. "Hang on." He made a few swipes and returned the phone to his pocket. Rolling his eyes, he said, "Sorry about that. I didn't mean to be rude, but that might have been an important email."

Dani shrugged. "I wouldn't know. Some of us don't have phones that do everything for us."

He laughed. "It doesn't do everything. I still have to do my own laundry." He rested his hand on the desk. "Am I all set, or do I need to do something else before I go down to the room? More convoluted copy jobs, perhaps?"

She grinned. "Nope. Copy Lady's back to work, so nothing extra today. You signed in, so you're all set."

"Great!" He flashed a charming smile at her, and she almost expected his teeth to gleam.

As he rounded the corner, Dani heard a door open. Curious, she half-stood so she could look around through the open front of the office. Alex emerged from his room, and he stood facing Phin. He opened his mouth to say something, but before either of them made another move, there was a commotion as two students came barreling down the stairs, jumping the last two and nearly colliding with Alex and Phin in the middle of the hallway. Dani suppressed a groan. It was Michael, her fifteen-year-old, and his friend Josue.

Alex put out a hand to stop them. "What's going on?"

"Sorry, Mr. Wells. We were just coming to get the copies Miss Del Rey asked for." Josue said. He looked down at the ground, appropriately apologetic; Michael scowled.

"Be more careful next time," Alex said. He stepped away from the boys, giving Michael a long look. Michael refused to return his gaze.

Dani let them into the office, and they made their way to the copy room. Phin and Alex still stood in the hallway. While she waited for the boys, she watched them.

Phin said, "You let your students get away with calling you 'mister'? You were pretty strict with me."

Alex chuckled softly. He leaned in and said, "Yep," letting the "p" pop just a little. He turned around and walked back into his office, shutting the door behind him and leaving Phin staring after him.

Dani shook her head and went back into the copy room. She ushered the boys out and then sat back down at her desk. Before the end of the day, she would have to put Phase Two of her plan into action, preferably without any interference from Alex.

That afternoon, Dani stepped away from her desk to deliver a message to a teacher she knew was in the staff room. When she returned, she found Michael sitting in a chair outside Gary's office. She sighed.

"Michael, what are you doing here?"

He scowled and slouched in his chair, arms folded across his chest. He wouldn't meet her eyes. "It doesn't matter."

Dani sat down in the seat next to him and put her hand on his arm. "It matters. What happened this time?"

Keeping his arms crossed, he turned away from her. "I glued the lock on Adam Fowler's locker."

"What? Michael, why?"

"Because Adam's a douche, Mom."

"Michael!"

"Sorry," he replied, but he sounded insincere. "He is, though."

"Fine." Dani adjusted, crossing her legs and making herself more comfortable. "And what, exactly, has Adam done to give you that impression?"

Michael sat up and flung his arms up. "I dunno, Mom, why don't you ask the sixth graders he keeps taking food from? He walks past them and just takes stuff off their trays. He's always acting like he's so awesome just because he's the star soccer jock. He's such a complete guy's guy, and he picks on anyone he thinks is too girly. And Nicki-Ann says her parents love him, but he's always being such a jerk to her. He treats her like he owns her, and they're not even going out." He flopped back against his seat and looked at the floor.

"Michael?" Dani put her hand on his shoulder. "Is this just about Nicki-Ann? Because I'm not okay with you taking things into your own hands, especially over a girl."

He shook his head. "Didn't you even hear me, Mom? It's not just about her."

"So, what happened?"

"Adam was after Josue. He says shi—stuff to Josue all the time. Like, calls him names and...things. Gives him crap because his brother works here, says Oscar cleans toilets 'cause he can't get a real job. And he's always just on him about everything. So I figured I'd just do one thing back, and he'd stop. But he made such a racket about it, and I got caught."

Dani huffed. "So you're not sorry you did it, just sorry you got caught. Michael, that's just not right. You need to say something next time."

Michael turned in his chair to face her. "You don't think I have? God, Mom. I'm not that stupid. But there's nothing else I can do because Josue can't even talk to his parents. And I get that, because I can't talk to you either, sometimes."

"What do you mean?"

"Nothing, Mom. Just go back to what you were doing. I can take the consequences." He turned away.

"Michael." Dani squeezed his forearm lightly until he looked up at her. "What aren't you telling me?"

He shook his head. "I'm not going to make it worse than it already is." His eyes were hard and his jaw set. "Alex knows. Ask him if you're that desperate. It's his fault anyway."

Dani looked at Michael without saying anything for a moment. She had no idea what Alex had done to make him so angry. They'd been at odds for some time, and Alex hadn't been any more forthcoming than Michael. She sighed. Her inability to communicate effectively with all the boys and men in her life was draining. She stood up. "All right. Ms.

Winthrop is in a meeting, but she'll be out in about five minutes. I assume that's why you're down here and not upstairs?"

"No. They thought you should keep an eye on me while I wait." He rested his elbows on his knees and stared down at his hands.

"That's what happens when you keep doing this kind of thing. Eventually, even I won't be able to do anything to help you."

"Right, Mom. Because this is about me and not about making sure you keep your job."

"Keeping my job *is* about you, as well as Carlie and Jake." She shook her head. "Try thinking of someone other than yourself for a change." She walked back to her desk and sat down, keeping her chair turned so that she faced away from Michael. It was a bit childish, but she couldn't take any more of his attitude.

As she wrapped up the last of her tasks for the day, Phin approached the desk. He unclipped his visitor's badge and set it in the basket on the desk. "Here you go," he said. He was entirely too cheerful for Dani's present mood, and she merely nodded at him.

"That kid in trouble?" he asked, tilting his chin towards Michael.

"Always," she replied.

"Sounds a lot like me at that age. I wasn't exactly one for rules."

Dani glanced back and saw that Michael was eying Phin from underneath his bangs.

Phin addressed him. "What did you do, kid?"

Instead of answering, Michael said, "I saw you this morning."

"Ah, right, when you nearly ran me over." Phin chuckled. "I see your day didn't get much better."

"My day was just fine." Michael glowered at him.

Phin only laughed harder. "I suppose that's why you're sitting outside the principal's office. So, let me ask you again—what did you do?"

"Glued a kid's locker shut," Michael mumbled.

"What was that? I didn't quite catch it."

"I said, 'I glued a kid's locker shut.'" Michael crossed his arms and glared at Phin.

"I have to admit, that's not one I ever tried," Phin said. "Creative."

"Hey!" Dani exclaimed. "Don't encourage him."

Phin put up his hand. "It's all right. I got it."

Dani pursed her lips. "Do not make this worse," she hissed.

"No problem," Phin replied. "What's your name, kid?"

"Michael."

"Okay, Michael. Why'd you do it?"

"Because the kid's a douche."

"Michael James Roberts! You will stop using that word immediately." Dani glared at him. When she looked back at Phin, his eyes were wide and his eyebrows raised. Dani explained, "He's my son."

"I see. Now this makes a lot more sense." He turned his attention back to Michael. "All right, so the kid's a jerk. Guaranteed, though, this isn't going to have been worth it."

Michael argued, "Yes, it will. He deserved worse."

Phin shook his head. "I'm sure he did. But since you got caught, he knows it was you. How much worse will it be tomorrow? Or the day after, since you're probably looking at a day's worth of in-school suspension."

"At least a day," Michael muttered. He slumped in his seat.

"Right. So, you got in trouble, and he looks like some kind of martyr. And if anything else happens to him, he'll think it was you, whether it is or not. Doesn't sound like such a good idea anymore, does it?"

"Well, then next time, I just won't get caught." Michael looked up at Phin.

"Uh-uh. He'll know next time. Look, I don't have any good advice for you, but I know revenge isn't the way to solve the problem. You need to be more subtle about it. I'll tell you what—I'll think about it and get back to you, all right?"

Michael raised his eyebrows. "I don't even know you."

Phin shrugged. "I'm just here checking out your school. I'll be around." He nodded at Dani. "Your mom will know where to find me." He grinned at Dani.

Dani snorted. "Seems like you're now in the business of sorting out kids' problems."

"Nah. I just like to help out where I can. Well, I'd better get out of here."

Sighing, Dani smiled a little and shook her head. She stopped him before he could leave, remembering what she'd planned to ask him. "Wait a moment. Before you go, I wanted to ask if you would like to have dinner on Friday." Before he could reply, she added, "At my house, with Vic and the kids. Vic says you two are old friends."

If Phin was surprised, he didn't reveal it. "Sure," he replied. "What time?"

"About five-thirty. I live in the house right next to the Railway Penny."

"I'll be there."

She let out a small sigh of relief. With the second part of her plan in place, she could focus on talking to Eunice and Gia as soon as they arrived at her house. She looked over her shoulder at Michael, who was no longer slouched in the seat. He had his legs crossed, one ankle resting on the knee of the other leg, and his hands clasped behind his head. What Phin had said had made more of an impression than most of a year's worth of trying to drag out of Michael what was going on.

Phin waved goodbye to Michael and reached down to pick up his bag. As he was straightening up, Dani saw his expression change from friendly to wary, and she followed his gaze. Alex was standing by the wall just past the open front of the office. Dani wondered how long he'd been there. She couldn't read the expression on his face, though his eyes never left Phin. Eventually, Phin turned away, and Dani watched him walk out the door. Alex relaxed.

Just as Dani returned her attention to wrapping up her final task for the day, Alex approached her desk. Dani's nine-year-old daughter, Carlie, was in tow. Dani groaned. She must have been there the whole time Alex was, hidden behind him. Fighting the urge to let loose on both of them, she looked up at Alex. "Now what?" she snapped.

Alex, whom Dani realized was not responsible for the previous fifteen minutes' worth of drama, looked taken aback. "Is this a bad time?"

Dani took a deep breath. "Sort of." She tilted her head toward Michael. She then turned her attention to Carlie. "Are you going back to class, or are you staying here for the rest of the day?"

"Can I stay here? It's only fifteen minutes. I could help you out." Carlie had a pleading look on her face.

"Fine. Go get your things from your classroom." Dani scrawled a note to Carlie's teacher. "Take this to Mrs. Fargo. Tell her she can come talk to me if she needs to."

Carlie skipped off down the hallway, and Dani called after her to walk. She slowed down for a pace or two and resumed her skipping.

When she was gone, Alex said, "I'm sorry." He grimaced.

"No, I shouldn't have taken it out on you. What's going on with Carlie?"

"She was in Jake's class again. It's becoming more frequent."

"She just decided to go down there?"

Alex shook his head. "No. Jake won't participate if she's not there. If it weren't the end of the school year, I'd tell you that you need to get a handle on this. As it is, I think it's time to consider referring him to someone else. You know I would do it, but he's family." His eyes flicked briefly to Michael before he returned his attention to Dani.

Dani looked over at Michael and up at the hallway where Carlie had disappeared. "I know. And I will, Alex. I promise that this summer we'll figure it all out. I just can't deal with it right now."

He nodded, and his expression softened. "Everything is going to be fine," he assured her.

"Yeah. Meanwhile, I have some things to do. I told Gia and Eunice to meet me after school."

"Oh?"

"Yes. We're about to find out what our Mr. Patterson is up to." She drew her brows together and gave Alex a hard stare. "Don't make trouble, or we'll never get anything out of him."

He put his hands up. "Okay, okay. Far be it from me to sabotage the plans of you three." He laughed. "Good luck, though. I have a feeling you'll need it."

"I'm not sure it's luck we need." Dani grinned at him. "You know that whatever it is, I'll have it out of him in no time—as long as Gia cooperates."

Alex raised his eyebrows. "I have a feeling I know what you're thinking."

"Probably." Dani winked. "Leave it to me, Alex. I've got this covered."

Alex finished one last stretch and stood to turn off the soft music. The five adults in his class rose to their feet as well and gathered their belongings. Before any of them left, Alex called them over.

"Fantastic job at the recital last weekend," he told them. "Now that crunch time is over, there's just one more class before the charity performance. If you're participating, don't forget to take an informational sheet from by the door on your way out."

The class filed out of the room, and Alex picked up his own bag, neatly stashing everything inside. He checked his messages, noting that

Dani had called while he was in class. There was just enough time to stop by to see her on his way home.

Dani's car was the only one in her driveway. Breathing a sigh of relief, Alex pulled in behind it. He knocked on her door, and Carlie answered. Alex hid a smile by coughing into his fist when he saw her. She was still wearing the skirt she'd had on at school, but she'd changed into a pink pajama shirt adorned with a sleeping panda. One of her feet was bare, and she had both a toothbrush and a book in her hand.

"Uncle Alex!" She grinned. "Did you come to read us a bedtime story?"

Dani stepped up behind her. "No, sweetie. Uncle Alex came to see me. Go finish getting ready for bed. We'll come tuck you in when you've finished brushing your teeth."

Carlie's face fell. She peered up at Alex. "Next time?"

He tugged her ponytail. "I promise."

"I'll meet you in the kitchen," Dani said. "I'm putting Jake to bed."

"No, you take care of Carlie. I've got Jake." He slipped up the stairs without waiting for an answer.

Once the kids were in bed, they sat down at the kitchen table. "What did you call about?" Alex asked.

"Phin Patterson, of course."

"I already told you what I thought, but you seem determined to keep me involved. I'm not interested." He folded his hands on top of the table and waited for her reaction.

"Mm-hm. And I already told you what I thought, too. Look, I think there's something else going on. On the record, he's supposed to evaluate our school for improvements—that's what consultants do. The real question is *why*. I know how this works, Alex. Our school doesn't have a choice anymore. We're going to face consequences no matter what because of the way the law is written. Given all that, why bother inviting him here in the first place? So I have in mind to figure out what he's doing and stay one step ahead."

Alex raised his eyebrows. "And you think I can do something about that?"

"Well..." She fidgeted. "Yes. He gets under your skin. I was hoping you could use that to our advantage."

"Right. What have you got Eunice and Gia doing?"

Dani laughed. "Eunice is just along for the ride. It shouldn't be hard to guess about Gia."

"Oh, dear god. You're serious?"

"Gia's good at reading men, Alex. Even you sometimes, as much as she pretends to be clueless."

He sighed. "I hope you know what you're doing. This could easily backfire. Letting Gia at him could get all of you in trouble."

"She's not going to do anything but show him a good time and get him to see beyond the walls of this building. It's about indifference. If he feels nothing, he'll do whatever he came to do. If he feels something, he'll either tell us why he's here or he'll help us. So are you in?"

Alex pursed his lips. "Fine. What do you need from me?"

"Well, first of all, I need you to do what you do best and find out what makes him tick. Then I need you to do exactly the opposite of what Gia's doing."

"Interesting. Maybe you could explain that a little more."

Dani grinned. "Gladly." She got up. "Tea? I have some of that blackberry stuff."

"Yeah, fine."

She put a mug in the microwave and handed him a teabag. "So, here's what I'm thinking. I asked him to have dinner here on Friday. The first thing you can do is just show up."

"Why?" Alex wrinkled his nose.

"I thought we should have the chance to talk to him when he's not in professional mode. Anyway, I invited Gia and Eunice to come over as well."

"Which brings me back to why you want me there. Honestly, Dani, I think you've got this covered." He blew on his tea and took a tentative sip.

She frowned. "I don't understand why you're so resistant to helping us."

"Because my help isn't necessary. You already have a plan and people willing to do it. Can't you leave me out of it?"

"No," she said. She sighed. "All right, fine. I might have a bit more in mind than just having Gia take him sightseeing. Are you happy?"

He set his mug down. "Of course I'm not happy. And I'm *still* not seeing what this has to do with me."

Dani's cheeks reddened. "After talking to the others, I might possibly think you have a better shot than Gia."

Alex's jaw dropped, and he stared at her for several seconds. He snapped his mouth shut and scowled at her. "I have no intention of making a pass at him."

"I'm not asking you to. I'm asking you to distract him. You do that however you want, but make sure he's focused on anything other than his job. I intend to get him to crack, one way or another." She crossed her arms and looked at Alex intently.

He sighed and closed his eyes for a moment. "Fine. I can't promise you anything, but I'll think about it."

She relaxed her posture. "That's all I can ask."

Alex rose from the table and bid her good night. He spent the entire drive home turning it over in his mind, trying to come up with a plan that fit what Dani was looking for. The only thing that occurred to him was to wish Phin Patterson had never shown up. He pulled into his driveway and sat there for a long time before getting out and going inside.

After he dumped his bag next to the door, he ascended the stairs two at a time. He rounded the corner and sped up the steps to the attic, heading straight for the stacks of boxes under the sloping roof. After a few minutes of rummaging, he withdrew a small, square box with a black-and-white pattern. He didn't open it there, opting to take it back down with him to the kitchen.

He set the box on the table and grabbed a glass from the cupboard. His hand shook as he ran tap water into the glass, causing it to tilt and water to splash over his hand. He snatched a dish towel and dried his hand and the glass before plunking his water down on the table. For a moment, he merely sat there, staring at the box. At last he opened it.

There were memories in there. Some, like the old photo of his great-uncle Alejandro—the one for whom he was named—made his heart ache. Others, like the note his first real boyfriend had slipped into his locker the day before spring break, brought a smile. But there were things in there that were best left buried in the past, and those were the ones he wanted to see. He put his hand into the box and brought out a few items to sift through.

It didn't take long to find it. Alex pulled out a piece of paper that had been folded several times. He stared at it, his heart thumping. Setting it down in front of him, he picked up his glass to take a sip. He hesitated, the glass halfway to his mouth, and put the water back on the table. He needed something a lot stronger before he could look at the note. He rose from his seat and crossed the kitchen to the liquor cabinet.

He didn't keep much in there, but he did have a few bottles of wine and a fine single-malt scotch an old boyfriend had given him. He reached for it but withdrew his hand. After a moment's hesitation, he grasped the bottle and took it out of the cabinet. He retrieved a shot glass from the cupboard and resettled himself at the table.

He opened the bottle and poured some out, recalling the last time he'd had any of it. It had been Christmas night. His ex had come to beg for another chance, and he'd brought the scotch. They'd taken their time enjoying it slowly until they were both fairly drunk, followed by an uncomfortable round of awkward sex on the kitchen floor. Alex's back had hurt for days afterward, and it hadn't been worth it anyway. In the end, he'd still refused to continue their relationship.

This wasn't the night for drinking it properly. In part to spite his ex's snooty insistence on the "right" way to drink, he downed the first shot as quickly as he could manage. He set the shot glass back down with a thunk and poured another one, which he left sitting there. It could wait until he'd opened the note.

Slowly, he unfolded the paper. It wasn't anything that would have appeared important to anyone else—just a request from a classmate to meet her in a designated location before a school dance. At the bottom of the note was a drawing, a rough cartoon of a boy and a girl leaning in for a kiss.

Alex had not, in fact, ever met the girl there or anywhere else. He'd gone, but not to see her. As he'd anticipated, she hadn't been there. What he hadn't expected was for a couple of Phin's friends to be waiting for him in order to humiliate him. They couldn't possibly have known anything; it was just a prank, a way to make him look foolish by replacing the girl they assumed he liked with a boy. The problem was that they'd inadvertently hit on the truth. Alex had gone there to find the person he knew had drawn that cartoon.

He didn't want to relive the rest of the memories of that incident. He downed the second shot and poured a third. Crumpling the paper, he slammed it back in the box. His reasons for having saved it in the first place were lost to him, other than that it was the only one of the dozens of drawings Phin had done for him that he'd kept.

This is ridiculous, he thought. *No reasonable person gets drunk over a stupid middle school prank.* He closed his eyes and drew in several tremulous breaths. *Unless the prank involves your former best friend and results in several years' worth of torture at the hands of the bullies he replaced you with. And also unless you really, really liked him before he pulled that shit.*

He stood up. Leaving the box on the table, he toted the scotch and his glass out to the living room. He set them down and flopped onto the couch, staring at the fish tank along the opposite wall.

"This is completely screwed up," he told the fish. "Dani thinks I can get inside his head. Hell, I can't even get inside my own head most days." He sighed and ran a hand over his face. "And now I'm talking to my fish. I can't decide if I've had too much booze or not enough. Think I'll go with the latter." He sloshed a bit more into the glass and sipped more slowly this time. He snorted at the fish tank. "You guys are lousy company. I need a dog."

He set the glass back on the table and stared at it, his head buzzing. *Damn,* he thought. *I have to work in the morning.* He shrugged and poured another shot.

Chapter Six

Chicken Not-So-Little

PHIN MADE his way down the hall in the C wing of the lower floor. When he had arrived that morning, Dani had informed him he would begin his observation in the Living Environment lab. He was glad to have the chance to see the school's emphasis on science in action. It would also serve as a welcome distraction. So far that week, he'd only seen Alex three times, and none of them had provided an opportunity for him to prove he wasn't the same person he'd been as a child. He needed some new strategies.

He knocked on the door of room 12C, and a dark-haired girl peeked out the window.

"Who are you?" she demanded without opening the door.

"Mr. Patterson. I'm here to see your teacher." He peered inside.

The room was large and square. There were a number of tables surrounded by more of the colored plastic chairs that Phin had noticed everywhere on the lower floor of the school. He couldn't see much else except that the students were milling around. He heard their voices and several other unidentifiable noises drifting from under the door.

After several minutes, a new face appeared in the doorway. The owner of the face was at window height, so Phin assumed this must be the teacher, Mrs. Fargo.

"When I open the door, come in quickly," she instructed.

Puzzled, Phin agreed. Mrs. Fargo hauled open the door and Phin rushed inside. She slammed the door behind him.

"What—" he started.

"I know you're here to observe my lesson, but at the moment, I don't care," Mrs. Fargo informed him. "We have thirty chicks on the loose and we need to round them up. Pitch in or get out." She turned her back to him.

Phin stood still for a moment, taking in the scene. Fifteen fourth graders were running around, stooped over. Phin looked down. The chicks were peeping and hopping away from the grabby little hands trying to wrangle them back into their crates. Some of them were disappearing underneath shelving and inside cubbies. He sighed. It couldn't be that hard to round up a few baby chickens. He rolled up his sleeves and set to work.

The chicks were in no hurry to be back in their wire prisons, and the children were not particularly adept at catching them. Phin caught two and put them back, only to have them escape the next time one of the students opened the cage to deposit his handful. It took another twenty minutes before they had all the chicks secured. By that time, Phin was more of a mess than he had been the first day he arrived at the school. Somehow, one of the chicks had christened his hair, and his clothes were covered in feathers. He sneezed.

The students, having accomplished their mission, obediently took seats around the tables in the center of the room. Mrs. Fargo, looking somewhat worse for wear, handed out packets of information. While she was circling the tables, someone knocked on the door.

Mrs. Fargo looked up at Phin. "Would you be so kind as to answer that, please?"

Phin pulled open the door to see Alex standing there. He groaned. "Can I help you?"

Alex's lips twitched and his eyes lit up. For a minute or two he stood there staring at Phin then leaned closer and whispered, "What happened to you? Get in a fight with a feather duster?"

"No," Phin said through clenched teeth. "I helped put chicks back in their pens. Why the hell are there live farm animals here?"

"No idea. Must be Jean's idea of teaching the kids about the life cycle." Alex straightened up and raised his voice. "Would you mind getting Carlie Roberts for me? I need to see her for a moment."

Phin turned around. He had no idea which was the right girl. "Mrs. Fargo? I believe Dr. Wells needs to see Carlie."

The dark-haired girl who had answered the door rose to her feet, then sat back down and raised her hand. Before Mrs. Fargo could call on her, she said, "May I go?"

Mrs. Fargo sighed. "Go ahead."

Carlie walked out, and Alex followed her. He reached around to close the door behind him. As he did so, he leaned in towards Phin for a second time. Softly, so the students wouldn't hear, he said, "By the way, you have something in your hair." He pulled the door shut, leaving Phin fuming.

The whole ordeal prevented Phin from being able to pay attention to the rest of the lesson. He didn't think much instruction was going on anyway. The children were still riled up from their chicken-catching adventures, and very little of what Mrs. Fargo was saying seemed to penetrate. She was struggling to help the students make a connection—any connection—between chasing chicks and the life cycle of birds. Eventually, whatever time they had in the lab was up and she instructed them to line up at the door. Phin tossed all of his belongings in his leather satchel-style briefcase, but he didn't bother to zip it. He followed the students to the door.

"My apologies," he said to Mrs. Fargo. "I need to clean up. I'll meet you back in your classroom in ten minutes. Which hallway?"

"The B hallway, number six. Third door on the right." She led her students out of the lab.

Phin stopped in the faculty restroom to sort himself out. It was as bad as he'd been expecting. He set down his briefcase, which tipped over and spilled its contents across the tile floor. He growled in frustration and hastily scooped everything back in. He carefully leaned the bag against the wall and half-stripped. After cleaning as much as he could off his clothes, he set to work on his head. He had to use school-issue soap and scratchy paper towels in a poor attempt at washing the chicken droppings out. At last he was satisfied that he was reasonably clean again, and he emerged from the bathroom.

When he arrived at room B6, the students were away from the room. Mrs. Fargo was seated at her desk with a stack of papers in front of her. Phin knocked, and she looked up.

"Come in," she said.

"That was certainly an interesting lesson," he commented. "Please, tell me more about the chicks."

Mrs. Fargo sighed. She took off her glasses and rubbed her eyes, then replaced the glasses. "It's not usually like that. One of the kids opened the cages and let them all out. Usually, we take them out carefully through the smaller door, then set them one or two at a time in the middle of our circle. Unfortunately, I have a couple of students who have trouble listening to instructions."

"Never a dull moment," Phin replied.

She shook her head and chuckled. "Nope. So, what would you like to know about the experiment?"

"I suppose my first question would be why you have a lab full of farm animals." Phin reached into his briefcase. "Pardon me while I make some notes here. I'll be using them to make my recommendations later." He didn't feel his phone, so he looked into his bag. *Shit. Where the hell is my phone?* It wasn't in there. "Um...hold on a moment." He must have left it in the bathroom when his bag spilled. He would have to make do for the moment and then search for it after he finished talking to Mrs. Fargo. He pulled out a piece of paper and a pen. "Okay. Go ahead."

Mrs. Fargo nodded. "We try to provide the students with educational experiences that line up with their own lives. In this case, one of my students, Maricela Alvarez, lives on a farm. Her parents generously donated the eggs, and they will take the chickens back once we are through here. Obviously, a child like Maricela has grown up around chickens and can provide valuable insight about their development. I can then use that to help all the students apply their experiences to general principles about the life cycle and so on. In fact, Maricela's brother works here as a custodian, but he's studying environmental engineering at the college up in Peroo. At some point, we'll have him in to talk to the class."

As Phin made notations, he considered what Mrs. Fargo was saying. Experiments with chickens made sense in a rural community, but it seemed disconnected somehow, as though the teacher was uncomfortable integrating both the hands-on lab experience and the skill set required by the educational mandates. There was a dissonance between her own life and education and that of her students. He could see how that might lead to a wide gap in student performance—those who understood would achieve high marks, while those who failed to make the connections would score much lower. It was a problem Phin would have liked to work on with Mrs. Fargo, but it wasn't the reason he was there; strangely, she wasn't even on his list of teachers to monitor.

He made a few more notes and slid the paper back into his briefcase. "You've been very helpful. Thank you. Where are your students now?"

Mrs. Fargo reached for her pen. "They should be back from art in about five minutes. Would it be too rude of me to finish marking these papers?"

"Not at all. I'll step out for a few minutes, and I'll return when the students are back in the classroom." He stood up. At least this would give him the chance to find his phone.

Without looking up from her desk, Mrs. Fargo nodded. She held up a hand in a quick wave, and Phin left the room. He headed straight for the faculty men's room, where he conducted a thorough search of the area. Nothing. Phin leaned against the outer wall of the stalls and huffed in frustration. He knew he'd had it when they were in the Living Environment lab because he'd been making notes about the chicks on it. He banged his hand against the stall. *Fuck.*

The only thing to do was carry on and hope that someone turned it in at the office by the end of the day. He wasn't interested in searching every place he'd been, and experience told him that it usually took a while before things turned up in the lost and found. He walked out, not noticing the small, black case wedged up against one of the pipes under the sink, hidden by the shadows.

Dani was in the midst of closing out the tabs on her computer so she could take a late lunch break when Oscar Alvarez, the part-time custodian, stopped by her desk. He had a small, black object in his hand.

"Ms. Sloane," he greeted her.

"Oh, hello, Oscar. You know, you really can call me Dani." She smiled up at him. "What can I do for you?"

"I found this in the men's staff bathroom." He held out the object.

It turned out to be a cell phone. Dani accepted it and thanked Oscar, who merely nodded and went on his way. She assumed one of the teachers had left it there, so she opened the phone to see who it belonged to. When she hit the home button and swiped the screen, she didn't see any immediate identifiers. She opened the calendar to see if there was a name listed there. When she tapped "accounts," the name that popped up surprised her: The phone belonged to Phin Patterson.

Of all the things that could have gone in her favor, that was at the top of the list. It couldn't hurt to do a bit of poking around. First, she opened the notes. There were several sections, each devoted to Phin's observations in the classrooms he'd visited. The notes were extensive and half written in educationese, so Dani left those alone; none of them made any sense to her. She scrolled through, searching for anything else that might be relevant.

That's interesting. She had come to a list of names. She recognized all but one of them as teachers in the building, including Gia and Eunice. The final name was one of the counselors. Dani frowned. What could Phin be doing with a list of teachers' names and content specialties? She quickly jotted down the list on her notepad.

Next, she opened Phin's contacts. She scrolled through the names, but nothing stood out to her until she reached the M's. There, she found *Murdock, Donald.* Dani recognized the name from some of the paperwork that had crossed her desk in the previous six months. Murdock was one of the people at the State Education Department with whom Gary had been corresponding. Dani opened Murdock's contact information. Sure enough, along with the Albany area code, Phin had listed Murdock's address as an office in the NYSED building. She added Donald Murdock's name to her list.

She continued to scroll through the names. When she came to *Patterson, Lorne,* she frowned. The name was vaguely familiar, but she couldn't place why. She assumed he was related to Phin. Out of sheer nosiness, she tapped the name. When the information popped up, she sucked in her breath. Her heart began to beat more rapidly; Phin had listed "Dad" as the nickname under the contact. That wasn't what had shocked her, though. Under "company," Lorne Patterson was listed as the CEO of EduText, the company Dani's father had worked for until she was eleven.

Just before Dani finished fifth grade, her father—along with hundreds of other people—had lost his job working for EduText when the company closed its operations in Peroo in order to move to Buffalo. People from all the surrounding towns had suffered the consequences. Some employees had been offered the chance to relocate, while others had simply been laid off; Dani's father had been in the latter group. The chain of events set in motion wasn't one Dani was likely to forget, especially as her family's life had been upended. Her parents never recovered from that setback. Her father was now long gone, and Dani had crawled her own way out of the misery EduText's closing had left in its wake.

Hand shaking, she closed the contacts and laid the phone aside. She took a few deep breaths to steady herself and closed her eyes, pinching the bridge of her nose. She reminded herself that there was no evidence that Phin had anything else to do with EduText other than sharing a name and some genetic material with the CEO. For all she knew, he didn't have much contact with the man.

Dani picked the phone back up and opened to the home screen. She tapped "phone" and scrolled through the quick-dial list. Lorne Patterson wasn't on it. While that wasn't evidence that Phin was not in contact with his father, at least it meant Phin didn't consider him worthy of being on his short list. She re-entered Phin's contact list and jotted down all of Lorne Patterson's information, making a note to check into what the senior Patterson was up to.

After looking through the phone for any other pertinent information and coming up empty, Dani closed the apps. She locked the phone in the file cabinet where they kept lost or confiscated electronics. She had pulled enough information from the phone to get started. Her lunch break long forgotten, she turned to her computer. A few clicks later and she had five tabs open.

The first thing Dani checked was the list of teachers. They were all over the building, at nearly every grade level, with a variety of certifications. She pulled up the calendar to see if they were among the teachers Phin was scheduled to visit. Sure enough, he had an appointment in every single one of the classrooms. The only name she couldn't find was the counselor. On closer inspection, Dani found that each of the teachers on the list had a second visit scheduled as well. Other than that, she couldn't find anything else they had in common.

She set that task aside, promising herself she would continue to work on it. She was about to switch to one of the other tabs when the door to the school opened and a tall, well-dressed man walked in. Dani stifled a groan. Ed Dunlop. Not only was he on the school board, his wife was the president of the PTA. Dani frequently entertained the thought that with Claire Dunlop at the helm, it would have been more appropriately named the "Pain in the Teacher's Asses" than the Parent-Teacher Association.

It was one of the pitfalls of working and living in such a small town; Dani knew every member of the school board outside of school, and Ed wasn't any better there. It didn't help that both Dunlops had a low opinion of Michael, especially since he and their daughter had been more or less dating for the better part of the school year. The Dunlops didn't quite believe that, however, and had discouraged the relationship. In their presence, Dani always felt like a naughty child who had been sent to the principal's office for behavior modification.

Ed glanced at Dani, turned up his nose slightly, and walked past to the office entrance. Dani had no control over whether he was allowed inside, so she paid no attention to him as he came in. Apparently, he wasn't in the mood to be ignored.

"Friendly as ever, I see," Ed commented.

Dani pursed her lips to keep from snapping at him. When she felt she was under control, she replied, "You appeared to know where you were going without my help."

He grunted and continued past her desk to Gary's door. No one answered his knock, so he turned to Dani, who was still watching him. "Where's Gary?"

"He's not in at the moment," Dani responded.

"Yes. I can see that. Where is he?"

"Out. He didn't tell me what he was doing. I'm not his mother." Dani turned towards her computer.

Ed inhaled noisily. "Right. Do you know when he'll be back?"

"Nope."

"Of course not." He made an irritated noise in his throat. "Just tell him I stopped by."

"Certainly." Dani continued to look at her computer screen.

Ed huffed. "Aren't you at least going to write a note?"

Dani looked up. "No need. I think I can remember to tell him you were here. You're hard to miss."

He went red in the face and opened his mouth, but he closed it again and merely sneered at her before he walked back out of the office. Dani waited until he was gone from the building to let out a sigh of relief. She would probably hear it later from Gary about how she hadn't been polite enough to him.

Dani opened up one of the tabs on her browser. She had done a quick search for Donald Murdock's name, hoping for more information besides his position with NYSED. She hadn't been expecting to find much, but when she saw his name associated with a school district in the Albany area, she clicked the link.

By the time she was three sentences in, she was frowning. Murdock appeared to have been involved in the conversion of several elementary schools into charters. That wasn't uncommon; with the new standards, many schools had failed to pass. Closing and reopening as charter schools was among the valid options. The problem was that Murdock seemed to have had a hand in at least three districts converting multiple schools to charters. Dani scribbled a note to check the records of the districts in question, comparing them to similar charter schools.

It wasn't until she clicked the link about Lorne Patterson's company, EduText, that she made the connection. A news report from two years prior showed Patterson at the ribbon-cutting of a brand-new charter school near Buffalo. According to the report, the financial backing and oversight for the school came from EduText. The company, which had started as a curriculum, textbook, and test-preparation distributor, appeared to have added educational management to its list of business ventures. About halfway down the article, Dani sucked in her breath. This particular school was one of Donald Murdock's projects.

Dani's heart rate sped up. In every case, the schools had hired "an independent consultant" to evaluate the public schools' performance. Each time, the recommendation had been not to close the school or restructure but to convert to a charter in order to remain open. Neither the consultants nor their affiliations were ever named.

"Oh, Phin. What are you really doing here?" Dani muttered, closing her browser.

At that moment, Phin approached her desk. Dani clicked furiously, closing all her tabs just in time. She cleared her throat and tried to compose herself. "What can I do for you?" she asked, forcing a smile.

"By any chance did someone find a phone? I think I left it in one of the classrooms." His posture was casual, but Dani heard the note of desperation in his voice.

"Let me check," she said. She went to the lost and found box and pretended to rummage around inside it. "Hm. It's not in here. Let me look in the locked file cabinet—we sometimes keep things in there that have been found or confiscated." Although she had her own key to the cabinet, she grabbed the one located on the wall in the copy room. She took her time, sorting through the few other things in there. "What's it look like?"

"Black smart phone, no front case."

Eventually, she pulled out Phin's phone and held it up. "This it?"

"Yes! Thank you so much. I don't know what I'd do without it." He accepted the phone from Dani.

"Didn't I warn you about phones that do everything?" Dani chided him.

He laughed. "I suppose you did. Good thing I had old-fashioned pen and paper with me." He signed the visitor's book and waved to her on his way out.

Dani sat back down in her chair and let out her breath slowly. Now all she had to do was set everything in motion when they gathered for dinner. Phin Patterson wouldn't know what hit him.

When Phin arrived back at the Railway Penny, he was exhausted. He figured a nice, long shower would take care of the problem. Besides, he still needed to thoroughly wash away anything left from his adventures with the chickens. He dropped his briefcase on the bed and stripped down, leaving everything in a heap on the floor; he would deal with it after he was clean. After adjusting the temperature, he stepped under the hot spray and exhaled, groaning pleasurably at the feeling of the water hitting his back. He felt better almost immediately.

Fifteen glorious minutes later, Phin shut off the shower and stepped out. He dried off and wrapped the towel around his waist, intending to get dressed immediately. He was distracted by the sound of his phone. When he picked it up, he had three new email alerts. After checking to make sure none of them were from Murdock or anyone else at either NYSED or the school, Phin closed his email. He decided to close out the other apps running in the background, a daily habit he'd developed to conserve battery when out in the field.

As he tapped, he frowned. There were three apps he knew he hadn't used since clearing them out the previous night: his calendar, the phone, and his contacts. Whoever had found his phone had probably just wanted to know who it belonged to and had opened a few things. He pulled up his calendar. Sure enough, someone had opened the section where his home and work accounts were listed. He frowned again. It didn't make sense for anyone to go searching for anything else after that. He closed the calendar app and opened his contacts.

Phin's stomach dropped—his contact list was open to his father, whom he hadn't called in more than six months. His hand shook as he closed his contacts. He tried to figure out who might have wanted to dig around. Aside from Vic, only two other people so far remembered Phin, and neither of them had mentioned anything about his employment at EduText. Alex had been his classmate, but the animosity between them had nothing to do with Phin's father or his business, at least not directly. Eunice Clark knew who his parents were, but she, too, had been only a teenager the last time she'd seen anyone in Phin's family, and at that time, his father hadn't owned the company.

Frustrated, he tossed the phone onto his bed and stood there in his towel, still wondering who might have had reason to snoop in his phone. While he was puzzling over it, there was a knock on the door. He called, "Who is it?"

"It's me, Vic," came the reply.

Phin barely restrained himself from stomping over to the door. As it was, he hauled it open forcefully. Vic looked Phin up and down and snickered. "What, no time to get dressed?" he asked.

"Oh, shut up," Phin grouched. "It's been a rough day. What do you want, anyway?"

"You didn't stop by the desk on your way in, so I came to see if you got Dani's invitation." He crossed his arms.

"Yes, I did, and I'll be there, fully clothed. Was there something else? Because I need to put something on."

"Go right ahead," Vic suggested. His lips twisted in a poorly disguised smile.

Phin glared at him. "In private."

Vic laughed. "It's not like there's anything I haven't seen before. How long were we friends? I was actually just going to ask how things were going, but I guess whatever I want to say to you can wait until you're not half-naked."

"Fine. Then get out." Phin ran a hand through his damp hair and relaxed his posture. "Wait. I'm sorry. It's just that I misplaced my phone this morning, and by the time I got it back, someone had looked through it. I have no idea how much other information they managed to get, but my contacts list was open to my father's number. Someone knows."

Vic's eyes widened. "I swear, I didn't tell a soul. You know I wouldn't. I already told you I can't get involved in that shit again."

"I know. That's why it's so weird. I've been trying to figure out who might want to know about that."

"You think maybe someone in the office? Like Dettweiler—the principal?"

Phin shrugged. "I doubt it. He already knows why I'm really here. It wouldn't even matter, but it looks suspicious if I'm associated with my father's company. If anyone makes that connection, I'm screwed."

Vic looked puzzled. "Why? I mean, I know why I don't want Dani to know, but why do you care if someone at the school finds out?"

Lowering his voice, Phin said, "With all the new Common Core testing, my father decided to get a piece of the market. EduText is one of the leading suppliers of test-prep materials. He's also started investing in charter schools, and there's been some question about the schools he's helped fund. At least one has ended up closing because he's removed his financial backing. It's his company that will be taking out the charter, and someone appears to have discovered that tidbit. It looks pretty damn suspicious that I'm here to force the charter through because of that connection."

"Fucking hell, Phin," Vic spat. "I told you years ago you needed to put some distance there." He blew out a long breath. "Nothing you can do about it now, but I sure hope you know what you're doing. Get your priorities sorted out so you don't leave the kind of mess behind you that your old man did. I never should have agreed to help you at all." Vic turned around and stalked down the hall, leaving Phin staring after him.

Phin shut the door quietly and retreated to the bed. He flopped down on his back and felt something behind his shoulder. Reaching around, he pulled out his phone. Huffing in frustration, he stared at it for a moment before sitting up and plugging it in. As he stood up to get dressed, he willed himself to calm down. There wasn't anything he could do at that point except continue to do his job and hope that whoever it was who had looked through his phone would have the sense to keep it quiet, at least until he'd investigated further. Somehow, that seemed like too much to ask.

Chapter Seven

What Your Kindergartner Doesn't Need to Know

PHIN PUT his worries in the back of his mind for the time being. He would deal with any consequences as they arose. In the meantime, he had dinner with Dani and Vic to look forward to. Unfortunately, before he could relax with friends, he had to get through a morning in Kindergarten and an afternoon with the physical education teachers. He was not looking forward to any part of that day. He could have done without gym class; he hadn't enjoyed it in school and didn't anticipate feeling differently as an adult. In all his time consulting, he had never once been asked to observe a gym class, as that was not considered to have much bearing on language arts and math test scores. He wondered what, if anything, had changed since he was in school.

The Kindergarten teacher he was scheduled to observe, Gia Scuderi, was on Murdock's list. From her file, Phin had learned she was young. That automatically made two strikes against her—she was a first-year teacher, and she didn't have any professional certifications. So far, this was the easiest recommendation for a lay-off he'd had to make.

When Phin entered the Kindergarten classroom, he immediately recognized the woman as the one he'd met in the copy room. She was in the middle of having her students clean up whatever supplies they'd had out on their desks, cheerfully singing to them about where the different items belonged. Phin barely refrained from rolling his eyes. This teacher reminded him of an over-eager puppy. He gave her credit, though—the children were picking up enthusiastically.

When the students had finished picking up and were all seated at their tables, she smiled brightly at Phin. "Good morning," she said, her voice cheerful. She turned to her students. "Class, this is Mr. Patterson. He's going to be visiting and having fun with us today. Would you all say hello?"

As one, the class said, "Hello, Mr. Patterson."

"Good morning, class," he replied. A girl with bright red hair in pigtails giggled. He raised an eyebrow at her, and she settled down. Phin was impressed; Gia obviously had them well-trained.

Much to Phin's consternation, they spent the morning immersed in a story about a woman who rescued chickens. He was beginning to sense a theme to his stay in North Cowell. He decided these people must have some strange chicken obsession, or else it was a building-wide mandatory unit. He hoped his afternoon would be chicken-free, and he prayed that Dani and Vic were serving beef for dinner.

Despite his initial displeasure with the topic, the students were thoroughly engaged. As it turned out, they had also been to visit the chicks in the Living Environment lab, and they were able to talk about how their chicks were better off because they could go live on a farm when they were done visiting the school. According to the story, roadside chicken dumping wasn't uncommon after educational hatching. At least three of the children lived on farms themselves, and they were eager to share their experiences. Gia steered the conversation expertly, gently redirecting when the inevitable unrelated five-year-old version of an overshare happened. When circle time ended and the children returned to their tables, Gia handed a stack of papers to the red-haired girl and told her to give one to each child.

Phin was sitting at a large table on one side of the room. When the red-haired girl passed him, she gave him a piece of paper. It had a blank square in the top half, and the bottom had lines for writing a story. Phin said to the girl, "Oh, no, thank you. I'm just here to watch."

The girl pouted slightly. "Ms. Scuderi says everyone participates, even if it's just a picture."

Startled, Phin replied, "All right. But I'll need a pencil. Do you have an extra?"

The girl pointed to a cup on the table. "There's some in there." She leaned a little closer and said in a loud whisper, "They're for people who don't remember to bring one."

Phin chuckled and took a pencil out of the cup. When the girl had finished passing out the papers and seated herself, Gia instructed the students to draw a picture, write a story, or both about what it might be like to keep a chicken as a pet. Phin set to work sketching. He drew a cartoon of himself with a fluffy chicken perched on his shoulder. In the cartoon, he was looking sideways at the chicken with a puzzled expression. Cartoon-Phin was covered in chicken feathers. His word bubble said, "Bawk?" and the one above the chicken said, "B'gawk!" He didn't bother writing a story.

At the end of the activity, Gia told the kids to find a partner and share their stories. She reminded them there would be one group of three, but the red-haired girl plunked herself down next to Phin at the big table.

"You can be my partner," she informed him.

They switched papers, and the girl described her pet chicken. It turned out that it wasn't too far from the truth—her parents owned an apple orchard, but they kept a few animals as well, including a couple of chickens. She pulled Phin's paper closer so she could look at it. She giggled.

"You draw pretty good," she said.

He smiled. "I've had a lot of practice."

"Does your chicken have a name?" the girl asked.

"Hm...I'm not sure," he admitted. "I didn't give him one."

"Are you sure it's a him? Because I think it's maybe a girl chicken. It doesn't look like a boy."

Phin laughed. "You got me. Maybe it *is* a girl. What should we call her?"

The girl looked thoughtful. "Dandelion," she said.

"Dandelion?"

"Yeah. Look, she has one of those fuzzy heads, like the one in the book. It looks like a dandelion."

"Sounds good." Phin took his pencil and wrote on the lines below the picture, "Mr. Patterson and his pet chicken, Dandelion."

The girl giggled. "Good job," she said.

Phin observed Gia as she moved gracefully among the tables, leaning over to offer praise and constructive feedback. She took her time with several of them, kneeling down so that she was at eye level with her students. As she spoke to each child, their faces flickered with a range of emotions—disappointment, confusion, joy. Seeing her competent interactions, Phin was puzzled as to why Gia was on his scratch list. Something clicked into place, and his stomach knotted unpleasantly. What a kindergarten teacher could possibly have done to incur Murdock's evil eye was beyond Phin.

For the better part of two hours, Phin watched Gia work and took notes on her classroom. At last the children put away their things and lined up for lunch. He stood up as well, stretching. The little red-haired girl happened to be last in line. She looked over at Phin and grinned. She was missing both her bottom front teeth. He smiled back. Suddenly, she broke away from the line and ran over to him. She wrapped her tiny, freckled arms around his waist.

Looking up at him, she said, "I'm happy you came to visit us today. Are you going to have lunch with us, too?"

He shook his head. "I'm going to stay here and talk to your teacher while you eat, and then I have to go play in the gym."

"Oh." She looked disappointed.

He crouched down to her level. "I'll be around, though, and I'm coming back here next week. Okay?"

"Okay." Her face brightened, and she hopped back in line.

He straightened up, and Gia looked over the kids' heads at him. She rolled her eyes and smiled before directing her students to file out of the classroom. She called over her shoulder, "Make yourself at home. I'll be right back."

While Gia was escorting her students to the cafeteria, Phin looked around the room. One entire wall was covered in student work. Their handwriting was scratchy, and many of the words were misspelled, but there was no doubt the students had put forth their best creative effort. Just as he was squinting in an attempt to read a poem scrawled by a girl named Megan, Gia returned to the classroom.

"That's our Wall of Fame," she said. "Everyone has something up there."

Phin turned to face her. "They're already writing poetry."

"Oh, yeah. I'm actually not all that good at poetry myself, but there are some fun books out there." She plopped down at her desk. "These guys wear me out," she said, giggling a little.

"I'll bet." Phin drew up a chair next to her. "Could I ask you a question?"

"Sure." She reached under her desk and came up with a bag. "Mind if I have lunch? I'm *starving*."

"No problem." He pulled out his phone. "I'm just going to take a few notes—"

Gia interrupted, "Ooh, nice phone."

"Uh...thanks. Anyway, I'm just—"

"Which note-taking app do you use?"

"Just the generic one that came installed on the phone. Could we—"

"I prefer to use an Internet-based one. I also have one that I use for lesson plans. Want to see?"

Phin was about to say that no, he absolutely did not want to see what sort of lesson planner she used, but he reconsidered on the grounds that it might prove useful. "All right. But first, I'd like to talk about the chickens."

Gia shrugged. "Okay. Well, what do you want to know? Oh! Wait—I was going to show you that note-taking app. I've got some stuff in there that's related." She rooted around in one of her desk drawers.

Phin shook his head, bemused. How anyone could go from teaching a high-quality lesson on chicken rescue to being so scattered she couldn't even stick to a single topic of conversation was beyond him. "Actually, I just want to talk about chickens, if it's all the same to you."

She popped back up from her search. "Never mind. I can't find my phone right now anyway. So...chickens. Right. Well, all the elementary classes have been in to see them. The fourth graders are studying their life cycle. One of the kids lives on a farm, so her teacher got the chicks for free. We thought it would be fun if everyone did something related."

"Makes sense. It's certainly been an interesting week, what with all the chicken-themed projects. If you don't mind my asking—"

Gia cut across him again. "I saw that you did a drawing this morning. Can I see it?"

Phin felt his temper rising. He breathed through his nose to keep from snapping at her. "If I show it to you, can we go back to talking about your lesson?"

"Sure."

"All right," he said. He pulled it out and handed it to Gia.

She grinned. "This is really good!"

"Please don't tell me you're going to say something about my nice use of the space or something."

Gia laughed. "Nope. I *do* know how to talk to adults."

Phin decided not to comment on that. "Your lesson this morning was excellent. You've really only been here a year?"

She nodded. "I student-taught here, and when the job opened up, I applied."

"You student-taught here?" Phin repeated. "There aren't any four-year colleges in the area."

"I went to SUNY Oneonta. It's a little over an hour away. I'm not from here, but I have an aunt in Peroo, so I stayed with her to make the commute shorter. I'm still working on my masters, but I'm taking a couple of classes online and a couple during the summer session. It's not so bad. Um, what were we talking about again?"

"Chickens. And your lesson."

Before they could resume their conversation, there was a light tap on the door. A young man in an old t-shirt and jeans poked his head inside the classroom. "Miss Scuderi?" he asked.

"Hey, Oscar. What's up?" Gia smiled warmly at him.

The young man's eyes lit up, and he returned the smile. "I think this is yours." Oscar extended his hand, in which he held a phone.

"Yay!" she exclaimed. "Thanks, Oscar. You're a life saver." To Phin she said, "Now I can show you that app. It's awesome." She flashed Oscar another grin before she turned her attention to the phone.

"No problem," Oscar replied and backed out of the room.

Phin and Gia chatted for a bit longer, until she had finished her lunch and indicated it was time to pick up her class. Phin rose from his seat. He had just enough time for a quick bite to eat before he had to find the gym. He gathered his belongings, bid goodbye to Gia, and made his way to the staff room, grateful for the break.

When Phin arrived at Dani's house, he heard voices on the other side of the door, and it sounded like general chaos. He rang the bell. After what felt like an eternity, the door opened partway and a dark-haired girl peeped out. Phin recognized her as the same one Alex had taken out of class the day he visited the chicks.

"Hi," she said, but she didn't open the door further or invite Phin inside.

"Hello," he responded. "Is there an adult I could speak to?"

She made a face at him. "Aren't you the man who was at my school this week?"

"Yes. May I come in?"

"I don't know. I have to ask." She turned around. "MOM!"

Dani appeared at the door. "Carlie, don't shriek—oh, hello, Phin." She gave Carlie the sort of look parents have perfected, something between exasperation and amusement. "Come on in, Phin. Carlie, go set the table."

Pouting, Carlie slunk into the kitchen. Dani opened the door wider, and Phin entered. There were already several other people in the house. Vic was helping Carlie and a younger boy set the table. Phin recognized the boy—he'd been in one of the gym classes that afternoon. When Phin attempted to smile at him, he scampered away into the other room with a handful of forks. The boy appeared around the corner a few minutes later, sans forks, eying Phin but remaining close to the wall.

Without stepping any closer, Phin crouched down to be closer to the boy's eye level. "Do you remember me? I was in your class today." The boy nodded, and Phin continued, "What's your name?"

"Jake," he whispered.

"It's nice to meet you, Jake. Is it okay if I help you with the table?"

The boy shrugged, and Phin stood up. He took a stack of plates from the counter and carried them to the table. He looked back over his shoulder at Jake, who moved closer to Dani and tugged on her arm. She leaned down toward him.

"Mama, that's the man from school today," he said. "He played the rubber chicken game with us."

"Rubber chicken game?" Dani asked, peering over Jake's head at Phin.

Phin chuckled. "Cross between tag, dodge ball, and capture the flag, only with rubber chickens." He shook his head. There was no escape from endless activities involving farm fowl.

The boy giggled. "I got him twice," he said. His eyes widened, and he clapped a hand over his mouth. He looked at Phin, who nodded and winked. Jake relaxed.

"Did you?" Dani asked. She glanced up at Phin again. "Hm." She smiled.

Behind him, Phin heard someone laugh softly. He turned around and found himself face to face with Alex. "Yeah, it's hilarious," Phin said, making a face.

"It is," Alex agreed. "I have to admit, I'm impressed you participated."

"When in Rome," Phin replied. "Just getting a sense of what it's like from the kids' perspective." He called to Dani, "Anything else I can do to help?"

Without preamble, she handed him a basket of dinner rolls. While everyone was busy preparing the table, the doorbell rang. This time, Alex answered. Phin glanced over to see Alex showing Gia and Eunice in. He raised his eyebrows. Dinner had turned into quite a gathering.

Eventually, everyone sat down around the table. Dani called up the stairs to Michael, who came down wearing the same sullen expression Phin had seen several days earlier. He gave Alex a long look and seated himself at the end of the table, not speaking to anyone. Phin glanced between the two, but nothing in their body language revealed a clue about why Michael was so angry. Meanwhile, in the scuffle to decide where everyone should sit, Phin ended up with Gia on his right and Alex directly across from him. He sighed. Gia wasn't entirely unpleasant company, and Alex had been nearly civil. He could make the best of it.

Over dinner—which, Phin was pleased to see, was *not* chicken—talk turned to the town. Dani asked Phin if he'd been sightseeing yet, to which he replied that he had not, other than a brief tour. He'd been around the town with Vic and up in Peroo for weekend entertainment, but that was all.

"Is there more to see?" he asked.

"Honey, you haven't seen anything until you've been up on the hiking trails or down in the orchards," Eunice told him.

"Or the vineyard," Dani suggested.

For the remainder of dinner, everyone was full of suggestions on what Phin should see over the weekend, including the kids. "I have no idea what to try first," he laughed.

Gia gave him a sly look. "I could show you around," she suggested. Phin felt her squeeze his thigh under the table and jumped a little, banging his other knee against the leg of the table. He looked sideways at her and then across to Alex, whose expression remained neutral. Phin turned to Gia and offered her a smirk. She winked back at him.

"All right," he agreed. "What time?"

"I teach a dance class at the community building from ten to eleven. You could meet me there." She giggled. "Or you could come to my class."

"Uh, I don't dance." Phin felt his face flush.

Alex laughed. "I'd hardly call what Gia does 'dancing.'"

She glared at him. "It is too! Just because it's a fitness class doesn't make it somehow not dancing." Gia turned to Phin. "He's just being a snob because he teaches there, too."

Phin was taken aback. "You still—that is, you do?"

"He teaches my class," Carlie put in. "If you come on Saturday, you can see us."

"Mr. Patterson is very busy," Alex told her. "I'm not sure he—"

"I'd love to," Phin said to Carlie. "What time is your class?"

"Ten," she replied. "And Miss Gia's is too, so you can see us first and then go to her class."

"Fair enough," Phin agreed. "Ten at the community building it is, then."

Eunice and Gia bid everyone good night, and Vic retreated to the kitchen, accompanied by Dani, to clean up. Michael had already slunk off to his room. Carlie and Jake wandered outside, followed by Phin. Alex offered a hand with the dishes, but Dani waved him off.

"Go see what the kids are up to. They'll want to say goodnight to you before you leave anyway," she said.

Alex stepped outside. Carlie and Jake were in the driveway, scrawling with oversized pieces of chalk. Carlie had drawn an elaborate maze-like structure that took up the entire lower half of the drive. Jake sat close to the stoop, making a series of small pictures—everything from flowers to dogs to geometric shapes. He silently passed a piece of pink chalk to Phin, who was seated on the stoop.

"Thanks," Phin said. Whatever he was drawing was hidden from Alex's view. He glanced over to Jake's drawings. "I like that one," he said, pointing. "The dog with the floppy ears." He chuckled. "I always wanted one like that."

"Me too," Jake whispered. He bent his head again and returned to his creation.

Irritation rose in Alex at Phin's familiarity with the children. "You're still here?" he asked.

Phin jumped a little and looked up. He stood, leaving the piece of chalk in the driveway and brushing his hands on his jeans. He ran his shoe over the place where he'd been drawing, smudging whatever had been there.

"May I speak with you for a moment?" Alex hissed.

"Certainly."

Jake eyed them warily as they stepped around to the side of the house, but he didn't say anything. Alex peered around the corner. Carlie was still at the end of the driveway, and Jake had gone back to expanding the circle of chalk drawings around him. Drawing in a breath, Alex faced Phin.

"Why are you here?"

"Carlie asked me to stay," he replied.

Alex crossed his arms. "And you thought that would be okay?"

Phin's eyes widened. "I suppose so," he replied. "I didn't see a problem, anyway. Carlie said she wanted to show me something, so I came outside with her. Believe it or not, I'm not a soulless jerk. I actually like kids."

"Do you realize how creepy that sounds?"

Phin's lips parted, and his eyes flashed. "Did you really just call me a predator? I think someone like you ought to know better."

"What's that supposed to mean?" Alex snapped back.

"How many parents have asked that you not be the one to work with their children?"

"None so far," Alex replied.

"Because they don't know you're gay? Or because this town is that open-minded?"

Alex ground his teeth. "Mostly the former," he admitted. "But that's not even relevant. I don't care what you do with consenting adults behind closed doors. You are a virtual stranger to these kids, and you have no business being around them uninvited."

Phin leaned in far enough to make Alex feel slightly claustrophobic. "I *was* invited. Dani asked me to dinner, and Carlie asked me to see what she was making. You saw yourself that I was doing nothing but sitting on the stoop." His nose was inches from Alex's. "Ask yourself this. If it weren't for who I am—or who you think I am—would you care at all?"

Alex slid sideways and backed up. "Just because you were asked here for dinner doesn't give you some kind of privilege. We're not your friends."

"I don't know about that. Gia seems pretty friendly to me." Phin's mouth curled up a little on one side in a way that made Alex want to shove him.

"You watch yourself with her." Alex gestured around. "With all of us."

"Thank you for your concern. Gia comes on a bit strong, but I think I can handle it. I'm sure I'll be fine with the rest of you, too."

"I wasn't worried for *you*."

Phin grinned. "I know."

An unwelcome wave of appreciation for Phin's sheer nerve passed through Alex, and he pinched his lips together. It was no use; an amused snort came out anyway. Phin's face relaxed into an easy smile, revealing a dimple in his left cheek. Alex's stomach swirled pleasantly, but he shoved the feeling away and turned serious again.

"I'm keeping an eye on you," he said.

Phin, too, dropped his smile. He leaned in again and murmured, "I'm counting on it." Straightening up, he said, "I should go. From the sounds of it, Gia's got big plans for tomorrow. I'll need some rest."

"Of course," Alex replied. "Have a good night."

Phin walked away. When he reached the corner of the house, he glanced back over his shoulder at Alex and smiled again. Alex merely stood rooted to the spot, incapable of reacting. Phin's smile faltered, and he turned back around. When he had gone from view, Alex stepped back around the side of the house and re-entered it.

Dani had just come from the kitchen, and Alex nearly ran into her in the entryway. "Sorry!" she exclaimed. She frowned. "What's the problem?"

"Phin. He was outside with the kids."

Her eyes widened. "Did one of them get hurt?"

"No," Alex replied, glowering at her.

Dani tilted her head. "You sound disappointed that he's actually a responsible adult."

He huffed. "I really don't think I can do this," he said. "He's just so...infuriating."

Laying a hand on his arm, Dani said, "Yes, you can. I know you. Don't let him get to you. At least, not until you wheedle some information out of him." She winked.

Alex rolled his eyes. "You're impossible too."

She leaned in and gave him a peck on the cheek. "You love me anyway. Now, go say goodnight to the kids and get out of here."

Chapter Eight

Gia's Guide to North Cowell

PHIN ENTERED the community building a few minutes early. He climbed the wide, flat steps, following two families with preschool-age children. Inside, the building was as active as the public school on an average day. Someone had set easels at the entry to each hallway listing the classes in the different wings. Dance classes were to Phin's right.

It didn't take long to find Alex's room. Eight children wearing various combinations of dance and athletic wear stood outside the classroom, neatly lined up and holding their street shoes. They all looked to be about Carlie's age; only one was a boy. Phin scanned the line for Carlie and spotted her talking to a girl with a tight blonde bun on top of her head. She looked up and waved when she saw Phin.

"Hi, Mr. Patterson," she greeted him.

"Hello, Carlie."

She pointed to each of the other kids in the line, naming them. About half of them looked familiar from classes he'd visited the previous week. He turned back to Carlie and asked, "So what kind of—"

He didn't get the chance to finish his question. Alex stepped out and invited the class into the room. He gave Phin a cursory glance, but said nothing and followed the kids inside. Phin hesitated. When he didn't move, Alex gave him a questioning look and made a motion with his hand. Phin took that as an invitation and joined them in the room.

"This is our last class for the year," Alex said to the children. "But if you want to sign up, we have summer camps going on in July, and some of them have dance classes. And of course, don't forget about the charity performance. If you're signed up, check in with me after class for some instructions." He looked at Phin, then back at the class. "This is Mr. Patterson. I think some of you may have seen him around school. He's here visiting us for a few minutes. Would you like to show him one of your dances from the recital?"

The students agreed enthusiastically, and Phin had to smile. At that age, any chance to show off was fun. Phin settled against the wall to watch the eight of them perform a jazzy dance to a pop song he didn't recognize. When they were through, he thanked them and apologized for having to leave so soon. They waved, after which Alex drew their attention to something else. Just as he was instructing them to line up, Phin ducked out of the room and went in search of Gia.

It took several minutes to find her class, but when he finally located it and peered through the window in the door, he laughed. He understood why Alex had poked fun at her. He had no idea what exactly she and her class were doing, but somehow, it involved three elderly women and two elderly men hopping around to the beat of something vaguely techno-punk. Whatever it was, it didn't look like any traditional form of dance Phin had ever seen. He watched for another minute or two until the song ended then knocked on the door.

Gia crossed to the CD player and turned it off before opening the door to let Phin inside. She gave him a bright smile and said, "Why don't you join us?"

Figuring it couldn't be too hard given the age of the participants, Phin agreed. By the time the class was over forty-five minutes later, Phin regretted his decision. He thought he might have discovered several muscle groups he hadn't used since college. He would have to ask Gia whether she minded if he went back to the Railway Penny for a shower before they headed out for the day.

She waved goodbye to her class, all of whom gave Phin pitying looks on their way out. He bit his tongue hard not to make snotty remarks to them in reply; after all, he'd been taught to respect his elders. When the last of them had gone, Gia turned to him and grinned.

"What'd you think?" she asked.

"Um. Could I answer that in an hour or two when I can feel my legs again?"

Gia giggled. "And Alex thinks it's not real dancing."

Phin grimaced. "I don't know. I might have to agree with him on this one. Don't tell him I think he's right, though. The shock may kill him."

"What shock is going to kill who?" asked a voice from the doorway.

Startled, Phin turned around. Alex stood in the doorway, arms crossed, wearing a subtle smirk. Phin's neck heated up. He turned away again, trying to adjust his clothes and smooth his damp hair into place without the others noticing.

Gia pouted. "Phin says he agrees my class isn't dancing."

Alex raised an eyebrow. "I guess we have something in common after all."

Phin risked another glance over his shoulder and then wished he hadn't. Alex was sizing him up, no doubt taking in his rumpled, sweaty appearance. Phin scowled. That only served to fuel Alex's fire; he snickered.

"Looks like Gia put you through your paces. Better you than me, I guess." He turned his attention to Gia. "Have fun with this one today." He jerked his head toward Phin.

"Oh, I plan to," Gia replied.

Alex addressed Phin. "If you want to know what real dancing is like, you should come here tomorrow morning when I do my warm-ups."

"No, thanks. I already told you I don't dance."

Shrugging, Alex said, "I figured you wouldn't really be up to it. If Gia's faux-dancing wore you out, I doubt you could handle my warm-ups."

That was a challenge if Phin ever heard one. "Oh, I'm up to it, all right. What time?"

"Five-thirty. And you had better not be late." Alex turned to go. On his way out, he called over his shoulder, "Wear something comfortable."

After Alex had gone, Phin groaned. *What have I gotten myself into?* He said to Gia, "Do you mind if I go change? I'm a mess."

"Actually, you'll probably want to wait until later. We're going to be outside most of the day."

Fantastic. Phin took a deep breath and let it out slowly before he asked, "Is there a bathroom nearby? I'd like to clean up a little, and then I'll be ready to go."

As the morning classes finished, the building emptied out in a steady stream of parents and children. Alex lurked in the entryway, watching Phin and Gia exit towards Phin's car before returning to his classroom. He shut the door and leaned against it for a few minutes until his legs were steadier. All the confidence he'd mustered not five minutes prior drained away. *What have I gotten myself into?* he wondered.

After a cleansing breath or two, he crossed the room to change the CD. He positioned himself in the middle of the floor, closing his eyes and listening for the first strains of the bassoon. Arching his back, he began his dance. Everything else faded away as the plaintive notes washed over him, flooding his soul until his heart beat in time with the rhythm.

He rehearsed a few more times then turned off the music and grabbed a towel from his bag. He spotted his phone and pulled it out, checking for messages. There was only one, from an unfamiliar number. He frowned and put the phone to his ear.

"This is Bettina Allen from the State University of New York at Plattsburgh."

Alex's pulse sped up as he listened to the rest of the message. He played it again, but when he heard voices in the hall, he stopped it and returned the phone to his bag. The door swung open, and Michael stood there with Carlie and Jake.

"Come on in," Alex said. "Go ahead and stretch while I change the music."

"Can you put in the CD with all the movie songs?" Carlie asked.

"Sure. You can warm up to that before we practice your dance."

Michael didn't say anything, nor did he make eye contact on his way past. He slouched to the other side of the room and dumped his bag on a chair then pulled off his sneakers, keeping his back to Alex the entire time. Alex sighed but didn't comment. Once the three of them had finished stretching and put on their shoes, Alex ran them through their warm-ups. He changed the music and sent them to their positions to practice their dance for the charity event.

The dance started off well, but halfway through Michael lost concentration and stumbled through a set of easy steps. Alex crossed to the CD player and shut off the music. "Michael, you've been doing this for years. Come on. These steps are at Jake's level." He repositioned them. "Try it again from right after the break. Five, six, seven, eight." They resumed their steps, and Alex called out the steps to them. "Heel, toe, heel, toe...good, keep going–Michael!"

Michael had stepped on Carlie, and she shoved him in retaliation. "Ow! That hurt, you jerk."

"Carlie," Alex warned.

She crossed her arms and pouted. "He's being a pain."

Alex glanced at Michael. "Yes. But that's his problem, not yours. Michael, is there something wrong?"

"As if you need to ask that," Michael muttered. "Fine. Let's just do it again. I promise not to do anything stupid."

"Maybe we should just practice another day."

Michael's eyes flashed. "Maybe we should."

Alex studied him for a moment. "May I speak to you in the hallway?" Without waiting for an answer, he crossed the room and stepped through the doorway.

Michael followed him out. "What?" he snapped.

"Talk to me," Alex said as he pulled the door closed. "You're usually right on top of this."

"Maybe I'm just having a bad day." Michael leaned against the wall and folded his arms, keeping his head turned away from Alex.

"That's fair. If you're not able to set it aside, we'll do this another time. We still have a few days, and you already know the dance."

"What if I don't want to do it?" He looked at Alex out of the corner of his eye.

Alex sighed. "You'd be letting Carlie and Jake down, but no one is going to force you into anything. If you don't want to do it, then don't. But at least give me a reason why you're acting this way."

"You should know," Michael said. "But I guess you weren't listening the last time I tried to talk to you." He glared at Alex.

"Then talk to me now," Alex pleaded. "I'm here."

Michael's laugh bordered on hysterical. "As if. You didn't understand at all when I tried to tell you about me and Nicki-Anne. You didn't even believe me when I said I didn't want to break up with her over Josue!"

"So this is about me? You're punishing me for some crime you think I've committed." Alex rested his fists on his hips.

"No, it's not about you. It never was. Why can't you understand? Nicki's not a cover for me and Josue." He blew out his breath. "Not everyone is like you, you know."

"Like me? Like me, how?" Alex frowned.

"I don't take it in the ass. I'm not a f—"

"Don't!" Alex spoke over Michael as the ugly word left his lips.

"Why not? It's what you are."

The blood drained from Alex's face; he put up a hand. "Don't you dare ever call me that again."

Michael made an irritated sound in his throat. "I'm done listening to anything you have to say."

"Was there a time when you did?" Alex snapped. He wanted to take the words back the moment they left his mouth.

Michael's expression darkened. "Fuck you," he spat.

"Your mom wouldn't be too happy if she heard you say that to me."

"You know what? I don't give a shit. I don't need you to tell me what to do, and neither does Mom." He pushed away from the wall and stepped close to Alex. "Don't you get it? We don't need you."

Alex stared at him, his mouth open, trying to find words. "I—"

Michael huffed and rolled his eyes. "I'm going to wait outside." He turned around and stalked off.

"You're still wearing your tap shoes!" Alex called after him; Michael gave him the finger.

Exhaling forcefully, Alex bowed his head and rested his shaking hand on the door for a moment before pushing it open and stepping back inside. Carlie and Jake were sitting in the middle of the floor, whispering. When Alex came back in, they both stared up at him.

"Did Michael go home?" Jake said, his voice quavering. A look of panic crossed his face. "He left us here!"

"Jakey, Michael wouldn't do that," Carlie soothed. She tried to grab her brother's hand, but he shrank away from her.

Alex knelt down on the floor and put a hand on Jake's arm. "No, he didn't leave. He's waiting for you outside. Let's just practice your part, and we'll worry about his another time. Okay?"

Jake's lip trembled, but he nodded. They stood up and resumed rehearsing the parts they didn't need Michael for. At the end of their session, Alex replaced Michael's things in his bag and sent it and Michael's sneakers out with Carlie. He collected his own belongings and straightened up the room. Just as he was locking the classroom, Eunice appeared around the corner.

"Hey there," she said. "I didn't know there was anyone else still here."

"Just practicing for the charity performance," Alex told her. "I thought your class was over."

"This was the last week. Then we're done until the summer session starts." She peered at him. "What's wrong?"

"Teenage drama. Michael's feeling like no one understands him." He shook his head. "No, that's not entirely true. He specifically feels like *I* don't get him, but he doesn't seem to want to explain that."

Eunice replied, "Ah, I see. Did you talk to Dani about it?"

"What for? He's not my son." Alex started walking towards the exit, and Eunice followed him.

"Wait a minute. Since when has that been a concern?" she asked.

"Since he assured me they don't want my help," Alex replied. "Leave it alone, Eunice. He's right—Dani doesn't need me to parent her kids."

They reached the double doors. Eunice put a hand on Alex's shoulder. "You going to be okay?"

"Yeah. I'm fine." He brushed her hand off. "I'm sorry. I'm just a little on edge. Dani asked me to help her out with this thing with Phin, so I need to take care of some stuff." He pushed the door open and looked back at Eunice. "See you Monday?"

"You know it." She grinned at him as they stepped outside. They headed in opposite directions.

When Alex reached his car, he tossed everything in the back except his phone. He sat down in the driver's seat and listened to the voicemail one more time. When it ended, he took a deep breath and called the number.

"Hello, Dr. Allen? This is Alex Wells. I received your message and I'm returning your phone call to set up an appointment."

When Phin and Gia left the community building, she had two backpacks with her that she assured Phin contained everything they would need for the day. She tossed them in his back seat and slid into the car. They set off in the direction of Phin's hometown, Morton Ponds. Her idea of sightseeing consisted of an array of outdoor activities ranging from berry picking to hiking trails, and she had come prepared.

"Mind if I turn on the radio?" Gia reached for the buttons on Phin's car stereo.

"Go ahead."

She picked a pop station that played mostly tunes Phin didn't know and sang along with the radio; her voice wasn't bad. Phin watched her out of the corner of his eye, amused. She was his idea of attractive—athletic but curvy in all the right places and pretty without being artificial or even overtly feminine. She had on very little makeup, but whatever it was shimmered slightly in the sunlight that played off the hood of the car. The window was down, and her short, dark hair ruffled in the breeze. He kept one hand on the steering wheel and reached out to her with the other, giving her hand a squeeze. She glanced sideways and smiled.

They stopped at one of the local farms which had a large, wooden sign advertising pick-your-own summer fruits. An hour later, they left with several pints of blueberries, raspberries, and peaches. Gia chose a spot in a small park where she produced a blanket from one of the backpacks and spread it on the ground. She pulled out a couple of water bottles and rinsed the fruit. While they sat in the grass and nibbled on the fresh produce and some nuts and cheese Gia had brought along, she explained that a number of the local families owned fruit groves and orchards.

"There's a nearby farmer's market where most of them sell their crops. It's not like those temporary ones they set up in cities—this one is a huge building that stands year-round. They sell other stuff, too, like fresh bread and pies. I'd have taken you there, but it's too nice to be stuck indoors, and anyway, it's more fun to pick our own, don't you think?"

Phin wasn't convinced, but Gia was nothing if not an enthusiastic tour guide. "Sure."

"We'll go another time, and you can meet some of the other families. Besides, if we'd gone to the market, you wouldn't have gotten to feed that goat. I think it liked you."

He grunted. The goat had been overly friendly, and Phin had been certain it would eat the clothes right off his body when it started using its teeth to tug at the hem of his shirt. He could cope with being isolated from civilization, having a thirty-mile drive to the closest decent grocery store, and hours of boredom, but he drew the limit at being munched by a goat. "Whatever," he muttered.

Gia laughed. "I take it you didn't return the goat's feelings. They do take some getting used to." She stood up. "Come on. We still have the hiking trails to explore."

North Cowell was far enough toward the southeastern part of New York that there were decent hills unmarred by interstate roads. Gia gave Phin directions to South Ponds Park, just outside Morton Ponds. She kept up a steady stream of chatter about the towns, the people, and the local culture. By the time they arrived at the park, Phin's head was spinning from Gia's endless commentary. He saw the public restroom by the parking lot and ducked inside, leaving her by the car.

When he returned, Gia had pulled out the backpacks. She handed one to Phin and took the other, and they set out for the hiking trails. It had been a long time since Phin had been there; in fact, he didn't remember ever hiking in these woods, not even when he'd lived there.

The weather hadn't heated back up to the near-record temperatures of the week Phin had arrived in town. It was warm, but there was a pleasant breeze and the trees provided ample shade. Phin was surprised to find that Gia knew her way around the hiking trails. They climbed higher and higher into the hills, Gia leading the way. Eventually, they came out into a clearing at the top of the hill. She took his hand and led him out of the trees.

"This is what I wanted to show you," she said, lacing their fingers together.

Phin looked down from where they stood. There was a wide expanse of trees thinning out at the bottom of the hill and melting into the fields beyond. Other than a few houses scattered here and there, this was empty, unspoiled land. He drew in his breath, his eyes widening at the spectacular view.

"Wow."

"Yeah. One of the perks of living here."

"So, you hike here often?"

She nodded. "There are other trails. I usually go on Sunday afternoons—there's a hiking club." She glanced at Phin. "There's a lot to do here. I know it doesn't seem like much, our little town, but it's there if you look for it. It's like the people—there's more to us than it seems."

They remained there for a few more minutes, and Phin absorbed her words. In the few days he'd been there, all he'd seen was the school and a small portion of the town. He'd had no idea any of this existed. His stomach twisted unpleasantly, and he shoved hard against intrusive thoughts about what Murdock's plan meant for the people living there.

It wasn't his job to analyze the outcome, only to trust that what he was doing was for the greater good.

Gia broke him out of his thoughts. "Ready to head down?"

"Any time."

As they hiked down the hill in silence, Phin watched Gia's back ahead of him. Experience was a good teacher; he knew the score. He had a very good idea why Gia had offered to show him the wonders of North Cowell and the surrounding area, just as he'd known exactly why Dani had invited him to dinner in the first place. The real question was whether or not he should play along. Phin had handled his father's most difficult clients often enough to know exactly what to give Gia under the pretense of appreciation for showing him the sights. Years of practice had taught him what to offer anyone in order to close a deal. Even after a single meeting, he always had all the information he needed.

He studied her, considering. She wasn't married, looking for danger and excitement, nor was she single and lonely. She wasn't like the ones whose religious convictions inspired pretending, just for a night, that this was what love really looked like. Every one of Phin's new acquaintances needed something different. Dani was looking for comfort, not a lover—she already had Vic for that. She wanted someone to sit in her kitchen, drinking tea and offering reassurance. Eunice enjoyed flirting and innuendo, but she wasn't interested in men and likely already had someone she saw periodically for romance or possibly more. She was the sort of woman who kept a collection of coffee table books expressly for the purpose of playing up a particular cliche. None of that fit Gia, but Phin had a good idea what might.

They reached the bottom of the hill, and Gia turned to him expectantly. All it would take was a few simple words, but they stuck in Phin's throat. Even studying her lovely face and her open, warm hazel eyes, he was torn. He knew she understood this wasn't permanent—just two people, crossing paths. He also knew it was just a job. A memory of the night before, of Alex offering a tentative genuine smile, came unbidden. What would it take to court Alex's trust the way he had already started to with the women? Phin refused to entertain those thoughts because heading down that path was far too painful.

Phin shook his head a little and stuffed everything down. He leaned in closer and touched Gia's arm, gently sliding his fingers down to clasp hers. Running his thumb in slow circles on the back of her hand, he pitched his voice low and soft. "So," he said. "I didn't have much chance to get to know you when I was in your class the other day. Would you like to go to dinner and talk?"

Dani was half asleep on the couch when the phone rang. She groped for it without sitting up. "Hello?"

"Hey, Dani. It's Gia."

"Hang on a sec." Dani sat up and switched the phone to her other hand. "So, how'd it go?"

"Had a good time. He barely kept up." Gia giggled.

"Oh yeah? I take it he's not still with you."

"No, of course not. He just left."

Dani snorted. "What'd you do all day?"

"I don't kiss and tell."

"Like hell you don't. Where did you take him?"

"All over. The farm, couple places in town, the hiking trails. He beat me to it and asked me to dinner in Morton Ponds, at that old sports bar there."

"Sounds like you had fun." Dani yawned. "So, what happened?"

"We came back here and messed around a little while we watched a movie. We didn't really have sex, exactly, but...you know. That ass of his is just as hot close up. Oh, my god, Dani, guys my age are so selfish, but he kept asking if I liked what he was doing. Seriously, dudes need lessons from Phin on how to give good—"

"Gia!" Dani squeaked. She felt herself flush. "Stop. Too much information."

"What? You asked what happened." Dani could almost hear the pout in Gia's voice.

"Urgh. Yes, but I didn't mean *that*. I meant, did he tell you anything?"

"Not much we didn't already know. Nothing about the school or whatever." There was a pause. "But, Dani, I think you need to have a talk with your boys."

Dani frowned. "Jake and Michael? Why?"

Gia huffed. "No. Your grown-up boys. Couple of things Phin said were...strange."

That got Dani's attention. "Strange how?"

"Well, he said something about his father and some company that I didn't quite understand, so I left it alone. But he mentioned something about when he and Vic were partners, and it didn't make sense. I thought I remembered that you said they went to school together, so maybe, like, lab partners? But that didn't fit with what he was saying. I don't know—it was just weird."

"What about Alex?"

"Well, that was off, too. I know Phin must've lived around here, since Eunice said she used to babysit him. Obviously, he moved at some point, because he knew Vic. But he made some comment like, 'if Alex ever gets over ancient history' and that he'd made a lot of mistakes. It was just as weird as the thing about Vic. Any idea what he was talking about?"

"No. That doesn't make any sense." Dani frowned. *Why didn't Alex say anything?* she wondered. "How on earth did you drag that out of him?"

"He thinks I have the attention span of a flea. Well, I do, but he thinks that means I don't listen to stuff. So he was just talking, and I'm not sure he even realizes I heard him."

"Nice."

"Yeah. Listen, you sound whipped, so I'm gonna let you go. I'll see you Monday."

"Okay. Good night." Dani hung up the phone and sat there, considering what Gia had said. It was finally time to push for the whole truth.

Chapter Nine

Jazz Shoes

Phin wasn't sure when being in his thirties had scarred him for life, but he could point with one hundred percent certainty to the moment he realized it. He was also certain that it was definitely—almost surely—*probably* all Alex's fault. He was still worn out from the previous day's activities, and getting up at five in the morning to do whatever it was Alex did on Sundays was not Phin's idea of a good time. He had only agreed to it because Alex had implied he wouldn't show up, and Phin took that as a challenge. Phin was never one to make light of a dare, even if it was far too childish for a man his age.

He entered the community building, glad there was no one else around to question why he was there. It was bad enough being awake at such an ungodly hour; he didn't need anyone else's company. He suppressed a yawn, wishing he'd thought to make coffee before he left. In a lame attempt to wipe the sleepiness away, he ran his hand over his face.

Phin made his way toward the same part of the building he'd been in the day before. The smell of industrial cleaner lingered in the air; he wrinkled his nose. A light overhead flickered slightly, and Phin's footsteps echoed in the silent, empty hallway.

Alex had said to meet him in room 127. On his way down the hall, Phin was greeted by the soft notes of orchestral music. It was familiar, but he couldn't quite place it. Curious, he followed the sound. He came to a stop at the room from which the music emanated. A glance at the door told him this was where he was supposed to meet Alex. The music which had piqued his interest was now featuring a haunting saxophone melody. Phin smiled; Alex had good taste. *Pictures at an Exhibition* had long been one of Phin's favorite pieces.

The door was ajar. Phin stepped closer and carefully pushed the door further open then peeked inside. At first, he didn't see anything. After a moment, a lone figure came into view and Phin realized Alex had previously been hidden by the shadows in the room. Phin could see him clearly now, and he sucked in his breath.

Nothing could have prepared Phin for how elegant and sensual Alex was as he moved across the floor. He had seen men dance before; his parents were cultural snobs, and he'd been going to the ballet since before he could walk. He had never seen anything quite like this, though. Alex wasn't a ballet dancer, and, being unfamiliar with dance styles, Phin didn't really know how to describe what he was seeing. He wasn't sure that graceful was the right word. That was something Phin associated with a certain delicate beauty, which was not how he would classify Alex or that form of dance. Yet Phin didn't think that power or athleticism fit either. Alex moved with the same fluid motion as a river, and it gave Phin the same sort of rush to watch. He appreciated it even if he didn't have the right word for it.

Alex was not particularly tall, but there was a long, muscular leanness to him. He was moving artfully with the music in a complicated pattern of steps and spins, his bare feet making soft thuds each time he landed a jump. He was clad only in a black tank top and a pair of black athletic shorts that ended just above his knees. The shorts were form-fitted, but they looked like they were made of very soft cotton. Phin had the sudden urge to reach out and touch the fabric to see if it felt as nice as it looked. His face heated up and his stomach tightened at the idea of touching Alex like that.

Phin closed his eyes, trying to settle down. He recalled the only other time he'd seen Alex dance. They had been ten at the time, and it was the day Phin had spent with Alex because his own mother was at a charity fundraiser. He'd been stuck riding along and sitting in the waiting area while Alex was in a class. The teacher had left the door open partway to keep the air circulating, and Phin had been able to watch, fascinated, as Alex and three girls worked on a performance dance. Just like it was now, his heart had raced and he'd been mesmerized by the way Alex moved, even if he hadn't quite understood why.

Extracting himself from the memory, Phin opened his eyes and watched the rest of the routine. The saxophone piece ended on a drawn-out note that grew fainter at the same time Alex was sinking down to the floor to end his dance. Phin stood rooted to the spot, his heart still pounding. He closed his eyes again, etching the details into his memory before they faded. While he was occupied with that pursuit, the other man had somehow managed to sneak up on him. Without warning, he was standing mere inches from Phin, who had an urge to back away from the room. He opened his mouth to apologize for lurking in the doorway, but Alex spoke first.

"See something you like?" His voice was low and warm.

"I—what?"

"You were staring." Alex had one hand on the door frame above Phin's head; it made Phin feel slightly claustrophobic, despite the fact that the open hallway was behind him.

"I wasn't staring! I was...appreciating your skill." Phin pursed his lips, tensing so he wouldn't squirm under Alex's gaze.

"Ah. And did you enjoy what you saw?" Alex withdrew his hand and straightened up.

"Possibly," Phin acknowledged, relaxing. "I'll know for sure when I'm actually awake."

Alex laughed. "Let's take care of that, then."

Phin wasn't sure if Alex had meant to have a juvenile tone, so he suppressed the urge to snort like a twelve-year-old. He was increasingly frustrated by Alex's hot-and-cold interactions. One minute he was making suggestive remarks and the next he was bordering on unfriendly. Phin brushed it off and followed Alex further into the room. Alex looked him up and down, frowning when he saw Phin's khaki shorts.

"What are you wearing? That's going to be too constricting."

"You said to wear something comfortable."

"Well, that's because I thought you owned something you would wear to work out and you were just too clueless to wear it yesterday for Gia's class." He sighed. "Never mind. I've got extra shorts in back." He disappeared into a coat room and emerged a moment later with an article of clothing.

"Better not be a leotard," Phin muttered.

It wasn't. Alex handed Phin a pair of soft cut-off sweat pants. Phin accepted them and made to retreat to the coat room to change. Alex rolled his eyes.

"I'm not going to ogle your ass, if that's what's bothering you. Just change here—there's no one else around."

Phin glared at him. "I'm just not comfortable changing in a room with a thousand windows." He gestured at the long wall in front of him.

"Yes, because there are so many people out there peeping in to see if they can spot some guy in his underwear. You're not even taking off your shirt. Phin, what I'm currently wearing reveals more than you would be."

Phin decided not to comment that he'd noticed that already. "Fine," he grouched, unbuttoning his shorts.

When Phin had donned the sweats, Alex led him to the middle of the floor.

"What are we doing first?" Phin asked.

"Just some basic stretches, a little yoga."

"Not going to teach me to dance?"

Alex chuckled. "Are you planning to teach me how to draw later today?"

Startled, Phin asked, "You remember that?"

"That you can draw? Yes. You used to draw cartoons of our teacher in class whenever we both got bored." He chuckled, but then his eyes clouded over. "God, I haven't thought of that in ages."

The knowledge that Alex remembered that part of their long-dissolved friendship was strangely appealing, as was the suggestion they might do something else together. Phin ignored the nagging thought that there was something off about the way Alex had actually been reasonably friendly in favor of being pleasantly surprised that he seemed interested in moving past their previous tension.

"I don't draw much anymore," Phin said. It wasn't exactly a lie if he didn't count all his random doodling on old papers.

"That's too bad," Alex remarked. He drew in a breath. "Right. So just something to get you warmed up for the day." He crossed the room and pushed buttons on the CD player until soft piano music began to play. Returning to Phin's side, he said, "Just do what I do."

Phin tried to imitate Alex's movements exactly, right down to breathing in rhythm with him. He wasn't used to the motions, however, and he didn't have quite the sense of balance Alex did. When he tried to stand on one leg, he tensed and overreached, toppling to the side. He grunted in frustration.

Alex released his pose and stepped over to Phin. "Just relax. If you strain, you won't be able to hold the pose."

"I can't help it," Phin spat. "My body doesn't go that way. I run or I work out at the gym—I don't stand around doing performance art with stupid names like 'pine tree' or whatever."

"Palm tree," Alex corrected, "And that was the last pose, not this one. It's all about balance. If you add this in, it'll help you stay in shape."

"Seriously, I don't care. This is ridiculous." Phin knew he sounded like a whiny child, but he wasn't interested in being mature at that moment. He was embarrassed that he was having a harder time keeping up with Alex than he'd had with Gia and her elderly class, and it annoyed him.

"Hey," Alex said. "It's okay. Let me help you."

"Fine. What do you want me to do?"

"Start by standing straight, keeping your hands at your sides."

Phin did as he was told. "Now what?"

"Relax, and let me move your body for you."

Phin closed his eyes. He felt Alex's hands on his shoulders, his fingers brushing, cool against Phin's neck.

"Now, reach down and grab hold of your ankle. Bring your foot up to your knee, just like I showed you."

After doing as Alex instructed, Phin asked, "Now what?"

"Now I'm going to raise your arms. This was where you had trouble last time." Gently, he moved Phin's arms upward. He let go and placed one hand on Phin's upper back and the other on his stomach. "Hold it there."

Several seconds passed, and Phin began to shake. Alex's hands were steady and calming, and Phin relaxed slightly into the stretch. At last, Alex moved the hand on Phin's stomach, and Phin released his pose. He realized Alex still had a hand on his back, and he leaned into the touch.

Their faces were inches from each other, and Phin's heart beat wildly against his chest. Although the music was still playing in the background, he was sure Alex could hear his pulse hammering. He swallowed, trying to calm the twisting in his stomach. It took all Phin's effort to resist the temptation to lean toward Alex; there wasn't a single thing that was appropriate about the way he was feeling. He turned slightly so he faced away from Alex, breaking the moment.

"Thanks," he said as Alex let go of him and stepped back.

"You're welcome. Ready to try something else?"

"All right. What do you have in mind?"

Alex grinned, and there was a wicked gleam in his eye. "Oh, don't worry. This will be fun. Trust me—after this, you'll think Gia's class was easy."

Phin could only groan in response.

Fortunately for Phin, Alex seemed to have taken pity on him. Once they were finished with the yoga, it wasn't nearly as difficult to keep up as it had been the previous day in Gia's class. When they were through, just as he was about to bid Alex good morning and head back to the Railway Penny for a shower, Alex stopped him.

"Why don't you get cleaned up and join me for breakfast? Say, forty-five minutes?"

Phin was surprised, then suspicious. He narrowed his eyes. "Why?"

"Just to talk." Alex's expression was unreadable. "Unless you're not up for it after our workout."

It almost sounded like a challenge, as when Alex had invited him to come to the community building that morning. Phin replied, "All right. Where?"

"We can just go to the cafe at the inn," Alex suggested.

"All right," Phin said again. He wondered what Alex wanted to talk about, but he didn't ask. He was afraid he might not like the answer.

They parted ways. On the way back to the Railway Penny, Phin went over all the possible points of discussion. None of them were pleasant, and it made Phin feel panicky. He tried to calm down by taking his time in the shower, but after ten minutes of doing nothing but letting the water pour over him, he was still shaking and his stomach was in knots. Quickly, he dried off and dressed, not wanting to be late.

He met Alex in the main entryway of the inn, and they proceeded into the cafe. As soon as the server appeared by their table, Phin ordered coffee. By that point, he was desperate, even though he'd been through an entire round of physical activity and a shower already. He looked over to see Alex, who had ordered only water, eying him, trying not to laugh. He scowled.

"It's my one vice. Let me have it," Phin grouched after the server had gone to put in their order.

"I didn't say a word," Alex replied.

"How are you so damn chipper, anyway? You had to have been up at least a half hour before me."

"I'm just naturally an early riser."

"I'm happy for you. The rest of us normal people don't get up at the crack of dawn to do yoga." Phin demonstrated his point by yawning; Alex only chuckled.

"Shouldn't you be more awake by now? I put you through quite a workout."

"Why do you think I'm so tired?" Phin stifled a second yawn, not wanting to give Alex anything else to mock.

Alex shrugged. "You know that staying properly hydrated has the same effect as drinking coffee, right?" He raised his glass in mock toast and took a sip. Phin glowered at him.

Once he had his coffee in hand, Phin was ready to get to the point. He said, "You're being almost nice. Why did you ask me to come see you?"

"Dani," Alex said. "She's beginning to trust you. Eunice already did, Vic knows you, and Gia obviously likes you, God only knows why." He turned his nose up slightly. "Dani thought it might be a good idea if I were a little...friendlier."

Phin hummed a little. "That still doesn't explain why you asked me to meet you this morning to practice standing around on one leg."

Alex snickered, but he quickly sobered. His eyes bored into Phin. "I didn't think you'd actually show up."

Phin narrowed his eyes. "If you thought I wasn't going to show up, why did *you* come?"

"I'm not cruel enough to ask you to meet me and leave you hanging." Alex's gaze was steady. "Or find another way to humiliate you."

It was the closest they'd come to acknowledging their shared past. Phin tried to keep his eyes on Alex, but he couldn't. He looked over at the other tables then down at his lap before returning his attention to his nearly empty coffee cup. "What would you have done if I hadn't?"

Shrugging, Alex replied, "Gone for a swim. Pool's open at five. Anyway," Alex continued, "I'm glad you did. After breakfast, I want to show you something."

"Was that why you asked to meet me here?"

"Yes."

Phin raised his head to look at Alex and nodded. "Okay."

Conversation during breakfast was strained but polite. Phin was grateful to Dani for whatever part she'd played in getting Alex to talk to him. Having a civil conversation over eggs and toast was far more than he'd expected. He braced himself for Alex to ask him pointed questions or make snide remarks the way he had in the bar, but he didn't. When they finished, they stepped outside to Alex's car.

Alex offered to drive, since he knew where they were going. A ten-minute ride later, they pulled into a parking lot. When Phin saw the building, his eyes widened. It was the last place he had expected Alex to bring him. A sign in front read, "St. Julian's. Worship 10am and 6pm." Alex chose a spot and parked the car. Phin sat back in his seat, leaving his seatbelt in place and refusing to move. He looked over at Alex and raised his eyebrows expectantly.

"You brought me to a fucking *church?*"

"You may wish to filter your language a little." Alex looked sideways at Phin. "This is where I go on Sunday mornings." He offered no further explanation. He got out of the car and stood next to it.

"You could've warned me. What if I were Jewish or something?"

"I know you're not."

With a sigh, Phin climbed out of the car. He didn't want to be rude, but he didn't want to go in, either. "I'm not really the church type."

Alex shrugged. "You don't have to come in." He started walking.

Another challenge. Phin frowned and said, "No, I'll go." He followed Alex toward the building and quickly caught up. "God. I haven't been to church in—what, fifteen years?"

"I promise, we don't bite." Alex tilted his head to the side. "You used to go to church?"

"My parents are Presbyterians, yeah." *Not that it made a goddamn bit of difference in their lives.* "You're Catholic?"

With a chuckle, Alex replied, "You're joking, right? *No.* This is a Lutheran church."

"Ah. Catholic lite."

Alex swatted his arm. "Jerk."

They entered the building, and Phin was struck by the dark elegance of the interior. It looked nothing like what he remembered of his parents' church, which had been open and full of light. That seemed ironic to him, given the secrets that church had harbored. His father had been an elder—religious power covered a multitude of sins. No one cared how he ran his business or what he did outside the walls of the church as long as he remained faithful with his giving.

St. Julian's had high, stained glass windows depicting various scenes of Jesus' life. Everything else was made from dark wood. It was small; Phin guessed that there weren't more than thirty or forty people in attendance. That didn't surprise him given the size of the town compared with the number of churches he'd seen. Phin thought that even if every single resident attended church on a given Sunday, they wouldn't fill them all.

An older woman greeted them. "Are you here for the baptism?" she asked.

Just as Phin was about to reply, Alex said, "Yes. Old friend of the family," and gave Phin a little push forward.

"Oh, lovely!" the woman exclaimed, handing Phin a bulletin.

Once they were past the entrance, Phin leaned in and whispered, "What the hell was that all about?"

"If they think you're here because of me, they'll start fussing over you."

The service wasn't long. Phin declined communion, though by this church's practices he could have taken it. He didn't feel right about it, though. He watched the others in attendance as they filed to the front of the church to receive the elements. It was different from the way his parents' church did things. He kept his eyes on Alex, watching him as he knelt beside the railing and accepted a small piece of bread and what Phin assumed was real wine—it was the wrong color for grape juice. He'd only ever had the juice, and it amused him to think about how real wine was a bit like being allowed to sit at the grown-up table. He was distracted and almost missed Alex forming the sign of the cross and rising from his place. It was a simple gesture, but it obviously meant something to Alex. Something about it pulled at Phin's gut in an odd way he couldn't quite identify.

At the end of the service, Alex said, "I want you to come somewhere with me. Here, let me get you out to the car before one of the grandmothers gets hold of you, or I'll never hear the end of it." He tilted his chin toward a tiny woman with permed white hair. Leaning in, he whispered, "That one is constantly trying to set me up with her grandson."

Alex cringed, and Phin offered a sympathetic nod.

Alex dragged Phin through the chattering congregants and out the door, leaving him by the car. "Hang on a sec. I need to get a few things first," he said. He disappeared back inside the church.

When he returned, he had a box in his hand. Without saying anything, he jerked his head toward the car, inviting Phin to get in. Alex drove them out of town in the opposite direction from the way Phin had come in the previous week.

"Where are we?" Phin asked when they pulled up in front of a series of abandoned railway cars.

"This is what I wanted to show you," Alex responded. "Get out of the car, but stay here." He stepped out himself and opened the rear door, retrieving the box he'd brought from church.

Alex went to the first railway car, carrying the box. By the time he reached it, there was someone else already standing outside the car. Alex took his time, talking with the person before opening the box. He pulled out various items, offering them to the man at the doorway. Phin's eyes widened. Alex had brought the communion elements with him—a loaf of bread, some wine, a stack of small cups, and a little tin of something Phin couldn't identify.

Pulling of a small piece of bread, Alex held it out. The person, whose face was hidden by the door frame, accepted it, followed by the wine. Alex touched the small tin with one finger and touched the person's head, making a motion. Afterward, he moved on from there, stopping at several of the cars, though not all of them. When he was through, he returned to where Phin was standing.

"What were you doing?" Phin asked, though he already had a good idea.

"I bring them stuff from the food and clothing boxes every week, and I serve some of them communion."

"Well, why don't they just come to church? It seems like they'd be welcome there."

Alex snorted. "Does it look like they have a way to get there? Not to mention how you might feel if you were homeless, walking into a church full of people who don't live anything like you. Not everyone is up for that."

They got back in the car, and Alex drove them back toward town. They stopped several times, delivering various items and occasionally communion. In between, they didn't speak at all. They passed ramshackle cabins and worn-down apartment buildings along their route. As pleasant and beautiful as his day with Gia had been, spending this time with Alex was the opposite. By the time they made their way back to the church so Alex could return the box and what was left of the communion elements, Phin was thoroughly discouraged. He waited by the car for Alex to emerge from the church.

When they got back in the car, Phin looked at Alex. "Why did you really bring me out here? You dragged me to church and then drove me around to the parts of town you thought I'd find most distasteful. Either this was some elaborate ploy to help me find Jesus or whatever you church-types do, or there's something you're not telling me."

"I don't know what—"

"Yes, you do." Phin paused to consider. "Wait. I think I know what's going on here."

"Oh?" Phin detected a note of false innocence in Alex's tone.

He sighed. "Yes. Gia was supposed to show me what wonderful things there are around here, how beautiful the country is, and what kind of community you have. Spreading the love. Now you're here to do the opposite. I take it this is all supposed to either make me spill my heart out about what I'm going to do to your precious school, or it's intended to make me reconsider doing something to turn your world upside down. How'm I doing so far?"

Alex didn't say anything for a moment. He rested his head on the back of his seat and closed his eyes. After a minute or two, he rolled his head to the side to look at Phin. "You're doing pretty well. Is it working, then?"

Phin ran a hand over his face. "Look. I'm not here to ruin your lives, as much as you might want to believe that," he said. "I was invited by your school board to come here and make recommendations about the future of the school. I haven't even started to put a report together yet—I still have to observe the high school classes, and I have a second round of observations among the elementary teachers. I don't know what you're looking for from me."

"I'm looking for some assurance that you're going to leave us in a better place than you found us," Alex replied. He looked steadily at Phin.

"I wish I could promise you that," Phin answered back. "But I don't know what 'better' means to you."

Alex drew in a deep breath and let it out slowly through his nose. "It means that these kids are going to be able to grow up to have more opportunities than they have in this small town."

Phin was taken aback, and he let his mouth drop open slightly. "I'm sorry...what? Did you really just say you think these kids have no future?"

"That is not what I said." Alex sat up and turned toward Phin.

"Oh, right. You said they don't have opportunities. Why? Because a lot of them are going to grow up to run their parents' farms? I thought maybe you all were going for the movie stereotype of poor equals good and rich equals bad—you know, we small town folks can win against the big, impersonal state board or whatever. At first, I thought maybe you were trying to take the spoiled, rich boy and make me see the error of my ways or make me so disgusted I'd leave you alone. But now I'm not convinced that's it. You know, for someone who thinks you're better than I am, you sure have a low view of the people here. Unless I'm missing something, of course." Breathing hard, Phin gestured at Alex, inviting him to prove him wrong.

"I don't know what gave you the impression that I don't think much of the residents of North Cowell." Alex crossed his arms.

"Gee, I don't know, maybe it's the fact that you seem to be keeping distance between yourself and them. Do you remember what you said to me the very first day I was here?"

Alex frowned. "Not really."

"When I asked you about your job, you said it was full-time because someone needed to test the kids. Not *help* them, Alex. *Test* them. That says a lot about what you believe."

"I—" Alex cut himself short and pressed his lips into a thin line. "No, you ass. That's the thing I say to self-important, unconcerned dirt-bags sent by State Ed to tell us that we're not even close to good enough for their standards, despite the fact that we do our best with our limited resources. Of *course* someone needs to take care of testing the kids, because that's all anyone cares about anymore." He was breathing hard, his nostrils flaring.

The words stung like a slap. He wanted to shout, *I do care, damn it!* But that level of investment hadn't gotten him anything except a parental seal of disapproval. Sitting in the car, staring at Alex, he found himself at a loss. They sat in silence for a long time. At last Phin said, "You're right. I don't have any attachment to this town, this school, or those students. But you do, and you have a strange way of showing it. You want me to care? Then help me. Give me more to go on than just a couple of drives around town for the high and low-lights." He turned away and leaned back against the seat.

Alex shook his head. "I don't know…" He trailed off and propped his elbow on the open window, looking away from Phin and resting his mouth against his closed fist.

Phin had a strange urge to reach out his hand, but he didn't. Instead, he said, "I didn't think so. Just let me do my job. Please. I promise if you do that, I'll be gone and you'll never have to see me again."

Alex didn't answer. Phin heard him draw in a shaky breath, and he wondered what was underneath the surface. He looked away when he saw Alex draw his wrist across his eyes, giving him a few minutes to compose himself.

"I'm sorry," Phin said, and he meant it. "I only wanted to ride you a little for being a self-righteous prick. I didn't mean—"

"No." Alex cleared his throat. "It's fine. I'll do it."

"Do what?"

"I'll give you more. This town—and the school—are worth saving, Phin. I—*we*—can't lose everything we've worked so hard to build."

Phin pushed away the feeling that he might regret his request later. "Okay, then."

They sat in silence, staring out through the windshield. After a few minutes, Alex asked, "Ready to go?"

"Any time," Phin replied, and they drove back to town without speaking another word.

Chapter Ten

He's More into You than You Thought

Dani busied herself with mundane tasks to keep from staring at the clock, waiting for Vic to finish work. Alex was spending the day with Phin—at her request—so she would have to wait for him to call to grill him on Gia's remarks. That left her ample time to confront Vic. He was only supposed to be at work until noon, going over some papers at the Penny. Another glance at the clock told her that he would be leaving any time. She spent a few minutes gathering her courage.

"Michael!" she called up the stairs. She heard him turn off the radio.

"Yeah?"

"I'm going over to talk to Vic for a bit. Think you can handle things here?"

"Okay."

They would be fine. She tried not to rely on Michael too often, but she had to admit that it was nice to have a reasonably responsible built-in babysitter from time to time. Fortunately, as much as Carlie and Jake could try anyone's patience, Michael managed better than most. She headed next door to wait for Vic to return from the inn. She sat on Vic's porch, humming to herself and trying not to look like she was up to anything.

At last Vic came home. He seemed surprised, though not displeased, to see Dani out front. She stood up and waited for him to open the door. Immediately, his expression changed from surprise to concern.

"What's wrong? Are the kids okay?" he asked.

"Let's go inside," she replied.

He opened the door and motioned for her to go in first. Once he was inside and had shut the door, she turned around to face him. "You're going to tell me everything. I'm tired of being patient with you."

Vic's mouth dropped open. He didn't say anything, just stood blinking at her. Dani crossed her arms and stood her ground. He shook his head and stepped around her toward the kitchen.

"I'm definitely not doing this without a drink. You want one?" He fished around in the refrigerator and came up with a couple of bottles of beer.

Dani made a face. "You know I don't drink that swill, and I'd rather be sober for this conversation anyway."

He sighed and put one of the bottles back in the fridge. "Fine." He opened the other one and sat down at the table. "What do you want to know?"

Sitting down across from him, Dani sighed. "Last night, Gia called me. She'd been out with Phin for the day, and—not surprisingly—brought him home with her. Apparently, his tongue was loose in more ways than one"—Vic nearly spit a mouthful of beer onto the table at that, and Dani rolled her eyes—"and he let some things slip when he thought she wasn't paying attention."

Vic coughed. "Such as?"

Dani wasn't falling for his innocent tone of voice. "Such as the fact that you and Phin used to work together. I'm not stupid, Vic. For years, you've kept us all in the dark about whatever secret past you have. Honestly, it's never felt like a big deal until now. But there's something going on, and you'd better tell me before I dig it up somewhere else."

"You want the whole story?" Vic set his beer on the table forcefully, and a little sloshed out of the top. "Fine. You're not going to like it."

She leaned forward. "I don't care. At this point, getting the truth is more important."

He looked intently at Dani and nodded. "I've known Phin since we were in high school. We were tight."

"Yeah, I know that already. You told me before. Start with what happened after high school."

"All right." He shook his head. "We were like brothers. We did everything together, even college. Afterward, we both went to work for his father."

Dani sucked in her breath. "EduText."

"Yeah. We worked together in the sales department, pitching textbooks to schools. The best assignments were the curriculum fairs—not too much drama. Just show up, explain the book, and let the schools decide if they liked your presentation or not. The worst ones were when schools would call us to meet with them for review. Phin liked to apply some...unorthodox methods. As in, everything from outright lying to fucking the curriculum supervisors for a deal." He cleared his throat. "I didn't know at first. We would meet with clients and they would agree to think it over. When we went back to them the next day, I pitched the materials again, and they bought whatever we were selling. Not all the time, but enough that I finally said something to Phin. He told me what he was doing. I tried to play along, but I got sick of it." He shifted slightly in his seat and fiddled with the bottle in front of him. He didn't meet Dani's eyes. "I left the company after working there for six years."

"There's something you're not explaining, Vic. Normally, people who quit their jobs don't move across the state and then hide in small towns, refusing to tell anyone why they're running away."

He sighed and stood up, pacing to the window and staring outside. When he turned around, his eyes blazed. "You're right that most people don't leave the way I did. I didn't have a choice. It wasn't just Phin. His father is a raging asshole who put me through a whole lot of crap. I knew he only hired me 'cause of Phin and so he could say he had minority employees. I never got half the recognition everyone else did. And he covered up a lot—not just Phin's behavior but stuff that was a lot worse. Right before I left, I found out what he was doing with his security investments. We lost a major contract with a district, so I wanted to know why. Turned out he'd mishandled funds, but there wasn't a trail. Like a fool, I went to Phin to tell him what was going on. Thought I could trust him. He didn't believe me, or didn't want to. I accused him of being involved. I still don't know whether he was or not. He must've told his old man, because they tried to fire me. I told them I'd bring a lawsuit about the blatant racism I experienced while working for them. They informed me I didn't have any proof, which was technically true. In exchange for not going after them, they said they wouldn't fire me. Instead, I was asked to leave quietly and say nothing. So I did."

"And how did you end up here?"

"Phin's grandparents all still live in Morton Ponds. Phin's father took over the company from his own father, so they were out of the question. But I was pretty sure Lorne Patterson's in-laws saw him for what he was. I was going to try to get to him through them. When I got there, they told me to leave it alone. They didn't want to get involved. I stopped here on my way out to get something to eat and clear my head, and I just...stayed." He turned around again.

Dani didn't say anything for a moment; she just sat there staring at Vic's back. "Why didn't you ever tell us?"

"Would you have believed me?" he countered.

"Why wouldn't we?" Dani frowned. "That doesn't make sense."

Vic balled his hand and looked like he might strike the counter, but he held steady. "Maybe because that's the way things work for people who look like me."

"I—" She didn't have an answer for that. "But this was *us*, Vic. You've known us for how long? At some point, it should have occurred to you that we'd have been on your side no matter what."

He sighed heavily. "Fear's a powerful thing, Dani. I didn't know what they were going to do to me if I told anyone the truth, especially after Phin's grandparents refused to help me."

"When Phin showed up, why didn't you tell me then?"

"Tell you what?"

"Everything. You didn't want me getting involved with him, but you wouldn't say why. How come you didn't tell me?"

Vic kept his back to her as he answered, "He asked me not to."

"What?" She stood up. "Why would he do that?"

Vic whirled around and threw his hands up. "I don't know. Maybe because there's a lot more to his job than just checking up on a random school in the middle of nowhere? Dani, leave it alone now. I've told you my story. I'm not gonna rat out Phin, too."

"Like you haven't already. Sleeping with clients isn't just some little indiscretion, Vic. I can't imagine he's stopped doing that since you left. You let me send Gia and Alex after him without warning."

"Stop. Please, Dani. Just stop now. Leave him alone to do whatever he's doing. You're not going to be able to prevent it anyway." He sighed and sank back down into his chair.

Dani remained on her feet, hands on her hips. "I'm not letting this go. What can't I prevent?"

Vic didn't answer immediately. He leaned against the counter, his arms at his sides, tapping his fingers against the cupboard doors. With a resigned sigh, he said, "His father is using EduText's management arm to take out a charter on the school. They come in, fire the principal and half the staff, and send in whoever they can get to do what they want in their place. It's an option for 'failing' schools. They don't have to worry about the Department of Education breathing down their necks, so they can teach however the hell they want, and it makes money for them and all their investors. On top of that, they get grant money from the state, which just pads their pockets. It's a done deal, Dani. Phin told me everything when he showed up. He's supposed to give the impression that he's creating a 'school improvement plan'"—he made air quotes—"but he's really scoping things out to give the go-ahead on the charter."

"I see. Well, things make a lot more sense now." Dani crossed her arms. "But it doesn't explain why you never told me what you knew."

Vic looked up at her, his expression pleading. "He asked for my help."

She stepped back a pace, feeling as though she'd been punched. "You agreed."

"Yes."

"Why?"

"You know as well as I do that the school is in trouble. The state's going to do something no matter what. By giving him what he wanted, I thought I could keep you out of it. All I told him was that you knew everything about the school because of your job."

"You actually sent him to me to work me over like you just said he does with all his clients?" She gaped at him.

"No! I made him promise he'd leave you alone. He wanted to use you to get information on some of the staff. He told me he'd find some-one else."

"And I handed her to him on a silver platter. What if he'd used Gia like that? You know what she's like. And there's something weird between him and Alex, too—I can see it whenever they're within twenty feet of each other. You didn't think to say something to me?"

"I didn't say anything because I didn't think it would matter to you what I did."

"You chose a liar with a dubious history over me." She closed her eyes. "Over us."

"Us?" He gestured between them. "There's no us, Dani. You've made that clear. We never made a commitment to each other. For more than a year, you've been using me. I wanted him to get in, do his job, and get out so that I could move on. You think you're the only one who's been tired of waiting? I'm sick of waiting for you to figure your shit out and decide what you want."

"What I want? Like you're just an innocent bystander, right? I don't recall you objecting to anything we've done. And now you're ready to just move on?"

He sighed. "Yes. I can't do this anymore. God knows, I've tried. I practically helped you raise Jake when his daddy died, but you keep shutting me out. I'm not your security blanket. You gotta move on, or I'll do it without you. I'm not asking you to forget Jim, but I sure as hell can't just be someone to keep you warm at night." He snorted. "As if you're even letting me that far in."

"So, you thought if you helped Phin destroy the school, that would— what? Force me to choose you?" She glared at him. "You know you've lost that chance now, don't you?" She stalked to the doorway. Out of the corner of her eye, she could see Vic rising from his seat and reaching out his hand to her.

"Dani, wait. That's not—"

She couldn't listen anymore. Ignoring him, she continued to the front door and walked out, pulling it shut behind her. She heard Vic call her name once more, and she almost turned around. Instead, she retreated to the safety of her own home, refusing to acknowledge the sound of his voice.

It wasn't until after taking care of the kids' needs that Dani had the chance to sit down for a good cry. She'd managed to drop Carlie off at a friend's house, wave goodbye when Michael left with his friends, and set Jake up with a movie in the play room. She sniffled her way through making a cup of raspberry tea and had just sat down at the table when there was a knock on the door.

Huffing, Dani remained in her seat and contemplated whether or not she should answer for so long that whoever it was knocked a second time. At last, she wiped her eyes and rose to get the door. She opened it to find Alex, fist raised to knock again.

"Uh…is this a bad time?"

"No. It's a fucking perfect time. Please, come right in and continue interrupting my perfect, sunshiny day." She pressed the heel of her hand to her forehead, trying to reduce the pounding.

"Dani?" Alex's eyebrows shot up, and he backed away a couple of steps.

She sighed. "I'm sorry." She gestured for him to come in.

Alex stepped inside, glancing warily at her out of the corner of his eye on the way to the kitchen. Dani ignored this and brushed past, pulling out another cup and a tea bag. Without bothering to ask first, she poured boiling water into the cup and set it in front of Alex. He didn't touch it.

"Did something happen with one of the kids?" he asked as she seated herself across from him.

"No." She buried her head in her hands, and finally the real tears started flowing. Alex slid out of his chair and into the one next to Dani. He put his arm around her.

After several minutes, she finally managed to calm down enough to wipe her eyes on a napkin. "God. I'm so stupid."

"What happened?" He made soothing circles on her back with his hand.

"I had a fight with Vic."

Alex withdrew his hand and looked at Dani, frowning. "A fight? It must've been pretty bad."

"It was. I guess I assumed he and I were on the same page. Turns out I was wrong."

"I'm not sure I understand."

"Yeah, well, of course you wouldn't. We didn't say anything."

Now Alex's features reflected his utter bewilderment. "Say anything about what?"

Dani sighed and looked up at the ceiling, then back at Alex. "We were sleeping together. Well, not so much on the sleeping part."

"Uh…oh. Okay." It was obvious he still didn't quite follow. "You were seeing each other?"

"Not exactly. It was mostly just sex. Well, not anymore." She turned toward Alex. "I finally made him tell me what he's been keeping from me. It didn't end well." She took a deep breath. "Maybe I should feel guilty for pushing too hard. You know what though? I don't. He's being an ass. And it hurts."

"I'm sorry." Alex put his hand on top of hers. "What did you fight about?"

She was quiet for a moment. She twisted her hands together and chewed a little on her lower lip. At last she said, "I don't know." She frowned down at her tea. "Us, mostly. Does that sound stupid?"

"No." Alex squeezed her hand and then withdrew his own to wrap it around the mug in front of him. "Tell me."

Dani shook her head. "It doesn't even matter. What's done is done, and I can't trust him anymore. He said he was protecting me, but I think he was just covering his own sorry ass."

"Why didn't you tell me there was something going on between you?"

In order to avoid answering the question, she countered, "Why didn't you tell me you knew Phin Patterson?"

"I have no idea what you're talking about." He refused to look at her.

"Yes, you do. He was with Gia last night, and she called after he left. Apparently, whatever they were doing loosened his tongue–" She glared at Alex, who was snickering. "Shut up. What is it with you guys and your junior high humor? Anyway, he said something about you and 'ancient history.' Any clue what he meant by that?" She applied the same look she gave her kids when she knew there was something they didn't want to tell her, and Alex shrank back a little.

"Fine," he said. "We knew each other when we were kids. We didn't get along any better back then."

Dani eyed him. "Yeah, see, you're doing the same thing Vic did. What aren't you telling me?"

"Nothing," he insisted. "He was just an obnoxious little brat back then, that's all."

"I see. And you didn't think this was important information?"

Alex shrugged. "Not really."

"Is this going to get in the way of following through? Because if it is–"

He held up a hand. "Not a problem." His eyes suddenly sparkled with mischief. "That's what I came here to tell you. It's a done deal."

"Already?"

He nodded. "Your suggestion worked like a charm." He grinned and shook his head. "I gotta hand it to you, Dani. I wasn't sure this was a good idea, but it's working out perfectly. He played right into your hands. What do you plan to do with him?"

Dani shifted uncomfortably when she recalled what Vic had told her. She squashed those thoughts and said, "I plan to find out who's head is on the chopping block, of course. I did some digging of my own, and I don't think he's just here to offer us some nice suggestions. Our school is in serious trouble, and we only have so many options. The school board is announcing the plans at the final meeting, but I intend to find out what's going on long before then. So, how'd you get him to go along with us?"

"Emotional manipulation." He rolled his eyes. "God, what is it about some guys that they can't resist the whole pouty thing? That breaks rule number five on my list of how to meet decent guys—stay away from the ones who attract drama."

Dani raised her eyebrows at him. "You're kidding, right? Alex, do I even need to remind you about the last several people you were even sort of serious with? I think you've already broken rules number one through four. Why stop there?"

Alex glowered at her. "Whatever. You do know those were actual relationships, right? This is different. Good thing it's not going anywhere."

Dani laughed. "Then why are you talking about it like it might be? Besides, I don't think it's possible to avoid drama. For what it's worth, I will never understand it either. Thank God I've never had to deal with that crap on the dating front." She sobered for a moment, thinking about both Jim and Vic. "I think it's that some guys like to be protective or something." She grinned. "Kind of like you. Which totally reinforces what I said to you that first night he was here—he is definitely your type."

"No," Alex hissed, "he is not. I do not want anyone who thrives on that kind of thing."

"But you like using your skills for reading people." She took a sip of her tea, peering over the top of her cup and waiting for him to respond.

"Not like that, I don't. I'd rather not play therapist for my men, nor do I want them messing with my head. That's not healthy."

She shrugged and hummed a little. "So, what happened after you melted his cold heart?"

"He practically begged me to make him understand why he should care about us."

"Wow. You must've done a number on him, then." She twitched an eyebrow. "What's your next move?"

Alex shifted slightly and tilted his head a little. "Dani, my part in this is done. You asked me to make sure he was invested, and now he is. Trust me, he's thoroughly distracted at this point."

"I was hoping you'd stay involved."

Alex shook his head. "I did what you wanted. I think you can handle it from here. He said he wants to know why he should care, and I think you're better off doing that than I am. Besides, you've got Gia for that. Apparently, she's good at—um—loosening him up, and you know how I feel about that."

Dani cringed. "Yeah, I don't plan to let Gia near him like that again. I don't think it's such a good idea. That's why I was hoping you'd help us out—you're not going to get sucked into anything."

Alex groaned. "Did you have to say it that way?"

Her face flamed. "Sorry! But you know what I mean."

He looked down at the cup in front of him. "I can't, Dani."

Dani set her mug down and reached for Alex's hand. "What is it?"

He glanced at her then looked away. "Just a lot going on right now."

"Is this about whatever happened between you and Michael?"

He sighed. "Yes, and the stuff going on at the school." He ran a hand through his hair.

"There's something else, isn't there?"

"I'm just a little run-down lately. Nothing I can't handle, but I'm not doing anyone any favors by continuing to spin my wheels this way. I just need to figure things out. I need some time."

"All the more reason for you to help me out with this, then. It'll take your mind off the other stuff. Come on, Alex. I've got plans here. We do this right and we can save our school." She leaned forward and squeezed his hand. "Please?"

Alex fiddled with the handle on his cup. "All right. But I don't have any good ideas. Isn't all this evil genius planning stuff your territory?"

Dani gave Alex a wicked grin and steepled her fingers in her best Evil Genius impression. "Not sure. I think he needs a better idea about what we do here. For sure we should get him to see the charity stage show and the science fair. Maybe the big music and arts festival at the

Performing Arts Center in Peroo? Some of our kids are playing there. Think you can manage to convince him he wants to see all that?"

"I don't think that will be a problem." He gave her a thin smile.

As they talked, Dani began to feel better again. She couldn't control how Vic chose to deal with their non-relationship any more than she could control what had already happened between them. She could leave it alone until they were through dealing with Phin. She only hoped that they hadn't run out of time and that she was doing the right thing by keeping the details to herself.

Chapter Eleven

The Tripping Point

Dani sat at her desk, flipping through files and flagging things for Gary to review and sign. She focused on the task at hand, shutting out any intrusive thoughts about Vic and their argument. When she came to the end of the stack, she left them for Gary and searched for anything else she could find to keep her mind occupied. She was in the middle of sorting through the morning mail when Phin arrived and approached her desk. Suppressing a groan, she attempted a warm smile but managed only a sort of grimace instead.

Phin's eyebrows rose. "Everything okay?"

"Um. Yes, thank you," she tried.

Phin shook his head. "I know that look. What happened?"

"I'm not sure we know each other well enough for you to ask me that or for me to tell you." She turned away to throw a handful of junk mail into the recycle bin. She remained bent over, pretending to search for something in the lower drawer of her desk.

"Actually, that's the best reason to talk to me," Phin reasoned. "I'm objective."

Dani snorted and straightened up to look at him. "Not in this case. If you must know, I had a fight with Vic yesterday." She raised an eyebrow at him. "You may have factored into it."

A look of panic flashed across his face before he composed himself. "I certainly wouldn't want to be the cause of stress between you two," he told her.

"Yeah, well, too late for that. Anyway, it doesn't matter." She sighed. "I think we've both screwed things up beyond repair at this point."

Phin tilted his head to the side. "It's never too late. I'll have to have a word with him later."

"Don't!" she begged. "It's actually not really your fault, and I don't want him thinking I ran to you the minute we had a little trouble."

Phin waved a hand dismissively. "I promise, I'll be subtle. I can do that, you know."

"I'm sure you can, but that doesn't mean I need you to. Anyway, we don't have time to talk about this now. You'd better get moving—you're upstairs today," she told him. "Marianne in the secondary office will take good care of you for the next two weeks. I've already sent her your schedule, and I printed you a copy as well." She hoped her meaning was clear: the conversation about Vic was over.

He took the hint and went along with the change of topic. "I think I'm going to miss it down here," he said. "Good thing I get to come back in a couple of weeks."

"Bet I know what—or who—you'll miss most," Dani teased, glad for the distraction. "I heard you and Gia had a good time the other night." She winked and tilted her head, waiting for his reaction.

"Mm-hm," he said. "Though I have to admit, she's a bit high-energy for me. I can still feel that hike in my calves." He shook his head. "When did I get so *old?*"

"You're not old!" Dani laughed. "You know, I usually have dinner with the guys a couple of times a week." She swallowed, trying not to think about what that meant in light of her argument with Vic. She cleared her throat. "You're welcome to come on over if you like. I can't imagine you want to eat in the cafe for every meal. I could invite Gia." She grinned and twitched her brows.

"Uh...okay," Phin replied. He glanced over his shoulder, and she followed his gaze.

Alex's door opened, and Phin's expression changed ever so slightly. His shoulders relaxed, and a tiny smile played at the corner of his lips. He turned his attention back to Dani. His face paled; he opened his mouth, but nothing came out. Dani smirked at him.

"I don't have to invite Gia," she said.

"No!" Phin replied. "It's fine. Gia's very...nice."

"Here," she said, handing Phin the copy of his schedule. "Looks like you get to see some of our secondary arts programs."

"What? Oh. Thank you," he responded, accepting the paper. "The secondary office is just at the top of the stairs to the left, correct?"

"It is. Have fun!" she called as he walked away. He waved back at her without turning around.

Dani stood partway up out of her chair and leaned over the desk. She kept her eyes on Phin the whole time as he stopped to talk to Alex for a moment. She couldn't hear what they were saying, but both of them laughed and they elbowed each other good-naturedly before Phin took the stairs to the upper grades. With a sigh and a shake of her head, Dani sat back down and returned to her work.

Phin spent the day listening in on instrumental music lessons with the band director. He learned that rather than a single band, orchestra and chorus, the performing groups were made up of smaller numbers of students interested in particular musical styles. The director explained how the program had been born from the town's diverse population. Students had brought in their own family's music and taught it to their peers. While Phin observed, Michael and his friend Josue's group played a piece of bossa nova-style music, the chamber woodwinds rehearsed an arrangement of a Mozart quartet, and the brass and percussion class played contemporary movie music.

Phin was disappointed but not surprised to note that three of the music teachers were on his short list. No matter how many times he'd consulted, the story was always the same. The arts were the first to go under the mistaken impression that the time and money should be funneled into literacy and math. He made a note to look into the history of the school's allocation of resources compared with their test scores. As he saved the note in his phone, it occurred to him Murdock wouldn't care. He growled in frustration and had to restrain himself from slamming everything back into his briefcase before leaving the music room.

After school, Phin returned to the Railway Penny. Putting aside his worries about his job, he went straight to the front desk at the inn. He hadn't seen Vic in days, thanks to Gia and Alex. By the time he'd returned to the inn after his excursion with Alex, Vic had already gone home. Rather than seeking him out, Phin had simply gone to dinner and back to his room; he had been too tired for anything else.

Vic was leaning back in his chair, a book in hand. He glanced up at the sound of the door. As soon as he saw Phin, he looked down at his book and made as if he were engrossed in the novel, angling his body away slightly. Phin ignored the signals and approached the desk. Whatever had happened between Dani and Vic was not his fault, regardless of what Dani had said earlier.

"You can't ignore me forever, so you might as well get it over with," Phin told his friend.

"I'm not ignoring you. I'm letting you know that I'm done with you." Vic's eyes never left his page.

"I see. You have one fight with your—what exactly is she, Vic? Your fuck buddy?—and you blame me. Good call."

Vic finally looked up. "Go to hell, man. You don't know anything about it. You came in here, expecting my help, so I gave it. Look where that got me. You're going to do whatever it is anyway. As long as you leave me out of it from now on, I don't care."

Phin snorted. "You do care. If Dani didn't mean anything to you other than being a warm body, you wouldn't be this pissed at me. Sort of reminds me of when you wanted to ask DeAnna Brooks out in tenth grade, and you blamed me for ruining your chances. Or after that thing with Yvonne McIntire freshman year of college. Or—"

"I had forgotten how you somehow manage to screw up all my relationships." Vic was still frowning, but his mouth twitched slightly.

Phin leaned on the desk. He lowered his voice and said, "If she matters to you so much, why didn't you tell her?"

Vic sighed. "How could I? She still thinks she's cheating on her dead husband." He looked past Phin to watch people drifting in and out for a moment, then returned his attention to their conversation. "Jim's been gone three years. I've waited long enough. Maybe you showing up wasn't all bad—at least now I know she's never going to let go."

Offering what he hoped was a sympathetic look, Phin said, "I doubt it's too late."

"Maybe. It's her call now." Vic shrugged. "Now, get out of here. I'm at the good part." He waved his book at Phin.

Phin laughed and straightened up. He bid Vic goodbye and headed for his room. Inside, he dropped his briefcase on the bed and pulled out his phone to check his email before changing to head to Dani's for dinner. He wasn't surprised to see a message from Murdock: "Final board meeting 3rd Tuesday in June. Have your reports ready by then. Email summary to me and CC Stevens." Phin closed out his email and sighed.

Not for the first time he wished he had said no when Murdock offered him this job. He no longer had it in him to ignore the potential impact on the lives of the students and staff. He tossed his phone on the bed and stood there, arms folded, staring at it. He knew he could always find and emphasize negative aspects of any teacher's performance. He'd been known to use that method more than once to recommend staffing changes. The difficulty here in North Cowell was that he had also seen plenty of instruction worthy of praise—from the same teachers he had been told to mark unfavorably. He needed a reliable way to appease Murdock without destroying the school.

He changed his clothes, trying unsuccessfully to put it out of his mind until after dinner. As he dragged on a clean polo shirt and raked his hand through his hair to settle it, he tried to clear his thoughts. Sitting down at the desk with his laptop open, he synced his notes from his phone and began to craft a report. Half an hour in and he was ready to call it quits. He slammed his hand on the desk in irritation.

He closed his eyes and concentrated on the classrooms he'd seen. Instead of lessons, all he saw were the people: Eunice in the copy room; Mrs. Fargo, wrangling chickens; Gia singing to her students; the red-haired girl and her gap-toothed smile; Michael and Josue in perfect rhythmic sync; Alex—

He opened his eyes and jerked himself out of that thought. His chest ached a little, and his head hurt. He rubbed at his eyes and attempted to continue his report, but it was no use. Giving in, he replayed his day with Alex. He shivered a little and sighed.

"I think I need help," he muttered, dragging himself back to his computer screen. He stared at it for a long moment before something occurred to him and he began to type.

It felt like a small eternity later when Phin at last closed his files. There was only one person he could think of who might be willing to take a chance on him. If he played it just right, he might have help after all. Phin put his key and phone into his pockets and headed for the door, still turning things over in his mind. If only he could be sure this would work.

For the third time in the past week, Phin was at Dani's house for dinner. Dani hadn't invited Gia to join them after all, and Phin wasn't entirely sorry. He tried feel at least marginally guilty that he didn't want to socialize with her in quite the same way as before, but he couldn't muster the emotional energy required for that. Pretending to be indifferent to Alex's presence—and discreetly scowling at Dani—took all his reserves.

Vic still wouldn't join them, and Phin decided that he was a fool for not even trying to make things right. Neither Vic nor Dani would explain with any further detail why they were bound and determined to continue not speaking to one another. They weren't actively making any steps to either end things for good or repair the damage. As far as Phin was concerned, they were both being childish, and he didn't want anything further to do with their drama.

In the meantime, he had plenty of opportunity to get to know Dani's children. As usual, Carlie talked his ear off all through dinner. Jake still didn't speak directly to him if he could help it, but he was far less wary of Phin than he had been at first. After dinner, Jake pulled out a big book on electricity and paged through it. For a six-year-old, he was obviously bright. Phin sat down on the living room carpet next to him. Jake glanced up briefly, blinked at Phin, and went back to his book. He was on a page detailing step-by-step instructions for how to make a simple project.

"You ever tried this one?" Phin asked, pointing at the page.

Jake shook his head.

Phin continued, "Think your mom would let you? Maybe I could help."

Alex looked over at them. "You know, Jake, the science fair is still a few days away. It's not too late to enter something. You can't compete, but you can make a display."

Jake looked over at Alex and then up at Phin. "You would really help me?"

"Sure. But I'll bet you know a lot more about it than I do." He ruffled Jake's hair, and the boy smiled.

"I know a lot about electricity." He looked thoughtful. "Okay. I'll do it."

Phin stood up. It had grown quiet, and he looked around to see what the others were up to. Michael was still in the room for a change; he usually skipped out as soon as he was through eating. He had a textbook open in his lap, but he was peering at Phin's interactions with Jake out of the corner of his eye. Phin nodded at him, and Michael rolled one shoulder in a half-shrug of acknowledgment.

When Phin retreated to the kitchen for a glass of water, Michael followed. Phin glanced over his shoulder briefly then returned his attention to the tap. He turned around and leaned against the sink sipping his water and studiously keeping his eyes trained straight ahead. Michael hovered in the doorway.

After several minutes Michael finally said, "Did you come up with anything?"

"Hm?"

"You said to give you a few days and you'd think about what I might do about Adam," he said. "You know, the douche—uh, sorry, I mean the jerk—who's been messing with us at school."

Phin coughed. "I'm not your mother, and I'm not going to rat you out for saying 'douche.'" He crossed to the table and set down his glass before pulling out a chair and taking a seat. He motioned to Michael to join him. "All right. The thing is, you need to get Adam to do something that makes him look stupid in a way that everyone can see what kind of person he is. If you do this right, you don't need revenge—you just need witnesses."

"Okay." Michael frowned, sliding into a chair. "So, what do you suggest I do?"

"Almost any harmless prank will do, as long as it's public. He's not going to tolerate that well. I'm not big on things that humiliate, but..." Phin trailed off, wincing. He brushed away the memory of a time when that hadn't been as important to him. He cleared his throat and continued. "But I think that in this case, some relatively mild embarrassment might do the trick. I have an idea. Got some paper?"

Michael handed Phin a note pad, and Phin scrawled a few notes and a sketch for Michael. When he turned the note pad upside down so Michael could have a look, the boy's face broke out in a wide grin.

"Yeah, we ought to be able to do that. Nikki and Josue—" He stopped. "Um. Well, anyway, I think it'll work."

"Josue's the one Adam's been after, right? Any idea why?"

Michael's cheeks turned pink. "Kind of."

"You don't really have to say anything," Phin told him. "I was just curious."

"No, it's okay. It's not really about Adam all that much anyway. It's about, um...me." He ran his trembling fingers along the edge of the table, and his knee bounced. When he finally raised his eyes to peer at Phin through his bangs, he said, "You're like me, aren't you?"

"You tell me."

Michael shook his head. "You went out with Gia. Kind of a date, right?"

"Sort of," Phin agreed.

"But you like Al—guys."

"Ah, I see," Phin replied. "Yes. Are you saying you're bisexual?"

"I don't really like labels." Michael fiddled with the edge of the tablecloth. Leaning forward, he whispered, "My mom doesn't know, okay? So you can't tell her. But Alex knows, and he was kind of an ass—uh, jerk about it."

"I'm listening. What happened?"

"I told him about something that happened between me and Josue and how Nicki-Anne's been kind of pressuring me lately. He thinks I'm using her. Said I should tell her before I hurt her."

"Oh, god." Phin scrubbed his face. "You want me to say something to him?"

Michael hunched his shoulders. "I don't know."

"He might listen to me. I have a little experience with this." He nudged Michael's arm.

Nodding, Michael replied, "Okay."

"We can talk more later if you want."

"Yeah."

Phin rose from the table and wandered outside to the back deck, still thinking about the conversation he'd just had. Alex was already there, sitting on the steps down to the yard. Phin sat down next to him, and Alex glanced briefly in his direction. Reaching into his pocket, Phin extracted a pack of gum. He held it out to Alex.

Alex scrunched his face a little. "Gum? Really? What are we, twelve?" He appeared to realize what he'd said, and his mouth dropped open slightly. He didn't take a stick of gum.

Phin chose to ignore the words. He shrugged and unwrapped a stick. "I quit smoking two years ago. I really want a cig right now, but I'd rather not go back to that. It's a shitty habit."

"Says the guy with a lot of other bad habits he hasn't bothered to quit."

Phin elbowed Alex. "How would you know?"

Alex ticked them off on his fingers. "Your caffeine intake, your potty mouth, and the way you're always hanging around. Oh, and Gia. What's going on with the two of you, anyway?"

"We're friends, apparently."

Alex snorted. "Friends don't give each other oral." He paused. "Well, no, sometimes they do."

Phin raised his eyebrows, wondering what Alex was thinking about. "Sometimes they do," he agreed, and then he frowned. "Wait...what did Gia tell you, anyway?"

"Enough." Alex chuckled. "The really fun part about being the token gay guy in your group of friends is that sometimes, women like to think you want to know *everything*. In vivid detail. Gia is the worst—she's like a teenage boy in a locker room, only the difference is, most of her stories are true."

Phin laughed. "Yeah, I could see that." He blew out his breath. "There's nothing else going on. Gia seems to me like a thrill-seeker, and she just wanted to have a good time. I gave her that."

"So I hear. Is that how you usually like to do business?"

"Sometimes."

Alex snorted. "Of course it is. Nice."

Phin glared at him. "You act like you know everything about me, but you haven't even bothered to ask. Kind of like some of the other people around you. Why do you think Michael's so ragingly pissed off at you? You do the same thing to him—pulling that counselor bullshit but getting it completely fucked up."

"I have no idea what you're talking about." Alex looked away again.

"The hell you don't. I had a long talk with him. I know, I know—not feeling 'understood' is classic teenage angst. But I think he's right. Believe it or not, I know a little bit about it." Phin shifted, waiting.

After a long pause, Alex turned his face toward Phin. "You think you know Michael better than I do."

"I didn't say that." Phin huffed. "I know what he's dealing with, though. He's confused and needed someone to talk to, and apparently, you dismissed him. To you, guys like us—we don't exist." He scoffed. "Or maybe you just think we shouldn't."

"What do you mean, 'guys like us'?" Alex drew his brows together.

Phin sighed. "In case it wasn't clear to you, I like men. I like sex with men. But, Alex, I like women, too. I enjoyed fooling around with Gia. Whatever else you may think of me, I wasn't play-acting or just trying to work her over. She's very sexy, and it felt good. That's all. With some guys, I feel like I need to fake it—to them, shame is respectable, but enjoying myself with women isn't. It would be easier for them if they thought I only ever fucked women because I was 'doing business,' as you said. Or maybe because I was still in the closet, I suppose. But I'm as out as I'm ever gonna be—I'm not hiding."

"What exactly does that have to do with Michael? I don't really care about your sex life or whatever you want to call it."

"God. You really are a clueless dick sometimes, aren't you?" Phin snorted. "Unless you're just fucking with me. Let me spell it out. Michael isn't hiding either, at least with his friends. He's pretending he is, though, because he thinks he has to in order to make you happy. The really stupid thing is, that's not even what he's confused about."

"I—what?" Alex looked genuinely perplexed.

Phin blew out his breath. "Did you or did you not tell him that it was okay for him to like boys?"

"Of course. I still don't see—"

"Did you tell him that it's okay for him to still like girls, too?"

"I...not exactly." Alex raked a hand through his hair.

"Right. That's what I thought. Which version of lying did you accuse him of?"

Alex drew his brows together. "Point taken. But that's *not* what he's confused about? I don't understand."

Phin shook his head. "He wanted relationship advice, you dolt, not advice on coming out."

Alex looked away. "I wish he'd said something the first time he talked to me."

"He says he did. Maybe you just weren't listening."

"No, I..." Alex sighed. "He tried to tell me again, but it turned into an argument."

"What happened?"

"I got after him for not talking to me. He called me—" Alex swallowed visibly. "Never mind."

"Oh." Phin reached out a hand to touch Alex's shaking hand but retracted it. "You're too close. He's family. Sometimes, it just takes someone else to figure stuff out."

"So now you're the expert." Alex scowled at Phin.

"This isn't about me. Are you paying attention to what I'm saying? God. No wonder Michael won't talk to you."

They sat in silence for a few minutes. Finally, Alex said, "So, what did you say to him?"

Phin lifted one shoulder in a casual shrug. "Just that I understood. That maybe he should talk to you again. I also gave him some advice on dealing with that Adam kid. You do know that this isn't like when we were that age, right? Adam is a privileged rich kid who thinks he has the right to dump on Josue for being anything other than that." He looked hard at Alex. "Your black-and-white thinking is hurting Michael. Consider that before you have a conversation." Phin stood up, pressing a hand in to Alex's shoulder. "I'll see you around, Alex." He turned to go back inside.

"Hey—are you stopping by the community center on Friday?" Alex sounded hopeful. "Charity dance performance is at seven in the auditorium."

Phin smiled to himself before looking back over his shoulder. He gave Alex a sly grin. "Maybe."

Alex nodded. "All right. Maybe—maybe we'll have lunch this weekend."

"Sounds like a plan." Phin turned back around and reentered the house. He hoped something of what he'd said had gotten through. Realization hit him that it wasn't for his own sake, but for Michael's. *When did I start caring about these people's personal issues?*

Chapter Twelve

The Pied Educator

Dani was making an early dinner before the charity stage performance. She had just finished slicing the cucumber and was reaching for a tomato when she heard the soft sound of throat-clearing behind her. She looked over her shoulder to see Michael standing in the doorway. She smiled.

"Just in time. Can you give me a hand?" She held out the tomato and the paring knife.

"Sure." Michael came further into the kitchen and accepted them from Dani's hands. He set to work next to her.

She pulled out a head of lettuce and a large knife and began to hack into it. "What's up?"

His shoulder brushed against hers as they worked, and she felt him shrug. He didn't say anything for several minutes. Finally he said, "Um."

Dani waited, continuing to chop. Michael cut the tomato agonizingly slowly, his hand trembling a little with each slice. The only sounds were the scrape of steel on the glass cutting board and the crisp crack of the lettuce coming apart.

After several more seconds without speaking, Michael said, "It's Nicki-Anne. And, um, you know," he lowered his voice, "sex." He quickly added, " And stuff."

Dani's heart sped up. She turned toward Michael, the knife still in her hand. "'And stuff'? What does that mean? Are you having sex with her? *Unprotected* sex? Shit. Oh, my god, Michael James, *did you get her pregnant?"*

"Mom! Calm the fuck down!" Michael slammed the last piece of tomato and the knife onto the counter and turned to face Dani, backing away a pace or two.

"You watch your mouth!" Dani snapped.

Michael's lips twitched, and he started to laugh. When he'd calmed down, he said, "Well, you said 'shit.' I kind of figured you were okay with the whole swearing thing now."

Dani relaxed enough to set her knife on the counter. She chuckled. "Yeah, well, I'm an adult. I can say whatever I want. You, on the other hand, need to watch your language."

"Real mature, Mom. And by the way, I'm not having any kind of sex with Nicki-Anne." His cheeks reddened. "Yet."

"Is that what this is about?" She tried to meet his eyes, but he was looking down at the floor.

"Yeah," he mumbled.

Dani returned to the vegetables. She handed Michael a pepper and pulled out the head of broccoli. "You're thinking about having sex?" Despite the fact that she wasn't sure how she felt about her fifteen-year-old having sex—as evidenced by her earlier outburst—she was proud of her kid for talking about it first. She mentally checked the "didn't completely screw up at parenting" box.

"Nicki-Anne wants to. She wants to 'take our relationship to the next level,' as she puts it." He shrugged.

Dani glanced at him. "But you're not sure."

"Yeah. I mean, how do you know you're ready?"

"That's a good question," Dani replied. "I'm not sure I have the kind of answer you want."

Michael sighed. "Any answer is good at this point."

Dani nodded. "Okay, then. Here's what I think—and you're going to make your own decision regardless of what I say, but I hope you'll listen."

"I will," he assured her.

She continued, "I think if you're not sure, then you're probably not ready. Sex is a commitment. Right now, you have enough to do just being fifteen without worrying about what kind of promise you're making to Nicki-Anne. I know a little bit about jumping into things before you're ready."

"You and Dad?"

Dani nodded. "Yeah."

Michael didn't say anything. For several minutes, the only sound was the knife on the cutting board. At last, he set the knife aside and said, "Did you love him?"

"Your dad?" Dani hesitated. "Of course I did."

Michael turned around and leaned against the counter. "What about Vic?"

"I'm not sure what you're talking about." Dani kept her eyes on the vegetables.

"You're having sex with Vic."

Dani jumped slightly and nearly dropped her knife. "What?"

"Mom, you heard me. Please don't lie. I know you're hooking up with him. But you're not even dating."

She looked sideways at him. "And you know this how, exactly?"

"I'm pretty sure you don't want me to answer that." He grimaced.

She cleared her throat and set down the knife. "All right. Yes, I *was* sleeping with Vic. It's...complicated."

Michael stared at the pieces of tomato on the cutting board. "Well, it's complicated with Nicki, too."

He was shaking a little, and Dani laid a hand on his arm. "It's okay. Can you tell me about it?"

"This would be easier if we were still cutting things up."

Silently, Dani set a bowl of mushrooms between them. She picked one up and began to slice it; Michael turned back around and did the same. For a minute or two, neither of them said anything. At last Michael said, "It's complicated because of Josue."

Dani frowned. "It can be hard to be the third wheel."

"No, Mom. That's not it."

"Does Josue like Nicki too?" She tossed a handful of mushroom pieces into a container.

Michael snorted. "I wish it were that simple." He added his mushrooms to Dani's and looked up at her. "If I tell you, you can't say anything."

"Michael, you know I can't promise you that. If one of your friends is in trouble—"

"Mom! It's not that kind of thing. No one's in trouble or anything. It's just...okay. Um." He blew out his breath. "Josue's gay. Now you see why you can't say anything? His parents don't even know, even though he's not really hiding it from our friends or anything. His family's kind of religious. I guess his brother knows, but that's it."

Dani looked intently at her oldest child, biting back her huff of exasperation. "Michael. What's going on?"

He pressed his lips together. "Josue told me that he likes me. You know, as more than a friend." He paused. "And I'm kind of okay with that."

"Are you saying you like him, too?"

"Yes. No! Maybe," Michael admitted. "I don't know. I mean, I've known that I like both girls and guys for a while." He looked sideways at Dani, clearly gaging her reaction.

Dani wasn't sure about proper etiquette. On the one hand, she was grateful to be having this conversation at all, especially given what Michael had said about Josue. It wasn't as if it was a surprise, either. On the other hand, Dani was disappointed that Michael hadn't said anything sooner. What was the right thing to say to him? She opted to remain quiet and just listen, but she reached out and touched his arm lightly with the back of her hand.

When she nodded at Michael, he continued. "I like Nicki, and she's my girlfriend. I like being with her." He flushed. "But I kind of feel like maybe that would be okay with Josue, too, except I'm not sure that I like him as much as Nicki, and now I'm stuck in the middle. Mom, is it even possible to like two people at the same time?"

Dani closed her eyes for a moment, fighting the sudden tightness in her gut and the burning behind her eyes. Memories of her life with Jim flooded her mind, only to be replaced with thought of Vic and the warmth of being in his arms. *Yes*, she thought. *It's entirely possible to love two people at the same time.*

Aloud, she said, "I think Nicki and Josue bring out the best in you, and there are things you like about both of them. There's nothing wrong at all with that. Liking—or loving—both of them is going to help you learn who you are and the kind of people you want to have in your life. And someday in your bed," she added, struggling a little to get the words out. "Though we should have another conversation about making sure you know how to be safe before then."

Michael resumed chopping. "Ugh, Mom. You already went over that about a million times already. Anyway, that's what Phin—uh, Mr.

Patterson"—he amended himself when Dani raised her eyebrow at him—"said, too."

"That you need to use condoms or that it's okay to love more than one person?" She hid a smile at Michael's blush.

"Both, actually." His flush darkened.

"Oh!" she exclaimed as something occurred to her, but she calmed herself. "Was this what you tried to tell Alex?" she asked more gently.

"Yeah, Mom. And he just...he didn't get it. Like, he thought this was about figuring out I like guys instead of girls. But, honestly, I just wanted some advice. It's okay, though. He and I worked it out the other night."

"I noticed you two were talking to each other again."

"Yeah." Michael grinned. "Thanks to Mr. Patterson. He said something to Alex."

"I'm glad." Dani smiled. "Now, want to help me put this out on the table?"

"No, but I'll do it anyway," Michael replied.

"Brat," Dani muttered, but she smiled and bumped him affectionately with her shoulder. His answering grin told her he understood what she hadn't said.

The charity performance sped by in a whirlwind of activity. Dani delivered the kids—all of whom were participating—to the dressing rooms at six-thirty, but she hovered close by, waiting for someone to retrieve her or for Jake to come looking. She continued sneaking peeks at the closed doors until one of the other teachers poked her head out and glared at her before asking her to find a seat.

She entered the auditorium and glanced around and finally spotted her friends, accompanied by Phin, sitting three rows from the front. It was hard to hide her disappointment, even from herself, when she didn't see Vic. She made her way down the aisle and slid in between Eunice and Gia, with Phin sitting to Eunice's right. Just as the house lights flashed a warning that the show was about to begin, Dani saw Vic slip in next to Phin. Relief and hope flooded her heart.

The performance couldn't have gone better. Carlie, Jake and Michael had been working on a tap routine for about a month, hammering out their steps in the basement and taking extra practices with Alex. Dani's heart swelled with pride at not only their skill but at how much they were enjoying being up on stage together. When they were through, it was Alex's turn.

As Dani had expected, he was marvelous. He'd chosen an unusual piece—part of the orchestral arrangement of *Pictures at an Exhibition*—and used modern dance techniques to interpret the saxophone solo. She'd never seen it all the way through, though she'd caught a bit of it every so often when she brought Carlie to class. She wondered what Vic thought of it and glanced in his direction before she could stop herself.

She was distracted by the expression on Phin's face. He was leaning forward in his seat, his lips slightly parted; his gaze never left the stage. Dani poked Eunice in the arm. When Eunice glanced at her, she nodded toward Phin. Eunice looked over and then back at Dani. They both smirked. Eunice leaned across Gia and tapped her hand, tilting her head in Phin's direction. Gia's eyebrows shot up, and then she frowned, pouting slightly. Dani snickered.

The sound alerted Phin, who took his eyes off Alex only long enough to wrinkle his nose at Dani and whisper, "What?" before looking back at the stage.

"You look like you're enjoying it. He's good, isn't he?"

Phin nodded. "Yeah. I've seen this before. That day I met him here."

"Ah," Dani replied, then shut her mouth to watch the rest of Alex's dance.

The performance ended with a crowd-pleasing number involving the full company. Afterward, Vic made a quick exit, and Phin followed suit. Only Eunice and Gia remained. They accompanied Dani when she went to round up the kids from backstage. When they arrived, Dani discovered that Phin had beaten them there and was talking to Alex.

Gia wrinkled her nose. "Why are all the good ones always taken?" She sighed. "He's a little old for me anyway. He's still cute, though."

"And has a nice ass," Dani and Eunice chorused.

"You've only mentioned that fifty times or so," Eunice said.

Gia discovered her inner five-year-old and stuck out her tongue at them just as Alex and Phin joined them.

"Great job," Eunice told Alex. "Very nice. I haven't seen you do that one before."

He nodded. "Just a little something I've been working on especially for tonight." He exchanged a glance with Phin, and Phin's cheeks grew faintly pink. Dani wondered what he was thinking about.

Phin changed the subject by turning to Gia and saying, "I heard what you said just now, and I'm flattered that you have such high regard for my ass. But you're selling yourself short. What about that one guy at school who brought you your phone? I think he likes you."

"Who? Oscar?" Gia frowned. "I don't think so. He hardly says a word to me."

Phin shrugged. "Then maybe you need to do the talking." He pulled out his phone and glanced at it. "Listen, I need to go. Dani, what time do you want me to come over to help Jake draw his display board?"

"Is nine okay? We need to be at the school by eleven to set up, and the fair starts at noon."

"Sure thing." He grinned at the group. "Good night, ladies. Alex." Once again, his face colored just a little when his eyes flicked to Alex. With that, he was off.

Dani watched him go, shaking her head. "Pied piper," she muttered.

"What?" Eunice asked.

"You know—the pied piper. He got everyone to follow after him, thinking he was solving the town's rat problem, only then he stole the children." She laughed. "I'm just being paranoid. Where are the kids? We should get going—long day tomorrow."

The science fair had gone as well as the charity performance. After picking up a pizza for dinner, Phin and Alex helped Dani wrangle the kids back to her place so they could all collapse. Before she could even begin to clean up and process everything from the previous week, both men stopped her.

"We've got this," Alex said.

"Right," Phin agreed. "You go talk to Vic."

Dani muttered, "Well, that was subtle." Somewhere between painting Jake's display board and grabbing dinner, they had managed to conspire against her.

"Go," Alex insisted. "We'll take care of everything. I promise."

Grudgingly, Dani agreed. Vic had been working all day, but she knew he would be home by then. She steeled herself and knocked on the door of his half of the house. When Vic opened it, his eyes widened in surprise. Without waiting for an invitation, she launched herself at him and kissed him. He tensed up slightly before he kissed her back.

After a long, breathless moment, Dani pulled back. She poked Vic in the chest.

"You are in big trouble. I'm still angry with you."

"Uh, come in?" Vic offered, a bewildered look on his face.

Dani stepped the rest of the way into the entryway and brushed past Vic to sit on the couch. He waited a moment then turned and walked into the kitchen. She could hear him opening a cupboard. After a few minutes, he returned, carrying two glasses of iced tea. She folded and unfolded her hands in an unsuccessful attempt to stop shaking. While she waited, she rehearsed what she would say.

When Vic was finally situated across from her, she blurted, "I'm sorry." That hadn't been how she had imagined starting this conversation, true though it might be.

Vic didn't say anything for a moment. At last he said, "Okay." After another long pause he continued, "Me too."

Dani cleared her throat. "I'm sorry for my part in this mess, but I'm still a little upset with you, too. I need you to listen. Can you do that?"

"I don't know. Will you be able to do the same?"

If Dani were honest with herself, she would have to admit she wasn't sure. Dani said, "Please. Just let me say this, and then we can go from there."

Vic looked away, resting his elbow on the chair and twisting his lip with his fingers. The space between them stretched until Dani's palms began to sweat and her heart thundered in her chest. She gripped her knees.

Just when Dani had made up her mind to get up and leave, Vic said, "All right. I'm listening."

She inhaled slowly, held the breath for a moment, and let it out as she closed her eyes. This was more than she had expected. "Give me a minute," she said. "I'm not sure how to begin."

Vic didn't respond, but he leaned back in his seat. He dropped his hands into his lap and trained his eyes on Dani. She nodded at their unspoken agreement.

"I loved him," she said.

"Who?" he asked, frowning.

"Jim, of course."

Vic scoffed. "Yeah. I got that impression. The whole married thing and all."

"I'm not sure you understand."

Vic sat up straighter. "I know you loved him," he replied. "What does that have to do with this?"

She tugged on her ponytail. "You don't know what he was to me. He was my whole world, Vic. He was my first crush, my first lover, and the father of my children. He took me out of the hell hole I lived in until I was eighteen. I loved him, and then he *died*."

"I was there for that part."

"I loved him," she repeated. She pinched her nose. "But I wasn't *in* love with him."

Vic's eyes widened momentarily, and then his expression hardened again. "Dani, why are you telling me this?"

"Please—I need you to listen."

Vic waved his hand for her to continue, but his expression remained unchanged.

Dani swallowed around the painful lump that was developing in her throat. "I was so lonely, even when we were married. We meant different things to each other. He was my way out, but I was his soul mate. Or at least he thought I was. I never gave him reason to think I didn't feel the same way." She sighed. "Vic, I've been half in love with you since—" She lowered her voice. "Since before Jim died." Four years' worth of guilt bubbled over and Dani struggled to hold back tears. Her stomach twisted.

"Dani, my god, why didn't you say anything?" Vic leaned forward.

"How could I have? I never would have hurt Jim like that." She shook her head.

"No, I mean after—after he died." He reached for her hand, but she pulled it away.

"Why didn't you?" she countered. "You kept telling me I should move on, but you never said it was because you wanted us to be together. Meanwhile, every time we were together, I felt guilty." She brushed at her eyes and tried to compose herself.

"So, is that what you wanted to tell me? That you're finally ready for more? You may be able to move on now, but it can't be with me. You still think you're betraying a dead man's memory. Dani, I hope someone can come along to give you what you need. But I'm not going to spend my life trying to convince you not to feel guilty."

Dani's eyes burned. "I'm not asking you to."

"Then what are you asking?"

"I want to start over. No more secrets. No pretending. Just us, working out our own issues."

"I don't know," Vic answered.

"I think we're worth saving." She closed her eyes.

There was a moment of silence before she heard a soft rustle indicating Vic had gotten up from his chair. She kept her eyes shut; she didn't want to watch him walking away from her the way she had done to him the week before. She was determined to wait until he had left before she got up to retreat to her own half of the house. She felt movement in front of her and risked looking up. Vic was kneeling by her chair. He reached out his hand and slid his warm palm against her cheek. She closed her eyes and leaned into the touch. When she opened them again, her gaze locked with his.

"On one condition," he told her.

"What's that?"

"We stop hiding from your kids. Dani, they're like family to me. Don't keep us in separate spaces like this."

"All right," she agreed.

He leaned forward. "May I?" he asked, his lips close to hers.

"Yes," she whispered.

He drew her in and kissed her, pouring into it everything they had both bottled in. All her fears shriveled and died, scattering like ash in the wind. They kissed and kissed, and Dani thought she might break in two from the joy of being in Vic's arms unashamed. At last he drew back and got up to sit next to her on the couch.

Vic extended his arm, and Dani curled against his side. He said, "What changed?"

She replied, "Phin showed up."

Vic held up a hand. "Not gonna go there. That man has caused enough drama for a lifetime."

"It's not a choice." Dani composed herself and straightened up. "You should have been honest with me, Vic. Which brings me to why I'm still mad at you."

His face softened. "You're right. I should've come to you."

"Why didn't you?" She shifted so she was half turned toward Vic and propped her elbow on the back of the couch.

With a sigh, Vic looked down at his hands. "Phin's father is a real piece of work. I would know—I used to work for him. When Phin showed up here, I had no idea how deep in it he was. I didn't want you getting mixed up in it. I know I should've told you, but I thought I could quietly just give him what he wanted and get him out of here. He told me what was really going down, but I was already in it by then."

"You should at least have asked me first." She looked down at her lap then back at Vic, steeling her gaze. "His father is a piece of work, you say? Well I already knew that. He's the reason my life was shit before Jim."

Vic drew in a sharp breath. "What?"

"Yeah. Asshole moved the company and fired half the employees, giving the rest the option to take pensions or move with him. My dad was in the half that didn't have a choice." She swallowed. "He's dead, by his own hand, because of that man."

"Aw, hell. I didn't know." Vic reached for her again.

Leaning into his side, Dani replied, "I'm not sure I'd have told you before now anyway." She took a deep breath. "I never meant to uncover all this shit. All I wanted was to find some dirt on Phin, something to keep us from losing our school."

"It's too late for that. Everything's moving too fast."

"You're wrong, you know. We still have a chance. I don't know what Phin told you, but the school board hasn't met yet. We can still do something."

Vic shook his head. "I'm not so sure."

"We have a plan, but we need your help. Are you ready to make it right for hiding this from me?"

"Does this plan involve handing Phin his own ass? Because I'd be cool with that."

Dani snickered. "That might be part of it." She grinned wickedly. "If Alex doesn't get to it first."

"God. I did not need to know that."

Dani gave a breathy laugh. "All right. Though, you were sitting next to Phin all last night. Surely you noticed—"

Vic groaned and leaned his head back on the couch. "No. No, I did not notice. I do not pay attention to these things."

"Okay, whatever. Anyway, I've been doing my homework, and I think we can bring everything out in the open at the board meeting. We just need you to make sure Phin doesn't figure out what's going on between now and then. Ten more days. Think you can handle that?”

"I'd better," Vic muttered. "Or it'll be *my* ass you're handing over."

Dani patted his knee. "You got that right."

He looked at her, his eyes full of tenderness. "You're a fiery woman. How could I not love you?"

She laughed and turned toward him, drawing him in for another kiss. This time, they didn't stop, letting heat and need build between them for several long, intense moments. Eventually, Vic pulled back slightly to look at Dani.

"Do you need to get back?" he asked.

She shook her head. "I'm not in a hurry. Phin and Alex are with the kids."

He eyed her. "And they won't wonder what happened to you?"

"No." She scrunched up her face and poked out her tongue. "And I hope they're not trying to guess, either."

Vic laughed and stood up, causing Dani to lurch sideways. She glared at him until he extended his hand to her, which she accepted reluctantly. He pulled her to her feet.

"Then let's take our time," he suggested.

He drew her up the stairs and into the bedroom. The early evening sun streamed in the window, muted by the partially drawn curtains. Slowly, they undressed each other, pausing in between to kiss and touch. They lingered, enjoying the freedom to be unhurried by their responsibilities and the need to maintain secrecy. In all the time they'd been together, they'd only ever used Vic's bed a few times, and they'd never been in Dani's. She shivered a little at the realization that they could be completely open now, and there was no longer anything to keep her from allowing him to stay with her.

They made love, kissing and moving together slowly, allowing their desire to build little by little until it threatened to consume them. Gradually, they increased their pace until they were both toppling over the edge, holding each other as the last of their shudders faded away. They lay quietly for a few minutes while their breathing returned to normal. Eventually, he withdrew from her and flopped onto his back next to her. She maneuvered so that she could lay her head on his chest. They didn't speak; for once it was good not to have to say, "I need to go."

At last Dani said, "We should get back. It's been a long day."

"We?" Vic extracted himself from Dani and sat up.

"Yes. *We.* You don't have to leave this time. Plus, I'm not going to tell the kids without you there."

He grinned at her and rolled out of bed to get dressed. "What are we waiting for, then?"

After Dani left, Alex sent Carlie upstairs to get a board game. She returned with an ancient something-or-other from her parents' childhood. Once she'd assembled it and dispensed cards and playing pieces, she stationed herself on one side of the board. Phin sat across from her with his back against the couch.

"Haven't seen this game since I was her age," he remarked. "I don't remember how to play."

"That's okay," Carlie assured him. "Me and Jake will teach you."

Alex grabbed a pillow from the couch and tucked it under his chest, laying stomach down on the floor in front of the game board. Jake curled his legs under him and leaned over to flick the spinner. He moved his playing piece and looked up at Phin.

"I landed on you," he said.

"Uh...what does that mean?"

While Jake offered a long run-down of the game rules, Alex glanced up at Michael. He was sitting on the stairs, a book in his lap, pretending to read while watching the others play their game. Alex caught his eye and Michael offered a tiny smile.

Alex returned his attention to the game, focusing his attention on Carlie and Jake. Every so often, his eyes flicked to Michael, but he always appeared absorbed in his book. In what felt like record time, Phin placed his last card and Carlie declared him the winner.

"Hey!" Jake cried. "You weren't supposed to win!"

Phin's face wrinkled in confusion. "Why not?"

"You were supposed to let me win!" He stuck out his tongue.

"Since when do we ever just let you win?" Alex asked.

"You don't. But I thought *he* might because he's new." He pointed at Phin.

Phin laughed and glanced at Alex. "He doesn't know me very well, then." He turned back to Jake. "I don't ever just let someone else win."

For a moment, Jake's lip quivered, but he drew it in between his teeth and gave Phin a steely-eyed glare. He darted his hand out and yanked a pillow off the couch. One resounding smack later, Phin's laughter was muffled by a mouthful of fabric. While he was still incapacitated, Jake tackled Phin. Whether out of surprise or because he'd let Jake take advantage after all, he toppled onto his back. Jake pounced on him and tickled him, causing Phin to squirm around. Alex watched them, focused only on Phin's delighted, flushed face. He was caught off-guard when Carlie, not wanting to miss out on the fun, attacked him.

"Umph!" he said, his face hitting into the pillow he'd left on the floor as he fell over.

They wrestled with the kids until Phin, in an attempt to wriggle away from Jake, rolled hard into Alex. They lay pressed together, shoulder to hip, and Phin froze.

"Sorry!" he exclaimed. He attempted to shift, but Jake sat on his chest and he couldn't get far.

Alex turned his head, and their eyes locked. He inhaled sharply, keenly aware of the warmth of Phin's arm against his own. An overwhelming desire for home and family and belonging, triggered by their impromptu tussle with the kids, hit him hard. His eyes stung as a flood of "what-ifs" crashed into him, and he had to breathe slowly to stem the rush of wishful thinking that rose in him.

Carlie noticed the pause and sat up on her knees beside him. "Uncle Alex?"

The sound of her voice broke his reverie, and he looked up at her. "Why don't you and Jake clean up the game and take it back to your room? Get your pajamas on, and when you come down, we'll put in a movie."

She crawled over to the game board, and Jake joined her. In short order they had the pieces back in the box. They pelted up the stairs past Michael to put the game away. Phin shifted and rolled onto his side, propping himself on one elbow. Alex shivered at the loss of contact and turned over to face him.

"You really do care about them, don't you?" he asked, tipping his chin toward the direction Carlie and Jake had gone.

Phin reached out for a moment, his hand hovering, and Alex thought he might touch him. He stiffened, but Phin merely placed his hand on the carpet between them. "I really do," he replied.

Alex nodded. Very quietly, he said, "Why are you here?"

"Helping you out with the kids like I said I would."

"But why? You have no obligation to fulfill." Alex studied him.

Phin drew his eyebrows together. "You promised to make me understand. I'm trying." He leaned in slightly.

Alex swallowed. His head felt thick, and his pulse jumped. "The kids—" he started.

"It's part of my job," Phin continued.

Sighing, Alex shifted away. His mind began to clear. "Your job. Right." He ran a hand through his hair. "Like all your other jobs. Are you actually here to help us? Is that what you think this is?"

There was a long pause. Phin curled his fingers and dug them into the carpet. "I always believe it is," he answered. Sadness flickered in his eyes, but the moment passed as quickly as it had come. He rolled over and sat up. "I think I need some water." He stood up and disappeared into the kitchen.

Alex watched him go then heaved himself off the floor. He wandered over and sat down on the stair just below Michael.

Before he could speak, Michael said, "You like each other."

"Michael—"

Michael shook his head. "Don't deny it. I saw the way you looked at him. Mom and Vic do that sometimes, when they think no one can see." His cheeks turned faintly pink. "I thought he was gonna kiss you for a minute there."

Alex chuckled weakly. "He wasn't. That would have been awkward and inappropriate."

"You're telling me."

"How do you know so much about this, anyway?" Alex asked. He nudged Michael's knee.

"You," Michael replied, lifting one shoulder casually.

"That surprises me," Alex said and laughed. "After the way I screwed up."

Michael looked down at him. "Yeah. But we're cool now."

"Thanks to Phin," Alex muttered. Michael smirked, and Alex elbowed him.

They were interrupted when Carlie thundered down the stairs, followed by Jake. The two of them were nearly tripping over themselves in the race to choose the movie. Alex stood up and stretched just as Phin emerged from the kitchen with a bowl of popcorn, several cups of water, and a bottle of wine on a tray. Alex raised his eyebrows, but Phin ignored him and set the tray on the coffee table. Michael followed Alex off the steps into the living room.

While the kids popped the DVD into the player, Phin poured the wine. He handed Alex a glass.

"Did this come from Dani's fridge? I doubt she'll be thrilled you helped yourself," Alex said.

"I brought it." Phin tilted his head at the television. "I thought we might need it."

Laughing, Alex accepted the glass. "We just might."

"Can I have wine?" Michael asked.

"Only if you come to church with me," Alex replied, and Phin snorted.

Michael scowled, and Phin handed him a glass of water. He grabbed a handful of popcorn and slumped into a chair. Alex and Phin settled themselves a respectable distance apart on the couch, and the younger two sprawled on the floor with the popcorn between them.

They were all of fifteen minutes and the first big musical number into the movie when the door opened. Dani and Vic entered, looking flushed and slightly rumpled. Alex exchanged a look with Phin, who mouthed, *I told you so.* Alex grinned.

Dani opened her mouth, but she didn't say anything. She pressed her lips together, turning to Vic, who merely offered a tiny shrug. She nodded and sank down onto the love seat. Vic glanced around before joining her and draping his arm around her shoulders. Whatever they'd planned to say evaporated, and the entire company turned their attention to the film.

All except for Alex. He surreptitiously glanced around the room, wanting to capture and hold the moment right there. Another wave of longing tugged at him. *I don't want to lose this*, he thought. *If only it were that easy.* He swallowed thickly and pressed his thumb against the corner of his eye. He trained his gaze on the television, hoping no one noticed he wasn't really following the movie.

Chapter Thirteen

Alex and Phin Are Friends

AFTER THE science fair, Phin finally had his chance to sleep late. He suspected Dani and company had intentionally kept him busy. What they thought that would accomplish was a mystery. When he eventually woke, it was earlier than he'd imagined. He rose slowly, sitting on the edge of the bed and contemplating his options.

He needed to talk to at least Dani and Vic about his problem. Now that they had resolved their issues, at least in some fashion, they might be able to do something for him. Reluctantly, he stood up and began to pull himself together. He looked at the clock. Alex was probably getting ready for church. An overwhelming desire to see him—to beg him for help, or maybe something else he wasn't ready to admit—gripped him. If Phin remembered right, the service was at ten. He had just enough time to get cleaned up and make it there on time. As unappealing as it was to attend another service, Phin thought he had a better chance of catching Alex and talking to him if he gave in on that point.

Phin rushed to make himself presentable then drove to the church to wait for Alex to show up. He felt like a stalker, sitting in the parking lot and watching everyone else enter the building. At last he saw Alex pull in, and Phin got out of the car. He leaned against it, arms and ankles crossed.

As soon as Alex shut his car door and turned around, he spotted Phin. There was too great a distance between them for Phin to read Alex's body language, so he just stood there until Alex came closer.

"What are you doing here?" Alex sounded wary, but not angry; that was a good sign.

"Waiting for you," Phin replied.

Alex raised his eyebrows. "Because you wanted to go to church?"

"Not really. I wanted to see you. I was hoping to talk to you."

"I see. Can it wait?" Alex gestured toward the building. "I don't want to be late."

"Of course. Did you want me to come in with you?" Phin tried not to sound like he was hoping the answer was no.

Alex sighed. "I don't think you want to, so no. I could meet you later, though."

"How about you meet me at the Railway Penny at noon? Outside, not in the cafe."

"All right." Alex looked over his shoulder. "I need to go."

Phin nodded. "Right. Remember, meet me at noon at the Penny. Don't be late."

"I won't." Without another word, Alex turned around and started walking toward the church.

"Railway Penny at noon," Phin called after him.

Alex waved without looking back. Phin shook his head. He hoped Alex would keep his promise and turn up.

Phin needn't have worried. Right on time, Alex arrived. He stepped out of his car and came over to where Phin stood by the entrance. Phin smiled at him and strode forward to meet him. He held out the basket he had in his hand.

"An actual picnic basket? Do people still use those?" Alex wrinkled his nose, but he didn't look serious.

"Lunch," Phin said by way of explanation. "I borrowed the basket from Dani. It seemed more authentic."

"I suppose," Alex said. He glanced up at the sky. "Sounds good, as long as the rain holds off."

Phin made a face. "Where's your sense of adventure? Besides, I doubt you'll melt."

They got in Phin's car and drove out to the other side of town. There was a small but picturesque park there, complete with a duck pond, a playground, and a small footbridge over the creek that ran through the north end. Perhaps because of the clouds, there weren't many people around. That suited Phin just fine. He grabbed the basket and a blanket, and they headed for a grove of trees out of the way of the main path through the middle of the park.

They spread out the blanket and sat down. Phin began to pull food out of the basket. While he was setting up their lunch, Alex said, "I almost didn't come."

Phin nodded. "I figured there was a chance you wouldn't."

Alex sighed and ran a hand through his dark hair. "I don't know what this is," he said. "I'm not even sure I should be here."

"Because of your job?"

"Partly. And partly because it's you."

Phin paused, his hand still inside the basket. "I don't follow."

"We don't have a stellar history. I would like to hope you've turned out well as an adult, but I'll admit, it's a little hard to trust you."

Leaving the rest of the items in the basket, Phin withdrew his hand. Instead of responding, he merely shrugged and returned his attention to the food. Alex didn't press, but his expression remained troubled. Phin decided to change the subject before the mood ruined the picnic faster than the clouds overhead.

"You talked to Michael," he said.

Alex nodded. "Smooth transition there. You are just about the least subtle person I've ever met," he said, his voice dry. "As much as it annoys me to admit it, you were right. He's fine, of course, other than the typical teenage relationship drama."

"He's a good kid. Lucky for him, he's surrounded by people who won't reject him." Phin inhaled deeply through his nose. "Things are a lot different than they were when I was that age."

"That what happened to you?" Alex asked, pulling out a sandwich.

"What?"

"Your parents."

"Oh," Phin replied. "Sort of. My mother threw a fit when I told her, but as I was an adult, I didn't really give a shit anymore about her drama." That wasn't strictly true; it had hurt. He knew Alex would be able to tell he was stretching the truth, so he added, "It sucked, but she couldn't kick me out, anyway. Besides, she still had her hope that I'd find the right woman and settle down."

"What about your father?"

"My father is a grade-A bastard. He found out because of something a client said to him about my...skills. He didn't care, though, because it got him an important account. I think his attitude was basically that he didn't want to know, and it was fine as long as he got something out of it. God. How fucked up is that?"

"Well and truly," Alex agreed.

"What about your parents?"

"It's just my mother, and she's always been supportive." Alex tilted his head to the side and looked at Phin. "I'm curious about something."

"You want to know why I let my father use me like that." It wasn't the first time someone had asked Phin that question.

"Yeah." Alex looked down, apparently just noticing there was food in front of him. He picked up an apple and bit into it.

"It wasn't like he sat me down one day and said he wanted me to do it. It just kind of happened. I was working at his company the summer after I graduated high school. You know, typical intern stuff—filing papers, coffee runs, deliveries. Dad sometimes took me along on sales calls, though, so I knew a few of his clients. Once, I overheard him complaining about a tough account. He referred to the client as 'that frigid bitch' and said she needed a good lay. To this day, I'm not entirely sure what he was thinking, saying that out loud."

"So, what happened?"

Phin snorted. "I took my father's suggestion literally." He bit into his sandwich and thought about her, wondering what had happened to her.

Alex's eyes widened. "My God. Did you—"

Realizing what it had sounded like, Phin rushed to explain. "Oh, shit. Sorry. No, nothing like that. It was mutually enjoyable."

"Wait...you said this was after high school? You would've been barely eighteen. And she was—"

"Don't get all judgy, all right? She was about the same age we are now. I don't think she knew I was that young, and I wasn't exactly inexperienced." He shrugged. "She signed a contract for five years' worth of textbooks and curriculum."

"And then what?"

"We had a relationship of sorts. Hooked up whenever she was local." He hesitated. "It didn't end well. She got married, but she claimed she and her husband had an 'arrangement' regarding her business travel. She wanted to keep on doing what we had been—I didn't." He looked away, bringing himself back under control before returning his attention to Alex.

It was obvious from his frown and slightly parted lips that Alex was on the verge of saying something, but he remained quiet, to Phin's relief. They ate in silence for a few minutes while Phin was lost in his own thoughts.

Eventually, Alex said. "So that's what you've been up to all these years."

"Yes," Phin replied. "I've been doing nothing but selling textbooks for the price of sex. Just like you've been doing nothing but providing IQ tests and dispensing well-meaning but misguided advice to your students and family."

Alex's mouth dropped open, but he quickly closed it. "All right. I suppose I deserved that. But you have to admit, that's a good example of what I meant before about trusting you. Conveniently, you avoided what I said earlier."

"I know."

"Why?"

Phin sighed and looked up at the sky. It had darkened enough that he thought they should probably start packing up. To that end, he looked down again and began scooping up their trash in an effort to draw out the time until he had to respond. He finally said, "I didn't want to talk about it yet."

Before Alex could respond, Phin stood up and extended his hand to Alex, who accepted it. He picked up the remains of their picnic and started walking. They headed toward the creek, where they crossed the little footbridge and stopped in the middle. Phin set the picnic bundle down and leaned on the railing. He looked over at Alex, who eventually gave in and joined him. Picking up a stick, he tossed it into the water and watched it float away from them.

"What about you?" Phin asked. "Besides the obvious, what have you been doing?"

Alex inhaled deeply and stared out over the water. "Not much. It's a small town."

Phin tilted his head and studied Alex's face; he couldn't read the expression. "Why didn't you leave, then?"

"I did, for a while. I came back to take care of my mother's uncle when he got sick. I didn't leave after that."

"Relationships?"

Alex laughed. "Are you asking if I'm seeing anyone?"

Phin felt his neck heating up. "Maybe."

"No. I'm not," Alex answered. "It's not like there are endless possibilities. The closest decent place to meet anyone is almost thirty miles away, and I'm not always keen on the prospects on those dating web sites." He shrugged. "I'm not usually what most guys are looking for anyway."

"What? That's ridiculous! Anyone would be lucky to have you." The words left Phin's mouth before he could stop them. He clamped his mouth shut and looked at Alex sideways.

Alex's lips twitched, and he looked like he might respond. Before he had the chance, three large raindrops splattered Phin's hair and face. They exchanged a glance. Phin reached down to pick up the basket and blanket.

"Let's go. I don't want to get caught in it," Alex urged.

Phin stared at him. "It's just rain. God, you're uptight. What's the worst that will happen, your hair gel will wash out?"

Alex glared at him. "You're serious."

"No, that's *your* problem—you're too serious. You need some fun in your life for once—like getting soaked in the rain."

"I have fun!" Alex insisted. "And how is that *fun*, anyway? I don't want my shoes all squelchy."

Phin looked down. "Sneakers will dry, and you don't wear them to work. It's not even raining that hard. What are you afraid of?"

Alex started to walk away, but Phin quickly caught up. He maneuvered Alex between himself and a pair of intertwined trees. Laughing, he blocked Alex from going any further. Alex glowered at him.

"What are you doing?" he asked.

"Proving to you that nothing bad is going to happen. We don't need to be in such a rush to get back." He put one hand firmly against Alex's chest and kept his gaze steady. "Let's just take our time, okay? We can always hurry if it starts raining harder." He didn't want to admit that he wasn't ready for their afternoon to be over.

"Fine." Alex sighed.

Phin tugged on Alex's arm and pulled him away from the trees. They wandered through the grove, droplets falling from the leaves and dampening their hair and t-shirts. Thunder rumbled in the distance.

While Phin was busy trying to come up with a way to extend their time together that didn't involve a thorough soaking, the skies opened up and rain poured down on them. He and Alex looked at each other. Phin grinned, but Alex just scowled at him. On a whim, Phin grabbed Alex by the hand and pulled as he began to run toward the car. Next to him, Alex ducked his head against the wind and rain and kept pace. At last they reached the car, and Phin stopped to catch his breath, letting water beat against his face. Alex hadn't let go of his hand, and for a moment, they stood there against the car, hands still clasped, breathing hard. Eventually, Alex broke the moment and pulled out of Phin's grasp.

As they climbed back in the car, Alex said, "We're getting your car all wet."

Phin shrugged. "It was worth it for your priceless expression. See? Nothing terrible happened." He shivered and turned on the heater.

"Look, why don't we stop at my house?" Alex asked. "It's two minutes from here, and we can both dry off before you take me back to pick up my car."

Surprised, Phin said, "You're inviting me over?"

"I should punish you for getting me soaked, but I'd rather change so I don't have to spend the next forty minutes like this." He made a face.

"All right. Where do you live?"

Alex directed Phin to a nearby street and told him to turn there. A moment later, they pulled into a long gravel drive leading up to an old-fashioned two-story house. It was white and featured the kind of ornate trim common on older homes. Phin liked it immediately and grinned as he looked out the car window.

"This is where you live?"

"No, I just brought you to some random house. Of course it's where I live."

"Sorry. Just surprised, that's all. I guess I pictured you in something less...quaint."

Alex ignored him and got out of the car. "You coming?"

The rain hadn't let up at all, so Phin dashed after Alex up the porch steps and inside the house. They removed their shoes and socks in the entryway. Alex led Phin toward the back of the house to a guest bedroom.

"There's some towels and a bathrobe you can borrow in the bathroom. Just go through the bedroom and you'll find it. If you toss your clothes out here, I'll throw them in the dryer for you." He shook his head. "Not much we can do about the shoes."

"No problem." Phin shut the door and retreated to the bathroom to change.

Five minutes later, wet clothes in hand, he emerged and returned to the living room. Just as he was about to sit down to wait, Alex came down the stairs. He had on only a pair of dry shorts, and he was rubbing his wet hair with a towel. Phin's throat constricted at the sight. He realized a moment too late that he'd been staring.

"What?" Alex was clearly trying to sound innocent, but he was smirking.

"Nothing," Phin muttered. He handed over his wet clothes and sat down on the couch, shivering slightly.

A few minutes later, he heard the sound of the dryer floating from somewhere toward the back of the house. Alex returned to the living room, this time fully clothed, and asked, "Want something hot to drink?"

"Sure."

After a short interval, Alex produced two steaming mugs of something that smelled of fruit and spice and set them on the coffee table. He flopped into an armchair across from Phin. Neither of them said anything.

After a minute or two, Phin couldn't stand it any longer. "This is awkward."

"What is?"

"I'm sitting here wearing another man's bathrobe, and I didn't even get to have sex first. Meanwhile, you're completely dressed. It's weird."

"No weirder than anything else you've done since you got here."

"This is definitely one of the more uncomfortable moments of my life."

Alex snickered. "As bad as Tina McAfee's sixth grade graduation party?"

Phin sat up straight and pointed at Alex. "Yes! You remember that?"

"How could I forget? It was the *worst*."

"It wasn't all bad." Phin smiled at the memory. "Well, except for her bizarre party icebreakers and that terrifying game of truth or dare."

He paused. "Yeah, you're right. That was definitely worse than this."

"Oh, yeah. I remember all that, too." Alex grinned. "Afterward, you stayed over at my house and..." He let his voice trail off, and his expression darkened.

"Right," Phin said. He tried to lift the sudden cloud over their conversation. "My turn. Mrs. Shirley—fifth grade. I sat behind you and flicked paper wads at you."

"Yes, only they weren't actually paper wads, they were drawings of Mrs. Shirley. Good thing she never found any of them."

"She did, though!" Phin laughed.

"What?"

Phin nodded. "This one time, you weren't in school for some reason—must've been sick, I guess. Anyway, I was supposed to make an extra set of class notes for you. I drew a bunch of pictures at the top for you, because I thought you were just going to get them in your stack of homework. Let's just say they weren't flattering. Instead of sending me to the office with the bundle, Mrs. Shirley collected everything before I could figure out a way to hide it."

"You must have been in huge trouble." Alex snickered.

"That was the worst part. She never actually did anything—just kept giving me these knowing looks for about two weeks after that. I lived in fear that she was going to find a way to punish me." He chuckled. "Huh. Well, I guess she did, really."

"You deserved worse."

"Hey!" Phin crossed his arms and made a face.

"Wish I'd known about that. Why didn't you ever tell me?" Regret crept into Alex's voice. "That was before."

"Right. Before." Phin knew exactly what he meant. For something to do, he picked up his mug and held it in both hands.

"Did you keep in touch with Tom Silas or Jay Andrews?"

The question took Phin by surprise. "Jay, yes. His family moved when mine did. He was an ass." He shook his head. "Last I knew, he'd become one of those fire-and-brimstone ministers."

"Oh, that figures."

"Yep," Phin agreed. "Same M. O., different context. Not Tom, though—we lost touch when I moved and his family decided to stay here."

"I hated him," Alex said. "He called me a fairy princess for three years. He stopped eventually." Alex snorted. "Probably because he found out I was dating his brother. His sister's still local—she's on the school board."

"Whatever happened to Tom, anyway?" Phin wondered where Alex was going with this.

Alex looked out the window. "He's dead."

"Dead? What the hell happened?" Startled, Phin set his mug back down before he spilled anything.

"Got drunk at Christmas party about six or seven years ago. Cornered me and apologized for being a dick when we were kids. Couple of hours later, he wrapped his truck around a tree. He wasn't wearing a seat belt. They said it was a drunk-driving accident, but I'm not sure." Alex sighed. "Did you really not know? Or care?"

"Both, I guess. I never really liked him."

"Sure could've fooled me. You were pretty tight with both those guys." Picking up his cup, Alex said, "What exactly is this, Phin?"

"What do you mean by 'this'? Us, spending time together?"

Alex nodded. "We're having a nice vacation in memoryland, but so far, we haven't even gotten to what happened the summer after Tina's party. Remember when you first showed up and you told me you hoped that was in the past? It's not like I've gone around carrying this thing with me since childhood, but we can't bury it until we deal with it."

Realizing that Alex had carefully orchestrated their entire conversation thus far, Phin frowned. Getting sucked in was his own fault for forgetting he was dealing with a professional. He replied, "You're really into talking about stuff, aren't you?"

"It's what I do for a living. So, yes."

"Fine." Phin took a sip of his herbal tea, trying not to make a face, and set it back on the table. "What is it you want to say to me?"

"Let's start with the fact that you and I used to be friends, and then you started hanging out with those two jerks." He looked Phin in the eye. "They had always bullied me, and you—what? Decided that if you can't beat 'em, join 'em?"

Phin cringed. "I'm sorry. Look, it's complicated. I can't excuse what I did back then."

"Complicated?" Alex looked over at Phin, and Phin felt small under his gaze.

"I didn't know how to deal with it." Shame welled up in him, making his face hot. He concentrated on his hands.

"You didn't know how to deal with what, exactly?" Alex frowned.

"My fucked-up life, for starters." Phin looked up. "It was easier to just take it out on you."

"Your life was a mess? Mr. Spoiled?"

Anger washed away Phin's prior guilt. "Yes. But I wouldn't expect you to understand, since your amazingly supportive mother was obviously perfect."

"My...what? You're not making sense."

"That was the worst summer ever. I found out that my father was cheating on my mother, and even though I didn't make sense of it all, I got enough of it. My father had just taken over EduText, and he insisted I had to be friends with those two assholes because it was good for business. And then I couldn't even hang out with you because my mother kept saying no, which never made any sense to me. Plus, we already knew then that we were moving. And as much as none of that was your fault, you were there, and you were an easy target." Phin was breathing hard by the time he finished.

Alex was staring at him, his mouth hanging open. "You could have told me."

"I was twelve. I didn't think these things through. I decided that if we couldn't be friends, then I could make myself hate you and we could be enemies."

"That's ridiculous. Why would you do something like that?"

Phin couldn't even look at Alex. He stared down into his cup, which was still sitting on the coffee table in front of him. "I liked you."

"No kidding. We were friends. I would hope you—" Alex stopped short. His eyes widened and his mouth dropped open slightly. After about four seconds, he blinked and inhaled sharply. "Oh."

There was something satisfying about taking Alex by surprise. Phin replied, "Yeah. I thought I liked girls. I mean, I did like girls, but I liked you too. After Tina's party, I knew you liked boys. I thought that's why my mother didn't want me spending time with you. We had to hear about it practically every week at church, and both my parents suddenly seemed unnecessarily invested in my social life. I was sure those feelings would go away if I convinced myself we hated each other. It didn't work as well as I'd imagined it would, but at least I still had your attention."

For a moment, Alex remained quiet. Then he said, "So that's what you meant about my mother being supportive. All right, I get that. But I think what hurt the most was that after the rest of your crowd played that awful prank on me at the school dance, you let them have it, and I thought that we could work things out. Only we didn't, and then you left. You never even said goodbye—or that you were sorry."

Phin frowned, puzzled. "I did."

Alex shook his head. "I would have remembered that."

"That doesn't make sense. Two days before I left, I went to your house. I didn't want to leave without talking to you. I at least wanted to try to be friends again. I thought maybe I could write to you, because no one would have to know anything about it—not even my parents."

"I never saw you." Alex shifted in his seat, and Phin looked up.

"Your mom said you weren't home. I gave her a letter for you. Well, not a letter, exactly, but a note. I came over to your house the day after school ended. Your mom said you weren't home, and I told her to give it to you. I knew I couldn't say everything to your face, so I drew you a cartoon. I put my new address in there, just in case. You never answered me, so I thought you were still mad."

Alex scoffed. "Well, something must have happened, because I never got any such letter." He furrowed his brow. "Wait. Did you say the day after school let out?"

"Yes," Phin replied. "Why?"

"Because I know I *was* home that day. I was supposed to leave for camp the next day, so I was home, packing. I remember that because I absolutely hated that camp. I came home after three days."

"Why—"

"I have no idea." Alex stood up, and Phin was afraid their conversation was over. Instead, Alex replaced his mug on the coffee table and offered Phin his hand. Phin allowed himself to be pulled to his feet.

"What is it?" he asked.

"I have a box full of letters I salvaged from my mom's house when she moved into an apartment. I think they're mostly from my dad to my mom, before she got pregnant with me, but there were some in there from other people. Maybe she saved your letter. Come on." He tugged on Phin's sleeve like an impatient child.

They dashed up two flights of stairs. Phin followed Alex into a fully furnished attic guest bedroom. On one side, there was a storage area stacked neatly with boxes. Alex dug through the pile, setting aside bins of holiday decorations, photo albums, and tea towels. At last he pulled out a long, shallow plastic bin. He carried it to a low table and set it down. Seating himself on the edge of the bed, he opened it. Phin peered inside. It was stuffed with old letters. Alex reached in and took a handful.

"Here," he said, handing them to Phin. "Start looking through these."

Phin sat down next to Alex. For ten minutes neither of them said anything; they sifted through the stack. Phin carefully examined each letter. He paused at one with a return address he recognized as formerly his, but it wasn't in his handwriting, and he knew he hadn't mailed his letter anyway. He set it aside. He was ready to give up when Alex made a noise of happy surprise.

"Found it!" he said.

Sure enough, Alex's name was written on the envelope in Phin's awkward, seventh-grade cursive. He felt his cheeks heat up at the memory of writing it and the way he had held out so much hope that Alex might want to make up so they could keep writing each other, even if they had to do it in secret. When he hadn't heard back from Alex, he had been certain that it was a sign of rejection. How much time had they lost because he hadn't tried harder?

Alex laughed nervously as he slit the envelope open. He pulled out a paper and unfolded it. It was the cartoon Phin had drawn: two boys, one with dark hair and the other fair hair. In each frame, the fair-haired boy made various attempts to get the other one's attention, including juggling and a one-boy band—but the other boy kept his back turned and his arms crossed. Finally, cartoon-Phin tapped cartoon-Alex on the shoulder. A tiny word bubble over his head said, "I'm sorry." In the next frame, the boys were smiling and shaking hands. Finally, Phin had drawn them walking with their backs to the viewer, their shoulders touching and their fingers just barely close enough that, had they been animated, they might have reached for each other. The word bubbles over their heads read, "Friends." Phin turned away so Alex couldn't see his face; he didn't want the other man to discern his emotions. When he was done reading, Alex folded the letter and slipped it back into the envelope.

Phin had been so lost in his thoughts he almost forgot where he was until he felt a gentle hand on his shoulder. Alex's lips were right next to

Phin's head and his breath tickled Phin's ear as he whispered, "That is the absolute cheesiest thing anyone's ever given me."

Turning to face Alex, Phin stared at him, open-mouthed. He said, "Are you kidding me? I was twelve!"

Alex snickered. "I know. But—oh, my god. That's just awesome." He began to laugh harder, almost sliding off the bed in the process.

Phin scoffed. He remembered exactly how long it had taken him to draw that. "You could at least accept my apology," he grumbled.

It took a moment for Alex to calm down. At last he said, "Apology accepted. I wish I'd known about this, though. I honestly don't know why my mom never said you'd come by. I never told her you'd been picking on me—I just said that we weren't really friends anymore after she stopped babysitting you."

"She must have figured it out," Phin said. "When I tried to visit you after—after the dance, she told me you were sick and didn't want to see me, and she wouldn't let me in."

Alex shook his head. "No, I don't think so. That was what she told everyone. She couldn't deal with the reality, so she just said I was sick or I was tired or whatever else she thought was close enough to the truth without giving anything away. I think it must have been something else, but I have no idea what."

They sat on the bed, shoulder to shoulder, staring at the piles of letters, and realization hit Phin. "Shit. Shit, shit, *shit*. Alex, I think I know." He dug through the letters, looking for the one that had barely registered in their hurry to find the one that he'd written. He knew he must look strange, sifting through the pile he'd discarded. At last, he pulled it out and held it up, looking at the return address. Now he recognized the handwriting as his mother's. "Fucking hell."

Alex frowned. "What?"

Phin handed him the letter, and Alex slid it out of the envelope. He scanned it quickly, his mouth dropping open as he read. "Oh, my god."

"It was her," Phin said. He put his head in his hands. "I knew. I knew he'd been screwing around—I told you that part already—because I overheard my mother refer to her as his whore. She said that he had to choose between them." He looked up at Alex. "I swear to you, I had no idea it was your mom."

"That explains a lot." Alex closed his eyes. "A whole lot."

Phin reached out and put his hand on Alex's arm. "I really am sorry."

Alex shook his head. "This isn't your fault." He turned so that he was facing Phin, and Phin released his grasp. "We are not our parents, and we don't own their mistakes." Alex put his hand on Phin's shoulder. "I wish I'd known," he said. "We lost so much time because of this."

With a deep breath, Phin took a risk and leaned closer. "It doesn't have to stay that way."

Alex slid his hand lower so that he was gripping Phin's upper arm, and Phin didn't care anymore. He didn't care about all the years they'd lost out on or about his botched attempts at friendship this time around. All he cared about was being two inches from Alex, his heart hammering and his hands sweating. Alex's breath came in tiny, quick puffs against Phin's cheek, and Phin's stomach tightened. He reached out and rested his hand on Alex's neck. When he received confirmation in Alex's eyes, Phin closed the gap and kissed him.

From the first hesitant brush of their lips, Phin was gone. A wave of intense pleasure rushed through him. He wondered if this was what it felt like to drown; if so, he thought that just might be how he would like to die. Instinctively, he wrapped his free arm around Alex's waist. Alex responded by drawing closer, slipping a hand down to rest on Phin's hip. Their embrace moved from shy and exploring to rough and raw and needy as they lost themselves in it. Phin parted his lips in invitation and was rewarded with Alex sliding his tongue against his own. As they kissed, Phin's senses were full of the sound of the rain on the roof, the taste of the herbal tea they'd been drinking, and the warmth of their barely-touching bodies.

It wasn't enough. Phin nudged, and Alex leaned back until he was lying supine on the bed. Eagerly, Phin kissed along his jaw and down his neck, while Alex ran his hands up Phin's back, digging his fingers in slightly. Phin slid his hand underneath Alex's t-shirt, inhaling deeply at the smooth feel of naked skin under his palm while he returned his lips to Alex's. They rolled so they were lying on their sides face to face, and they pressed their bodies together, arching into each other and kissing hungrily. Phin worked both his mouth and his hand lower, reaching for the button on Alex's shorts. He flicked it open deftly and unzipped the fly, but Alex grabbed his wrist.

"Wait," he panted. "We can't just—"

Phin stopped and raised his eyes. "Because you don't want to?" He mouthed Alex's bare stomach, making him squirm a little.

"No." Alex inhaled sharply. "Because I don't have any—" He cut himself off, groaning when Phin licked his navel. "—condoms," he finished breathlessly.

"Ah." Phin kissed his way back up. "It's okay," he murmured. "We don't—" He paused to kiss Alex on the mouth. "—have to fuck. We can just—" He pressed his lips against Alex's jawline. "—do this instead." He pulled his wrist free to slide his hand inside the opening in Alex's shorts and applied gentle pressure, causing Alex to gasp and push into him. "Yeah?"

"Oh, yes."

Alex to tugged at his clothes until he was half undressed. Phin undid the sash on the robe, allowing it to fall open, and together they pushed his briefs out of the way. They continued to kiss as they sought release by each other's hands. With each stroke, Phin silently pleaded his apology for all the things that had passed between them. Every answering touch felt like an offer of forgiveness. Desperately, Phin clung to Alex as their mouths and hands and bodies merged and moved together. Everything narrowed down to the moment of release, intensifying until they tumbled over the edge, groaning and spilling onto each other.

They lay unmoving in a boneless heap of tangled limbs, their hands still resting between one another's legs. The rain slowed its dance on the roof in concert with their heart beats, and they leaned their heads against each other, catching their breath.

"Jesus," Phin said when he could speak again. His voice shook a little.

Alex chuckled faintly. "So you found him after all." He rolled onto his back.

Phin looked at him sharply. "What?"

"You said, 'Jesus.' Remember when I took you to my church and you accused me of trying to help you find Jesus?"

"Oh, god." Phin groaned and shoved Alex lightly with his shoulder. "Nope, just me."

"Jerk." Phin silenced Alex with a kiss, which quickly led to another and another. Phin couldn't remember the last time he hadn't wanted to stop, though he knew they should.

He pulled away. Alex grinned and leaned his head back against the pillows but made no move to get up. In the meantime, Phin looked down at their half-naked bodies and grunted. He glanced around for something to clean them both up. He snagged a box of tissues from beside the bed. Hesitating for only a moment, he pulled a few out and gently went to work on Alex first.

"What are you doing?"

Phin stilled his hand and leaned in for another kiss. "I'm not really sure. Just seemed like the right thing to do. Do you want me to stop?"

Alex shook his head. "No. It's...nice." He closed his eyes, and they kissed slowly while Phin wiped away the remnants of their activities.

When they had put themselves back together, they sat down on the edge of the bed to take care of the letters that they had strewn across the table and the floor. In a few minutes, they had everything tucked neatly away in the bin. Alex returned it to storage and replaced the other boxes he'd moved.

"Your clothes are probably dry by now," he said.

Reluctantly, Phin followed Alex downstairs. The rain had slowed almost to a stop. Alex retreated to the back of the house to retrieve Phin's clothes and returned a moment later with them in hand. Phin escaped back to the first-floor bedroom to change. He hung the robe neatly back in its place and emerged to find Alex waiting. When Phin attempted to put his still-damp sneakers back on, he reflected that Alex had been right about one thing—they were unpleasantly squelchy. He decided not to admit that.

They drove back to the Railway Penny in companionable silence. The gray skies gave way to blue, and the sun made its first appearance of the day. Alex flipped stations on the radio until he found a station playing classic rock and pop. Phin refrained from rolling his eyes; the afternoon had ended too well to make a big deal out of a difference of opinion on music. When he heard the next song, though, he laughed.

"Appropriate, if cliche," he remarked.

Alex grinned at him and rested a hand on his knee, singing along. "...the smiles returning to the faces..."

Phin snorted and focused on the road. The song ended just before they pulled into the parking area at the Railway Penny. When Phin stopped the car, Alex remained seated.

"Come with us next weekend," he said, jarring Phin out of his thoughts.

"Where?"

"There's an arts festival at the community college outside Peroo. We usually spend the weekend there. They have concerts, lectures, and exhibits—it's a lot of fun." He quickly added, "Some of our students are playing, so you'd get a feel for why we do things the way we do here."

Phin considered it. It was his last weekend in town, and it wasn't as though he had plans. His heart sped up just a fraction at the thought of two whole days with Alex, even if he had to share him. He might even be able to negotiate for time away from the others. "All right," he said.

Alex grinned. "Good. I'll give you the details later this week." He got out of the car. For a moment, it looked like he might just go straight to his own vehicle; instead, he rounded the front of Phin's car and came to the driver's side. He knocked on the window.

When Phin rolled it down, Alex leaned in and pressed a relatively chaste kiss to Phin's cheek that made his face flush and his pulse quicken. He reached up and drew Alex down for a proper kiss. At last they parted, and Alex headed to his own car, waving over his shoulder in his familiar style. Phin sat for another minute before getting out and heading inside the inn.

It wasn't until he was back in his room, changing and gathering his clothes for a trip to the laundromat, that Phin realized he'd never gotten around to the real reason for their date.

Chapter Fourteen

The Decay of Dishonesty

ALEX DRIFTED into wakefulness, a hint of sunlight filtering around the curtains. He stirred and rolled onto his back, drawing the covers closer under his chin and letting out a soft sigh. He'd been dreaming, but he could only just grasp the edges of whatever it had been about. It involved Phin, but the details were already fading like the darkness. Alex kept his eyes closed, trying to hold the last bit of the dream before it was entirely gone.

It was no use; the only thing that came to mind was Phin's face, without any context from the dream. Alex decided that was good enough and gave in to recalling their afternoon together. His neck heated up and his gut swirled pleasantly at the memory of fooling around like teenagers. The feeling was compounded by a tightness in his chest that had more to do with Phin's intimate confessions in the park than the feel of his hands on Alex's body.

He smiled as he reached down to run his hand over the outside of his pajama pants. Thinking about Phin—his soft, honey-blond hair; his eyes the color of the summer sky; his perfect, round ass—was plenty to make Alex's body take notice. Keeping his eyes closed, he shoved both the covers and his clothes down.

He hissed a little as he wrapped a hand around himself, moving slowly and savoring every stroke. He brought to mind the sensation of Phin's fingers around him, firm but not too tight, tugging at him. His lips parted, a small gasp escaping as his skin began to tingle. This wasn't going to take long. He slid his other hand down his chest, reaching towards the juncture of his thigh and—

The cell phone on his night table went off.

"Shit!" Alex let go of himself and sat bolt upright, his heart thumping wildly. He panted, swallowing in between gasps and rubbing his eyes with the heels of his hands. On the fifth ring, he reached over and picked up the phone. "H-hello?" he choked out.

"Uh...hello? Alex? It's Phin."

Damn it! His cheeks burned. "Hey, Phin." He flopped backwards onto his pillow and ran a hand through his hair. He frowned. "How did you get my number?"

"Called Dani. Did I wake you? You sound...tired or something."

"N-no. I was just getting up." He glanced at the clock and grimaced. "What's up?"

"Wondered if you wanted to have breakfast with me. I think—" There was a pause. "I guess maybe we should talk. I need to tell you something."

"No!" Alex winced at his tone. "Uh, I mean, I can't."

"Oh. I was hoping you were free." Phin sounded a little upset. "I'm—I'm sorry." He paused again. "Did I do something wrong? I mean, I kind of pushed—"

"Ah, god, no, babe. I just..." Alex struggled to come up with an excuse. "I'm running a little behind already. How about lunch?"

"'Babe'?" Phin chuckled. "Sure. I'll see you at school."

"Right. Yes. See you there."

Alex ended the call. He flung one arm to the side and draped the other over his eyes, groaning. When his heart rate had finally slowed down to normal, he uncovered his face. He glanced down at himself and sighed before dragging his clothes back on and rolling out of bed. Might as well head to the community center for some mind-clearing exercise.

A brief swim, a rushed shower and shave, and a hurried bite to eat later, Alex was on his way to work. He barely acknowledged Dani on his way in, ignoring her bemused expression as he flew past into his office. Once inside, he shut the door and sat down at his desk, resting his elbows and gripping his head. He took several long, calming breaths before pulling a stack of files toward himself and opening the top one.

He never did meet up with Phin; somehow, they kept missing one another. By the time all the students had left, Alex's whole body ached with tension. He tried to finish the last of his reports, but it was no use. The text swam before his eyes, and he couldn't formulate a coherent sentence. Shoving the stack aside, he stepped back out of his office and approached Dani.

"You see Phin leave yet?"

Dani gave him a puzzled frown. "No, actually. Why?"

"I just need to talk to him about something. We were supposed to have lunch, but we were both too busy."

"Hm. I thought he was going to call you earlier. It's a good thing I had to be here for the support staff meeting or I'd have been pissed that he called me so ridiculously early to ask for your number."

"He did call, but I was kind of in a rush, so I didn't have a chance to find out what he wanted."

"I bet I know," Dani muttered.

"What?"

"Nothing. I can let you know when he—" She glanced past him. "Never mind. He's right there."

Alex spun around. "Hey, Phin."

For a moment, Phin's eyes lit up, but the spark faded. He stopped a few paces short of the desk. "Hey." He gave a half-smile.

Frowning, Alex asked, "Everything all right?"

"Sure." His face softened. "Sorry I missed lunch."

Dani hadn't moved from her spot. She wasn't even pretending to work instead of listening in on their strained exchange. When Phin turned to the desk to retrieve a visitor's badge, Dani shook her head a little. "Where'd you spend your day this time, Phin?"

He chuckled weakly. "Middle school phys ed. That was a joy. Thank god I didn't actually have to participate this time." He looked at Alex one more time, and his smile faltered. He unclipped his visitor's badge and dropped it in the basket. "I'm just going to use the restroom before I go." He brushed past Alex, heading down the hallway past the staff lounge.

Dani peered at Alex. "Are you okay?"

"Not exactly."

"Did something happen?" Her eyes narrowed.

"No. Yes. I mean, nothing bad." He made a frustrated sound. "Phin's acting weird, that's all."

She opened her mouth, snapped it shut again, and pursed her lips. Rolling her eyes, she tilted her head in the direction Phin had gone. Alex nodded and escaped from the front desk and down the hall. He pushed open the door to the men's room.

Phin stood in front of one of the sinks. Before he could move, Alex wrapped his arms around him. "Hey."

Turning to face Alex, Phin replied, "Hey, yourself." He pushed at Alex a little. "Let me go. I came in here for a reason."

"Yeah, and I followed you for a reason." He slid his hands to Phin's arms. "I didn't mean to be such a jerk this morning. You, uh, caught me in the middle of...something." He hoped the dim light hid the flush rising in his cheeks.

Phin's eyebrows rose. "I did?"

"It was just bad timing. I didn't mean to snap at you."

"It's fine."

Alex leaned up and placed a soft kiss on Phin's lips. After a slight hesitation, Phin kissed back more firmly. Alex took that as license to slide one hand to the back of Phin's neck and the other to cup his cheek. Phin put his hands on Alex's waist, and they stood there for some time, the sounds of their kisses echoing slightly against the tile walls. Alex opened his mouth as invitation, but Phin broke away.

"Stop. You're going to get us both in trouble, you know."

"No one's in here. They've all gone home."

"Yeah, except for anyone like us who's working late. They could walk in at any time. What's gotten into you, Mr. I-Follow-All-the-Rules?"

"Maybe I don't want to follow them right now." He kissed Phin again, more urgently this time.

"Alex, stop." He was breathing hard. In a harsh whisper he said, "We can't get off in the staff bathroom!"

Alex looked up at him and snickered. "Presumptuous, aren't you? Who said anything about getting off? Thought we were just kind of making out a little."

"Look, I still need to piss. We can save this for another time." He unwound Alex's arms from around him and stepped back, his brow creased. "I..." His face crumpled slightly, and his shoulders sagged. "I just think we need to slow down."

"I see." Alex crossed his arms. "That's not how it seemed yesterday." Impatience bubbled up in him.

Phin ran a hand over his face. "Maybe that shouldn't have happened."

The words stung like a slap. "I should've known. You didn't sound like you had regrets with Gia."

"That was different!"

Alex gaped at him. "Why? Because Gia's a woman? Or because you think she's easy?" He turned away.

"No, wait. I didn't mean it like that." Phin put a hand on Alex's shoulder and drew him back in. He leaned down so their noses almost touched. "I meant that I want to do this properly for once in my life. I just need a little time, okay?"

There was a long silence. Alex studied Phin, trying to read his expression. Giving up, he said, "Okay." He leaned up for one last kiss, putting as much promise into it as he could before he withdrew.

He wasn't a moment too soon. The door opened, and they sprang apart just as Gary Dettweiler walked in. "Gentlemen," he said, nodding at Alex and Phin. He turned away from them and stepped over to the urinals.

Alex grinned at Phin behind Gary's back. "Guess we were lucky," he whispered, tilting his chin at Gary. "See you around." He walked out, glancing back to see Phin's mortified expression.

Phin's desire to see as much of Alex as possible warred with his instinct to avoid him until he worked out how to tell him the truth. They'd missed their lunch, thanks to several unruly classes and Alex's work load. Then Alex had cornered him in the staff men's room, nearly nullifying his commitment to honesty before pleasure. Afterward, Phin alternated between imagination—following Alex into his office and kissing him senseless—and reality—sneaking around corners to be sure Alex wasn't standing there waiting for him.

He headed down from the secondary school determined to have a word with Dani on his way out. When he reached the bottom of the stairs, he heard Dani's voice, and she didn't sound happy. Phin stepped quietly to the corner of the hallway and peered around to see into the open front of the office. Dani stood about six paces from a motley crew of boys in various states of injury and disarray. To the left of the principal's office door, three of them sat lined up. Michael was on the far left, a bag of ice over one eye. A burly boy with sandy hair sat next to him, holding a cold pack just above his right ear, and a slender, dark-skinned boy bearing a strong resemblance to Oscar the custodian sat on the end, a wad of blood-stained tissues covering his nose and mouth. On the other side of the door, a tall, lanky boy with wavy brown hair slouched in his seat, scowling. He had a scrape along his jaw and his knuckles were bruised and bloody.

Dani was controlling the volume of her voice, but Phin could still hear the fury. "What were you all thinking? This is the last straw, Michael. I have had it. You couldn't have waited just seven more school days to deal with your personal problems?"

Michael didn't answer her. He looked up at her, his mouth set and his eyes hard. Phin was surprised it had come to this; he had hoped that Michael would take his advice and the situation would resolve itself. His stomach twisted with guilt. He stepped out in front of the desk to take responsibility.

The minute he rounded the corner, Michael turned to look at him. A grin stretched across his face. Phin stopped, startled.

"Michael?" he asked. "What—"

"It worked!" Michael's grin widened. "I did just what you said, and it worked!"

"Then why are you sitting here looking like you've been in a fight? I don't understand."

"Well, I may have modified your idea a little. We sent the texts, just like you suggested, from Nicki-Anne. But we decided that instead of anything embarrassing, we would just find enough people to get in his face and tell him to quit being a dou—jerk." His eyes darted to the other boys, but none of them said a word.

"All right." Phin frowned, trying to imagine how it had gone from one thing to the next.

Michael continued, "When he showed up, there were like a dozen of us waiting for him in the cafeteria. We told him we weren't going to take his attitude anymore." He looked over at the tall boy sitting by himself. "That's Adam," he said in a loud whisper. The boy turned his head and glared at Michael.

"So, how did you end up here?" Phin had to admit he was impressed by Michael's resolve, though he had never intended a fight to break out.

"Well, he was mad because it was a bunch of us instead of just Nicki, and he took a swing at Josue." Michael nodded toward the boy with the bloody nose. "Then Olin here"—he jerked his thumb at the boy next to him—"threw a sandwich at Adam to stop him beating Josue up before a teacher got there."

Phin looked at the burly boy, who shrugged and gave him a weak smile in return. Phin caught himself before he laughed, though he couldn't quite keep his mouth from moving slightly when he pursed his lips to stifle the snicker. "I see."

"Yeah. It ended up in a food fight—they're still cleaning it up—and all of us trying to pry Adam off Josue. We got hit in the process. I took an elbow to the eye, and Olin somehow banged his head."

"How in the world are you four not covered in food?"

Michael shrugged. "We were too busy fighting. It was completely worth it, though. Adam's through."

Shaking his head, Phin said, "You may be too, you know. You shouldn't have put your hands on him."

"Nah. Olin and I won't get more than a day of in-school, and Josue won't do time at all. Adam's the one who has to worry. Even if they check Nicki's texts, she didn't say anything mean—just to meet her in the cafeteria."

"If you're sure."

Michael nodded. "I'm sure. Adam's done. Everyone saw what happened, so he can't lie about it."

While they were talking, Oscar rounded the corner. His eyes widened and he said, "Josue? *Que lo que?*"

"*Tato,*" Josue replied, removing the tissues. "It's cool."

Stepping into the office, Oscar examined his brother's nose and mouth. "No, it's not. You're a mess."

"I'm fine," Josue insisted, but he let Oscar turn his face side to side.

"You're gonna be in trouble at home." Oscar frowned.

"Nah. I told you, I'm *fine.*"

Oscar shook his head and looked like he was going to say something else. At that moment, the door to the principal's office opened and Dettweiler himself strode out, followed by two men and a woman. Dettweiler didn't seem to see the boys at first. His attention was on Phin.

"Good. You're still here. Mr. Patterson, I'd like you to meet three of our school board members—Ed Dunlop, Jason Meyer, and Pepper Britt." He turned around partway to look at the three people behind him. None of them had their attention on Dettweiler, and he looked around to see what had distracted them. He jumped a little when he saw the boys. "Good lord!"

A muscle in Ed Dunlop's jaw twitched. "What is all this?"

Dani intervened. "These boys are waiting to see Mr. Dettweiler. It is my understanding that this one has been antagonizing some of the other students." She indicated Adam, who merely scoffed.

"This is ridiculous." Dunlop looked furious. He turned to Michael. "That's the last straw. You are not to go near my daughter again. If you do..." His voice trailed off ominously.

"Are you threatening my son?" Dani asked.

Dunlop turned to face her. "Not threatening—warning. I've warned you, too. Now see what happened."

Michael straightened up and looked Dunlop in the eye. "You'll have to take that up with Nicki. You don't own her, you know. Oh, and you might not want her to hang out with him, either. Look what he did to Josue."

Speechless, Dunlop just stared at Michael, his face red and his mouth set in an angry line. Dettweiler was trying to calm Jason Meyer down. He hovered over Olin, alternating among examining the injuries, glaring at Adam, and shooting equally angry glances at Dettweiler.

"I hope you're planning to do something about this," he said to Dettweiler. "This situation has clearly gotten out of hand. Were you even aware that this was happening?"

While all this was going on, Oscar had started lecturing Josue in a mixture of Spanish and English. Josue shrank into his seat, not daring to meet his brother's livid stare. Dani, Michael and Ed Dunlop were still arguing. Dettweiler seemed incapable of giving Meyer a straight answer. Pepper Britt just stood there, her attention shifting from one argument to the next and back again.

Phin barely held himself from rolling his eyes. He looked at Dani, who had gone to stand with Michael. *What a mess.* He cleared his throat and raised his voice to be heard over the ruckus. "Could you all be quiet for a moment?"

Slowly, the talking died down and nine pairs of eyes locked onto Phin. He waited until he was sure no one was going to interrupt him.

"It seems to me that this would best be resolved if you just let the boys have their say. I won't justify their fight, but you may want to listen to them." He flicked his gaze to Michael, who relaxed slightly. "From what I understand, if you can't clear this up now, there are plenty of other witnesses who would be willing to tell you what happened."

Adam immediately said, "He started it." He pointed to Olin. "He threw a sandwich at me!"

That set off another round of bickering. It was a minute or two before Phin could calm everyone down again. "Why don't you give us your version, Michael?"

Michael sat up straighter. "Adam's been after Josue all year." He looked at Oscar apologetically. "We decided it needed to stop."

Phin waited long enough to make sure that the conversation wasn't going to take any unpleasant turns. After a while, he could tell that meaningful dialogue was happening, so he quietly backed away from the circle of people. No one seemed to notice. Relief washed over him as he headed for the door. Having missed his opportunity to talk to Dani, he would stop by the desk at the inn and find out from Vic if he could meet them at Dani's later, provided Alex didn't also decide to join them.

Eunice and Gia sat at Dani's kitchen table, waiting to hear what Dani had in mind for the school board meeting. She would have liked to tell Alex, too, but she hadn't been able to reach him. She suspected there was a reason for that—possibly a blond with a fine ass—but she chose not to antagonize him about anything that made him smile the way he had been lately. Before they started talking about school politics, she filled the other women in on her day's unexpected chaos. She had just finished explaining to them about the latest in Michael's saga with Adam when the doorbell rang. She excused herself and answered it to find Phin standing there.

"Phin! Did you come to check on Michael?"

"Uh...no." He stood there for a few seconds before he said, "By any chance is Vic here? He wasn't at the desk at the inn."

"He's home, changing. He should be here in a few minutes. Want to come in and wait?" She opened the door wider.

Stepping through, Phin said, "How is Michael, by the way?"

Dani sighed, then chuckled. "He's fine. No school tomorrow, of course. He was wrong about that—Dettweiler was trying to save face with Ed Dunlop, of course. At least it's only the one day."

"I suppose." There was tension in Phin's voice.

When they reached the kitchen, Phin stopped and looked at Gia and Eunice. He shifted on his feet and rubbed the back of his neck, refusing to meet Gia's gaze. She exchanged a glance with Eunice. *Okay?* Dani mouthed, but Gia just gave a tiny shake of her head and mouthed back, *Later.*

"Why don't you have a seat?" she offered to Phin. "I was just telling the others about what happened at school this afternoon."

Although he made small talk, Phin's face was strained. He twitched his hands, his leg bouncing under the table. He didn't even crack a smile when Dani explained the sandwich that started the food fight. He kept his eyes trained on the table in front of him. Eunice kept sneaking puzzled frowns at Dani. It was a relief when Vic turned up a few minutes later, until he saw Phin and his expression darkened.

"Phin, what's going on?" Vic demanded. "You look like hell."

"I need to talk to you and Dani about something." Phin sighed. Glancing at Gia and Eunice, he said, "You might as well hear this too."

"Thought I told you last night I don't have any need to hear about you and Al—" He looked around at the women all of whom were staring at him open-mouthed. "Never mind."

"It's not about that. Thanks for telling everyone, though."

Vic pulled up another chair and sat down next to Dani. "All right." He gestured to Phin to enlighten them. "Then what is it?"

Phin ran a hand through his hair and tugged slightly. "I haven't exactly been honest about a few things with my work at the school."

"I was wondering when you were going to get around to telling us," Dani said.

Phin looked up at her, eyebrows raised. "You knew?"

"Of course. But there really wasn't anything I could do about it, other than—"

"Set your friends on me, yeah. I got that." Phin drew a deep breath. "There's more to it than you know. I already figured out you snooped in my phone a couple of weeks ago, so you know about my connection to EduText. They didn't hire me, but they're the ones who will be taking on the charter for your school."

"So it's true, then," Eunice said. "They're closing and reopening as a charter."

"That's the plan," Phin confirmed. "Donald Murdock is the assistant Commissioner assigned to the task of monitoring the progress on your school, since you had some previous problems meeting the standards under the new regulations."

"I'm confused," Gia said. She glared around the table when all four of the others tried to mask their amusement with varying success. "Yes, I know that's not unusual. I'm not stupid, you know. What I don't get is why Murdock hired you. Isn't it the *schools* that usually bring in someone to fix their problems so they *don't* get taken over by educational management organizations?"

"Usually, yes. But for some reason, Murdock made a deal with Dettweiler to bring me in. No one was supposed to know the official plan. The charter was already on deck, and Murdock has a list of teachers he wants removed. The easiest way to do that was to hire me under the pretense of observing the staff and making recommendations for improvement."

Dani said, "Officially, you're on Dettweiler's pay, then." When Phin nodded, she continued, "And that must be what the list in your phone was for."

"Yes. Those are the teachers I was supposed to find reason to terminate. That part is subsidized by Murdock's department, though I'm not entirely sure how he's billing it."

Gia asked, "Why does Murdock want those particular teachers fired? Was there anything they all have in common?"

"That's what I've been trying to figure out as well. His claim is that everyone on the list is somehow a threat to progress, but I couldn't find a connection. They're not even poor or mediocre educators. Most of the teachers on the list are highly competent. I can see why EduText wants to remove some of them—they're closer to retirement than not, and I'm sure they want to avoid larger pensions. The charter will mean pay cuts for everyone. But they don't even need a reason to fire Gia—sorry—because she's only been there for a year."

"I can answer that," Eunice said. "It's because we were the ones who pushed the school board to consider other options. We've been fighting with Ed Dunlop and Pepper Britt over this since last year's test scores came in. They want everyone out of there who had anything to do with trying to stop the school from closing. A few of us have been very outspoken, but the rest are probably the ones who have supported our efforts or voted for board members who preferred another option."

"Right," Dani said, remembering. "We only had a few choices—all of which involved firing a minimum of half our staff. No one was happy about that. Dettweiler has been keeping staff mostly in the dark about it."

"Yeah, I think he's pretty much sold out, poor man," Eunice said. "He loses his job no matter what, so I think he's trying to find a way to save his own ass. Not that I blame him—he has a wife and kids to consider."

Vic frowned. "I know I have very little to do with this, but why the hell does Murdock even care about all this, anyway?"

Phin shook his head. "I can't answer that, either."

"I can." Dani looked Phin in the eye. "Are you telling us the truth? You really don't know?"

"I promise you that I am. I never asked that question when he hired me." He shrugged. "It was a paycheck."

Dani nodded. "All right. This is what I wanted to tell you all about. After I did some digging, I made a few phone calls. The closest I could get to it was that he has some investments tied up in L and M Securities." She drew her eyebrows together. "Your father has some as well. Murdock is connected to EduText, and he clearly has personal reasons for seeing this succeed."

"Wait...L and M Securities? That's my grandfather's investment firm."

"I thought your grandfather had owned EduText." Dani crossed her arms and waited for Phin to notice that she knew about that.

He didn't seem surprised. "That was my father's father. My mother's father is in finance."

Vic pounded his fist on the table. "Damn. No wonder your grandparents didn't want to speak to me when I came looking for some help after I left there. They were still knee-deep in it."

"Yes," Phin replied. "They always were." He shot Vic an apologetic look.

"But why is Murdock investing in securities with Phin's father?" Gia asked.

The color drained out of Phin's face, and he slumped down in his seat. "Oh, God. Murdock..." He closed his eyes and pinched his nose. "Murdock is investing in charter schools, but he's hiding the money in securities so State Ed doesn't find out."

A chorus of "What?" rose up among the group. Only Dani remained quiet. She caught Phin's eye, and he nodded.

Phin explained, "Charter schools run by Educational Management are for-profit, so anyone investing in them stands to make money. The problem is, most of the places turning schools into charters are urban centers with few resources. The profit margin is higher if the schools are suburban. I'm not certain about rural schools, but in this case, you're a sure thing—you only have one school in the entire district, so there's no choice. Murdock must have gotten sick of seeing the schools fail and wanted to invest in something he considered more stable. Because of the lack of options, there is greater pressure to demonstrate academic success. In your case, that means cutting any programs deemed unprofitable and replacing them with whatever they think will improve test scores."

There was silence while everyone processed that information. After a few minutes, Vic said, "So, why are you coming to us now? You've been here for weeks, man. You could've easily told us sooner. Unless... you were going to just screw us over and get the hell out of town." Vic frowned. "You were, weren't you?"

"I was going to finish what I started and hope it was enough to get Murdock to rethink his strategy. There's nothing in it for me but a paycheck. After seeing the schools practices, I was considering whether I should just cut my losses and take the paycheck from the school and not the extra stipend. I wasn't even going to say anything, just finish up and get out. I didn't know Murdock was personally involved."

"What changed?" Dani asked. "Why did you decide to tell us?"

Phin's cheeks reddened slightly and he didn't say anything. Dani watched him, trying to read what he was thinking.

Vic leaned forward and peered at Phin, then burst out laughing. "Oh, man. You have *really* got it bad. Look at yourself." He continued to snicker quietly.

"No, I don't," Phin said.

"You do," Gia picked up. "We all saw it."

Eunice reached across the table and laid her hand on Phin's. "Does he know?" she asked, her voice gentle.

Phin shook his head. "I wanted to tell him. We spent Sunday together, and I was supposed to talk to him about it then. But we—I got distracted." He cleared his throat and looked away.

Vic was still grinning. "You're in a lot of trouble."

"I know that!" Phin snapped, glaring at Vic.

"You need to tell him," Dani said. "If you don't, I will. We need his help, and I'll be damned if I'm going to watch you break his heart over this."

"No!" Phin said. "Please," he begged. "He asked me to go along for the arts festival up in Peroo, and I'll talk to him while we're there. Just... please don't say anything, all right? I don't want him to think that I lied to him just—"

"For sex?" Gia giggled.

"We didn't have sex, exactly." Phin huffed. "And that's not why I came to talk to you, anyway. I need your help."

"What can we do?" Eunice asked.

"I have to send Murdock the report. I wrote two different ones—the real one and the one that implies you're all a bunch of incompetent, lazy fools. If I send the real one, I lose my stipend, which doesn't really matter, but it won't make any difference to the charter going through. If I send the other one, it makes it easier for EduText to use it later when they make staffing changes."

"Send the fake one," Dani advised. "But tell him it's in draft mode and you'll have it finalized by the board meeting on Tuesday."

"What? Why?" Gia asked.

"I have an idea. But you'll just have to trust me. Phin, can you send me a copy of the real report?"

Phin nodded. "I can do that. I'll also send Murdock the other one—I can certainly make it look a bit rough. He'll be annoyed that it's not the final copy, but he'll understand. I hope you know what you're doing."

"I do," Dani assured him.

Standing up, Phin said, "I believe you."

"So we can count on you?" Dani asked.

"Yes. Whatever you need from me, I'll do it." His shoulders relaxed, and he offered them a small smile. "I'm going to go finish that report so I can send it tomorrow."

"Not staying for dinner?"

He shook his head. "I have to get this done."

Dani showed him out.

After she closed the door, she stood in the entry for a moment. It would only take a couple of phone calls to set everything in motion; she would take care of the details after dinner. She returned to the kitchen.

"How many extra places should we set tonight?" she asked the others.

Chapter Fifteen

The Very Drunk Caterpillar

Alex met Phin at the Railway Penny so they could drive up to Peroo together. Vic had chosen to ride with Dani and the kids. When Phin had offered Gia a ride as well, she had blushed furiously and said that she would ride up with Oscar when he brought Josue to perform. Eunice also declined, as she had chosen to stay with "a friend" for the weekend. Phin took that to mean her sometime-partner, which Eunice confirmed when she invited them to stop by for a party after they arrived and settled in.

Their rooms for the weekend turned out to be in the only student housing at the college, a row of townhouse-style dorms. Each one consisted of two small apartments, one upstairs and one downstairs. Their group had an entire townhouse to themselves; Dani and the kids took the first floor, and the men had the second. Inside, there were three bedrooms furnished with a pair of twin beds with matching dressers and desks, a common area with a couple of office couches, a bathroom, and a small kitchenette reminiscent of a hotel.

Once they had deposited their bags, Alex pulled out the schedule and handed it to Phin. "You can look at this if you want. It lists everything for the entire weekend. Michael and Josue are playing in the jazz ensemble tomorrow afternoon, so we won't want to miss them, but otherwise, it's up to you."

"All right." He laid the schedule on the table in the kitchenette. "What time are we supposed to meet up with Eunice and...uh..."

"Renee."

"Right. Renee. How big is this party, anyway?"

"Not sure. I think it's something for a couple of friends of theirs who just got married. I didn't catch all the details." Alex put a hand to his pocket. "Hang on, I just got a text. Maybe that's them." He withdrew his phone and looked at it. "Crap. It's from work. I need to send a file before Sunday morning. Hopefully the campus library is open." He huffed.

"I brought my laptop. You can send it from there," Phin offered.

"That would be great. I'll do it when we have more than a few minutes to spare."

At that moment, Vic arrived, and both the text and the laptop were forgotten as they made plans for the evening. Dani had planned on staying back, but Michael told her that he didn't have anything to do until Josue arrived anyway, so he was willing to stay with Carlie and Jake. There were some children's activities set up for early-arrival families, and Michael suggested taking his siblings. Dani had raised an eyebrow at that, and Phin suspected there might be some other reason Michael was so agreeable about babysitting. No one questioned it, though, and the adults set off for Renee's house after Dani reminded Michael not to keep them out too late.

Renee's home was less than ten minutes from the college. She taught there, and Alex had been right—it was a mid-sized party to celebrate her co-worker's recent marriage. They gave a few details, but Phin still wasn't clear on them. The whole situation already felt slightly awkward and surreal. After about fifteen minutes—most of which was spent being introduced to a lot of people whose names he promptly forgot—Phin began to wish he hadn't come. Parties were not his style; he was used to entertaining clients alone or in small, private groups. Alex, Dani, and Vic moved through the house, catching up with friends.

At first, Phin remained at Alex's side, but at some point, Alex became caught up in a conversation Phin wasn't following. Somehow, they ended up separated, and Phin found himself at the edges of the party. Eventually, a chatty young woman brought him a cup of some kind of punch with berries floating in it. Phin sniffed it; the drink smelled fruity with vague alcoholic undertones. He took a tentative sip and decided it wasn't repulsive. He downed it, deposited his empty cup on a table, and spent several tedious minutes listening to the woman talk about a lot of things Phin didn't quite catch. When he finally extracted himself from her company, he went in search of Alex. Before he got very far, someone else handed him a cup of the blackberry punch. Phin tried to decline, but she pushed it into his hand.

"Here—you have got to try this," she said. "It's amazing."

"What exactly is in it?"

She shrugged. "I don't know. It's not very strong, though." She held up her cup. "Cheers!"

Phin relaxed and finished the second drink then tried again to find any of the people he'd come with. It shouldn't have been hard, as it wasn't crowded. For some reason, Phin seemed to be getting further away from the center of the house where he assumed the others had ended up. Before he could accomplish his mission, another guest handed him a cup of something similar to his previous two. Phin protested, "I really don't drink."

The man, who looked like he might have been trying to relive his parents' hippie adolescence, dismissed him. "Nah, there's nothing in this one. It's the one with the blackberries you want to watch out for."

The beverage passed the sniff test, so Phin drank it more slowly this time while the other man tried to engage him in a pseudo-intellectual conversation about the upcoming weekend. Phin didn't want to be rude, but he hadn't studied the program outline Alex had given him and was therefore lost in the details. He managed to discern that the weekend had something to do with cultural influences, but by then, Phin was starting to feel light-headed. He thought maybe the man he'd been talking to had either lied or been mistaken about what was in the punch. Phin deemed him an ass and decided to look for the others again.

Just as he was about to move on, the man grabbed his arm. "Where're you going, babe?" He leered and leaned in a little too close for Phin's comfort.

Phin had had enough. "Oh, fuck off, will you? I'm here with someone else." He shook himself free and tried to disappear, not checking to see if The Ass was following him.

On his way through the crowd—which seemed to have grown exponentially since Phin's last attempt—at least three more people offered him a drink. Someone finally just shoved something at him, and Phin had to take it in order not to slop liquid all over himself. He frowned and looked for a place to get rid of it. What was wrong with people at this party? He couldn't find a table, so he sipped some off the top to keep it from sloshing over the side while he weaved among people. At one point, he thought he spotted The Ass and quickly ducked behind someone to hide. Unfortunately, his legs didn't seem to be working properly either, and he bashed his shoulder into the wall.

"Ow," he said loudly enough that a couple of people turned to look at him, puzzled frowns on their faces.

When Phin finally spotted Alex again, he was talking to an attractive man with a long ponytail. Phin thought they were standing a bit too close together, but he wasn't sure if that was because whatever he'd been drinking was already causing him to feel fuzzy. He hadn't had nearly enough to eat, and he wasn't much of a drinker. This was definitely not pleasant.

By the time Phin reached Alex, he knew he needed to get out of there. He was grateful that Vic was with him and Ponytail was gone. "I'm really not feeling great," he managed. "And a pretend hippie who apparently finds me hot might or might not be looking for me." The hand holding his cup shook, and Alex took it from him.

"Are you okay?" Alex asked. The concerned look on his face made Phin feel unsteady and too warm.

"No. What the hell is in that punch?" He rubbed his face.

Alex's eyebrows shot up, and he exchanged a glance with Vic. "I don't know."

The Ass, who obviously had been looking for Phin, appeared seemingly out of nowhere. Phin groaned, and Alex shot him a look of confusion before addressing the other man. "Oh, hey, Dave." He leaned in, and they exchanged a quick, chaste peck on the cheek.

Phin felt slightly nauseated at the sight. "Wait, you know The Ass?" He hadn't meant to say that; his private nickname for the man just slipped out. "Shit. Sorry."

Dave laughed. "Nice. Alex, tell me this isn't your date for the night."

Alex glanced over at Phin. "Sort of, yes."

"You might want to get him out of here before he does something stupid."

"I'll keep that in mind. Speaking of that, I think I've reached my limit for the night. Would you mind telling Renee thank you for us? We'll see ourselves out."

Phin tried to step forward and stumbled, knocking into Alex, who held Phin's half-empty cup over his head and backed up. He turned around and set the cup behind him somewhere then reached out to steady Phin. He extended his other hand palm up.

"Phin, give me your keys. No way are you driving back like this." To Vic, he said, "Help me get him out to the car."

Later, Phin couldn't recall how he'd gotten out of Renee's house and back to the townhouse. The details were blurry, in part because he spent the entire car ride trying not to throw up as the dizziness increased. He felt better once they weren't moving, though he struggled to remain steady on his feet on the way up to their floor. He leaned heavily on Alex as the other man half carried, half pushed him up the stairs and into their rooms. Once inside, he slumped against the door, but he didn't let go of Alex's waist. The warmth felt nice against his side, and he didn't want it to stop. When Alex tried to pull free, Phin grabbed his shirt.

"Nuh-uh," he murmured. "Stay here."

Alex gave in and leaned against the wall next to Phin. He turned his head so they were looking at each other. Phin wasn't sure if the swirling in his stomach was from all the alcohol or from his proximity to Alex. He stretched out his arm and ran a hand up Alex's chest, causing Alex to twitch and pull away slightly. Phin dropped his hand.

"You need to lie down," Alex said.

"Not yet. I have to tell you..." Phin squeezed his eyes shut. He wasn't entirely sure what he was supposed to say. He pushed away from the wall and swayed a little as he moved to face Alex.

"Tomorrow. Let's just take care of you for now." Alex tried again to move, but Phin put out a hand.

"I luff—luff—" Phin slurred. "Fuck." His mouth wasn't working properly. He tried again. "I love you." He leaned in and overcompensated, falling heavily against Alex, who winced. "Oops."

Alex put his hands on Phin's shoulders, and Phin took that as his cue. He decided his coordination wasn't good enough to hit the mark on the first try, so he wouldn't even bother going straight for Alex's mouth. Instead, he pressed his face into the front of Alex's shirt and began to kiss a path upwards until he finally made lip-to-lip contact.

Phin felt Alex tighten his grip on his upper arms. He tried to shift, but Alex was resisting. "Want you," he mumbled against Alex's cheek.

"Stop. God, how much of that punch did you have, anyway?"

"Not sure. Can't rem—remem-ember."

"Well, you're completely trashed. Come on, you need to get to bed."

Phin tried to ignore the way his stomach was rolling. "You come too," Phin suggested. His brain wasn't functioning well enough to get any more out.

"Not like this." Alex's voice was firm.

"Okay. Let's talk instead." Phin leaned up and pressed his lips against Alex's, attempting a chaste but uncoordinated kiss.

"No." Alex wound his arm around Phin's waist and nudged him forward. "Not until you're sober."

"I didn't want this, y'know." Phin frowned. That hadn't been exactly what he'd meant to say.

"Didn't want what?" Alex asked. Even in Phin's drunken state he could tell Alex sounded confused.

Phin gestured around. "Y'know. This. People. You an' me. I was jus' fine *alone*." He drew out the last word for emphasis.

"I can see that." Alex sounded amused, and it annoyed Phin.

"No. Not tonight. Forever." He waved his hand and nearly smacked Alex.

"This probably isn't the best time—"

The effects of his inebriated haze made Phin impatient that Alex wasn't understanding him. He stopped walking. "I haff *thins* to tell you. Imtortant *thins*."

Alex nudged him again. "You're drunk. You're going to say something we both regret."

Anger bubbled up inside Phin and he shoved Alex away from him. "Do you ever fucking stop playing therapist? Shut up. Just shut the fuck up."

"I–I'm sorry." Alex sounded surprised. "I didn't mean to upset you. Please, just let me—"

"You don't know anything at all," Phin accused. "This wa'n't s'pposed to happen. I was s'pposed to come in, do m' job, an' get the hell out. But *you*"—he reached over and poked Alex in the arm—"had to completely ruin that." Phin gave up on making sense of anything he was thinking or saying. He moved so they faced each other, wobbling a little. He put out a hand to steady himself. "It's all your fucking fault."

Alex took hold of his arm. "Tell me," he said softly. "Tell me what I did."

"You made me care about shit, dammit!" he shouted. His stomach lurched and he pulled out of Alex's grasp. "Oh, god. Shit. I'm going to—"

Alex didn't wait for Phin to finish that sentence. He hauled him into the bathroom just barely in time for Phin to kneel down and retch into the toilet. He gasped for breath and leaned back a little. He looked over at Alex, who was standing at the sink, wetting a washcloth. A fresh wave of nausea hit, and Phin gagged and vomited again.

A warm hand rested on Phin's back. He risked glancing to the side to see Alex, his eyes soft and his face relaxed and open. "Here," he said, handing Phin the washcloth.

After emptying his stomach another couple of times, Phin decided the worst of it was over. Whatever had been in that punch had been strong, regardless of what The Ass had said. Phin wasn't used to having more than the occasional beer or glass of wine with dinner; this had been far too much at once. He wiped his face and collapsed into a sitting position with his side against the tub. He laid his cheek on the cool ceramic and closed his eyes.

He heard Alex move. After a couple of minutes, he felt Alex sit down next to him, and he opened his eyes. With a groan, he shifted so his back was to the tub. Alex handed him a glass of water.

"You'd better drink this or you're going to feel like hell in the morning," Alex said.

"Thanks." Phin sipped gratefully at the water. His head still felt fuzzy, and he couldn't organize his thoughts properly. "You're amazing," he said then frowned. He'd meant to say something else, but whatever it was wouldn't come out.

Alex didn't respond directly. Instead, he reached out and began gently massaging Phin's neck. "You okay?"

Phin slumped down so he could lean back against the edge of the tub, and Alex withdrew his hand. His head was starting to hurt, though he felt somewhat more clear. "God. I am too fucking old to get drunk like this." He ran a hand over his face. "I feel like shit."

"Are you going to puke again?"

Phin started to shake his head and decided that was a bad idea. "I don't think so. I just need to sleep." He made a face. "After I brush my teeth." He shifted so he could stand. "And take a piss."

Alex stood up and held out his hand. "Need some help?"

"I don't need you to hold my dick for me," Phin grouched.

Sighing, Alex rolled his eyes. "Yeah, I meant help getting up."

"Oh." Phin accepted the proffered hand, and Alex pulled him off the floor.

When Phin emerged from the bathroom after satisfying his immediate needs, he found Alex leaning against the wall, waiting for him. Together, they made their way to Phin's room. Alex said something Phin didn't quite catch—or that didn't quite register—about getting something and left the room. Meanwhile, Phin somehow managed to change his clothes without passing out or tangling himself in his pants. When he was done, he slid gratefully into bed.

Alex returned with a second glass of water and a couple of aspirin. "Take these and leave the glass by your bed," he ordered.

Obediently, Phin downed the aspirin and settled down under the blankets, finally allowing himself to drift into blissful oblivion.

For having been falling down drunk the night before, Phin felt surprisingly tolerable when he woke. He had a mild headache and his mouth tasted awful, but nothing else seemed to be amiss. He played it safe by rising slowly. When he sat up and dangled his feet over the edge of the bed, he glanced to the side and smiled. Alex had left a fresh glass of water, two more aspirin, and a couple of pieces of lightly buttered toast on the bedside table.

Phin felt even better by the time he emerged into the common area. He had nibbled the toast and downed the aspirin before heading to the shower. Now clean and fully dressed, he thought he might be able to face the day. Neither Alex nor Vic were anywhere in sight. Having learned his lesson the night before, he opted not to attempt going out on his own. Instead, he plugged in his laptop and turned it on.

He might have felt a little guilty about checking on work while away for the weekend, but they had the whole rest of the day ahead of them. He could get this out of the way first and be ready for whatever the others had in mind. With a click, he pulled up his email. There were several new messages, including one from Murdock. Phin frowned. What could Murdock possibly want? Phin opened the message.

Received your report, and everything is in good order. Please present the final copy to my representative before the board meeting. Your recommendations on staffing changes and other updates are in line with our original agreement. The charter should be wrapped up and the contracts signed within the next week. After the board meeting, please schedule an appointment with my secretary. At that time, we will complete the terms of the contract, including payment, with options for further involvement once the new policies are in effect. If you have any further questions, contact me at the number listed below.

The email concluded with Murdock's official signature. Beneath that were three attachments, which appeared to be his original document—presumably with any alterations Murdock wanted—some information about the board meeting, and another document which, strangely, appeared to be a copy of their original agreement. He frowned at the screen. What did Murdock mean by "further involvement"? As far as Phin was aware, this was it. He would complete the assignment at the board meeting and be free to move on. A pang of regret caught him as he thought about what that meant for the tenuous friendships he'd built. He refused to acknowledge how it would affect his relationship with Alex.

Phin dragged himself out of his thoughts and read the email several more times, contemplating a reply. He hoped fervently that Dani knew what she was doing because if anything went south, he was the one Murdock would ruin. The sound of the door opening made Phin jump. He couldn't deal with it at that moment, not with Alex there and a full day of music, art, and lectures ahead. There would be plenty of time later for Phin to try calling Murdock to get some answers. He closed the laptop just as Alex returned to the room.

"Oh, good, you're up," Alex said. "I wasn't sure, after last night."

Hot shame crept up his cheeks as he recalled his behavior when they had returned to the room. He was a little hazy on the details, but he knew he hadn't been at his best. "Yeah. I'm—I'm sorry if I did anything I shouldn't have."

"You don't remember much of what happened, do you?"

"Not exactly." Phin didn't want to admit how much of it he did recall until he had a better idea how Alex had taken it. "Care to refresh my memory?"

"Which version do you want—SportsCenter recap or Lifetime Movie of the Week?"

Phin groaned and buried his head in his hands. "That bad?"

Alex laughed. "No, not really. First you called one of my old boy-friends an ass and nearly spilled punch on him. Next, you confessed your undying devotion, tried to make out with me but failed the coordination test, and yelled at me that something—who knows what—was all my fault. After that, you puked a lot and went to bed after assuring me I didn't need to help you pee."

"Oh, my god. Please tell me I didn't."

"You did. Sorry."

"Shit. See, this is why I don't get drunk. Look what ridiculous things happen."

Alex snickered. "Were you ever? Drunk, I mean. It didn't take much to get you wasted."

"Only once," Phin admitted. "I've never been much of a drinker, and I get stupid when I have even a little too much. Last time I did this was back in college."

The corners of Alex's mouth twitched. "What happened?"

"It was a party at a house my friend shared with a couple of other girls. I ended up making out with her. When her boyfriend caught us, I thought he'd be pissed. Instead, he asked to join in, only it turns out I was the one he wanted to fuck. He finally admitted to her he was into guys too, and, possibly because they were both either high or trashed, they thought that a three-way with me in the middle sounded hot. I didn't. But I was drunk too, so all I did was yell at them—in public—about how I didn't want to be their experiment, and then I hurled into the rose bushes."

Alex had a hand over his mouth in a poor effort to stifle his laughter. When he had calmed down, he said, "I guess I can see why you don't do this very often, then. It's still surprising that with all your other vices, this isn't one of them."

Phin rolled his eyes. "You and this hang-up of yours about my sins. Besides, I'm not a teetotaler. I do have a beer now and again, or sometimes a little wine. I just don't care for most of the other stuff, and definitely not in excess."

"Ugh. You're willing to drink something that tastes like cat pee, but not much else?"

"While I'm dying to have you explain how exactly you know what cat pee tastes like, I'm just going to switch topics and apologize again. I really hope I didn't do anything that made you think I don't respect you." Phin silently pleaded with Alex to understand his meaning.

He did. He stepped closer and laid a warm hand on Phin's shoulder. "It's okay. You stopped when I asked you to." Alex smiled down at him. "Anyway, you seem much better this morning."

Relief washed over Phin. "You took very good care of me." He frowned, remembering something. "Wait...did you say that you dated that one guy?"

"The one you said was a—what was it? Oh, yeah—a pretend hippie? Yes."

"I'm sorry. Though, he didn't exactly seem like your type."

Alex chuckled. "Why do you think we're not dating anymore?" He picked up the schedule from where it still sat on the table. "We already attended a photography exhibit and a lecture while you were still asleep, but there's plenty more to do. Are you feeling up to it?"

Phin nodded. "I'm absolutely fine, thanks to you," he assured Alex, who still looked concerned. "I'm ready to check out whatever is going on today any time you are."

"Great. I brought back some breakfast, so let's enjoy that first."

Phin stood up and pressed a quick kiss to Alex's lips in thanks. The result was several distracting minutes that threatened to extend into something else. They might have finished what they started if Alex hadn't pulled back to remind Phin they had other things to do. Reluctantly, Phin agreed, but he couldn't resist sneaking in one more kiss before they sat down to eat.

Chapter Sixteen

The Pilgrim's Undress

Dani and Vic caught up with Alex after returning from a final round of children's activities. Dani had missed the previous night's excitement, but Vic had filled her in on the basic plot. When the men emerged from the townhouse, Dani tried to figure out just how hungover Phin was. She was surprised that he actually seemed to be in decent shape, so she politely refrained from asking any questions. She also chose not to comment on the fact that Alex was distinctly more disheveled than he had been before he went in to retrieve Phin.

Alex and Phin remained in almost constant light contact: Alex's hand on Phin's back; Phin bumping Alex's shoulder; the backs of their hands brushing lightly. It wasn't enough to be uncomfortable, but it was more than casual. Dani frowned at their backs, but no one else made any remarks or even gave them a second glance. She looked for an opportunity to pull Phin aside and ask him just what he thought he was doing.

That was easier said than done. Alex barely let Phin out of his sight. She finally had her chance after they caught up with Eunice, Gia and Oscar before the boys' afternoon performance. Oscar had brought along his younger sister, Maricela, and Renee had joined Eunice before having to stop by the lecture hall to make sure no one needed anything. For a few minutes, there was a confused mess of several people talking at once, all trying to figure out who needed to be where. Dani seized her moment and pulled Phin aside.

"Well?" she demanded.

Phin shook his head. "Didn't anyone say anything to you? I was pretty out of it last night."

"Yeah, I heard. But you had all morning."

"No," Phin huffed. "Alex let me sleep while you all went off to see some exhibit. When would I have talked to him?"

Dani glowered at him. "Oh, I don't know, maybe when you were busy fooling around earlier?"

Phin scowled. "We weren't fooling around." When Dani raised her eyebrows at him, he amended, "Much."

"When are you going to explain this? We need everyone to be on board here, Phin. If you don't talk to him, I will."

"Just give me time. I'll do it tonight."

She jabbed a finger at him. "You'd better."

"I swear it," he said.

"Good. Let's get back before someone misses us."

They rejoined the others in time to hear Oscar talking about the college. For all the time they'd worked together, Dani had never known that Oscar had been taking classes part-time.

"...transferring my credits to SUNY Oneonta in the fall," he was saying.

"I think I missed something," Dani said, slipping in between Eunice and Gia. "Oscar, are you leaving us?"

He nodded. "Yes. I'm going to finish my degree in Environmental Sciences. Then I want to come back home and make our farms more environmentally friendly."

Dani thought that might be the most she'd ever heard Oscar speak at one time. "Oscar, that's fantastic. But I'm sorry to see you go."

Gia sighed. "Me too," she agreed.

Oscar reached out for her hand and squeezed. "I'm staying at home. I just won't be at the school anymore."

While that was going on, Michael and Josue had approached Phin, along with their friend Olin. "Hey, Phin," Michael said.

"Hey yourself. That eye's healing nicely, I see."

Michael laughed. "So worth it. You've met Olin, right?" He indicated the other boy.

"Not formally." Phin exchanged a fist bump with Olin. "How're you doing?"

"Good," Olin replied.

Phin turned to Josue. "Adam leaving you alone now?"

Josue grinned. "Yeah. But I think it's 'cause he's afraid Olin will sock him with another sandwich."

Dani turned away from the conversation to talk to Eunice and Gia. Out of the corner of her eye, she caught Carlie and Jake showing off the prizes they'd won at the games. Alex and Phin both leaned in to talk to them, and Phin ruffled Jake's hair. Jake looked up at him with wide, adoring eyes, and Dani's heart constricted a little. She sighed and stepped into the middle of the group.

"So, are we ready to go?" she asked.

They spent the rest of the day taking in the festival. The afternoon featured lectures on the history, influences, and styles of jazz as well as performances by the top three student ensembles from the spring competition, including the one from North Cowell. Somewhere along the way, Nicki-Anne joined them with three of her younger siblings in tow. She made a comment about wishing they still had the kids' tents set up the way they had been the night before, and Dani raised her eyebrow at Michael. He merely shrugged and offered her a sheepish smile.

After Michael and Josue's group played, there were art exhibits, one of which displayed college student and faculty work inspired by musical compositions, and more music on the main outdoor stage. The featured performers for the evening were a local Dominican-roots jazz group. Dani and the others set up a place to eat and watch the concert, slowly unwinding after the long day. A relaxed mood descended on the group. As daylight faded into evening, more people joined the crowd. Dani leaned comfortably against Vic, who slid his arm around her.

All around them, people stood up to dance. Carlie pulled Jake and Maricela by the hands and began making up her own moves. Michael, Josue, and Nicki-Anne brought the other kids into the mix, and Dani laughed when Michael attempted to teach them a few steps. They mostly ended up giggling and chasing each other around.

The music shifted to a set of slower songs. Michael invited Nicki-Anne to dance, and they began swaying awkwardly in time with the music the way only teenagers can. Carlie and Jake danced too, laughing and exaggerating their imitation of the adults in ballroom fashion. Oscar invited Gia to join him, and he turned out to be surprisingly good. Gia grinned and winked as they passed, and Dani gave her a thumbs up.

Vic withdrew his arm from Dani and stood up. He extended a hand to her then pulled her to her feet. They stepped out among the other dancers, where he held her close, his arms encircling her. As they turned, she looked over to see that Alex and Phin were still at the edges of the crowd, among the few people not reveling in the joy of the warmth and the stars and the music. From just a few feet away, Dani watched them.

Alex held out his hand. "Come on."

Phin shook his head. "You know I don't dance."

"I've seen you," Alex replied, laughing. "Yes, you do. Now come over here."

"I don't know." Phin hung back, his arms crossed. He looked around. "Are you sure it's okay?"

Alex, replied, "Look around, Phin. No one cares if you're a little clumsy."

"Not what I meant..."

"I know."

While they were talking, Olin stood up and offered a hand to Josue, whose face registered surprise. He shrugged and stood up, letting Olin pull him out among the dancers. They struck an almost comical ballroom pose, but Olin wasn't a bad dancer, and in a few minutes they found their stride and swayed with the rhythm.

Phin, too, gave in and accepted Alex's hand. In a moment, they were dancing between Michael and Nicki and Dani and Vic. Phin still seemed hesitant, but he soon relaxed and moved along with Alex. He caught Dani's eye, and she smiled. Dani took a minute to look around. In every direction, all different sorts of couples—young and old, children, men, and women—danced together in many configurations.

Leaning towards Michael, Phin nodded to Olin and Josue and said, "Are they a thing now?"

Michael snickered. "Nah. Olin's completely straight. He's just really cool and didn't want Josue to feel left out with all this mushy stuff."

Phin threw his head back and laughed, his face open and free. He leaned into Alex and gazed down at him, his eyes sparkling in the light from the paper lanterns. He laid a hand on Alex's face, brushing his cheek with his thumb. He hesitated, moving closer, but then he withdrew his hand. Dani studied him, her head tilted. She decided to give them a little push.

Leaning up a little, she whispered to Vic, "Stay with me tonight. It won't matter. There's plenty of space."

"Are you sure?"

She looked at Phin and Alex again and sighed softly. "I'm sure. It's our last night, and we've never stayed at the festival as a family before." She gasped a little at her own bold words, putting a hand over her mouth.

"Family?" he asked. He tilted his head to the side, a thoughtful expression on his face.

"Um...yes?" she whispered. He was focused entirely on her, and she felt too warm under his steady gaze. She met his eyes and tried to calm her thundering heart.

"You think of us as a family." He rested his forehead on hers and brushed their noses together.

There was nothing to do but tell him the truth. "Yes, I do," she said firmly. "And maybe it's time we did something about that."

"Just what do you have in mind?" he asked, his voice low.

She took a deep breath. "For now, stay with us tonight. Tuck the kids in. Sleep in my room. Tomorrow, make plans for our future."

He nodded. "That sounds just about right to me." He folded her back into his embrace and swayed with the music.

Before Dani let go of herself and drifted away on the low, sweet tones of the saxophone, she took one last glance at Phin and Alex, offering them a subtle nod. Just as the song ended, Alex pulled Phin away from the crowd and they slipped away back towards the townhouse. Dani closed her eyes and leaned into Vic, crossing her fingers that somehow, everything would work out.

The heat and the music and watching the other couples hold each other had been almost more than Phin could bear. His whole body thrummed, and it was all he could do to refrain from kissing Alex right there in the middle of the crowd. He was grateful when the song ended and Alex looked at him questioningly. Alex's eyes were bright, and his breath was shaky. At least Phin hadn't been the only one. He nodded, and Alex edged away from the crowd. They broke away and retreated to the townhouse.

Once they had closed the door to their suite, Alex had Phin against the wall before Phin could blink. His mouth was on Phin's, effectively preventing any conversation for the moment. Slowly, he traced a path along Phin's jaw and up toward his ear. Meanwhile, he had snaked a hand up under Phin's t-shirt. Phin suppressed a groan. He just hoped Vic wouldn't walk in on them. This time, he was sober enough to enjoy every second of what Alex was doing.

They ground against each other, and Alex's hands roamed downward. He tucked two fingers just inside the top of Phin's shorts and left them there while placing light kisses all over his face. Phin squeezed his eyes shut, trying to close his mind to anything but the feel of Alex's hands and lips.

Alex slid his free hand to rest on Phin's hip. He withdrew his fingers and touched the button on Phin's shorts lightly. "Can I?" he murmured.

A wave of guilt hit Phin, breaking his concentration. His gut twisted, and his eyes burned. Alex deserved the truth before they went any further. Phin lifted his hand so it was flat against Alex's chest and pushed lightly. To his relief, Alex backed off a bit.

"Wait," Phin said. He took several deep breaths.

"What is it?" Alex looked surprised.

"I—there's—there's something I need to tell you." He put his hands on Alex's arms just below his shoulders.

Alex smirked. "I know you're not going to tell me you're a virgin."

Phin looked him directly in the eye. "This is serious."

"Apparently. Serious enough to stop us in the middle of an excellent round of foreplay, anyway. Maybe we should sit down." Alex drew Phin to the sofa.

Once they were seated, Phin cleared his throat a couple of times. At last he said, "I'm not staying after my job is over."

Alex frowned. "Yeah. I know that."

"And you're okay with this? With having just a few days before I go?"

With a shrug, Alex replied, "You mean, am I okay with what we're doing now? Yes. After all, last night, you confessed your undying love—"

"I did not!" Phin shoved Alex lightly with his foot. "Anyway, I was drunk."

Alex laughed. "Whatever. You made your feelings clear, even if you were drunk." Alex put his hand on Phin's cheek. "I'm glad we found each other again. Tonight, we both know what we want, and we have this moment to share it. We'll figure out the rest in the morning." He leaned in and took possession of Phin's lips again.

They stayed that way, the kisses light at first and then deepening. When Alex ran his tongue over the seam of Phin's mouth, desire conflicted with the need to make good on his promise to Dani. Reluctantly, he pulled back.

"There's something else."

Alex didn't let go this time. Instead he pulled Phin closer and ran his lips across Phin's forehead and down the side of his face. "Tell me." He pulled the neck of Phin's t-shirt out a little and traced his tongue along his collarbone.

Phin shivered; he wasn't sure he could manage to talk with Alex so close. He opened his mouth and all that came out was a faint squeak. He coughed. "You...need to stop...for a moment."

With a sigh, Alex withdrew. "Does it have to be now? Can't it wait until morning? Or at least after we have sex?"

Phin grunted in annoyance. "No. It can't wait."

Alex backed off and settled himself into the couch. He looked at Phin expectantly. "Well?" He gestured for Phin to explain.

Phin closed his eyes. Alex wasn't going to like what he had to say, and it would very likely result in Phin having to take a long, cold shower. He opened his eyes again and looked straight at Alex.

"I'm not..." he started, but he let his voice trail off. He tried again. "I haven't told you the whole truth. I'm not who you think I am."

Alex said, "Well, I already know *that*. Though I'm glad you've finally admitted it. I was wondering when you'd fess up. We all knew you weren't here to help us improve our state test scores, of course. Why do you think Dani asked us to keep an eye on you? You were looking for dirt on our school to give the state an excuse to change our programs. Probably come back to them with a list of classes to cut and teachers to fire."

"How long have you known?"

"A while. Maybe the second week you were here or so? I can't say."

"So Dani told you?"

"Of course she did."

Phin scowled. "I'm still pissed that she got hold of my phone."

"Is that how she knew?" Alex smirked. "Apparently, you need to put a passcode on your phone."

"I know that now," Phin snapped. "If I'd been more careful, I wouldn't be explaining myself to you right now."

"Oh, please." Alex rolled his eyes. "You didn't think you were being completely obvious as it was? You stick out here like a sore thumb, but not just in the way some low-level state rep would. Plus, it's not like we don't have the Internet in North Cowell. You would've been explaining yourself all right, but probably not right before getting it on with your twenty-years-past crush. Lucky for you, Dani's pretty capable. She's assured me that you're willing to help us."

Phin groaned and slouched down. He covered his face with his hands. "Yes, but Dani didn't tell you everything. There's still a lot you don't know. It's more complicated than you think."

"And I'll be happy to hear it. *But not right now.*" Alex was firm. He tugged at Phin's hands, and Phin dropped them to his thighs. Alex leaned in and whispered, "Right now, I'd like you to show me *exactly* how you used to convince people to purchase textbooks from your father's company." He slid his hand upward from Phin's knee and applied just the right amount of pressure to make Phin squirm.

"Oh, god," Phin choked. Alex chuckled.

That broke the last of Phin's resistance. Within what seemed like the span of a heartbeat they were entangled in each other once more, pressing their bodies together. Alex reached around and hitched Phin's leg over his own, cupping his backside and humming a little. He murmured against Phin's lips, "Mm. Gia's right. Your ass is hot." He resumed his kissing.

Phin, nearly dizzy with anticipation, broke off their kiss and grunted softly. He tipped his head back and panted, "Sl—slow down."

For the third time, Alex drew back. "What is it this time?"

Phin was afraid to open his eyes. He was sure Alex was going to kill him. When he finally risked looking, he saw that Alex appeared more amused than angry.

"Are you okay?" Alex asked. "We don't have to do this. No matter how much I want to, if you want to stop, we can. I know things have gotten intense between us pretty quickly, so it's okay if you're not ready."

Phin's mouth dropped open, and he sat there staring at Alex for a moment. "Are you seriously psychologizing me before we fuck? I thought I told you last night to cut it out."

"'Psychologizing'? Is that even a word?" Alex wrinkled his nose.

"And *that's* the one thing you remember saying to me when you were trashed? No, I just—I want to make sure this is what we both want. I want to make love with you, but not if you feel like I'm pushing you."

"I do *not* want to make love." He sneered a little.

"You don't?" Alex seemed puzzled, and perhaps a little hurt.

"God, no. That makes it sound like all hearts and flowers and shit. I want to *fuck*. But I want to be naked in bed with you at the time, not on a dormitory couch. If we don't move now, we won't get that far. So can we skip to the stage where we're doing that, please? Just preferably with a lot less therapy-babble."

Alex's eyebrows rose. He stood up, turned around and made for the bedroom, leaving Phin staring after him wondering if he'd said the wrong thing. When Alex reached the doorway, he looked back over his shoulder. "Well? Are you coming with me or not?"

Phin rose from the couch and followed. Once he was inside, Alex shut the door, shoved him up against it, and kissed him so hard Phin felt it all the way into his toes. Alex pulled back and said in a low voice, "Is this what you want?" Before Phin could answer, their lips were joined again, and anything he might have said was lost in heat and need. Hurriedly, they yanked at each other's clothes, kissing and continuing to grope one other in between tugging off each article. Alex turned Phin so his back was to Alex then ran a finger lightly along the snake that slithered across Phin's shoulders. Phin shivered at the touch.

"Someday, maybe you'll tell me about this," Alex whispered, pressing hot, open-mouthed kisses along the ink as his hand traveled lower.

"Someday," Phin agreed. He spun around so he was facing Alex. "But not now. I'm busy." He pushed Alex backwards onto the bed and climbed on top of him, straddling him and kissing him heatedly. Alex attempted to roll Phin onto his back, but the dormitory bed was narrow and all he succeeded in doing was forcing Phin to smack into the wall.

"Ow. Dammit!" Phin growled. He readjusted and gave Alex a moment to move.

Alex ran his hands down Phin's chest and abdomen, chasing them with kisses. "Better?" he asked, his voice muffled by Phin's stomach.

Breathlessly, Phin replied,"Yes. Do you have—"

Alex sighed and retreated, huffing a little. "Yeah. They're in my bag." He crawled off the bed and fished around in the inner pocket of his duffel.

"Well, you sure come prepared," Phin commented. Not that he was complaining. He admired Alex's naked backside while he rummaged.

"Naturally," Alex said. "Never know when I'm going to end up with a hot guy in my bed." He winked at Phin.

"Oh, fuck you."

"That was the idea, yes." He dropped a handful of foil packets and a small bottle on the desk beside the bed.

Phin's eyes widened. "*Really* prepared. You were relying pretty heavily on my endurance, there."

"No, I was relying on the fact that the best you've had in at least five weeks was a few hand jobs, possibly including your own." He settled back onto the bed beside Phin, jostling the desk and sending several of the packets sliding onto the floor.

Phin reflected briefly that Alex's tendency to overanalyze everything did come in handy once in a while. He leaned over to grab a condom and the lube from the desk. Brushing the bottle with his fingertips, he stretched slightly further, overshot, and–

"Shit!"

Alex flipped over and peered down at where Phin lay sprawled on the floor. "Need a hand?"

"No," Phin huffed, hauling himself up. "Damn narrow bed. I haven't fucked in a space this small since I was twenty."

Alex buried his face in his arms, and his shoulders shook. Phin smacked him soundly on the rump, eliciting more laughter. Reaching over, Alex picked up the the necessities and silently handed them to Phin, who snatched them out of his hand and resettled himself on the bed. They lay facing each other, Alex's back against the wall. He traced his thumb down Phin's cheek.

"Are you all right?" he asked, his voice soft and warm.

"Yeah."

"Come here." Phin shifted closer so Alex could wrap his arms around him. Cupping his chin, Alex brushed his lips against Phin's. "Now, is that the last of the interruptions?"

"I promise. No more interruptions." Phin crossed his heart.

"Thank God," Alex mumbled against Phin's cheek. "Now maybe I can help you find Jesus again."

Phin opened his mouth to say something, thought better of it, and instead rolled them both over so that he was on top with Alex pinned beneath him. "You," he said, pressing a kiss below Alex's ear, "need to shut the fuck up. Please," he added, silencing any comments about his vocabulary by capturing Alex's laughing mouth with his own.

Everything else was soon forgotten. Despite what he'd said about wanting to go hard, Phin lost himself in the pleasure of exploring Alex's bare skin. He mapped it, memorizing every inch of his body and every touch that made Alex gasp and sigh and groan, his own flesh heating in response until he thought he might be consumed. He reveled in tasting Alex and the feel of being skin-to-skin. They wrapped themselves in each other, moving with increasing urgency until they were breathless and straining against each other. They shifted positions again, this time with more finesse, so Alex was on his stomach.

Phin looked down at Alex, and a flood of tangled emotions washed over him. "God, you're gorgeous," he muttered before bending forward and laying a kiss on Alex's cheek. He slid his hand down the curve of Alex's spine, relishing the feel of Alex shivering, then ran his fingers along the rise of Alex's backside. Phin slipped his hand down between the cheeks and stopped, his fingers teasing. He remained still, waiting.

"It's been a while," Alex murmured.

"I hope not so long you've forgotten how."

"Jerk." Alex swatted the outside of Phin's thigh. "Just...take it easy, okay?"

Phin nodded and withdrew his hand. He leaned down along Alex's back. "Tell me," he breathed. "Tell me what you want."

Alex twisted around a little and they locked eyes. "No," he answered.

Sucking in his breath, Phin pushed himself up a little. "Please," he begged. "Let me make you feel good."

"No," Alex repeated. "Make *us* feel good."

Phin let out a shaky whimper and bowed his head, resting his cheek on Alex's shoulder briefly. He located the lube and poured some out. Slowly, gently, he began to open Alex up. While he worked his slicked fingers, he pressed kisses along Alex's neck and shoulders, drawing soft grunts. He took his time, waiting until Alex began to move against his hand. He withdrew his fingers and sat back, picking up one of the condoms on the way. He rolled it on and positioned himself. Alex drew up his knees, and Phin leaned down as he slid inside.

"Fuck," Phin groaned. He held still, tensing all his muscles and listening to Alex breathing deeply. He rubbed Alex's neck and kissed his upper back. "*Fuck,*" he gasped again, drawing out the word so that it was almost multiple syllables.

"Yes," Alex said.

That was all the encouragement Phin needed to move. He began to thrust, longer each time as momentum grew. Alex grasped the sheets and rocked back against him, their movements in perfect rhythm. Phin braced his hands on either side of Alex, gaining leverage. The small bed swayed with them, sliding a little on the floor with the force of their motion. Every one of Phin's nerves tingled with anticipation as need built until he couldn't hold on any longer. He let go, muffling a shout of pleasure by pressing his mouth into Alex's shoulder. He rode the aftershocks, shaking and gasping.

When he could move again, he slid out and pushed his finger back in, maintaining the pace he'd set. Alex moaned into the pillow, pressing back against Phin and sliding a hand underneath himself. Every exhalation ended in a shuddering grunt. "Yeah?" Phin asked. Instead of answering, Alex threw his head back, crying out and breathing hard as he came.

They collapsed together to wait for the roaring in their ears and chests to die down, lying molded together for some time. Phin was reluctant to move, but eventually, they shifted to clean up. Afterward, they settled back down in each other's arms, remaining connected in the narrow space. Before he drifted off to sleep, Phin had just enough time to realize Vic had been absolutely right—he had it bad. He reflected that maybe he needed Jesus after all, because it was going to take a miracle to make it through the rest of his assignment.

Chapter Seventeen

The Kill-Joy of Sex

PHIN STRETCHED. His muscles were pleasantly sore in all the right places. He smiled when he recalled their night. It had been a long time since sex had meant remaining wrapped in someone else's arms, moving among wakefulness, lovemaking, and sated sleep all night. They hadn't gone through all the condoms Alex had with him; Phin supposed it was a good thing they were headed home that afternoon—maybe they could work on that, hopefully in a more comfortable space.

He rose from the bed and dragged on pajama pants and a t-shirt. After another good stretch and a yawn, he emerged from the bedroom. Alex was seated at the table in front of his laptop. For a moment, he was surprised, until he remembered that Alex had wanted to email a file. He didn't turn around when Phin entered the room. Phin grinned and padded softly across the carpet, coming right up behind him.

Phin leaned down and whispered in Alex's ear, "Good morning." He made an attempt at kissing Alex's cheek but was surprised when Alex resisted. He backed off. "Everything okay? I thought—"

Alex turned toward Phin, and his eyes were rimmed red. He shook his head a couple of times and looked up. "You complete bastard."

"I—what?" Phin stepped backwards, stung. "What did I do?"

Alex glowered at Phin. "I read your email."

"What the hell? Why would you do that?" Phin crossed his arms and scowled.

Alex huffed. "You left it open. I thought I'd get that file sent while you were still in bed so we could enjoy the rest of our day. When I opened your laptop..." Alex let his voice trail off and looked back at the screen.

Dammit! Phin had forgotten to close his email when he shut the laptop the previous morning. They'd been out all day, and then they'd been so wrapped up in each other the night before that he hadn't gotten back to it. "It's not what you think."

"No? So you weren't actually here to fire half our staff and then have your father's company come in and privatize our school with a charter? Because that's pretty much what it looked like to me. God, I am so stupid." He balled his hand into a fist. "You're profiting from this yourself, and you used me just like your other clients."

"No! I didn't—"

"Save it." Alex stood up. "God. I trusted you! I let you—" He made a frustrated noise.

"Excuse me?" Phin was suddenly angry. "You 'let me' do what, exactly? Let me fuck you? Or maybe you meant let me suck you off? Oh, wait—I know. You meant let me give you *my* ass. Seemed to me like you were a pretty damn willing participant every time. Or was I mistaken about that?"

"That was before I knew you were lying to me!"

"I have never lied to you. I tried to tell you last night, but you wanted to save it. Hell, I even tried to tell you when I was too drunk to get the words out properly."

"You didn't tell me anything. You made some cryptic remarks about not being what I thought you were. Well, that's for damn sure." Alex stood in front of Phin, his hands out in a pleading gesture. "I trusted you," he said again, a note of pain in his voice this time. His face contorted in anger. "I trusted you, but you were selling god-damned boys' bands."

"I—what? I don't even know what that means. I'm not selling anything!"

"Just that you're a liar and a fraud, getting all of us to believe your scheme and fall for your games. Using us to make money, hiding it by sucking up to—or sucking off—whoever you needed to so you could distract us."

"I wasn't trying to distract anyone. Will you please let me explain?" Phin reached for him, but Alex pulled away.

"Maybe I should ask Gia just how distracting you were. How's that line go again? 'I suppose I'm not the first to find it easier to think clearer when not under the spell of your salesmanship.' Should I ask her if she's thinking more clearly now?"

"What the fuck are you talking about?"

Alex threw his hands up. "Never mind. Forget I said anything. In fact, forget all of this ever happened." He turned his back to Phin.

"If you would just listen to me—" Phin tried.

Without turning around, Alex replied, "Listen to you explain how you got me to trust you with sex? Or listen to you tell me that what you're doing to my school isn't personal—it's just business? No, thank you." Alex stalked to his room. He turned around at the threshold. "I'm getting dressed and going out for a while. I want you out of here before I get back. I think you should just go back to town."

Phin swallowed. "How—how will you get home?"

"I'll ride with Dani and Vic, or one of *my* other friends will drive me. Just get out." Alex turned and went inside his bedroom, shutting the door behind him.

For a moment, Phin just stood in the lounge. His chest constricted, and his throat burned. Shaking, he breathed through his nose, gripping the back of a chair to steady himself. He felt as though he were frozen in place, incapable of moving or making a decision. He remained in place so long that Alex emerged from his bedroom, fully dressed and on his way out. Phin made one last desperate attempt.

"Wait," he pleaded.

Alex ignored him and brushed past on his way to the door. When he had opened it to leave, he turned enough to meet Phin's gaze and give him one last pitying look. He walked out and slammed the door behind him, leaving Phin still rooted to the spot, staring at the townhouse door.

"Dani!"

Dani gasped and sat up in bed. Someone was pounding on the door and calling her name. Deciding to answer before whoever it was woke up the whole campus, she climbed out of bed and grabbed her robe.

"Dani!" The voice was more insistent this time. "Open the damn door!" It was Alex.

She flung open the door just as he was about to pound on it again. "Alex, what do you want? It's early, and everyone else is still sleeping. I hope," she added, thinking they probably weren't anymore.

Alex pushed past her and started pacing the common area. Dani muttered, "Come right in."

He stopped in the middle of the room and looked at her. His eyes were blazing. "Why the hell didn't you tell me, Dani?"

"Tell you what?" She crossed her arms.

"About Phin. You knew, and you didn't tell me." He sat down in one of the chairs. "Why didn't you say anything?"

She sighed. "Would you have believed me? I saw what was happening. You were happy, Alex. For the first time in years, you were really, truly happy."

He flung out his arms. "But now look at me! If you'd told me, I could have walked away. What did you think you were going to accomplish? Were you using me too, the way you tried to use Gia?"

"No! I never intended anything to happen between the two of you. But, Alex, you're in love with him. I don't care that it's only been a few weeks. I can see it even now." She bowed her head. "I wanted it all to work out."

"Yeah, well, it didn't, and that son of a bitch has everything to do with it." Alex pounded his fist against the arm of the chair.

Dani crossed the room and sat down opposite Alex. "I take it Phin didn't tell you this himself, so how did you find out?"

"He left his email open, and I read it. The deal's signed, Dani. Edu-Text, which is apparently owned by his father, is taking over. No wonder State Ed sent him. Obviously keeping it in the family."

"Alex, did he explain what else was going on?"

"There's more? Oh, why am I not surprised by that?" He growled in frustration.

"It's not quite what you think. He's prepared to help us—"

Alex's head snapped up. "You still believe that, don't you? You didn't see the email, Dani. There's nothing he *can* do, even if he lied and said there was."

Dani sucked in her breath. "I—I don't know, Alex. He said he would do what he could. Why?"

"Oh, maybe because someone named Donald Murdock at NYSED says everything is already in place. It was all in the message, including

Phin's contract and the report he sent."

"Yes," Dani said. She breathed a sigh of relief. "I told him to send it. He's on our side. We've got a plan for the board meeting. The report he sent is just part of that. I have the real one at home."

"The real one?" Alex furrowed his brow.

"Yes. He wrote two. The one he sent Murdock is just a decoy. I trust him to do whatever he can for us at that board meeting."

Alex scoffed. "You're too soft. Look I need to get back to town. I have work to do, which I'd have done if this hadn't happened. After that, I'm leaving for a couple of days. I was about to call and say I wasn't taking the job interview after all, but with all this going down, I don't see what choice I have, so I'll need to make arrangements. Are you heading back early too, or should I find another ride?"

"I was planning on heading home before lunch. I don't think the kids will want to stay for everything. We might hear the PCC Symphony play first, but that's about it. Looks like the rest of the day is just lectures." She frowned as what Alex had said registered. "Wait a sec. What job interview? Where are you going?"

Alex didn't say anything for a minute. He stared at his clasped hands on top of the table. Finally, he looked up at Dani. "I had an offer for a faculty position up at SUNY Plattsburgh. The interview's just a formality."

Dani's mouth dropped open. She quickly recovered herself. "When did this happen?"

"A while ago. Before Phin showed up." He wouldn't look at her.

"You were hedging your bets. You didn't trust us." She felt sick.

"Dani, it's not personal. When the state comes in and takes over the school in whatever way they see fit, most of us will be gone anyway. I'm not going to stick around and watch it happen and then have to look for something after the fact."

"So, you'll just—what, move up north and leave us to pick up the pieces? What are we supposed to do?" She didn't add "without you," but they both knew she meant it.

He finally met her gaze. "You don't need me anymore," he said quietly.

"But Michael—"

Alex shook his head. "He's fine. He'll just need someone he can talk to. And Carlie, too—she'll be okay as long as Jake is. You promised you'd take care of what he needs this summer, and you know I can't help you with that anyway."

"But how will we manage all of that?" Her voice broke.

He shrugged. "I guess that's up to you and Vic to figure out."

"I guess so." She took a deep breath and swiped her thumbs under her eyes. "You'd better gather your stuff so we can get out of here."

"Fine. As soon as Phin gets his slimy ass out of our room, I'll get my things together. I told him to be gone before I got back. I also need to go over to the campus library and send the documents they want before my interview."

Dani sighed. "I'll get you some breakfast." She stood up and began to go through the last of the food they'd brought. This wasn't working out the way she'd had in mind. She wished she could talk to Gia and Eunice—together, they might figure out what to do next. She decided it was the last time she would ever get involved in something so far beyond her control. Before she could entertain that thought any further, she realized it was probably the last time she would ever have the chance, if Alex was right. As she dropped two pieces of bread into the toaster, she steeled her resolve. There was nothing for it but to walk into that meeting on Tuesday and do everything in her power not to lose her school.

After Alex left, Phin packed his bag, throwing everything in haphazardly. He emerged from the bedroom to retrieve his laptop, still open on the table. He hesitated only a moment before closing the email, shutting it down, and tucking it back into its case. He glanced around to make sure he hadn't left anything behind before leaving the townhouse.

For most of the early part of the day, Phin searched for Alex at the festival in hopes he was still in Peroo for the remainder of the scheduled activities. He even endured a particularly dull lecture about Russian influences on twentieth century American composers, hoping Alex might have stayed for that one—it sounded like his kind of thing. No luck. When he didn't find any of them in Peroo, he hoped Alex and the others had merely left before Phin could catch them, and he began searching the minute he returned to North Cowell. Alex wasn't waiting at the Railway Penny—not that Phin had honestly thought he would be—nor was he at Dani's. In fact, Dani herself seemed out of sorts and wouldn't give Phin much information except to say that Alex wasn't there.

Phin's desperation led him to drive to Alex's house, but no one was home; Alex's car was gone, and he didn't answer the door. The only other place Phin could think of was the community building where Alex had his studio. Phin headed there next, praying Alex would be seeking solace in his art. It didn't really matter whether that was a ridiculous idea stolen from too many over-the-top romantic movies; it was his last hope.

He raced from the parking lot and up the steps of the community building. When he tried the doors, they were locked. He peered through the glass, but there were no lights on anywhere. In frustration, he slammed the side of his fist against the building. He reeled back. "Ow!" he yelled. He cradled his sore right hand with his left. The combination of pain, exhaustion, and disappointment overwhelmed him; he sank down onto the steps and put his head in his hands. For the first time since Alex had left, he allowed the tears to come.

He felt movement beside him, but he kept his head down. A warm pair of arms encircled him, and he smelled delicate floral perfume. Curiosity got the better of him, and he looked up briefly to see that it was Eunice. He gave in, buried his head in her shoulder, and sobbed. Eunice didn't say a word; she just sat there, holding him the whole time, gently stroking his back.

Eventually, drained of his grief, he raised his head. He brushed his wrist across his eyes and tried to compose himself.

"What are you doing here at five on a Sunday evening, honey?" Eunice asked.

Phin sniffled a little and cleared his throat. "I, uh, I was looking for someone." He pulled back, and Eunice dropped one arm, leaving the other loosely around Phin's shoulders.

"I see. Alex?"

"Yeah. We, um, had a fight."

"Oh." Eunice squeezed his shoulder. "All couples fight, honey. It'll blow over."

He shook his head. "I don't think so. And we weren't exactly a couple." He grunted. "Or maybe we were. I don't know."

"You slept with him, didn't you?"

Phin jumped a little. "I can't believe you just asked me that. How did you know, anyway?"

She smiled and shook her head then reached out to pat Phin's arm with her free hand. "We've all seen you together. I knew it was just a matter of time. You look like hell, though. What happened?"

"I probably shouldn't tell you this, but..." Heaving a great sigh, Phin began to fill Eunice in on the details. He managed to leave out anything too personal, hoping to convey the story without going in depth. It was all he could do to hold it together while he talked.

When he was done, Eunice just sat there looking at him for a long, silent moment.

"Phin, what is it you expected?"

Startled, he turned to stare at her. "What do you mean?"

"I mean, what did you think you were going to do when you came here?"

"I thought I'd find Alex and explain things." He furrowed his brow in confusion.

"No, not here to this building. Here to this town." She gestured around.

"I thought—I thought maybe I could make a difference." He sighed. "I don't think I cared how I accomplished that, so long as I did my job and got paid. I trusted that Murdock knew what he was doing. When I found out he was a liar, I thought maybe I could fix it. I was determined to rescue the princess and collect my reward."

"And then what?"

"And then maybe the knight in shining armor could rescue *me*." His eyes stung.

"Mm-hm. And did it occur to you that nobody needed rescuing at all?" She folded her arms.

"I—" He paused. "No," he said at last. "Someone was always going to have to be the hero."

"Well, there's your problem right there. Go home, Phin. You're not our savior any more than State Ed is. Think about it, and while you're at it, stop looking for someone else to save your sorry ass." She stood up and looked down at Phin. "Give him time, honey. You're gonna have to show him that he meant more to you than whatever you thought you could get out of him to avoid screwing us over while still claiming your bonus check."

Phin watched her walk away, remaining where he was. He sat there until his legs were stiff and his back hurt from sitting on the concrete. He rose and drove slowly back to the inn. When he arrived back at the Railway Penny, Nicki-Anne was working at the desk. She waved cheerfully, but Phin could only muster a half-hearted wave and an incomplete smile.

Back in his room, he pulled out his laptop and turned it on. He opened his mail folder and located the email from Murdock then pulled out his phone. As he scrolled down his contacts list, something caught his eye. The phone number in Murdock's email signature was wrong. He glanced from the computer screen to his phone several times to make sure, but it was clearly several digits off. He sat back in his desk chair.

Puzzled, he stalled, staring at the screen. His fingers hovered over Murdock's name. "Screw it," he muttered, and pulled up the numeric pad instead. Carefully, he tapped the numbers from the email and hit "call." The phone rang several times before someone picked up.

"Hello?" The voice on the other end was unfamiliar.

"This is Phin Patterson. I got your email." Phin held his breath.

Several seconds passed in silence. Finally, the voice said, "Thank God. Phin, we need to talk. This is Greg Stevens at the State Education Department."

Phin was momentarily confused. "Who?"

"Greg Stevens. I was with Mr. Murdock in our meeting back in April."

Oh, my God. The baby-faced assistant. "I remember," Phin said.

"This isn't the time. We need to talk in person. I don't think you understand what's going on. Can you meet me tomorrow?"

"Where and when?"

"Let's meet up in Peroo at noon. I'm in Syracuse, but I'm headed home, and I can stop there."

"All right." With the details of their meeting secured, Phin hung up. He hoped Stevens could provide some answers.

Chapter Eighteen

Board of the Rings

PHIN SHOWED up at the school just long enough to let Dettweiler know that he would be in again the next day if he wanted to discuss anything before the board meeting. Dani was still a little touchy, and Alex hadn't shown up at all during the half hour Phin was in the building. Phin sensed there was more to it than just the argument he'd had with Alex, but there wasn't time to sort it all out before he had to be up in Peroo.

When Phin arrived at Sherry's Diner for the meeting, Greg Stevens was already there. He motioned to Phin from a corner booth where he sat with a table full of papers. He quickly swept them into a stack and slid them into his briefcase before standing up.

Stevens extended his hand. "Mr. Patterson," he said. "Thank you for meeting me like this." They sat down and Stevens continued, "I know you must have a number of questions, and I'll do my best to answer them."

"I actually only have one," Phin replied, sliding into the booth. "Why did you want to meet with me?"

"Ah. Of course. Well, I got your email about the board meeting in North Cowell, along with the draft version of your recommendations."

Phin frowned. "Right. And you said we needed to talk, so here I am. What would make you think I have any questions?"

Stevens leaned back in his seat, extending his arm of the back of the booth. He tapped the fingers of his other hand on the table, seemingly lost in thought for a moment. After a few minutes, he said, "Do you really not know what you're tangled up in, Mr. Patterson?"

Surprised, Phin said, "No, not at all. Would you mind filling me in?"

"Perhaps I should go back to our introductions. I'm not actually from NYSED." He sighed. "I was appointed by the state Attorney General's office to investigate certain educational management organizations and uncover any possible relationship with employees of the State Department of Education."

Phin swallowed. "You're investigating my father. That's why you thought I would have information."

"Partly," Stevens agreed. "But you also work with Donald Murdock. That wasn't an accident, by the way."

"I'm not sure what you mean." Phin narrowed his gaze.

"Your connection to your father made you ideally suited to being part of the investigation. You've worked with Murdock in the past, so it wasn't a stretch to bring you in again."

"Hiring me was your idea?"

"Yes and no. I suggested Murdock might like a closer connection to his, how do I put this, business associates. Obviously there are only so many consultants with ties both to NYSED and EduText."

Phin felt slightly sick. "You used me to get to my father."

Stevens cocked his head to the side. "You might say that, yes. And also to get to Murdock."

The conversation Phin had had with Dani the previous week replayed in his mind. "He's profiting from companies like EduText."

"Yes. We've nearly got him nailed down, and I was hoping I could count on you to help see it through."

"With all due respect, Mr. Stevens, I have no idea how I could possibly—"

"You've already done it. The report you created casts enough doubt to warrant further investigation into Murdock's practices, especially when it comes to overseeing schools that have failed to meet state standards. There's no chance the school closing won't be seen for what it is."

"But that's not the real report!" Phin protested. "One of the school employees found out what was happening, and she came up with a plan for how to stop this charter from going through. I gave her the real report, which is vastly different from this one. I only said it was in draft to keep Murdock from knowing the truth before the board meeting."

"I'm sorry that you already had something worked out, Mr. Patterson. If you'd sent this earlier, or if I'd known something of what was going on, I'd have advised you differently."

Phin glared at Stevens. "Differently, how? What would you have had me do?"

"For one thing, I would've told you to stay away from talking to any of the employees about this. That was a foolish thing you did," Stevens admonished him. "At this point, the important thing is that you know now, so you can act accordingly. This charter needs to go through, or we won't be able to catch Murdock. Those papers will be signed and ready to go by the day after the board meeting. Once we have that in hand, we have enough information to make sure Murdock is arrested for fraud."

"If I go along with this, it will ruin my career."

"You already played with fire by making a deal with Murdock," Stevens reminded him. "And besides, your report here isn't the real issue. It's making sure that those papers get signed. You're not on Murdock's payroll, you're on the school district's. No one's going to touch you. This is about weeding out corruption at the state level."

For a moment, Phin's mouth hung open. "You would really sacrifice the school for this? Murdock is worth that much to you?"

"The charter isn't really going to happen, Mr. Patterson. You know that. It's only the signatures and only for the sake of taking out Murdock." He looked at Phin, and his eyes flashed. "We go after EduText when we're done."

"That isn't what I meant. You and I both know that with North Cowell's failure to achieve the state standards, they will have no choice but to take other disciplinary action against the school. Jobs—people's lives—are at stake here. The town is trying to save their school."

Stevens shrugged. "So, tell your school to take it up with the NYSED people. I'm sure there's a way to buy some time. But not until after this whole thing goes down," he warned.

Crossing his arms and sitting back, Phin said, "And what if I refuse to comply? I made a promise to them."

"Then un-promise it," Stevens told him. He leaned forward. "I have enough dirt on you, Mr. Patterson, to last a lifetime. You think I don't know about all those little games you played when you worked for Edu-

Text yourself? Or the ones you used as a consultant?" Stevens wasn't blushing this time when he referenced Phin's less orthodox practices.

For half a second, Phin was tempted to simply say, "Fuck you," and walk away. He didn't, though. He sighed and ran a hand through his hair. "What do you need from me?"

Stevens replied, "Just show up at that meeting with your report in hand. The one you sent me, not the one you claim is the real one. For now, that's all we'll require." He smirked. "Unless we need you to testify against your father, of course."

Phin stood up and grabbed his bag from the seat. "Fine. I'll do it. But don't come crying to me if this blows up in your face. You've no idea who you're messing with by taking on the people in North Cowell. They're not going to take it lying down."

"And you have no idea who you're messing with right now," Stevens shot back. "But by all means, go ahead and try to stop this train wreck of an educational system we've got going. This isn't personal, Mr. Patterson. It's all about making sure people like Murdock can't take advantage of the process anymore." He gestured at the seat across from him. "Now, why don't you sit back down, and we'll have some lunch."

"No thanks," Phin responded. He turned around and walked three paces before looking back at Stevens. "You're wrong, Mr. Stevens. It *is* personal. It's *always* personal." He shifted his bag higher on his shoulder and walked out of the diner.

Inside his car, he turned it over in his mind. He wasn't sure if he entirely believed Stevens' claim that his role at the school board meeting was that important. On the other hand, if Stevens was right, it could stop Murdock from doing something similar in another district. Phin only had two choices, and he had less than two days to figure out which one he would make. He didn't even have the option of asking Dani for help; there was no way she could be objective.

There wasn't anything left to do but drive back to North Cowell and hope that he made the right decision when it came down to it.

All day before the board meeting, Dani was on edge. She noticed that Phin seemed distant as well, but she chalked that up to the tension from the previous weekend. Alex hadn't returned yet, which she thought was probably good; the last thing Phin needed was to have another argument with him right before the board meeting.

Everything was in place. Dani had called Anita Silas to confirm that she was ready for the meeting. The only problem was that she still hadn't had a chance to go over plans with Phin. He'd been in to school briefly to talk to Gary and tell him something had come up. Even when he returned, he'd been mostly unavailable except for a few minutes when he arrived and when he left. When she had tried to give him the papers for the meeting, he had told her he would collect them later. Every time she saw him, he appeared to be rushing off somewhere. A NYSED representative was supposed to be present at the meeting, so she assumed that was part of what Phin was dealing with. As long as they caught up before the board meeting started, she could give him what he needed then.

Now, shortly before the board meeting was scheduled to begin, Dani stood outside the doors of the lower gymnasium, waiting for Phin. She had told him to find her there so she could give him the copies of his report for the school board members.

When Phin showed up at last, he rushed up to her. His face was pale and drawn. "I'm sorry I'm running late. Just give me what you need to and let's get in there."

Dani handed him the papers. "Are you feeling okay? You don't look good."

He accepted the stack. "It's nothing. I'll be fine."

She frowned. "If you say so. Anita Silas already knows about this, and she's prepared to bring it up. I already told her to wait until after Pepper Britt or Ed Dunlop unveils the school improvement plan. Either of them is a likely culprit in this whole mess."

"Uh..." Phin replied, but he didn't have time to follow that up with anything. A bland, baby-faced young man showed up at his side and greeted him, drawing him away from the crowd of people heading into the gym.

Dani wrinkled her nose and put her tongue out. She'd expected to have a few minutes to go over what Phin intended to say regarding his recommendations for a school improvement plan. Her stomach clenched, and she remembered what Alex had said about trusting him, but she closed her mind to those thoughts. She slipped inside the gym and looked around for Gia and Eunice. When she finally spotted them, she hurried over to claim a seat before someone else did.

"You ready for this?" she asked.

"Honey, bring it on. I'm ready for anything," Eunice said. "Are you sure our Phin's ready, though? He looks a little green." She waved her hand toward the row of chairs at the front of the room.

Dani shrugged. "No idea. He's been a little off all day, but I think he's just still feeling upset about what happened with Alex."

Gia leaned over. "What did happen with Alex?" she asked.

Before Dani could answer, the moderator stepped up to the podium. Dani whispered to Gia, "I'll tell you later."

Once everyone settled down, the moderator called the meeting to order and announced the agenda. They suffered through several items of business unrelated to the charter before the moderator introduced the topic.

Ed Dunlop stood up and crossed to the podium. He cleared his throat and glanced back at the other board members. Returning his attention to the assembled teachers and parents, he said, "I'm sure many of you are aware that our school has faced some challenges with the new Common Core and the increased number of state-required tests." There was a general murmur of assent, and Ed continued. "I am disappointed to report that our school has failed to pass an adequate number of students for the past two years. This year, should the numbers remain below expectation, we will have no choice but to restructure the entire North Cowell school system."

A cry of surprise rose up from the audience. Several voices could be heard saying, "No!" Chatter escalated to a volume unsuitable for continued dialog, and the moderator banged his gavel for silence.

Ed held up his hand. "We're joined tonight by a representative of the New York State Education Department who has been working with us on our situation." He indicated the dull young man Dani had seen with Phin earlier. "We have explored several options, and we have concluded that the best one available to us is to allow an educational management organization to help us put a charter in place. That would mean having someone else do the work of sorting out the challenges and deciding which of our programs to change or remove in order to focus more time and energy on meeting the standards. We have already had a visiting consultant in the school for the last several weeks, making notes on where we can improve the learning environment." He gestured to Phin.

Phin stood up and approached the podium slowly. He took his

place beside Ed, who continued speaking. "Phin Patterson was recommended by NYSED and hired by Principal Gary Dettweiler to observe patterns within our school that could be detrimental to the learning environment. He will now give us a summary of his findings." Ed stepped aside to let Phin have the microphone.

For a moment, Phin seemed to hesitate before taking Ed's place. Dani felt just a little sorry for him. Ed was unpleasant on his best days and intimidating on his worst; Phin must have been feeling the strain. He cleared his throat and looked back at the young man who had accompanied him in. The man gave a curt nod, which Phin returned before addressing the assembly. "I have spent the past five weeks visiting classrooms, taking notes and talking with teachers and other professionals in the building." His voice shook a little. "I feel that the school's programs are unique and offer a taste of the local culture of North Cowell. When carried out under ideal circumstances, those programs would be an excellent addition to any school district."

He stopped talking, and Dani wondered why he was stalling. He looked slightly sick, and she hoped he was all right. It occurred to her that he could face consequences from what she had planned. The thought made her uncomfortable on his behalf, but she determined that it was worth it. If he hadn't wanted to go along with her plan, he would have said so—she was sure of it.

After a moment, Phin continued. "Unfortunately, the conditions are not ideal they rarely are." His voice grew stronger, and he held his head up. "My recommendations are as follows. Eliminate unnecessary positions and remove problematic staff members. I have compiled a report, which the board members have in hand, detailing which teachers should be considered for removal or relocation within the building, depending on their evaluations. I strongly urge the school board to sign the necessary papers in order to form a charter school overseen by Edu-Text."

Dani's mouth dropped open. She looked up at Phin, and their eyes met. For just a moment, she saw a flicker of something—remorse? apology?—before his gaze steeled and he looked away. Determined not to let it go, Dani stood up.

"That hardly seems like a reasonable solution," she said, speaking loud enough to be heard over the ensuing chatter. "I'm sure there are other options—"

Ed cut in and waved his hand dismissively. "This is just a formality to confirm our decision. We are already proceeding on the charter."

Someone in the crowd called out, "What was the point of having a consultant, then? I thought this was a meeting to decide what we were going to do."

"No," Ed replied. "This was a meeting to inform you of our decision."

"What if the consultant had reached a different conclusion?" Dani fired back, trying to give Phin a path back to their original plan.

Ed didn't respond, though it was hard to tell whether that was intentional or if he simply couldn't hear or be heard. Her voice was drowned in a chorus of parents and staff members all talking at once. It was obvious she wasn't the only one blindsided, but she was the only one who knew the truth. What had happened that Phin hadn't stuck with their plan? She tried to catch his eye again, but he wasn't looking in her direction.

By that time, general pandemonium had broken out. Angry parents demanded an explanation, and board members were attempting to speak over them in order to bring the discussion back around. The moderator looked bored; he wasn't bothering to control the audience at that point, opting to let them go.

"What the hell just happened?" Eunice asked, turning toward Dani.

"I have no idea," she replied. "That was definitely not part of the plan. I hope Anita can do something, because at this point, I'm at a loss."

Anita was trying to get the moderator's attention. After several minutes, she succeeded, and the moderator banged his gavel. When the crowd didn't immediately respond, the moderator motioned to the security guard, who shifted menacingly. The furor died down, and Anita stepped up to the microphone.

"Mr. Patterson, it is my understanding that you have some association with the company that holds the charter. Is that correct?"

Phin fiddled with his cuffs, and he leaned around behind the person next to him to say something to the NYSED representative. The young man replied, but Dani couldn't hear either of them.

"Yes," Phin told Anita. "The company is owned by my father. However, I am not on the payroll of EduText in any way. I was contacted directly by NYSED and hired independently by the district. My financial records are available publicly, and anyone who wishes to do so may check." He glanced briefly over at the man from NYSED before continuing. "I do strongly suggest that you look into the records of anyone else who may or may not be connected with the process." The NYSED representative didn't look happy, but he didn't make any objections.

"This is highly questionable," Anita said to Ed. "Had I known about all of this, I would not have agreed on this course of action."

A parent in the back of the room asked, "So, there's nothing we can do about this? Nothing at all?"

"Of course there is," Ed replied. "You can make sure your children are attending school and doing their work. If this option doesn't appeal to you, children who choose not to participate in the charter may be homeschooled or sent to one of the surrounding towns. I'm sure the half-hour drive will be worth it." Dani heard the slight sneer in his voice.

"I've got nothing to lose," Eunice whispered. She stood up. "What about you, Ed? What are you getting out of this? Surely you want your children to have the best education possible."

"Of course I do," he replied. "Which is why they will be attending the private Catholic school in Morton Ponds."

The sudden collective outrage was so forceful that Eunice was startled off her feet and back into her chair. There was no recovery at that point; the board meeting had devolved into a shouting match with everyone demanding to know why Ed thought his children were special and didn't need to be educated at the local public school. Dani was surprised that people weren't actually throwing things at Ed by that point.

No matter how hard the moderator banged his gavel, no one paid any attention. The security guard looked at the moderator for help in figuring out who to remove, but there was no way to tell where the greatest part of the chaos was being generated. Anita and Ed had started a heated debate, most of which was lost because of the shouting in the crowd. The other board members remained frozen in their seats, looking from Anita to Ed while they argued. The NYSED representative looked unconcerned.

Phin leaned over again and tapped the man on the shoulder. They had a brief exchange, after which Phin slid out of his seat and walked out. Dani wasn't about to sit there waiting for the meeting to be over before she confronted Phin, so she excused herself from Gia and Eunice, both of whom wore identical mystified expressions. She rolled her eyes and scooted out of her seat.

When she caught up with Phin, he was on his way out of the building. "Phin!" she called, trying to control her anger.

He spun around to face her. "I can't talk to you right now," he said. He sounded tired.

Rage surged up in Dani, and she stepped into Phin's personal space. She reached out and slapped him as hard as she could. He reeled backward, his hand flying to his face.

"You absolute fucking bastard!" she screamed at him. "You coward! You spent five weeks lying to us, screwed us all, and now you won't even talk to me?"

"I can't!" he yelled. "I can't say a damn thing to you. Leave me alone, Dani. You have no idea what's going on. Stop fucking around with things you don't understand before something else happens you can't control." He turned away from her and began walking.

"Alex was right about you!" she called after him. "He said you would do this to us. I didn't believe him. I chose someone I barely knew over one I've known over half my life. I hope you're happy!" She wished she had something to throw at him; the slap hadn't done nearly enough to dampen her fury. "Fuck you, Phin Patterson!" she screamed after him.

Phin never responded. He continued to walk away, leaving Dani staring after him wondering what had gone wrong.

Chapter Nineteen

Tapestry of Failures

WHEN THE dust had settled from the board meeting, Phin stood beside his bed at the Railway Penny, neatly folding clothes and laying them in his suitcase. The television played quietly in the background; Phin had turned it on in a poor attempt to distract himself from the misery of his own making. He'd spent his last days in North Cowell avoiding coming into contact with anyone associated with the school. It wasn't as hard as he'd imagined. Sneaking out early, arriving home late, and spending time in neighboring towns had been plenty. The real problem would be checking out. He thought he might just sit in his car and stalk the inn until he saw Vic leave so he could deal with one of his employees instead.

Just as he was putting a t-shirt away, something on the news caught his attention. The warm voice of the noontime news anchor intoned, "And in other news, Donald Murdock of the New York State Education Department has been arrested on charges of fraud. No word yet on whether there was involvement by any of his associates. The State Attorney General's office could not be reached at this time for comment. NYSED is expected to issue a statement later today in a press conference. We'll bring you live coverage as the details unfold."

Phin clutched the t-shirt tightly, anger flaring in his chest. Stevens had gotten his man, all right, but the price had been paid by the students and staff of the North Cowell school. Phin slammed the shirt into his suitcase and reached for another. After taking out his frustration on several more shirts, Phin had had enough. He left his belongings strewn around the room, grabbed nothing but his keys, and headed out. On his way past, he saw that Vic wasn't at his desk, which meant he was probably with Dani. Phin wasn't sure whether that would make much of a difference.

When he reached Dani's house, he knocked forcefully on the door. "Dani?" he called, banging harder. "Dani! Vic! Open the fucking door!"

To Phin's surprise, it was Jake who let him in. The boy's eyes were wide and his mouth was open a little. Looking past him, Phin saw Carlie peering around the corner from the kitchen. She had a hand over her mouth, suppressing a giggle.

"You said the f-word," she told him. "Mom's gonna be mad."

Dani appeared in the doorway to the kitchen. She frowned at Phin then turned to Carlie. "I'm sure you and Jake have heard Michael say it plenty of times. And that's the least of my problems with Mr. Patterson at the moment. Carlie, could you take Jake upstairs for a little while so the grown-ups can talk?"

Carlie shrugged. "C'mon, Jake. Let's go play a game." She leaned in and stage-whispered, "If we leave the door open, we'll hear everything anyway."

Dani gave Carlie a threatening look as the children walked past to the stairs. She turned her attention to Phin. "What the hell are you doing here, Phin? I don't have anything else to say to you."

"You do seem to have said it all with that slap, yes. But *I* have something to say, and I need you to listen."

She sighed. "Fine. You get five minutes. If I don't like what you're sharing, you shut up and get out of my house. Agreed?"

"Agreed."

Dani stalked into the kitchen, and Phin followed her. She didn't offer him anything, and he didn't ask. It was enough that she was willing to give him a few minutes to explain. He sat down at the table, but she remained standing, leaning against the counter with her arms crossed.

"Well?" she said. "I'm waiting."

"Did you watch the noon news?"

"No," she huffed. "I don't have a lot of extra time for that sort of thing."

"Well, I did. Donald Murdock has been arrested."

Dani's eyebrows rose, but she didn't say anything.

Phin continued, "That's what this was about. On Monday, Greg Stevens from the Attorney General's office came to see me. He told me to make sure your plan failed and that Murdock wasn't exposed as a fraud at the meeting so that the dirty board members couldn't find a way to cover his tracks for him. Stevens is going after my father, and he threatened to go after me as well if I didn't do as he said."

"Why didn't you say anything?"

"I wanted to tell you—I really did. But I couldn't put Stevens' investigation at risk."

Dani shook her head. "Phin, even if what you're saying is true, why did you go along with it? You knew that either way, we were finished. Was it just to save your own ass?"

He shook his head. "No. In fact, I wasn't even going to do it at first. But, Dani, if I hadn't, you would've been in much more trouble than what actually happened." He looked down at the table, fighting the well of emotions threatening to erupt again. "Because of me—what I did while I was here."

"You mean who," Dani muttered. Louder, she said, "Because of Alex."

"Yes. I didn't want any of you to get in trouble because of—because we slept together." He shook his head. "It wasn't professional, on either of our parts."

Dani tilted her head to the side. "You really are in love with him, aren't you?"

He nodded miserably. "God, Dani. I'm so far gone." He ran his hand through his hair and took a minute to get hold of himself. He didn't need Dani to think he was using his emotional response to get to her. "But it's not just Alex. It's all of the rest of you, too. I let myself get too close, and I got caught up in it. Stevens knew about my history, and he wouldn't have cared who was in his path if he went after me. I couldn't let you be punished for my crimes."

"You should have let us be the judge of that," Dani said.

"Yeah, I know that now. I had in mind to just quietly leave after I was through and wait until I heard something from Stevens about the situation. He said that once they had a case against Murdock, your school could pursue action to prevent the state from forcing changes until you've had the chance to clean up from Murdock's mess. I was going to contact you later and tell you that. But since I'm still here, I think I can help you."

Dani scoffed. "Haven't you 'helped' us enough already? I don't think there's much you can do."

"Actually, there is. I know someone who can represent you legally, and you can petition the state to give you time to find a better solution. I give you my word, I will do whatever I can for you to make this happen."

"You would do that for us?" Dani sounded surprised. Her posture relaxed.

"Of course. I helped create this problem, so it's my job to give you a hand sorting it all out. Please, Dani," he begged, "don't give up on this." He cleared his throat. "Don't give up on me."

She studied him, her expression still hard. "All right. I'll consider it."

At that moment, Vic walked into the house carrying several bags of groceries. When he entered the kitchen, his attention immediately focused on Phin. "Aw, hell. Man, what are you doing here? I thought you were gonna be gone by now." He dumped the bags on the counter and began emptying the contents, setting things on the counter forcefully. He kept his back to Phin.

"I'm trying to make this right, Vic."

Vic offered a humorless laugh. "Right. A lot like how you've made so many other things right since you got here. You are out of your damn mind, Phin. You hurt all of us with this crazy-ass shit you've pulled. Now, get out."

Dani put her hand on his arm. "Wait. Phin, why don't you explain to Vic what you told me? See what he has to say."

Spinning to face Dani, Vic said, "Are you shitting me, Dani? You can't possibly believe a word he says at this point." He glared over his shoulder at Phin. "I should've known better. It's not like you weren't clear about it when you showed up here."

"Please hear me out," Phin said. "Donald Murdock was arrested."

"Who in the ever-living hell is Donald Murdock?"

"The NYSED asshat who hired me," Phin replied. "Don't you remember me telling you that? He was charged with fraud. That's what this whole thing was about, Vic. I was planning to do whatever Dani wanted me to, but Greg Stevens from the Attorney General's office showed up saying he was after Murdock. He threatened me and basically said I was impeding his investigation if I didn't go along with my contractual obligation. My hands were tied until the arrest, but now I'm advising Dani on what to do next."

Vic sighed. "I want to believe you, Phin, I really do. But how can I know you're telling us the truth this time?"

"Because I'm willing to go all the way to Albany to petition for your school to have time to find a solution before they take disciplinary action. With Murdock gone and the public eye on the oversight of districts not meeting the standards, we can force their hand on this. They won't want a repeat of this problem."

Vic crossed to the table and sat down, followed by Dani. "So what do you propose we do?"

"I'm going to start by calling my lawyer friend. Meanwhile, Dani, why don't you talk to Gia and Eunice? We'll need representatives of the school to go to Albany, and having respected teachers do it isn't a bad idea."

Dani sat looking at Phin for what felt like an eternity. He grew hot under her fierce gaze. Finally, she said, "In my mind, I know that it's not a good idea to put any further trust in you. But something in my heart wants to try one last time. If you do anything that looks like another lie, though, you are going to wish you'd never set foot in North Cowell. Stevens thinks he has dirt on you? Good—I'll find a way to get it out of him, add my own to the extent it doesn't screw up our lives, and make sure you never work anywhere near another school. Clear?"

"Perfectly," Phin replied. "Now, if you'll excuse me, I'm going to call my friend. I'll let you know what she wants to do." He turned to Vic. "Looks like I may need to stick around for a bit. Okay with you?"

Vic shrugged. "Long as I get paid, it doesn't matter."

"Fine." Phin stood up. "I'll talk to you in the next day or so, Dani. We'll get this worked out somehow."

On his way back to the Railway Penny, Phin reviewed what he was going to tell his lawyer, hoping she was up for the challenge. If not, he would need to manage on his own—there was no way he would let Dani and the others down again.

Before Phin entered the Railway Penny, he heard a voice behind him.

"Wait."

He turned around. Vic stood there, arms crossed.

Phin sighed. "What?"

"I wanted to talk to you without Dani. You may have her fooled, but I know the truth."

"You know what, Vic? Go to hell." Phin turned around again, only to feel a strong pair of hands turning him and shoving him roughly against the wall of the building. He wriggled to get free, but Vic had him held fast.

"I did everything I could for you, and you screwed us over. Now, you are going to listen to me, or so help me God I'm going to carry out Dani's threat to ruin you."

Phin stopped struggling. "Fine. What do you want to say to me?"

"I want to know what you're getting out of this. You've flipped so many times since you've been here that I've lost track. Even if you do what you promised, there's nothing that says you won't go back home and do it all over again in some other tiny town that doesn't have the resources to fight you." Vic's nostrils flared and his eyes were hard. He didn't let go of Phin's shoulders.

Phin wanted to look away. His heart pounded and sweat broke out on his forehead. It was time to stop running. He took a deep breath, swallowed his pride, and said, "I let myself get caught."

Vic's expression changed from angry to confused. "I'm not sure what you mean."

"I spent a long time playing people, telling myself it didn't matter as long as no one knew and no one got hurt. Except *I* got hurt, Vic. It hurt from the first time. Do you remember Meredith Hill?"

"Oh, hell. You were in love with her, weren't you?" Vic loosened his grip and shook his head. "I thought you just liked the power trip."

"No." Phin huffed. "All right, I did actually enjoy that. And it wasn't always bad, either. It was fun when it was with people like Gia, who didn't have any expectations other than having a good time. But it didn't change that I was lost and couldn't find my way back after she left me."

Vic dropped his hands. "You never told me what happened."

Phin ran a hand through his hair. "Eight years, Vic. She'd signed a contract with the company, so she was in town whenever we had new materials for her. In between, she wrote to me—long, poetic letters about how much I meant to her. I went out with other people while we were in college and even afterward, but she was the reason I was never serious with anyone. I thought she was waiting for me."

"But she wasn't."

"Yeah, only I didn't know that. When she told me she was getting married, I begged her to give me a chance. Do you know what she said to me? She said she thought I understood it was just sex. I'd saved every fucking letter she sent to me, and after that, I burned them all."

Vic said, "I always thought you were already using your skills to make sales before then."

Phin shook his head. "Not like that. I was full of shit back then—even you know that. It was a lot of talk. No, I was just good at reading people and giving them a bit of wish fulfillment. It wasn't anything more until after *her*."

"Fine. I get that you're a misunderstood hero. But what the hell happened here that you're ready to suddenly go all noble?"

"You don't know? You said it yourself."

Vic's mouth dropped open. "Alex."

"Yeah."

"I was joking," Vic said. "I just wanted to give you a rough time 'cause you seemed like you had kind of a thing for him. You were serious?"

"God, yes. Right now, he won't even talk to me. But I'll be damned if I'm going to lose him the way I lost her."

Vic stepped aside and leaned against the wall next to Phin. "I know how that feels."

"Dani?"

"Yeah. I owe you for that. If you hadn't shown up, I was going to give up on us. Damn it, I hate admitting you did anything good while you were here." He chuckled.

Phin relaxed. "I'm sorry I never told you. I didn't think you'd understand."

"I probably wouldn't have at the time."

Rolling his head to the side so he could look at Vic, Phin said, "Are we cool?"

Vic raised his fist, and Phin bumped it with his own. "Yeah. We're cool." His expression darkened slightly. "You'd better fix this, Phin. You pull it off and I swear I will throw you the biggest fucking victory party you've ever seen. Blow it, and I'll make it my life's mission to destroy you."

Phin laughed. "I believe that. But you'll have to take a number because Dani's going to get there first. Listen, I need to go call my lawyer. You remember Sue, right?"

"She's a lawyer now? Damn. Always knew that woman was brilliant. I'm not surprised. If she's your lawyer, you're in good hands."

"I know it. I'll see you later." He pushed off the wall and stepped around Vic. Before he entered the Railway Penny, he glanced back over his shoulder and gave Vic a sly grin. "We've got this." He waved and gave Vic a thumbs up before pushing open the door and stepping inside.

Back in his room, he pulled out his phone and scrolled through his contacts until he found the number he wanted. Susan Wilson-Howard was Phin's personal lawyer as well as a friend. She was an expert in education law, and he had worked with her before in situations where a school district was forced to make a decision regarding disciplinary action. She was as willing as Phin to adopt unorthodox methods if she felt the situation called for it, but she also knew what she was doing. Like Phin, she had become frustrated and concerned with the direction for-profit education was headed. Unlike Phin, she'd already started doing something about it.

When Phin called her, he discovered she had been following the news with interest after learning of Murdock's arrest. "I saw the whole thing," she said. "What I don't understand is how on earth you got mixed up in this whole thing."

"Murdock sent me to the school," he said. "It was my job to evaluate them for the charter to go through." He took a deep breath and started talking.

After he explained what they needed, she was eager to help. "How soon can you return to Buffalo to meet with me? We need to go over a strategy. I have an idea, but I want to show you everything and map it all out in person. There are several ways we can do this. For one thing, Murdock tried to move before having the district's test scores in hand. That's poor form. It's our job to persuade NYSED to give the district more time so they can find their own solution, and that could be one way to do it."

"While I was here, I saw their programs firsthand. What I don't understand is why their scores are so low in the first place. They need some help tightening up their methods, but that's easily done." He thought for a moment. "You know, Al—the school psychologist suggested they've seen some growth in recent years. The town has expanded, and they've implemented some new things. I wonder if there's any correlation."

"There could be," Susan agreed. "Can you get the records from the last several years for comparison?"

"Absolutely. I'll bring them when I see you."

"In the meantime, have someone at the school put together a proposal. They need to at least have some idea what they need time for. Whether that's to tighten their programs, as you say, or for some other purpose, NYSED will need action steps."

Phin replied, "Good thinking. First, I need to talk to Gary Dettweiler, the principal, to get him on board. I'll take care of all that and meet you in a few days." When he hung up, he called Dani to tell her what was going on.

"I'm going to stop by the school on Monday to talk to Gary about this, and then I'm headed back to Buffalo for a bit," he told her.

"When will you be back?" she asked.

"End of the week. Susan thinks we need some time to draft a proposal and develop a plan. After that, we'll need to go to Albany."

"All right. I'll fill Eunice and Gia in, but I expect you to stay in contact while you're gone. I'm wary, Phin. Very wary."

"I know. Listen, I'll call you from Susan's office so you can hear our conversation. Will that help?"

"It's a step," Dani replied. "Listen, I need to go. I'll see you tomorrow."

"Sure." He ended the call and sighed. It was the best he could do, but it still didn't seem like enough.

He resumed the packing he'd previously abandoned, leaving out only whatever he might need for the next couple of days. When he opened up his briefcase to tuck some files away, a paper, folded in half twice, fell out. He picked it up and unfolded it.

"Damn it to hell," he muttered and promptly had to fight back tears. It was a bulletin from the church service Alex had brought him to.

He wasn't sure why he'd bothered to save it. He crumpled the bulletin and hurled it at the wall. It dropped harmlessly—and unsatisfyingly—to the floor. Phin sat back down on the bed and flopped backwards, running his hands over his face. For some time, he lay there, staring up at the ceiling.

He needed to do something. He thought showing up at Alex's church again might be in poor taste. If Alex didn't want to talk to him, it might cause a scene. Much as he wasn't sure he personally cared about disrupting a church service, he was certain it wouldn't drive Alex to listen to him. He had to think of something else. He sat up and leaned his elbows on his thighs, looking around the room for inspiration.

He spotted the desk in the corner, a small tablet and a pen sitting off to the side where Phin had pushed them to make room for his own papers and laptop. He crossed the room and picked up the pen, turning it over in his hand. Not having an alternative, it would have to do. He sat down at the desk and pulled the pad of paper toward himself then closed his eyes, thinking. When he opened them again, he set the pen to the paper and began to draw.

Phin arrived just as classes were starting. It was the first day of exam week, so the secondary students' schedules were odd and the teachers in the upper grades were all proctoring tests. He hoped Gary would still be in his office rather than in a meeting. Phin stopped by the desk to talk to Dani for a moment.

"Morning," he said, trying to sound more casual than he felt.

"Hello, Phin." She didn't look up from whatever she was typing.

"Is Gary in?"

"Yes. But if you want to see him, you'll have to do it right away. He said he has a meeting later this morning."

"Well, that's why I'm here," Phin told her. "Can you see if he's available?"

She shrugged and picked up the phone. "Gary? Mr. Patterson's here to see you." She paused. "Sure." As she hung up the phone she said, "You can go in."

Before Phin stepped around to the door into the office, he held out an envelope to Dani. He cleared his throat. "Could you do me one other favor?"

She eyed him. "That depends on what it is."

He took a deep breath. "Alex won't see me, but I need to give him this. Please," he said. "It's important."

Dani looked from the envelope in Phin's hand to his face. "All right." She accepted the envelope.

Relieved, Phin thanked her and rounded the corner to the office door. Dani let him in, and he crossed the office to knock on Gary's door. After a moment, Gary appeared and beckoned Phin inside.

The office was in disarray. There were a couple of boxes filled with books and another one with personal affects. Phin frowned in confusion, but he had more important concerns. He remained standing awkwardly just inside the door, noting that both chairs were taken up with stacks of papers.

"I came to talk to you about the school," Phin said.

"What's there to talk about? You did what you were supposed to do, and now it's over. It's just part of all the growing pains with the new standards." He tossed a handful of papers into the recycle bin.

"Surely you've seen the news," Phin said.

Gary scoffed. "Of course I have. Why do you think I'm packing up my office?" He gestured around. "I told you before that it didn't matter what you did here—I was gone either way."

"It doesn't have to be like that," Phin told him.

After putting a picture frame in one of the boxes, Gary stepped around his desk to stand in front of Phin. "You and I both know that after what happened, there was no way I could keep my job. Either I was gone because of the charter or I was gone because of the shady dealings of Mr. Murdock and three members of our school board. No matter how you look at it, I was always going to be caught in the middle. Just one of the perks of being the principal."

"But that's what I came to talk to you about," Phin said. "We're not leaving things like this. I don't know what can be done about the school board, but I've hired a lawyer. She wants to take your case to NYSED and plead for more time."

"That's not how it works, Mr. Patterson."

"It does in this case because of Murdock. He worked for them, and it caused harm to a school district. My lawyer recommends that your school have a plan in place for an alternative. You at least need to do something until they figure out what to do with you."

"*I* don't need to do anything," Gary informed him. "I don't work here anymore." He sighed. "And really, it doesn't matter."

"Doesn't it? It's your job. How can it be so unimportant to you?"

Suddenly, Gary laughed. "Did you know I hated this job?" When Phin said nothing, he continued. "Oh, not right away. But I grew to despise it. I thought I could make a difference. I had a handful of idealistic teachers who wanted to make this school like some of the ones we'd heard about that used a wider range of creative learning strategies. We focused on the arts and sciences, and we hoped it would be enough. Until it wasn't. I couldn't do anything about the bigger issues—we never really resolved them, just kept adding new things to make them go away."

"Your methods are actually on the right track," Phin said. "I've been at this long enough to know that much. If you kept going, tweaked it a bit—"

Gary cut him off. "You think you can make that happen? Be my guest. As for me, I need to get out of here. I'm sure I'll never work as a principal again, and quite frankly, that suits me fine. I'd rather be back in the classroom anyhow, if I can get a job."

"Why not stay here? I really think you need to listen to me," Phin begged. "I'm not giving up on this school. I lied, Mr. Dettweiler. I played along at that board meeting because of the investigation into Murdock's tactics. But this is what I really saw here." He handed Gary a copy of the report he wished he'd been able to share at the meeting.

"I don't have time for this," Gary said, tossing the papers onto his desk. "But you're welcome to share it with Karen Winthrop. She's an assistant principal, and she'll be taking over my place until they hire someone."

Phin changed strategies. "You don't have to stay on as principal. Just don't leave until we've made our case to the state. Please. We're going next week, and I want to take people from the school with me."

Gary turned back to his packing. "By all means, go for it. Just don't involve me." He looked up at Phin. "Take Dani. She can represent me as my administrative assistant. Or rather, former administrative assistant. I suppose she works for Karen now."

"All right. I'll need a couple of your teachers as well."

"You figure that part out, Mr. Patterson. I told you, I don't want to be part of this."

"Fine. Just don't do anything until we get back. The world could use more idealists, Mr. Dettweiler."

Gary grunted. "Tell that to people like Murdock who are ready to take advantage of us."

Phin turned around to leave. As he put his hand on the door handle, he said, "Just think about what I said."

"I will," Gary replied, though he didn't sound convincing.

Stepping out into the office, Phin pulled the door closed behind him. He approached Dani again. "I talked to Gary, but he's not interested in helping us. Can't say I blame him, but it's too bad he doesn't want to see this through. Listen, can you be free to make a trip to Albany next week?"

Dani swiveled around in her chair and looked up at Phin. "What?"

"Albany. Next week. Gary said I should take you as his representative." He grinned. "You, Gia, Eunice, and me. That could be an interesting road trip."

"I don't know..."

"Come on, Dani. I made a promise to you, and I intend to keep it. Truth is, I think the three of you could do this without me, but I'm already involved. Don't leave me hanging."

She chuckled. "Fine. I'll make arrangements. I'm sure my mother will watch the kids for a couple of days. When?"

"Early next week. I'm going home tonight, and I need a few days with Sue to work out the details. She'll set up the meeting for us."

"Okay." Dani shook her head. "What is it about you that I just can't help myself?"

He grinned broadly at her. "It's my natural charm."

"Yeah, right. More like your superior skills of manipulation." She tilted her head to the side. "Underneath it all, I think you're actually a decent guy, Phin. I just wish you would find a way to be that person on the job and not just when you're solving people's personal crises."

"I'm working on that. See you next week, then?"

"Next week," she agreed.

Phin left the office and walked out of the building into the bright sunlight. He breathed in deeply and exhaled slowly, steeling his resolve. It was time to do this.

Chapter Twenty

Phin Patterson and the Chamber of Education

WHEN DANI told Vic what was going on and how she was involved, she half expected him to put up a protest. The last time she'd seen Phin, Vic had been beyond angry with him and had followed him to give him a piece of his mind. He hadn't told her the result of that conversation, and Dani assumed Vic wouldn't want her to go to Albany. Instead, he grinned and told her how proud of her he was. He also told her to make sure to keep an eye on Phin the entire time so he couldn't worm his way out of anything. She assured him he wouldn't have any escape and that he didn't want to face her wrath.

She offered to ask her mother to take care of the kids while she was gone, but Vic protested, saying that if they were a family, it was his responsibility to take them. That resulted in kissing him so assertively that her children made faces and asked them to stop because they were embarrassed. Dani ignored them and finished thanking Vic despite their protests.

The day she left, she pulled him aside so they could say goodbye properly. There wasn't any better way she could think of to let him know how much he meant to her. Fortunately, Vic understood. She left the house to the sound of Vic turning up the stereo and asking the kids if they wanted to bake some cookies. Dani didn't quite have the words for how good and how whole it made her feel to let go and trust him.

Dani, Gia, and Eunice met up with Phin at the hotel in Albany. Once they were all together, Phin gave his name to the woman at the desk. While they were occupied, Dani looked at their surroundings. It was a fairly posh hotel; Phin had good taste. Her eyes traveled back toward the desk, and she noticed that the well-dressed businessman behind them in line was eying them. He sneered when the woman handed

Phin both key cards. Phin quirked his eyebrows at Gia and Eunice, and Dani could see he was about to have some fun. Hitching his bag higher on his shoulder, he stepped away from the desk.

He leaned in toward the businessman and said in a low voice, "I saw you watching us." He eyed the man up and down, making it obvious he was assessing him. "I wouldn't be against bringing in another man. You're welcome to join us in our room later if you like." He chuckled at the businessman's expression, which fell somewhere between horror and curiosity, before turning his back on him. He extended one arm each to Gia and Eunice. "Ladies?"

They took his arms, Dani walking on Gia's right, and headed for the elevators, leaving the businessman staring after them. "Take a picture, honey. It'll last longer," Eunice called over her shoulder.

When they were safely enclosed in the elevator, they all broke out in peals of laughter. "You all are horrible!" Dani told them.

They entered their room, and Gia immediately staked a claim on one of the two queen-sized beds by throwing her duffel on it. The others set their bags under the coat rack. Phin hung his suit neatly in the recessed closet before turning to the rest of the group.

"There's only two beds. I'll be happy to camp out on the couch for the night," he said.

"Don't be ridiculous," Eunice told him. "You can share with me. I don't snore, and I don't bite." She arched an eyebrow at Phin. "Much."

He snorted, but he said, "All right, if you're sure."

"I'm sure. You need your beauty rest, Prince Charming. You'll need to be fresh for that meeting tomorrow."

Dani began pulling things out of her bag and setting them aside. "I'm just going to go clean up. I feel gross after that long drive."

After a quick shower, Dani joined the others in the room to find them talking about Gia and Oscar's budding romance.

"You sleep with him yet?" Eunice asked.

"Eunice!" Phin sounded shocked. "I honestly don't need to know that. God, Alex was right about you all."

Eunice shrugged. "Gia's a kiss-and-tell kind of woman, and I want to know."

"But I don't!" he protested.

Stepping over to the bed where they were all seated, Dani put in, "Phin, ignore them. They do this all the time."

"Right," Gia agreed. "And Alex always gives me good advice on men."

Phin laughed. "Because he's *such* an expert on straight guys."

"No," Gia replied. "Because he's a psychologist, you dork. Also, not all the guys I've been with are straight, thank you very much." She raised her eyebrows at Phin.

Huffing, Phin said, "I still don't want to hear about your sex life."

"You've seen the goods, baby," Gia shot back. "Jealous someone else is enjoying them?"

"Shut up, both of you," Eunice told them. "I want an answer to my question."

"Fine with me," Gia said. "Long as there are no more interruptions from the class." She looked pointedly at Phin, who rolled his eyes but remained silent. "Yes. We slept together."

She flushed, and Dani was surprised. She wondered if Gia's embarrassment had something to do with Phin.

"And?" Eunice pressed.

"It was...nice," she finished.

"Gia, coming from you, that's not a ringing endorsement. That bad, eh?" Eunice snickered.

"No! It wasn't like that," Gia replied. "Um. If you must know, I was his first."

"Really?" Dani squeaked, interested despite herself. "Oh, Gia. So, what happened?"

"Will you all please stop it now?" Phin said. "Gia, you answered the question already. I can leave, if you want to discuss the details."

Gia looked up at him. "I don't want to discuss the details, for once. I was only going to say that he was worried he might not be very good, but actually, it was fine." She blushed again. "I really, really like him, you guys. It's different, with Oscar. I don't want him to just be a one-time thing."

"Good to know. *Now* can we stop talking about this?" Phin shifted in his seat, and Dani could tell there was something else to his discomfort with the subject. She had her suspicions about what it was.

Gia beat her to it. "Oh, I see. You think if we're going to have girl talk we expect you to join in." She grinned. "Maybe we should."

Dani said, "Gia, I don't think—"

Ignoring Dani, Gia continued. "So, tell us. Did you and Alex finally get it on, then?"

A long, uncomfortable silence followed. Dani tried to put her hand on Phin's arm, but he shook her off. His face tensed.

"Yeah," he said. "We did." A muscle in his jaw twitched.

"What?" Gia asked, looking around at the others, a look of genuine confusion on her face.

Gently, Dani said, "Alex took off right after. He thought Phin was playing us." She looked at Phin, who was shaking slightly; his eyes were red and a little too bright.

"Oh, God. I'm sorry!" Gia's eyes widened, and she put a hand to her lips.

Phin cleared his throat. "You didn't know."

Eunice reached out and patted his hand. "Ah, honey. I told you—give him time."

"I don't think that's going to work." Phin shook his head. "Even you thought I'd lied to you after the meeting. It was all I could do to convince Dani to listen to me for five minutes to explain." He glanced sideways at her. "I think you all were willing because we didn't have any extra baggage." He sighed. "Did he tell you?"

"Tell us what?" Gia asked.

Phin slouched down in his chair. "It's not just the sex. That's part of it, but we sort of have a history."

"I questioned Alex about that ages ago," Dani said. "He never did tell me what it was."

"Short version," Phin said. "We were best friends until we were twelve. Then my father had an affair with his mother, my mother found out, and I wasn't allowed to see him." He swallowed. "I liked him—as in, twelve-year-old-boy *like* liked him—and tried to get rid of my crush by being a dick to him for an entire school year. My friends played an awful prank on him at the seventh grade dance, which I won't detail for you here, and I told them off for it. Alex missed that part, and my family moved before I could make it up to him. Until a month ago, we hadn't seen each other since." He sat back. "So now you know."

Gia sighed. "Oh, that's so sweet," she said. "And you finally got to be with your one true love—"

Phin scowled at her. "That's pushing it a bit."

"Whatever. But you're like star-crossed lovers." Gia gave a second, more dramatic sigh.

"Seriously, Gia. This is not a Harlequin romance novel. Alex is pissed off at me, probably for all the right reasons, but damn it, I want him back." Phin huffed. "I was only just getting to know him again."

Eunice shook her head. "You will. I know Alex, and he'll come around—especially after everything you've done for us this week."

Phin still looked hurt, and Dani saw it would be better to change the subject. "Maybe we should just talk about what we're going to do at that meeting tomorrow," she suggested.

"Oh, no," Gia said. "Not before you get your turn in the hot seat. Spill it, Dani. What's going on with you and Vic?"

Dani felt her face heat up. "Well..."

"You're together officially now, right? So it's not secret anymore?" Gia asked.

"So you knew?" Dani wasn't really surprised.

Gia nodded. "Oh, yeah. I don't know what made you think you were hiding anything, Dani. You two were always together. 'Just friends' my ass."

"Yes. It's all out in the open." Dani squeezed her eyes shut for a moment then opened them and grinned. "I was going to wait to tell you until after the meeting, but...we're getting married."

Gia squealed and jumped up to grab Dani in a fierce hug. "So, how did he propose?"

"Um...he didn't," Dani replied. "*I* did."

Eunice laughed and clapped her hands together. "Good for you, lady!" she said. "Did you get him a ring?"

"No. But I want to. I was going to ask your advice on that when we got back home."

"Now, this is where we need Al—" Gia stopped herself. "Yeah, we'll help you after we get done with this meeting."

"We should go over our strategy, then." Dani said firmly, more than ready to move away from discussing relationships.

Phin offered her a tiny, sad smile before he stood up and grabbed his briefcase. He pulled out a handful of papers and opened his laptop. "You already know what you need to do. Let's just go over how we're going to present it."

"Sounds good to me," Dani agreed. "Let's do this thing."

They laid out the relevant documents on the table so everyone could look them over together. Just as they were about to begin, Phin's phone rang. When he picked it up, his frowned and made a motion to the others to wait.

"Hello?" he said. There was a long pause, then, "I see. All right. I'll let them know, and we'll be there. Thanks." He ended the call and turned to the others. "That was Susan. She wants to meet us for breakfast in the morning before the meeting. Something's come up, and she doesn't want us to be surprised. It sounded like a good thing, but it was hard to tell."

"But we can't wait until then to go over this," Gia protested.

Phin shook his head. "We don't have to. We'll prepare everything, and if we have to make adjustments, we'll do that after we talk to Susan. We're supposed to meet her in the restaurant at eight. That should give us plenty of time to fix anything before the meeting."

There was nothing else to do but agree and get to work. Dani hoped that the last-minute changes wouldn't prevent them from making their case. She also hoped she was wrong to worry that once again, her trust in Phin was misplaced.

In the morning, there was a mad rush to get four people ready and out of the hotel. Amid the chaos, Phin, who had managed somehow to be the first one finished, kept giving them last-minute instructions. Dani politely refrained from making snide comments to the others; Gia wasn't quite so kind.

"Do you think you could shut the hell up for five minutes so I can put on my lipstick in peace? Thanks." She stalked into the bathroom.

From inside, Dani heard Eunice yelp in surprise, and she turned to exchange a glance with Phin. She expected him to look harried, for all the frantic orders he'd been barking at them. Instead, he actually looked calm and collected.

"You all right?" she asked.

He looked up from a paper he was holding. "Hm? Oh, yes. Just making sure everything is ready. What about you?"

"I think so. I've never done anything like this before."

"It's not so bad. Have you ever been in the NYSED building?"

Dani shook her head. "I haven't had any reason to." She was a little embarrassed as she admitted, "I've never been more than an hour from home."

"Don't worry. I'll be there with you." He squeezed her arm as he walked past, then turned to look at her. "I'm not the hero, here, Dani. You three are going to be fine. I'm only there to provide support and give them my *real* observations about your school." He handed her the document. "You can go over it, if you like. I promise—no surprises this time." He ducked into the closet to grab his suit jacket.

Dani scanned the report, her eyes widening as she read. If this was what Phin thought of the school, they would have no problem carrying out their plan. She flipped to the last page, where he had outlined his own recommendations. She couldn't help rolling her eyes when she saw that he suggested bringing in a consultant on an ongoing basis until they had fully achieved the markers of success he'd detailed.

Gia and Eunice emerged from the bathroom, and Phin finished tying his tie. Dani set the papers back on top of Phin's briefcase. "Ready?" she asked the others.

"Let's go," Phin urged. "I'll drive. No need to bring two cars."

They drove to a small diner about halfway between the hotel and the NYSED building. When they arrived, a woman in a neatly tailored gray suit waved to them from in front of the restaurant. It was impossible to tell from her expression whether they were there to hear good news or bad.

Phin greeted her warmly and introduced the others. "This is Susan Wilson-Howard, the lawyer who will present your case," he told them.

Once they were seated, Susan said, "Phin sent me everything, including your proposal. It all looks good. But there's been a last-minute addition, and I didn't want you to be surprised at the meeting. You need to know in case it changes anything."

Eunice eyed her warily. "What exactly would we need to change?"

Susan shook her head. "Nothing about your proposal, just how you might go about it." She took a sip of her coffee, and she looked like she was trying to figure out what to tell them. "Someone from EduText will be there today."

"At the meeting?" Phin's cool, calm demeanor from earlier vanished.

"Yes," Susan replied. "But I think you'll like the reason. They're withdrawing their petition for the charter."

"What? Why?" Dani asked. "I mean, not that I'm upset, but I'm a little confused."

Phin nudged her and leaned in to whisper, "Susan must have something on them."

Susan heard him. "You bet your ass I do. Phin, I've got dirt on that company going back at least ten years. Your father is a slimeball." She shrugged. "Sorry."

"No worries." Phin chuckled. "I already know that." He cleared his throat. "How much of your information involves me?"

"You have nothing to be concerned about. Your business practices weren't stellar, but that's not what I've got on them. It's mostly financial and has to do with the charters they've created."

"I don't mean to sound dense," Eunice said, "but what in the world would that change as far as our proposal?"

"Ah," Susan said. "There's more." A devious smile spread across her face. "EduText is planning to offer a charitable donation to the school in North Cowell to compensate for any damage done as a result of Mr. Murdock's involvement."

Phin's mouth hung open for a few seconds, and then he laughed. "Oh, that's good."

Eunice grinned. "That means we won't need as much time to plan and collect funds to open the school under our own charter!"

"Right," Susan agreed. "This should make your position that much stronger. You can tell them that what you need is time to bring the community on board."

Dani looked around the table then back at Susan. There was definitely something she wasn't saying. "What's the catch?"

Startled, Susan turned to Dani. "Only that if you can't make it work, we need to concede to the state. They will maintain the right to take one of the disciplinary actions available to them according to the law. But I don't think you have much to worry about. We can probably negotiate for another year to take the necessary steps. The Commissioner's office didn't have a choice except to make an official statement about Murdock, but they want to keep everything else as quiet as possible. They don't want people to know that Murdock was in the business of destroying a small town's educational system. So no one is going to do anything unless they absolutely have to."

"Good," Phin said. "Do you have anything I could take a look at for the meeting so I know what's going on with this?"

"Absolutely." Susan reached into her briefcase and pulled out some documents, which she handed over to Phin. "Read through this."

They spent the rest of their time going over the plan, making sure everyone had it down to the last detail. When they were through, it was time to put it all into action. Susan rose from the table.

"I'll see you there. I need to meet up with the representative from EduText and make sure there won't be any surprises."

Phin stood up and offered a hand to each of the others. "Let's go." They returned to his car.

The four of them arrived at the NYSED building, and Dani stared up at it in awe. It was gorgeous, with its wide, stone steps, tall columns, and a multitude of windows. Dani was momentarily intimidated by its grandeur. Beside her, Phin chuckled.

"It's overly impressive," he said. "And a little out of place." He gestured around. "Welcome to Albany, home of Frankenstein's architecture. No two buildings are alike."

Dani laughed. "I guess I'm just used to home." She shook herself. "I'm ready."

They stepped inside the building and made their way to the conference room where they were to meet with Susan, the EduText representative, an official from the Commissioner's office, and Greg Stevens, who would confirm the details of the case against Murdock. There would likely be other people there too, but those were the ones Dani knew for sure. She hoped they were thoroughly prepared.

Before they entered, Phin turned to Gia. "One last piece of advice—don't talk to them like you speak to us. Talk to them like they're your class of kindergartners. I've seen you teach, Gia."

Gia nodded. "I know. I just get nervous about this stuff." She brightened. "Can I pretend they actually *are* kindergartners?"

Phin grinned. "If it helps." He raised his hand to knock. "Ready?" he asked.

"Ready as we'll ever be," Eunice replied.

"Good."

He rapped soundly on the door, opening it when a voice from within answered, "Come in."

The meeting lasted less than an hour, during which Susan explained the situation and turned it over to Eunice to outline North Cowell's plan for change. For nearly the entire previous school year, Eunice had been the head of a small committee put together by two members of the PTSA. Their sole focus had been finding a solution to the school's failing test scores. As it turned out, although they were still below the standards, test scores had been steadily rising. They'd brought in school board members Anita Silas and Jason Meyer to help them organize a plan. The best option they'd found was to create their own charter—that would eliminate the need to fire any staff and would give them greater flexibility in trying new methods. It also took advantage of the state's increasing preference for creating charter schools, only with the added bonus of community support and local resources.

In order to prove that the school was making an effort to improve the quality of education, Phin neatly summarized his report, providing a full copy to everyone in the room. He explained that the methods matched similar ones found in private and Montessori schools and, given enough time and the right training, would produce superior results. He detailed his recommendations for adjusting to the rural setting and the needs of the large population of students whose first language wasn't English.

None of that mattered nearly as much as convincing the Assistant Commissioner to allow them the time required to create the charter and the new educational programs. Disciplinary action was inevitable at that point unless the situation with Murdock was enough to cast doubt on whether an overhaul was necessary yet. That was where Susan came in; she gave it everything she had, including explaining the presence of the EduText representative.

It was enough—North Cowell had one year to work out whatever they needed. At the end of that, they would either have their own charter or the state would force another solution on them.

At the close of the meeting, they rose and shook hands with everyone around the table. Phin thanked them for their time and began packing away his things. "Susan, I trust you'll send me a copy of this when you bill me?"

"Sure thing." She smiled at him and turned to Gia, Dani, and Eunice. "Very nice work, you three. It sounds like you've been hammering out that proposal for a while—it's brilliant."

Eunice nodded. "Seven months. We knew this was coming, and we'd hoped to have time to finish it. Got a little blindsided by the school board when it turned out they had other ideas."

Susan nodded. "Money talks. They obviously didn't see your solution as profitable enough." She closed her briefcase. "Phin, I'll see you back in Buffalo, right?"

"For a couple of days, yeah. I think I may have another job lined up." He winked at her.

"I'll bet. It's always something with you. Stay out of trouble this time, will you?"

"I'll try." He shook her hand and gave her arm an affectionate squeeze before she walked out of the room.

"You know," the NYSED official said to Phin, "we could use someone like you. Would you consider coming to work here in Albany?"

Phin shook his head. "Not a chance. I like my freedom too much." He extended his hand. "It was good to meet you. If you ever need some consulting work, you know where to find me." He turned to Stevens and said, "Good luck."

Stevens chuckled. "I may need it. Murdock's not the only corrupt soul here." He eyed Phin. "Sure you won't change your mind and cast your lot with us? You don't have to work with these people." He jerked his thumb at the NYSED official, who merely rolled his eyes.

"I'm sure," Phin answered. "I admire you—I really do. It's pretty bold to take on these corporations the way you're doing. But I don't want to live like that. I think it's time I tried for being completely honest in my life for a change. I'd be happy to go in on something again, but next time, warn me before you throw me in the deep end." He laughed softly. "It's been quite a ride."

"That it has," Stevens agreed. "I'll be in touch."

They shook hands, and Phin picked up his things. He nodded his head to Dani, Gia, and Eunice, who stepped around the table to join him. They exchanged handshakes all around; with that, it was over. They walked out of the conference room together.

They waited all the way until they were inside the elevator before all three of them rushed to embrace him simultaneously. Phin found himself at the center of a laughing, crying group hug. He disentangled himself. "Don't get too comfortable. There's a lot of work to do. You've only been given a grace period of one year, so you'd better get moving once you're back home. If you'll have me, I'm in for the long haul. I can help you, if you want."

Dani nodded. "We'll take it. If it wasn't for you, we never would've gotten this far."

Phin turned to her and took her shoulders. "No. This wasn't about me. You three did it—you made your case, and you had a perfect proposal. I'm only sorry I screwed things up for you first."

"Oh, Phin." She wrapped her arms around him. "Thank you."

They made their way back to the front lobby. Before they stepped outside, Phin grabbed Dani's hand and squeezed. She pressed her fingers into his palm in return, and they exchanged a long look. He knew that she had forgiven him. Looking to Eunice and Gia, he could see they felt the same way. He only hoped that would be enough for Alex when they returned to North Cowell.

"When we get back, I'm going to find Alex and make things right," Phin said to no one in particular.

Dani touched his arm, and he looked at her. She shook her head. "I know you want to, Phin, but that might be harder than you think."

"What? Why?"

"I didn't want to spoil this by telling you sooner, but the reason he left was for a job interview up in Plattsburgh. He wasn't planning on staying in North Cowell. It may be a while before you can do anything about it."

"Oh." There didn't seem to be any more to say. He tried to ignore the shattered feeling in his chest in favor of enjoying their victory.

He closed his eyes briefly then stepped through the doors into the bright June sunshine. He blinked a few times to adjust to the light and almost missed someone standing on the steps of the building. When he saw who it was, he stopped in his tracks. There, about to go in, stood Alex.

"Looks like you won't have to wait that long after all," Dani said. She leaned toward Eunice and Gia. "Let's give them a minute." She urged them to move away.

Gia made a sympathetic pout at Phin, and he gave her a half-hearted smile in response. The three women descended the stairs, leaving Phin and Alex alone.

"Hi," Phin said. It sounded lame even to his own ears.

Alex offered a tiny smile and a faint snort. "Hi."

"I really am sorry," Phin told him. "I shouldn't have kept the truth from you." He held up a hand when Alex started to speak. "Let me finish. I knew Murdock wanted to turn the school into a charter, but I figured everything was fine because you were already in trouble. I didn't know that he'd done this before, and I didn't know he was invested in it personally. It wasn't until talking to Dani before the Peroo Arts Festival that I put two and two together and realized Murdock had a stake in it himself and was just firing anyone who might get in his way." He looked Alex in the eye. "Please believe me," he begged.

Alex sighed and closed his eyes. "I know all that now. Dani called me a few days before you all took off to come here. She said you were going to make it right."

Phin grinned. "We did. It turned out that Greg Stevens was in on it from the beginning, working from the Attorney General's office to catch Murdock. I was pissed when I found out they'd used me to get to Murdock, but it all worked out. I bought you some time."

"How much?"

"A year. You have one more year to do what you need to."

"A year?" Alex asked. When Phin nodded, Alex grabbed his shoulders. "A year!"

"I'm sorry," Phin said. "I wanted to do more, but—"

"No! Don't be sorry. You did it!" Alex dragged Phin in roughly and wrapped his arms around him. "You did it," he whispered.

"I did? I mean, we did?"

Alex held him at arm's length. "Yes. A year is enough time for us to get everything in order to start our own charter."

"That's what Eunice said. They brought their proposal to the meeting with the lawyers and the NYSED official, and they have time to bring staff and families on board. It was an excellent strategy. I couldn't have come up with a better one myself. I just hope we're right and we—I mean, you—can pull it off in that amount of time."

Alex stepped back. "What do you mean, 'we'?" he asked.

"Um. I sort of promised Dani that I would help you. In between my other consulting work, of course."

"So…you're staying in North Cowell? Or you'll consult from Buffalo?" Alex's tone was difficult to read.

"I don't know," Phin said. "I'm not sure I have a reason to stay in North Cowell."

"I could give you one."

Without warning, Alex pulled Phin close and kissed him, right there on the steps of the New York State Education Department building. From somewhere below where they stood, Phin could hear someone whistling and calling at them; he couldn't have cared less. He laid his hand on Alex's neck and kissed him back, long and deep. It was several wonderful moments before they released each other, and Alex rested his forehead against Phin's.

"What about your job in Plattsburgh?" Phin asked, a little breathless.

Alex backed up and withdrew something from his pocket. He unfolded it, and Phin saw that it was the drawing he'd made the previous week—the one of the two of them, wrapped in each other's arms. It wasn't one of his typical stylized cartoons; it was raw and sensual, despite the fact that it wasn't particularly graphic. Phin flushed.

"Dani gave me this last week, along with your note apologizing. That, and Dani's phone call, changed my mind. I'm not taking the job."

"You're not? I hope it's not just because of me. I don't want—"

"No. Dani didn't want me to give up on the school, either. She was pretty fierce. Said I'd invested too many years not to see it through and I could always find something else if it didn't work out."

"So, what will you do?" Phin wanted to know.

"Stay on at the school. Teach a class or two up in Peroo to keep things fresh. Maybe publish a paper." He grinned. "I can think of other things that might keep me occupied, too. That is, if you're staying."

Phin made up his mind. "I am. I'm invested now as well, and I want to see where this goes."

Alex smirked. "Are you talking about the school or about us?"

"Maybe both." Phin's heart beat wildly as he said, "I'm in love, Alex—both with the town and with you."

Alex kissed him again, and it was a long time before Phin's brain shifted into gear and he remembered there were people waiting for them at the bottom of the steps. He withdrew reluctantly.

"Are you staying the night?" he asked. When Alex shrugged, Phin continued, "I shared a room with the others last night, but there's no reason at all I couldn't ask for a second one."

"That's probably a good idea," Alex replied. "I'm not sure I want an audience. You know how Gia talks."

Laughing, Phin reached out his hand to Alex. "Come on, then. We'd better go disappoint her."

Together, they descended the steps of the NYSED building to where the others stood. Eunice winked at Phin behind Alex's back; Dani gave him a surreptitious thumbs up. He offered them a small smile.

"You know," Dani said, "it's still early. I'll bet we could head back home today instead of tomorrow."

Gia scowled. "But we haven't even seen the city! I want to—"

"There's not that much to see, honey," Eunice interrupted. She gave a slight nod to Dani. "Besides, I'm more than ready to get out of here."

"Can we at least have lunch first?" Gia whined. "I'm starving!"

"Of course we can," Phin said. "I know just the place. It's on me."

As they walked towards the cars, Phin hung back with Dani for a moment. He leaned in and whispered, "Thanks."

She grinned at him. "No problem. You two deserve some time alone." Her expression turned serious. "Be good to him, okay?"

"Count on it," Phin replied. His face grew warm, and Dani's eyes lit up; she knew what he wasn't saying.

Before she stepped away from him, she gave his hand a light squeeze. "I'm glad you're staying."

His eyes flicked to Alex, who was laughing with Eunice about something Phin didn't catch. "Me, too," he replied.

Alex and Phin enjoyed a leisurely lunch with the women then bid them goodbye. Dani kissed Alex on the cheek and gave him a long, meaningful look before settling herself in the back seat of Eunice's compact car. The men leaned against Phin's door, watching until the others were out of sight.

Phin turned to Alex, pulling out his phone. "I'll text you the address of the hotel. Let's take your stuff back there, and then we can decide what to do next."

Alex could think of several things he wanted to do, none of which were appropriate in public, so he agreed. "I'll meet you there."

As they pulled out onto the street, Alex caught a brief glimpse of Phin looking back at him in the rear view mirror. He winked, and Phin glanced back, grinning. A moment later, Phin darted out between cars, and Alex lost sight of him. He snorted and took his time squeezing into traffic, exercising considerably more caution than Phin had.

Alex arrived at the hotel, unsurprised to see Phin's car already there. He retrieved his bag and shouldered it then stepped inside to where Phin stood just beyond the doors. Phin was whistling, hands in his pockets, pretending not to notice Alex.

"Looks like you could use some company," Alex said, sidling up to him.

Phin eyed Alex sideways, and his mouth curled into an inviting smile. He tilted his head toward the elevators. On the way there, they passed a man in a suit carrying a briefcase. His eyes locked on Phin, and his jaw dropped; Phin winked at him. Alex just stood there watching the exchange, his eyes traveling between them.

"You were serious," the man muttered.

Phin tilted his head to the side. "About what?"

"Last night. About…" He leaned in and whispered, "Adding another man."

Amusement flickered across Phin's face. "Still want in on that?"

The man recoiled. "No!" He pressed his lips together and glared at Phin for a moment, but then his face relaxed. "Uh, maybe."

Phin smirked. "Too late. I'm spoken for." He turned around and walked away, leaving the man staring at his back. The man glanced at Alex, who shrugged and hurried away to catch Phin.

"What was that all about?" he demanded when they reached the elevator.

Phin laughed. "That tool kept sneering at us last night. I may have implied that Dani, Eunice, Gia and I were…well. You know. I offered to let him join us."

They stepped into the elevator. Alex said, "You're awful, you know that?"

"That's what Dani said, too." Phin grinned, but his expression quickly sobered. "You know nothing happened, right?"

"I know." Alex fidgeted a little.

Phin shifted so they faced one another. "First of all, *nothing happened* with the women. Period. I have no interest in any of them. Besides which, Dani's engaged, Eunice is a lesbian, and Gia and I are just friends." He flushed a little and added, "Friends who will never, ever have any kind of sex again. Second, even if that guy had been looking to hook up with us, that wasn't going to fly. He was being a jerk, making assumptions, and I wanted to dig at him. That's all." He leaned down and kissed Alex, who let his eyes drift closed. Phin's breath tickled Alex's ear as he whispered, "Third, I meant what I said. I'm yours."

Alex turned his head and reached up to grab Phin's chin. He angled it so they were looking at each other. "Prove it," he murmured.

Phin's lips twitched. "Right here?"

Alex dropped his hand and laughed. "I think we can wait until we get to our room."

When the elevator stopped, Phin grabbed Alex's arm. They dashed down the long hallway, laughing. At the door, Phin spun Alex around and trapped him against the door while he fumbled with the key card. As soon as the door unlatched, they tumbled inside. Phin's mouth was on Alex's long before the door clicked shut. Alex dropped his bag and let Phin tug him to the bed. For several moments, everything was a jumble of heated kisses and hands everywhere and desperate pulling at clothes. Phin groaned loudly as the last of the material separating them landed on the floor.

"Shh!" Alex hissed. "What if there are people next door?"

Before Phin could answer, voices drifted through the thin wall from the next room. It was impossible to hear the specifics at first, but within moments, the talking had given way to a rhythmic squeaking punctuated by the occasional faint moan.

Phin chuckled. "Looks like we weren't the only ones," he murmured. His eyes twinkled. "Think we could give 'em a run for their money?"

"Hell, yes." Alex paused. "But could it be a quieter one?" His ears heated up.

Phin looked down at Alex. "Anything you want." He kissed him. "Condom? I don't want to break momentum later."

"Yeah. Hang on." Alex shoved Phin off and leaned over the side of the bed to retrieve his wallet. When he sat back up, Phin's face was alight with amusement.

"Are you a fucking teenager?" He threw his head back and laughed.

Alex elbowed him. "No, you jerk. I just...wanted to be prepared." His face flamed. "I was hoping."

Phin stopped laughing, but his eyes still shone. He pushed Alex back down onto the mattress, straddling him. "Then I have a promise to make good on."

"What's that?"

"To compete with the people next door. I want to make you scream. Silently, of course," he added, smirking.

Alex shut him up by dragging him down into a kiss that was anything but delicate. They moved together, wrestling and rocking, sweat making their bodies slick as they pressed and slid against each other. Phin pushed away a little and tore open the condom, his hands shaking and his chest heaving.

"God, I'm so fucking ready," he groaned.

"Yeah." Alex made to roll over, but Phin stopped him.

"No. Like this, on your back. So I can see you."

In a series of fluid movements, they joined their bodies together. The air filled with the sounds of their skin-to-skin contact, everywhere from their greedy kisses down to the slap of their bodies pounding together. Phin slid his hand between them to stroke Alex, causing him to gasp and shudder. He wrapped his legs around Phin, drawing him closer. Fire coiled low in his belly; the tingling spread out until it reached his limbs. His toes curled as he arched his back, digging his fingers into the flesh of Phin's shoulders. The hot waves of his orgasm washed over him, and the tension bled out until he was spent and trembling.

Regaining awareness of the man still thrusting into him, Alex was just in time to watch Phin come undone. He inhaled sharply at the beauty of Phin's face as it contorted—the way his eyes pressed shut, his lips drew up over his teeth, his nose wrinkled. He uttered a long, shaking whimper as he emptied himself, and his features relaxed once more. Slowly he opened his eyes and looked down. Alex shivered and reached up to cup Phin's cheek. He ran his thumb along his jaw, enjoying the rough texture.

For a quivering, breathless eternity, they didn't move. Phin leaned in, and Alex pressed brief, grateful kisses to his lips and jaw. At last Phin withdrew, and they stretched out together on the bed. Alex's eyes drifted closed as he nestled against Phin's chest.

The peaceful moment was shattered by a long, drawn-out moan from the room next door. Phin jumped. They exchanged a glance and burst into fits of silent laughter.

"Ours was better," Phin remarked.

Alex smacked his arm. "How would you know? They sounded... pleased."

Phin adjusted so he was on his side. He held Alex's gaze. "Because it was with you." He gave Alex a peck on the cheek and sat up. "I'm not feeling all that sleepy anymore. Want to come somewhere with me?"

Alex propped himself up on his elbows. "What do you have in

mind?"

"Hm...have you ever been here before?"

"Nope." Alex shook his head. "I mean, yes, I've been in the NYSED building before, but I've never done anything else in Albany."

"There's a lot to do here. We can stop at the desk for a guide book. Did you know there's a dance museum in Saratoga Springs? And there's some great local entertainment, too. If you like opera, we can try to get tickets to the Saratoga Performing Arts Center. Or we could just visit Thatcher State Park, if that's more your thing. Oh! And I *have* to take you to eat at Jumpin' Jacks. They have the most fabulous onion rings." He was almost bouncing.

Alex laughed and held up a hand. "Slow down! We only have so many hours."

Phin shifted closer and pressed his lips against Alex's. "Stay here with me for a few days?" he asked. "Then I can show you everything. I mean, if you don't have to get back..."

"I don't. School's over, and I don't have to work again until the summer schedule starts." Alex stood up. "Sightseeing it is, then. But I want to shower first." He stretched and ambled towards the bathroom. He stepped inside and peered around the door frame. "I may need some help, you know."

"Oh?" Phin grinned wickedly. "Maybe I can be of service." He got up and made for the bathroom.

Alex shot out a hand and dragged him inside before turning on the taps. As steam filled the room, Alex stepped close to Phin. His chest constricted when he recalled Phin's words outside the NYSED building. Unthinking, he murmured, "I am too."

Phin's brow creased. "You are what, too?"

"In love," he said.

With that, he pushed the door closed, effectively shutting out everything else.

About the Author

A. M. Leibowitz is a spouse, parent, feminist, and book-lover falling somewhere on the Geek-Nerd Spectrum. She keeps warm through the long, cold western New York winters by writing romantic plot twists and happy-for-now endings. You can follow her writing at amleibowitz.com or follow her on Twitter (@amyunchained) or Facebook (www.facebook.com/UnchainedFaith).